A KINGDOM OF CURSED LIES

LAUREN LOWTHER

Visit my website at www.laurenlowther.com
Cover Designer: Books & Moods, www.booksandmoods.com
Editor: Jovana Shirley, Unforeseen Editing, www.
unforeseenediting.com

This book is a work of fiction. Names, characters, places, and
incidents either are products of the author's imagination or are
used fictitiously. Any resemblance to actual persons, living or
dead, events, or locales is entirely coincidental.

ISBN-13: 978-1-7390333-0-9

*For those lost souls who look for themselves in
the pages of books.*

Pronunciation Guide

Diana (Dye-an-uh)
Spense (Spence)
Aedan (Ay-den)
Maisie (May-zee)
Vera (Vare-uh)
Embris (Emb-ris)
Alwyn (All-win)
Sorin (Sore-in)
Badras (Bad-rass)
Olys (Ole-us)
Jweira (Way-ruh)
Jamey (Jay-me)
Eira (Air-uh)
Meske (Mess-kee)
Ryen (Rye-in)
Aislinn (Ash-lin)

PROLOGUE

The well inside was a constant swirl of magic. By binding myself to her, the chosen one, I had a way to use it again. She was strong and light and determined—everything she had been prophesied to be.

So alike to the first of her name.

Eight thousand years in limbo sounded like a long time to average ears, but to me, it had passed in a blink. That day—my last day—seemed like mere hours ago.

But the time had aged me even if I didn't acknowledge the passing of centuries. Millennia.

I was wiser, possibly. Stronger, most definitely. Vengeful? That was yet to be seen.

So, it was no surprise to me that my own well of magic, of Source, mixed easily with hers. She drew from it as simply as if it were her own.

And, I supposed, it was now. As long as I let her have it.

It was refreshing to feel the cool breeze of magic against my soul even if I couldn't use it myself. It was almost a relief.

"Jweira, I need more!" The girl with the chestnut hair pulled at me, at my Source.

She did not need to ask. I had already given my consciousness to her.

But I agreed anyway. On this plane, they needed constant reassurance.

"Take as much as you need."

I was aware of more souls surrounding us, using their combined strength to pass through onto this plane for a short window. They were encouraging her, giving her as much as they could spare.

She was a healer. Of course she could heal the portal. It felt silly to me that this was all so dramatic.

She was the chosen one. She would bring balance back.

The pull from my magic to hers was warm and blindingly white. If I were no wiser, I would think I was finally being called home.

But I was destined to stay in this soul prison a little longer. The end felt near though. My respite was coming soon. Thank the gods.

The girl was slowing, her job nearly done. But she was going to stop before the last lines of it were healed.

"Keep going."

"I don't want to harm you," she whispered, her voice almost pleading.

"You cannot harm me." I pulled away as much as I could, baring the well of my magic to her. *"Do what must be done."*

With a final heave, she pulled from me, more and more until it was done. She was drooping, exhaustion settling deep into her soul. She still had a job to do, and my consciousness was only going to drain her more.

I settled myself into a deep rest, away from this plane, where she could do her job without my interference. When she was ready, I would be back to help her again.

"Wait, where are you going?" She scrambled around, looking for me.

"You did well, Diana."

With a last push, I fell back into limbo.

PART 1

ONE
SHRIVELLED FRUIT

DIANA

I hated sand.

I hadn't always. The beachy shoreline of the Southern Isles back home was incredible. It stretched on for eons, seamlessly blending into the water and eventually the sun-speckled horizon. It used to be my dream to spend an entire summer there one year.

But now, through my tiny, barred window, all I could see was sand. Dry and yellow-white and never-ending. Aside from the small, spiky plants scattered around, the only other thing to look at was the impossibly high metal fence that, no doubt, enclosed the fortress I was being kept in.

So, now, I hated sand.

It was one of an impossibly large number of changes I had seen in the last two days. Gaia, had it really only been that long? Two days since I had become a killer, two days since I'd found my soulmate, two days since I'd betrayed my own kingdom.

Although it wouldn't be truly fair to say that things had only started changing two days ago. The day of my ascension ritual weeks and weeks ago was when a mysterious and annoyingly handsome enemy wreaked havoc on the course of my life—and I hadn't stopped changing since.

While I had known deep down that my involvement with Spense couldn't end well, I certainly hadn't thought it would land me here, in the heart of the Unseelie, with no allies to be seen.

My only company was that of a quiet young servant named Laith, who dutifully brought my meals. She was less inclined to converse than a tree would be. Her name had been given to me only this morning, a bone she threw my way to shut me up.

Inside the lavish, albeit impersonal, room, clothes had been left for me, all lightweight and tan-coloured. The dress that I had worn through the portal—once the most beautiful piece I had ever seen— hung at the back of the closet. The sparkles caught my eye every time I opened it. And every time I stuffed it under the bed or balled it up and threw it at the door, it always reappeared, wholly intact. An ever-constant reminder of my failure.

I would've burned it myself if Urdan hadn't stemmed access to my magic. I had not believed it possible, but I was severely cut off. Unlike the magic-binding bracelet Spense had worn, I could still feel my magic. But it was weak and dry, like a shrivelled fruit that had sat in the sun too long. Just trying to pull some forward had me exhausted, to the point that my knees shook and the world started spinning.

It was embarrassing that I had believed Spense would have come for me already. How long did it take to recover from having your memories unceremoniously dumped back into your head? More than a few days?

Urdan had made it very clear he wasn't keeping me around for my sparkling conversation skills, so the one thing I was sure about was, Spense was alive. Otherwise, I wouldn't be.

Which led me to a painful train of thought. It was entirely possible that with his old life returned to him, Spense had become someone I didn't know, and he didn't care for me anymore.

The longer I sat on this, the harder it was to convince myself that what we'd shared was real—the soulmate tattoo, the stolen kisses, the secret truths. Before I'd left Eira, he'd quickly become my only confidant, someone I trusted with my life. Would I still be able to place that trust in him?

A small rap at the door had me lurching off the chair I'd been perched on. The well-worn leather squeaked in protest.

Laith had only left an hour ago. I wasn't due for another meal until dinner.

Before I could make it to the door, it glided open. Standing in the doorway was a very small creature. His face looked childish, but there was something in the way his eyes were sunken and hollow that said he was a lot older than he seemed. But what stood out the most about him was the bright blue tinge of his skin and the skinny tail that flicked around him. I couldn't stop myself from staring at the first Folk I had ever encountered.

The strange creature swept into a bow. "It is a pleasure to make your acquaintance, Lady Diana. I am Pik, head servant of the Crown."

He spoke to me like I was an esteemed guest—polar opposite to how Urdan had treated me.

"I wasn't aware prisoners were treated so well here."

Pik shifted on his feet. "Ah, yes, well, the situation is indeed unfortunate. But it is my nature to see that all who stay in Ivywall are treated well. I am sure—"

"Ivywall?" I interjected.

"That is the name of our palace grounds, lady."

The use of *lady* irritated me. I was a high princess, an heir to an entire realm. I pushed that ugly piece of pride down deep. I didn't deserve the title anymore anyway even if I could somehow get back to Eira—an impossible idea without my magic. Jweira wouldn't be able to help me either, considering her noble sacrifice.

I placed a hand over the emerald on my chest as my heart clanged painfully. A sacrifice I didn't deserve. I would do whatever I could to make sure it was not in vain.

"Where's Spense?"

Pik clasped his hands in front of him. "That is actually why I came to see you. The prince is awake and healing well. He should be up on his feet again by the end of the day."

My heart fluttered. I needed to see him before he was mobile, before he could leave and never come back for me. Needed to speak to him and see for myself what, if not all, had changed.

"When can I see him?" I didn't bother hiding the eagerness in my voice. "Can you take me to him?"

"I'm afraid I don't have the clearance to accompany you anywhere," Pik said, shaking his head. "But no fear, my lady. I would wager he'll be at this door the very minute he is cleared to leave the infirmary." He smiled knowingly, eyeing my tattoo.

Had he spoken to Spense? How could he be so sure?

I nodded because it was all I could do at this point. A strange knot of anxiety wound its way into my stomach. I could be seeing Spense *today*. I'd been thinking about what I'd say to him for two days straight, but now faced with the thought of actually seeing him sent unease through me. I couldn't help but wonder what the new—or, I supposed, *old*—Spense would be like. If I would know him still.

"Is there anything else I can help you with?" Pik's voice interrupted my wandering thoughts.

I was struck by the desire to ask what Spense was really like. Pik seemed nice enough, and his position would certainly bring him close enough to know. But I wasn't ready to trust this goblin yet. And also, it was maybe a little embarrassing.

"If it's not too intrusive, would you tell me, erm … what you are?" I cringed at how that had come out. "I've just never met anyone of the Folk before."

"Not at all. I am a goblin, specifically from the mountains of Err. I am, regrettably, the last of my clan." Pik smiled tightly. "Sad as it might be, I believe that is quite the nature of things when you get to be my age. I must be off, but I am sure we'll see each other again soon. Should you need anything at all, do not hesitate to call for me." With a last nod, he backed out of the door, shutting it softly behind him.

My spirits lifted slightly, a small weight off my heavy heart. Urdan certainly fit the bill of the nasty, malevolent Dark fae—*Unseelie*, I corrected myself—that I'd been raised to believe in. But Pik was like Spense, seemingly kind so far. Perhaps Urdan was the anomaly.

Maybe Spense was still the same kind, confident, funny soul I knew.

Maybe.

TWO
ONCE FORGOTTEN

SPENSE

The sun beat down across the desert, creating wiggling lines above the sand on the horizon. I was dressed in complete battle armour, covered head to toe in heavy equipment, but it didn't weigh me down. It fuelled me.

The house on the outskirts of goblin territory was small and unassuming, a typical dwelling of a farmer or hunter. Built into the side of the mountains where the goblins had tunnelled inside, it was hidden in rock.

But I knew where to look. I never lost sight of my marks.

My knuckles hit the door once, twice, and I waited. There was scuttling inside, and then a small, round head peeked out. Fae, no doubt, but small and childlike, with wispy, long hair and blue skin.

"Lord Spense, what a surprise. I hadn't expected to see you until the next council meeting."

"Sedal, I have a matter to discuss with you. Won't take long. May I come in?"

Sedal, being the smart goblin he was, eyed up my armour and where my hand rested on the marble pommel of my sword, Bloodletter. He barely disguised a nervous swallow and swung the door wide for me to follow him in.

Considering the goblin race was probably a third of my size, I ducked to *get in and stayed that way until we reached his sitting room, where he had put in a large ceiling to accommodate guests.*

"Please, sit." Sedal busied himself at the drink cart in the corner.

Even from behind, it was impossible to miss how his hands shook. Good. He should be scared. He knew the consequences of going against Ivywall. Against me.

"I'd rather stand."

It took two steps for me to cross the room, and the only warning Sedal got was the hiss of metal before Bloodletter was pressed against the back of his neck.

"My lord, I can explain."

"The king is not interested in excuses."

The goblin was visibly shaking now. "Please, let me explain. My daughter—"

The tip of the sword pressed into him, drawing a thin trickle of blue blood along the blade. The sword's red hue glinted in the low light, seemingly delighting in adding to its collection.

"Your daughter was not worth the lives of countless Unseelie," I hissed, stepping closer. I grabbed Sedal by the back of his tunic and twisted him roughly to face me. "You are nothing but a coward and a traitor."

"They knew. I don't know how, but they targeted me. They knew I was among the trusted in Ivywall. They sought to exploit me for my knowledge. I didn't know the information I gave them would have that result. They were going to kill my daughter."

"And where is that daughter now?"

Sedal's face fell, shame clouding his eyes. "Do it then. Kill me. Release me from this nightmare. It's a losing battle, you know. Life. Every time you think you're getting ahead, it beats you back, more broken than the last time. Just do it."

Life was not fair or kind. I knew just as well as anyone what it looked like to be dealt a shitty hand. But I got up each day and faced it because I was no coward. I was no loser. My father had raised me with a strong hand, and that was what I expected from the world in turn.

There was no easy way. If I had to live through this hell, they did too.

"Death is hardly a punishment, Sedal. For someone like you, it is a reprieve. If you had anyone left you cared about, today's payment would be their lives. But the humans have taken care of that for me. How sad, to think that you gave up your own king and they didn't keep their end of the bargain. Humans cannot be trusted. And your blatant disregard for the safety of Ivywall means you can no longer be trusted."

Sedal took a shuddering breath and went still. "I understand."

"It didn't have to be this way."

"If only you knew."

Bloodletter paused, my arm halfway extended. "Knew what?"

"If only you knew that it did *have to be this way. That the love of a family, a partner, is unlike any other feeling. If only you knew that when given a choice between their lives and others, there is simply no other option. If only you knew that there are more important things in life than wars and getting revenge. If only—"*

Whatever nonsense that was about to spill from Sedal's mouth disappeared with a gurgle. I pulled my arm back, Bloodletter sliding free, its blade coated blue.

The goblin's body slumped to the floor, small and soft.

I didn't spare it another glance as I ducked through the house and back into the desert heat.

I took a rag from my pack and cleaned my sword before sheathing it. The familiar weight at my side balanced me as I started toward my next mark.

My ears rang uncomfortably.

Light was coming in through a slit in the window shades, causing me to squint as I looked around the room. The air felt dry, the walls starkly white. This didn't feel like the healer's ward that I'd recovered in before. Had they taken me to another region?

I shifted a little in the small bed I was almost too big for. A groan escaped me when my head pounded painfully.

Movement in the corner of the room caught my eye. Four fae sat on various mismatched chairs that obviously didn't belong here. Eight identical brown eyes stared at me widely. I stared back.

Confusion gave way to recognition in a split second that ripped through my brain in a sharp pulse.

The four anonymous fae became Sorin, Alwyn, Badras, Olys.

My siblings.

A grin spread across my face as I let out a relieved laugh. My brothers and sister! I was in Ivywall, my home.

They returned the smile, gathering around my bed. Alwyn grasped my hand, her fingers small and warm.

"Brother," Sorin said, patting me on the shoulder. "The gods have brought us together again."

I shared his sentiment. I had been prepared never to see my siblings again on that fateful day when I stepped through the rift into Eira.

Wait. Eira.

I frowned. "How did I get back here? The last thing I remember is being in Eira, and Father—he showed up, and …" My head hurt, trying to pull forward what I had last experienced.

Oh gods, the portal. Father had taken my memories. He was the reason for my amnesia. He had also given them back. Then, I blacked out.

I had been pulled back into Rathe while I was unconscious.

Sorin handed me a small cup of a foul-smelling liquid, intending me to drink. "This will help soothe you while you transition into your own mind again."

I took the cup and, without looking away from my eldest brother, hurled it as hard as I could against the wall. Olys leaped out of the way to avoid the flying liquid, which landed against the wall in a satisfying splat. I felt Alwyn's hand leave mine as she backed up a step.

"I don't need to be *soothed*. I need to know what you're not telling me!"

Sorin pursed his lips together. "Always with the dramatics, Spense." He flicked his hand once, and the liquid on the wall disappeared. "We're not keeping anything from you. We just want to help."

I didn't like his tone of voice. "Where's Diana?" A pit of fear had inflamed in my stomach at his words. They wouldn't be dragging it out like this if there was good news.

Badras exchanged a look with Sorin, who cleared his throat. "None of us were present when you arrived back home. This information comes from Pik. From what we've been told, there was quite a commotion with the girl—"

"Where is Diana?" I repeated.

My siblings shifted, having silent conversations with each other.

Finally, Olys rolled his eyes and stepped forward. "She's being kept under guard in your room."

"*What?*" I roared, leaping forward, trying to launch myself out of bed.

Badras put a hand on my chest, a small zap of his electric magic paralyzing my limbs for a second.

Sorin frowned. "You must understand, brother, what this looked like. The three of you came barrelling through the portal, you were unconscious, Father was half lucid, and she's the high princess of our enemy. It was for the safety of everyone involved. I promise you, we haven't harmed her."

"And the portal?"

"Closed."

His words settled me, even as hot anger still held on, its hooks deep. Sorin was always the reasonable one. Memories flooded me—of our protocols and how many years we had been suffering because of the Seelie. It felt like a slamming headache every time I remembered something.

Gods, that was painful to endure.

These memories were like a tap I couldn't turn off. For all the time I'd spent in Eira, willing something, anything, to appear, now, I wanted them to leave me alone.

And it wasn't that I was ungrateful. I was ecstatic to have my mind back, my life. Truly, it was a huge sigh of relief to look upon familiar faces and walls. The problem was that I now felt like I was two separate Spenses. The Unseelie version and the Seelie version.

"See, told you he'd be back to himself in no time." Alwyn's ever-chipper voice pulled me from my thoughts. "Our reasonable Spensey."

"Don't call me that," I grumbled, the words coming unbidden, before I could even think.

Alwyn laughed, her eyes alight. With a jolt, I realized how much I had missed that sound.

"How'd you get that one?" Badras was pointing to my most recent scar—a jagged pink line slashed across my abdomen. "Don't tell me a Seelie was able to get that kind of shot on you." His words were teasing, but I knew my brother and how disappointed he'd be to hear that I'd been bested by the Lights. He was three parts pride, one part ferocity.

I grimaced. "That was the result of rift-jumping."

Olys grumbled, "Idiot."

Badras, all muscle and stature, bumped him with his shoulder, pushing Olys's tiny frame a few steps back. "Spense did what none of us would."

They were, of course, referencing the reason I'd willingly hurtled myself through an unstable portal. It made me feel grimy inside to remember. That could stay tucked away for the time being. I had learned so much in Eira, with Diana. My soulmate.

I pushed back the sleeve of the shirt I wore and examined my arm. The mating tattoo was still there, inking from my shoulder to my wrist in waves and swirls. My heart jolted when I saw it again. The gods had blessed me by intertwining my life with such a force of nature.

Alwyn let out a low whistle. "You really went and got yourself mated, huh?"

I looked up. They were all studying my arm intently, making me sink back into the bed at their scrutiny.

"I've never seen one spread so far up," Sorin remarked. Perhaps unconsciously, he flexed his left arm, where his own tattoo swirled from elbow to shoulder.

Warmth spread across my chest as I remembered his lovely wife, Meske, and their young daughter, Aislinn. I had never understood the intrigue and pull around soulmates. Sorin being mated was all I'd ever known, but it had come as a shock to us all when they announced their pregnancy and Sorin stepping back from his role in Ivywall. Although I had been excited to inherit his job, it had been utterly confusing as to how a soulmate and family could make him change so much. But now, I understood.

"I have to see her. Have I been cleared to leave?" I sat up again, this time slowly, eyeing Badras warily to avoid another shock.

Sorin placed a hand on my chest to keep me from standing up. "We have to talk about Father."

I frowned. "Back in one of his *moods*, I presume?"

My eldest brother nodded, grimacing. "He was lucid for so long. He went through the portal and came back, and his mind was still there. We thought maybe, this time, it would stick. But this morning, Pik reported he was in an unbearable rage. He was asking for you. It's unlikely he remembers anything from his trip to the Seelie realm."

"I have nothing to say to him."

"That might be the case, brother, but we do have pressing matters to discuss now that you're home. We'll reconvene in the conference room for a quick recap before dinner." The way Sorin spoke made it clear that this was not up for discussion.

I got up off the bed, the room spinning a little. I had forgotten how much taller I was than my siblings. The closest to my height was Badras, who wordlessly placed a steadying hand on my back. I must have looked wobbly.

"Fine," I agreed. "But I won't come without Diana."

Badras made an unhappy growl in the back of his throat. "Not a chance."

I spun to face him. "I'm not in the mood, Bad."

We stared each other down until Alwyn slipped in between us. It was almost comical, considering her head didn't even reach either of our shoulders. "Now, now, boys. Let's play nice. Of course Diana is welcome. She's one of us now, isn't that right?" She glanced at Sorin, expecting him to back her up.

Sorin took a deep intake of breath through his nose and finally agreed. "It would hardly be fair to exclude her."

Badras stalked out of the room, letting the door slam behind him.

With eyes on the door, Olys said, "I'm not very comfortable with it either, Spense. But I suppose we don't have a choice. I will see you all there." He left the room as well, his wavy hair disappearing, much more swiftly and silently than his brother.

Alwyn reached up on tiptoes to kiss my cheek. "I, for one, cannot wait to meet her. It will be nice to have a female voice on the council!"

Sorin made a befuddled face. "Meske has been on the council for years."

Alwyn shared a discreet look with me. Sorin was so blissfully unaware that Meske offered little more on the council than an extra vote for him. We all loved her, but she was the polar opposite to Alwyn and always erred on the side that was least confrontational.

"A *fresh* female voice is all I mean," my sister said. She gave me a hug, squeezing tight. "I've really missed you," she whispered into my chest.

I wrapped my arms around her tiny frame. "I've missed you too."

And it was true. Of all my siblings, Alwyn and I had always been the closest. My heart ached that I had once forgotten her.

She stepped back. "All right, go get her already!"

Sorin held out a hand, which I accepted. We grasped each other's arms. "It's good to have you back."

My chest was tight with all the emotions I was trying to keep inside. Having my siblings back was finally a puzzle piece that felt *right*. I couldn't wait to introduce Diana to this world.

Sorin and Alwyn stepped back so I could head to the door.

"Dinner's in an hour!" Alwyn called as I left.

I barely registered her words. It was all I could do not to run down these familiar halls. Ivywall was just as I remembered. The reddish adobe walls led me along, smelling like clay and sand. Like home. When I passed the first window, I had to stop for a second to take in the desert views I had grown up memorizing. The sun beat down outside, and it was starting to stoop low on the horizon. It cast shadows on the cacti and aloe plants, making them seem tall and lonely.

There was so much I had to atone for. So many things I wanted to say to Diana, to apologize for, to explain to her. She must have been so scared and lonely, so confused.

Well, maybe not scared, I amended. That girl was a force to be reckoned with.

After twists and turns and stairs that all seemed entirely too long, I found myself staring at the familiar doors to my chambers. A guard had been posted outside, who looked shocked to see me.

"You're relieved," I said as I grasped the brass door handle.

"But, sir, I cannot—"

"Go. Now." I didn't wait to see if he obeyed me, but the footsteps trailing away confirmed he had. I swung open the door, standing in the threshold as I took her in.

Diana's mouth was agape, and she stood frozen halfway to the door. She was still as beautiful as ever, her hair trailing over her shoulders in a chestnut wave. But the lines on her face made her look worried and the shadows under her eyes unbearably sad. The princess looked lost.

"Spense," she breathed.

I walked into the room to meet her, stopping before I closed the gap too much. A lot had happened since I'd seen her last. I didn't want to overwhelm her even if it was all I could do to keep myself from wrapping her in my arms.

She smiled faintly, and I nearly melted. I was lost in her eyes, the evening sun making the hazel shine. She took a step, and I waited for her to move first. Diana was coming closer, looking up at me, unguarded.

Which was why I was completely unprepared when she slapped me across the face.

THREE
FROZEN HEART

MAISIE

The palace was darker without her. The sun's rays still shone into the large windows, but they were weak and lacklustre. Even the servants and workers struggled to lift their smiles higher than polite greetings. It was fitting, I supposed, in a deeply ironic way, that *he* was to blame. The dark one. The one who had sucked the life out of her and pitched the kingdom into night when he stole her away. It was my fault. I had seen her becoming consumed by him. I should have stopped it.

The heavy energy of the palace was not helped by the subsequent funeral of Anten, a longtime trusted soldier in the queen's army. I couldn't believe my own eyes when I saw the body, and I'd thought my ears also betrayed me when I was told Diana had been his demise.

She couldn't have done this, I'd wailed. *Diana is the purest of us all!*

That remained true. It might have been her hand that slayed her own, but I knew better. It was him controlling her. Twisting her.

I stood in the palace kitchens, looking out the window into the gardens that were littered with patrons in varying shades of green—the colour of life and death. My mother, Ada, came behind me and wrapped a heavy arm around my shoulders. I leaned into her warmth.

"There's still time for you to join the ceremony," Ada said.

I shook my head once. "I'd rather be here with you." I couldn't face them all, knowing I could have prevented his death if I'd been smarter.

She gave me a pat on the back and resumed her baking. She would be at it until the early hours of the morning, cooking just about every dish possible for the hundreds of guests at Anten's funeral. Staying here was not only a great help to the kitchen staff, but it also provided hours of mindless work, where I could just be unfeeling for a while.

It certainly worked, for I was astonished when the last tray of pastries went up to the guests and the fires winked out. When I looked outside, moonlight shone back at me.

I had just plunged my hands into soapy water and was picking up a brush to start scrubbing dishes when Jilly, one of the young girls running food, came bursting into the room.

"How many times do I have to yell at you girls not to run in my kitchen?" Ada exclaimed as Jilly narrowly avoided skidding into a towering pile of plates.

"Sorry, chef, but I was sent to tell you, Grea took a fall down the stairs!" Jilly was still breathless from her run, and the time she took to gulp a few breaths of air was far too long for the workers to stay silent.

"Is she okay?"

"Did any of the royals see?"

"How many plates did she break?"

"Enough!" Ada's voice rang through the kitchen. "Jilly, spit it out already. What happened exactly?"

Jilly nodded so fast that I was surprised her head didn't fall off. "She was taking the west stairs—avoiding Lord Rentin, of course—"

The workers nodded in acknowledgment. It was more than common to be trapped in a corner with Rentin's wandering eyes and ale-crusted beard while he asked for more than expected from a servant.

"And nearly collided right into Deputy Captain Thesand, coming in the door! So, she threw herself out of the way and ended up falling right down the stairs. It made a huge commotion, and they took her to the healer's ward."

Ada shook her head. "Dumb girl," she said softly.

There was no conviction in those words; we all would have done the same. It was the mark of a good servant to put the royals before themself even if it involved taking a tumble down the stairs. It was really too bad the efforts had been wasted on Aedan Thesand. He would much rather take a plate full of food on his clothes than have someone fall down the stairs on his account.

My mother turned to me. "Go check on Grea."

I balked. "I'm sure Jilly is more than capable," I said. The very last thing I wanted right now was to pick my way through the palace guests to spend time in the healer's ward. That was one place I avoided whenever I could—servants had a tendency to get roped into changing bedsheets and other more unsavoury jobs the healers didn't enjoy.

Ada settled her signature stern gaze on me, lifting one brow warningly. "I wasn't asking, Maisie."

Feeling like a scolded child, I left the kitchen without another word. Heat was rising in my cheeks, as much as I willed it to go away. The interaction only solidified my stance on my aversion toward confrontation. Never did me any good.

The servant hallways took me the long way to the healer's ward, but they were blissfully empty. The lowly lit orbs on the walls weren't much help in the growing dark, making me trip over more than a few cracks and steps. So, I decided it was worth the risk to keep all my limbs unbroken and ducked out into the main hallway.

Right into Deputy Captain Aedan Thesand.

My apologies were extremely muffled, my head jammed into his large chest. Our bodies were touching everywhere, and I tried to pry myself away from him without feeling him up. An endeavour that was only partly successful. Was there a single part of this male that wasn't covered in muscle?

When we were at last untangled, the stream of apologies still pouring from my mouth, Aedan touched my arm gently. "Don't apologize," he said, his eyes kind. "I believe the problem might be myself tonight."

I met his grim smile with one of my own.

"Yes, I'm actually on my way to see your first victim right now."

He gave an apologetic smile.

I'm sure you're used to females throwing themselves at *you, not away.*

My face still felt hot, and I was sure I looked like a tomato, which was entirely embarrassing. I had been a mess of a servant since Diana's disappearance—something that I knew had been a big part of the gossip around here. I did not relish the fact that I was now adding *almost tackled the deputy captain* to my list of misfortunes.

Even in my misery, I could see that Aedan was struggling as well. His eyes were gaunt, haunted. He had been present during the famed portal incident, and he had known Diana as long as I had.

He understands.

Maybe it was that realization, or maybe it was something entirely out of my control, but I said something I hadn't spoken aloud yet.

"I miss her."

Aedan's eyes softened, the pale blue colour looking like a sad, cloudless sky. "I do too," he said, his voice barely louder than a whisper. "I can't help but feel like I could've done something to stop it."

"It's not your fault," I assured him. Because it wasn't his fault. It was mine.

"You weren't there, Maisie. No offense, but you don't know that."

I lifted a shoulder passively. I wasn't about to pick a fight with him. It wasn't even my place to speak with him if he didn't want me to.

"How is the queen?" I asked tentatively.

The queen of Eira had allegedly been injured in the struggle. She hadn't left her room in the two days that followed Diana's departure.

Aedan's lips thinned. "She is recovering."

"You don't seem happy about that."

Aedan clenched his jaw as he stared past me at a painting in the hallway. "I would be handling it differently if I were in her shoes—that's all."

The unspoken words hung between us. He wished action were being taken toward retrieving the princess. That made two of us.

"If I could go retrieve her myself, I would." The words spilled from my mouth. It was unlike me to be … *chatty* with those of authority, but this didn't feel like idle chitchat. This was something we both needed.

He gave me a crooked smile, one that hid his usually present dimples. "I would join you," he said. "I keep thinking there has to be a way to get to her. There has to be someone in Eira who can make another portal, right?"

I shrugged. "Magic is not my strongest suit, unfortunately. Nor have I had the time as of late to search for someone who can help."

Vera should be the one searching, I thought angrily. Instant guilt followed for thinking ill of my queen.

"You believe nothing will be done by the royals then?" I asked, disheartened.

Aedan sighed. "I hope that isn't the case. There is talk of a council meeting when the queen is healed. I would imagine the regions all have something to say on this matter."

When *didn't* the princes have something to say? Unbearable, stuck-up pricks.

I nodded.

"I could let you know what they decide, if you wish."

I looked up at him, meeting his eyes. I didn't welcome the thought of the deputy captain seeking me out, but it was overruled by the desire to know what the officials planned to do about their missing high princess.

"Yes, please," I said, dipping my head in gratitude.

"Perhaps you could return the favour by seeing what you can find out about portals. We could form an … alliance." Aedan's lips curved up on the word.

I crossed my arms. "I don't know where you got the idea that a palace servant has the time to pour into research," I said, a little offended. "But I suppose it is a fair trade."

Aedan nodded.

He opened his mouth, but I cut him off before he could speak. "As long as you can keep up your end of the bargain. I wasn't under the impression that deputy captains were invited to meetings of the officials."

A ghost of a smile appeared on his sallow face. "I have made many friends on the inside, I promise you. Have you no faith? I am closely related to the captain, remember." It was a weak attempt at easy confidence, but it was nice to see some semblance of *Aedan* return.

"Yes, well, when a girl throws herself down the stairs to avoid making contact, it doesn't give me a lot of trust in you."

He was trying not to smile and losing the battle. "Oh, are we joking about this now?"

There was no one else I would have been so brazen with—save for

Diana. A tiny speck of warmth crept into my frozen heart.

We chuckled together quietly until a servant running through the halls broke the tension.

Aedan placed a hand on my forearm and grew serious. "I'll find you in a few days."

His skin was hot, and when he pulled his hand away, I had to ignore the impulse to rub my arm.

Aedan bade me good night and left me in the hallway. Was this dumb? My stomach rolled anxiously. Was I conspiring against the queen—against the North? Nothing I was doing could really be considered treason, but it still felt wrong. I would hate myself if this backfired on me.

I would hate myself even more if I didn't at least try to help get Diana back.

FOUR

LIABILITY

MAISIE

After assuring that Grea was recovering well—the bruised ego seemed worse than her broken rib—it was late. The party had dissipated, the patrons shuffled up to their beds, and the staff were touching their hands to the orbs on the walls, causing the lights to wink out.

I wanted nothing more than to crawl into bed and be done with this day, but I knew my mother would be waiting up for me to give her news of Grea.

At the end of the hall, I saw the doors to the queen's council room open. A figure was coming toward me, tall and dark in the shadows of the darkened palace. When we were a few paces away, I recognized the figure to be Prince Leo from the Southern Isles.

My heart rate quickened. I hadn't expected to see him tonight—or any of the high nobility I was used to entertaining. And it was too late to avoid him now.

I curtsied, keeping my eyes down. "Prince Leo."

He paused, his gaze slowly snapping to attention. He had been lost in thought—damn it. I probably could have walked right by without notice. The smell of the sea had begun to strengthen around me. I used to dream of seeing the ocean one day, sailing on the blue waters and even bluer skies with the smell of the salty breeze in the air. But now, my stomach churned at that scent.

His adder-like smile was not as predatory tonight. "Maisie," he said. "I trust you are well."

I could only nod. My body was tight everywhere. He seemed different.

"I find myself needing a good night's rest," Leo continued, his expression pleasant and vacant. "If you'll excuse me."

My throat felt thick with relief, which was why my voice came out pitifully small when I clarified, "You have no desire of me tonight?"

He crossed the space between us, his long legs making quick work of the gap until he was staring down at me. He drew a slender finger from the base of my throat up to my chin, tilting my head back to look at him. We were so close that I thought he might kiss me. I shouldn't have questioned my luck.

I felt Leo's breath on my lips as he spoke softly. "As enjoyable as I find your services to be, tonight, they are not required."

Despite myself, a shiver ran up my spine—a muscle memory. A small, vain part of myself was proud. He thought our time together was enjoyable. Even if I didn't.

I was relieved when he finally stepped away. I shook my head once to clear the air.

Leo was already walking down the hall, his crisp suit still in perfect condition, even after hours of wear. Incredibly on-brand for him. "Another time," he called over his shoulder.

There was something off about the prince. His unflappable attitude was gone, along with the hideous overconfidence. It relieved me to no end to see him walk away, to have avoided what I rarely did, but it still surprised me. He was reacting to Diana's disappearance more than I'd thought him capable of.

Still didn't improve my opinion on the snake.

The soft whispering of voices drifted toward me. Slowly, curiosity getting the better of me, I crept toward the council room that Leo had just come out of. The door was open a crack, and I stopped myself just outside, trying to calm the heartbeat roaring in my ears.

"… getting to be too much," Queen Vera was saying. "Leo is a liability."

I covered my mouth before I gasped audibly. The queen was out of her rooms, taking meetings in the dead of night. Why so secretive? Surely, the North would have loved to see their queen at the funeral of one of her most trusted and loyal soldiers. If she was able to be mobile, she should have been taking action.

"I'll keep an eye on him."

I recognized Embris's gruff voice. Of course he would be involved, as the captain of the queen's army. Was he keeping this from Aedan— or was Aedan keeping this from me?

"See to it that you do. I don't want any surprises when I meet with the council in two days' time. I expect a report on all the region heads by the night before, understood?" Embris must have nodded in affirmation because she continued in her queenly manner, "I will need your help to get the support of the others. And Aedan—I think it is time he stepped up, joined the inner circle."

"I would agree, My Queen."

"Good. I have big plans for him."

The sounds of creaking floorboards and shuffling chairs became too loud to ignore. They were leaving the council room. The clickety-clack of claws on the hardwood confirmed that the wolf, Delios, was with them. He would detect me soon if I didn't leave.

As quietly as I could muster, I crept away from the door and ran the rest of the way to the kitchens, hoping that my presence had gone unnoticed.

My head whirled. The way the queen had sounded just now—sneaky and conniving, doing her business in the dark—was not the Vera I knew. Nausea curled in my belly. I didn't like change, and my life was completely overloaded with it right now. This was going to end badly for me—I just knew it.

I greeted my mother with a tight smile and assured her of Grea's well-being, all the while preoccupied with what I'd just witnessed. Ada could tell I wasn't acting myself too. Another thing I would have to stay on top of.

My heart panged for Diana. She had made it seem so easy, balancing everything that was expected of her with such poise. I would never be that way.

Diana, please come home soon.

FIVE
RUTHLESS FLIRTING

AEDAN

Two days had passed since Anten's funeral, and I still felt like absolute garbage.

The scene at the portal kept playing in my head, over and over again, a continuous loop that I couldn't snap out of—Diana healing the portal, Vera slipping into a fit of rage, Anten flying across the clearing and breaking his neck on a tree. The blood seeping from his head and the absence of life in his eyes. The worst part of it all had been the sound. I could still hear his neck crack, and it made me shudder to my core.

Anten had been a mentor to me, a friend. I hated myself for how I had failed to save him. And I hated myself for how I still couldn't think a single condemning thought toward Diana. Because the truth was, my heart had been hers since the day we'd met.

Wiping the sweat off my brow with a towel I kept in my training bag, I finally allowed myself to sit for a second. I had worked the soldiers of the queen's army hard today, relentless and long. None had complained, but I could see it in their faces.

"We are preparing for the worst," I'd told them through my own sweat as we went into the half-hour mark of holding our bodies in a plank position. "We are the protectors of Eira."

My father, Embris, had been adamant that training pick up significantly now that Diana had been taken and Urdan had proclaimed his plan to take this realm. I was happy to oblige, seeing as the workouts were the only thing keeping the darkness at bay right now.

Ryen approached me as the soldiers cleared off, his forehead shiny with sweat. "Please tell me this training schedule is not permanent." He gestured to the parchment I had nailed to the door of the training building, where it outlined specifically by day what the soldiers could expect to work on in the next month. "It will not make you very popular at parties."

My second had never been timid to speak his mind. If he thought my idea was dumb, he was going to tell me flat out. But that was part of the many reasons I trusted him to be my second-in-command. Between his candour and his strive for excellence, he was perfect for the job.

He reached out a hand, which I accepted, and helped me stand.

"Good thing I don't really care."

Ryen narrowed his eyes. "You used to care."

I only shrugged.

"All I'm saying is that if you work them too hard, too quick, you're going to lose them."

"The soldiers knew what they were signing up for, Ryen. This is how we prepare for the unknown. We've had it easy, and that's made us all soft. Myself included. It's time to step up and be a real army."

"So, you think there will be war?" Ryen never missed a beat.

"I haven't been told anything, only to prepare for the worst. There is a meeting tonight, where I hope to learn more."

Ryen scratched at his stubble. "I suppose the queen will be quite adamant on getting her daughter back. If she's still alive."

I stilled. Of course Diana was still alive. She had to be.

Great. I had just gotten her out of my head.

"If you don't need me for anything, I'm going to go for a jog. I'll see you for evening training."

I made to step around my second to head toward the exit, but he braced a hand on my chest to stop me.

"You're going *running*?" he asked incredulously.

"In case you missed our entire conversation, Ryen, I am in preparation mode."

"You know what I think, Deputy Captain?" he hissed, stepping into my space.

I raised an eyebrow at his boldness.

"I think you're in hiding mode. You're hiding from the guilt, you're hiding from the pain, and you're hiding from *feeling*. It is not healthy. Working out might feel good now, might keep your mind quiet, but you're pushing it too far. As your second, I feel it's my duty to tell you that you are close to your breaking point."

I shoved Ryen's arm off my chest and stepped into him, causing him to retreat a few steps. "You don't know anything about my breaking point."

I threw my towel over his head to the cleaning basket without breaking eye contact. I waited for him to look away first, but the moment never came. We both startled at a female voice behind us.

"Am I interrupting?" Jamey Pinois stood just a few paces away, looking completely out of place in a sweaty training room with her coiffed hair and perfectly tailored riding tunic.

Obviously, you're interrupting. I never understood why statements like that were made. For attention probably.

Years of etiquette burned into me insisted that I step forward, take her hand, ask what I could do for her. But I wasn't feeling in a polite mood, so I let Ryen take the lead.

"Of course not, Lady Pinois. What brings you down to the training centre?"

"I was looking for someone to assist me in going for a ride. It's a lovely morning for one." Jamey clasped her hands in front of her, smiling expectantly.

I knew for a fact that she had the ability to get a horse ready to ride by herself. She was just enjoying the North's hospitality.

In my opinion, the West had overstayed their welcome.

"I would be happy to accompany you. Just let me—"

"Actually," Jamey cut in, "I would love to catch up with my dear friend, the deputy captain. If you don't mind, of course."

Ryen gave me the smile he usually reserved for when he bested me in the training ring. "Not a problem at all. I'll leave you to it."

I walked with Jamey down to the stables, inwardly cursing my second the whole way down.

"I imagine you are quite busy with everything that has happened. I appreciate you taking the time to ride with me."

"No problem," I lied.

"Anten's service was beautiful," Jamey said conversationally.

It killed me to speak of him so casually. I could only nod and let her chatter as we walked.

When we got to the barn, I sought the head stable hand, Rolfo, right away.

"Ah, Deputy Captain! I was wondering when I would see you here again!"

I clasped Rolfo's arm and couldn't help but smile at his ever-present happiness. "I've been busy, but how long can one really go without a trip to the stables?"

He grinned his gap-toothed grin. "I'll get Kali saddled for you right away," he said, referencing my grey mare. "And who might the lady be suitable with?" Rolfo noticed Jamey and swept into a dramatic bow.

I opened my mouth to tell him any of the guest horses would work when Jamey spoke up. "This one is gorgeous. I'll take her."

With a heart-dropping realization, I recognized which horse Jamey was standing in front of, admiring. Finnvarra lifted her head from her hay, regarding us warily. The fiery-orange mare's ears flattened against her head as another horse walked past, and she lunged at the bars before returning to her meal.

"No." It was highly rude of me. But Gaia help me if anyone attempted to ride that horse.

"Excuse me?"

"Absolutely not. She's too much to handle."

Jamey crossed her arms. "I am an extremely competent rider, thank you very much. I can handle myself just fine."

Rolfo looked between us nervously and, catching my pointed glance, cleared his throat. "Ah, perhaps the deputy captain is right. The mare has not been right since the princess … well, you know. I do worry about her unpredictability right now."

Jamey didn't look convinced, but stayed quiet.

"Plum will do," I told Rolfo.

He set off, visibly relieved to be out of the tension.

It wasn't until we were mounted and walking down the path into the forest that Jamey spoke again. "I think I know why you snapped at me," she started.

How presumptuous. I waited for her to continue, but she was silent, waiting for me to bite.

"Do tell."

"The mare—she belongs to Diana, doesn't she?"

I scoffed. "You expect me to believe you didn't already know that?"

She ignored the question, reaching out to place a hand on my arm. "Diana is smart and capable. I have every faith she will find her way back to us."

I wanted to scream in frustration. What if she couldn't? What if she was hurt or being held captive? What if, what if, what if. But I had no way to emote that didn't involve a punching bag. So, I just stared ahead through Kali's ears, my jaw clenched.

"And, yes, I did know that Finnvarra belonged to Diana. Admittedly, I was trying to see where your feelings stood with her. Immature, I know. But I can't help it when I'm horribly jealous of those feelings."

Was I that easy to read? It was horrible to think of how many might know my feelings if someone from another region could guess. Oh *Gaia*, what if Diana had known?

But wait. Was Jamey saying what I thought she was? I looked sideways at her, grateful to find she wasn't staring expectantly at me, but instead playing with Plum's mane.

"You're jealous of what feelings? Which, by the way, I'm not admitting to."

Jamey smiled. "Is it so hard to believe that I'd be interested in a handsome, kind, strong male such as yourself?"

Ruthless flirting—that was what this was. I wanted to laugh, but it seemed inappropriate in the situation.

"I am one of thousands with that description in this region alone, I can assure you."

"Ah, but I've never met anyone with dimples like yours," she said, the corner of her mouth twisting up. "They're endearing."

I shook my head softly. Jamey could flirt all she wanted. It didn't change where my heart lay. And truthfully, it felt like a compliment.

"Come on. That's enough heart-pouring. Let's race." She laughed.

Through the thundering hooves and whipping of the wind, I could hear her giggling carrying back to me. It was infectious, bringing a real laugh to my lips for the first time in a while. Kali was eager for more, and I let her out, easily overtaking Plum. I couldn't help matching Jamey's grin as I passed her.

When we finally returned to the stables, my heart felt lighter.

The clouds darkening around my head had lifted significantly. And through the new clarity, I could see something that was certain. I didn't have to wait around for orders to take action.

I could get Diana back myself.

All I needed was a little help.

SIX

LOST IN THE MAZE
DIANA

My hand stung uncomfortably, but I didn't mind. It reminded me that some of the pent-up emotions had left my body. It reminded me that he was real, he was here.

Spense.

He'd come into the room like a storm, door swinging wildly. He was unkempt and tall and handsome, just like the first day we'd met. His black curls flopped on his forehead, and his eyes of steel, they were looking at me with such emotion. An emotion I was afraid of. He was so open and raw, and there were too many things between us. It was too much. I'd had to defuse it somehow. The slap had seemed to fit the bill.

Plus, I might have had some residual anger built up.

Now, as he rubbed his already-reddening cheek and furrowed his brow in confusion, the idea to slap him seemed like maybe a poor choice.

"I-I'm sorry," I began. "I don't really know what possessed me to do that."

Spense lowered his hand from his face and smiled, although he kept the space between us. "Don't be. I think I had that one coming."

It shouldn't have been a surprise to see him act normal, but it was.

I had been convinced the events leading up to our portal trip would change him. It was uncomfortably odd to look at Spense's familiar face, his strong features, and prominent horns and know he was a stranger to me now.

No matter how much he charmed me, I had to be vigilant.

"How are you doing?" I ventured.

"I don't think I know how to answer that." He laughed.

I had to agree.

Spense slowly reached out and grabbed my hand in his. "I'm sorry you were here all alone. Were you treated well?"

I spared a glance around the furnished room. It could have been worse. "It was frustrating. But I wasn't mistreated."

He nodded, relief spreading on his face. The idea that he had been concerned for my welfare scared me. Who had he thought would hurt me?

When I met his eyes again, he was staring at our joined hands, at the dark ink decorating the arms that were held out. I swallowed.

"We have a lot to talk about," Spense said, his voice low.

I nodded.

He continued, "And I want to tell you everything. But first, we're expected to meet my siblings for a council meeting."

My stomach leaped in shock. "Siblings?" I breathed.

Spense smiled, real emotion on his face. "Four. I can't wait for you to meet them." His eyes flicked once to my neck, where Jweira lay. "You might want to take that off before we go."

I placed a hand protectively over the emerald. "No. It stays with me."

He furrowed his brow. "I know you know who she is. You told me, remember?"

Yes, I did remember. That night was seared into my brain. It had been the night of our first kiss.

"Jweira was once our sister. My siblings might not take very kindly to you wearing her as jewellery."

His tone was not accusing, but I still felt anger spitting in me at the insinuation.

"I'll tuck her away then," I said. "But she doesn't leave me."

Not until I knew more about the Unseelie. Not before I knew what they planned to do with her. She had given her life for me, and I wasn't going to hand her away like a broken toy.

Spense nodded apprehensively as I unclasped the chain from my neck and tucked Jweira into the deep pocket of the borrowed tan pants I wore.

He cleared his throat. "I, uh, want to just say that … I've got your back."

My heart clenched. Whatever Spense this was, the version I knew or not, he was trying to express emotion, which he clearly hadn't had a lot of practice with.

I should return the sentiment, tell him I had his back too. But did I? Of course I wanted to fall back into this easiness with him, but I couldn't let myself. Not yet. And I should be honest with him about it.

"Thank you," I replied. "Look, I want to trust you. It's just … a lot has happened. I don't think I'll be myself for a while. I need some time."

"Of course. I want to earn your trust again."

"You can start by telling me everything."

Spense wet his lips and glanced around the room. "And I will. But first, the meeting." He squeezed my hand once. "As long as you're up for it."

Like hell he was leaving without me even if the thought of being in a room full of Dark fae terrified me. I wouldn't be holed up in

Spense's room, hiding from the scary stories I'd been told as a child.

"Lead the way."

Spense offered me his arm, and I took it warily. Being so brazenly *with* him made me uncomfortable. Our arms might be yelling at the world that we were a package deal, but I wasn't so ready to declare it yet.

I felt his sweet, soothing magic reach out to mine, which did not respond. Damn.

He frowned. "Are you all right?"

"Like I said, just not feeling like myself."

Spense nodded once, and I saw hurt splash across his face before he could hide it. My stomach clenched, but it was better for him to think I had rejected his magic than to risk the disability of mine getting out.

Wanting to move on from that awkward encounter, I asked, "What can I expect from this meeting?"

We left his room and started down hallways made of an unfamiliar substance—it looked wet and dry at the same time. Unlike the palace in Nevelyn, there were hardly any windows. Considering the desert climate, I assumed that was to keep the heat out. But I didn't like how close and tight it felt.

"Well, my siblings will all want to meet you, of course. And go over the events of the portal." He gave me a sideways glance to gauge my reaction, to which I kept my face neutral. "But other than that, it should be business as usual. The heads of the departments will give reports, and we will decide together the course of action for each."

"Are you a department head?" I asked.

Spense smiled wryly. "I am."

Despite myself, I pushed my shoulder against his arm once to get him to continue, earning a huff of laughter from him.

"I manage the Unseelie army." His tone was light, but the words fell heavy between us.

"That would explain your fighting proficiency then," I managed.

"It's a fairly new role for me. I only took over for my brother six years ago, when his daughter was born. He wished for a role that would keep him close to home," Spense said.

He led me down a plain set of stairs into a foyer that branched off into no less than eight different hallways. I would have to be careful not to get lost in this maze.

"Six years does not seem like a new role." I glanced up at him in time to see him run a hand through those black curls. My treacherous heart skipped a beat.

"You're right. It has been a while. I suppose I still don't feel as if I have earned it. To me, it still seems like Sorin's job. I should count myself lucky that he worked so hard to shape the army into something that I've never had to spend time changing. There is a really good system in place."

Finally, we were getting somewhere. Hope lifted, warming me from the inside. Spense was open; he was talking to me. Even if the trust was still being earned back, this was a good start.

Right as we rounded a corner, Spense dropped my hand and snatched something in the air that had been running away as quickly as it could from the sound of our footsteps.

"Hey! Put me down!" A small child's face emerged from Spense's arm, properly disgruntled.

"What do you think you're doing here, Ash? Running away from your governess again?" he chided, placing the girl back on her feet.

She looked up at him with wide brown eyes, her shiny black hair a mess atop her head.

"Spensey!" She ran back at him with all the force she could, wrapping her tiny arms around him.

"There you are!" A tall, lanky female with catlike eyes ran over to us, wrenching Ash back to look her in the eyes. "Do you know how much trouble you're in, little lady? Your mother has been worried sick."

"Don't blame her," Spense cut in, smoothly transferring the attention to him. "She was just excited to see her uncle again."

The female righted herself, pulling at her sleeves primly. "Yes, well, whatever the case might be, Aislinn knows she is not permitted to wander the premises on her own. Should she have asked, I would have gladly brought her to visit you."

The little girl rolled her eyes, and then her gaze caught on me. "Who are you?"

"I'm Diana," I told her. "I'm a friend of Spense's."

Her eyes shifted to our clasped hands and then back up, wariness crossing her features. "Are you going to the meeting? Father says there are no outsiders allowed. You can't go."

I looked to Spense, who was laughing quietly.

"She's a special friend, Ash. Don't worry; you'll be joining us in those meetings before you know it."

Ash pursed her lips at me but smiled when she looked back to her uncle. "I'm happy you're back."

"Let's go, Aislinn," her governess said, steering her away. "Let them get to their meeting. You don't want to be the reason they're late."

"Be good. We'll see you later." Spense smiled at her retreating form before shaking his head once and continuing to lead me down the hall. "That's Sorin's daughter."

"She seems like a handful," I remarked.

"You have no idea. She goes through tutors like you wouldn't believe."

I opened my mouth to ask about her, but my question died on my tongue. We had halted in front of a giant set of double doors. I blinked. Had I been transported? Unlike the entirety of Ivywall that I'd seen, all unimpressive reds and browns, these doors were made of marble, as black as obsidian. The brass handles were long bars that rested across the middle of the doors in a gentle swoop. They were grand and inviting, looking for the first time like they belonged in a palace.

"Ready?"

No, not really.

But I nodded anyway. Pulling away from my arm gently, Spense pushed open the doors and guided me inside.

SEVEN
HIDING SPOT

MAISIE

"Oh, shut up," I grumbled under my breath as the third servant in a row gave me a weird look.

I'd deserved it though, for having my ear stuck to the side wall of the queen's council room. It was blatantly clear that I was unsuccessfully trying to eavesdrop through magic-enforced shields.

The queen had called the meeting with her high officials, just as I'd heard her say to Embris two nights ago. I'd watched them all file in, region after region, wearing finery and conversing like it was a leisurely visit. There was no fire, no urgency. It made me wonder if they even cared.

Two guards had closed the doors, and the servants of the officials were all sent outside. They had gleefully disappeared to enjoy their unexpected time off, leaving me alone in my pitiful spying attempt.

I was finally contemplating giving up when a flurry of movement from down the hall caught my eye. Kitchen workers were heading toward the council room, laden down with giant plates of food. I recognized Jilly among them, who waved at me.

The guards began to open the heavy doors for the food delivery. Now was my chance. I stepped in front of Jilly and pried the silver dish of poached eggs from her grip.

"Maisie? What—"

"Let me do this. I'll owe you one."

Without another glance, I followed the party into the council room. The massive table was filled, the patrons sitting so close together that arms were brushing. Even with the far window open to a lovely breeze coming off the River Nord, the room was stiflingly hot. Spring was turning to summer, and these bodies crammed together wasn't helping. I looked at the plate of eggs I was carrying and wrinkled my nose. They would not be my first choice in this heat.

As I walked around the table and set my plate in front of a disgusted Prince Leo, I caught Aedan's eye. I raised my eyebrow ever so slightly, to which he responded with a barely noticeable nod. I breathed a silent sigh of relief.

I faded into the back of the room, hoping to remain unnoticed. Prince Kashdan of the West spoke as he scooped a heaping amount of raw salmon onto his plate. It was a favourite of his; whenever he visited, the kitchens would be filled with the fish.

"It is safe to assume that no living entity has the knowledge of how to create a portal. Is that correct, My Queen?"

"To the extent of my knowledge, yes." This was the first I had laid eyes on Queen Vera, who was looking regal in an emerald dress that matched the jewellery with which she was bedecked. She was her usual poised self, albeit the dark circles under her eyes told a different story. Her wolf companion, Delios, lay off to the side, panting in the heat.

Lord Nimshar, the haughty representative of the East, drummed his fingers on the table. "My lady knows of magics long forgotten. It is possible she has the knowledge."

He referenced the royal he served, Princess Hollaina, who had not been seen in another region for many years. I'd always been told she had lost her wits in a horrific accident and was not of sound mind. From the looks of the officials around the table, they seemed to share that notion. All avoided eye contact with Nimshar, fiddling with their hands or helping themselves to food.

"Forgive me, but was it not your own magic that closed the portal?" Prince Leo asked the queen, his voice as sharp as a blade.

At that moment, Vera looked directly at me, sending a jolt to my heart. "Servants, you are dismissed."

All I could do was bow my head and follow the others, who were shuffling out. I tried to walk as slow as possible without arising suspicion.

"That is not common knowledge, and I'd thank you not to repeat it," I heard Vera hiss. "It is true I was forced to close the portal, but that is an entirely different type of magic. To destroy is much easier than to create."

If Leo had a rebuttal, I did not hear it. As soon as I left the room, the wards kicked in, and all I could hear was the blood roaring in my ears.

My eavesdropping had been a bust, but I'd heard enough. There was no way they knew how to get a portal open. With a heavy heart, I disappeared into the servants' corridor to find some way to keep busy until I could meet with Aedan.

I waited for the bastard deputy captain to show up the whole rest of the day, finding inane things to keep me busy in the servants' quarters. I figured it was best to stay in one place so he had a better chance of finding me.

But he never showed. When night fell, I took a tour around the palace, but still could not find him. Frustrated, I pushed the glass doors open into the gardens and set out. The air was still warm with a crisp wind that was a huge relief from the stuffy palace. I let the fresh air in my lungs calm me. If I did not see Aedan on my way back through, I would go to bed and try again tomorrow.

"There you are!"

I spun to see the aforementioned bastard deputy captain striding toward me with the gall to look annoyed.

"I've been waiting for you all day," I said. "I haven't moved!"

"That's the problem," he said, catching up to me. We went farther into the garden, away from any residual palace light. "I couldn't just walk into the servants' quarters and ask for you—that would have been entirely questionable. We aren't known as friends."

That stung, considering how many hours of my life I'd spent just a few paces behind him and Diana as they attended a party, or visited the theatre, or raced their horses through the fields. It was a sharp reminder that I was invisible to him as a friend. I was only a servant, helping him with what he needed.

"Right. Well, I never thought of that."

"It's fine. We're here now. Should we make this our meeting spot from now on?"

I looked around the grove we'd stopped in. It was one of Diana's favourite spots with an abundance of lobelia and irises. She had loved to sit on the wooden bench years ago while she studied. It felt appropriate.

You will see this place again, I promise.

I nodded. "What did you learn in the meeting?" After the snippet of conversation I'd heard, I was not feeling very optimistic.

Aedan ran a hand through his golden hair. He kept it short, as was expected in the army, but still was able to tug on a few strands absentmindedly. "There was so much needless reiteration that it made it hard to keep the topic on track. The meeting ended with, 'Let's all reconvene in a week, when we have more information.' As if anything will change."

My heart sank. "So, there is no plan?"

"Not as of yet. Without the means of creating a portal, they are at a loss as to what we can do."

"Are they at least going to enlist the help of scholars on this?" I tugged at a piece of my curly hair and chewed the inside of my cheek. "The more eyes, the better."

Aedan sighed. "The queen only wants the most trusted scholars from the academy to help. It will slow things down, but at least it's something."

I plopped onto the bench. "This is so frustrating."

Aedan sat beside me, looking straight ahead at the purple irises in full bloom. "I know. But they're charging on ahead in their plans to learn how to make a portal. What they will do once they figure that out is another story. And I expect it will mean another frustrating day spent in that sweltering room."

I shuddered at the memory.

"The queen says she believes this is all part of Gaia's plan and that the ancestors are watching over Diana."

"Why doesn't she commune with her ancestors then and find out?"

"The thought crossed my mind as well."

I shoved his shoulder once. *"Why didn't you speak up?!"*

Aedan's blue eyes turned cold as he leaned closer to me, his jaw working. "I would have thought you would understand how status works, Maisie." His stormy look sent a shiver down my spine. "I am not someone in a position of *speaking up*. I do as I am told without question—that is my role until my father concedes his captain's badge to me. I was lucky to have been in the room at all!"

Clearly, a nerve had been struck. Guilt bloomed in my belly.

"I'm sorry. I don't mean to berate you," I said.

His face softened.

"I'm on edge right now. This isn't right."

Aedan sighed. "I know. Between you and me, I have been thinking of ways to figure this out myself."

Sharply, I looked at him. "How so?"

"Well, you keeping your end of the deal would help," he said, nudging my knee with his.

It was true; I had come up short on that. Embarrassment flamed through me. I would not come to another meeting empty-handed, I vowed.

"I want to see if I can pull up water from the Well and use it to channel enough magic into creating the portal. If I do, I can slip in much quieter than the queen and her army. I know I am simplifying it completely, but I believe I can grab her and get out much faster and safer than whatever the council decides."

Hope fluttered in my chest. The Well! It was a long shot, but a shot at last.

"That is promising. But how will you get permission to use the Well?"

Anyone who wanted to attempt to pull water from the mystic well had to first be given the okay from the queen herself.

"I'm still working on that." Aedan looked sheepish.

These army males were so proud that they couldn't stand to be caught with an unfinished plan.

"And there's something else."

I looked at him, moonlight splashing over his face.

"The shadows have taken another victim."

Horror washed over me. "I thought they were gone."

Aedan nodded grimly. "We all thought they would disappear with the portal. Personally, I was under the impression that *he* was controlling them. But now, it seems they are something else entirely."

"That is troubling."

"To say the least."

"So, what do we do?"

"Not much we can do. Keep vigilant for them, although the safest place right now would be the palace. They are only attacking in quiet, rural areas so far."

I nodded. "All right. So, we go ahead with our plan. By our next meeting, I will have better information about making portals, and you will have a cover story for using the Well."

Aedan smiled. "Deal. You sound like an official with these demands," he teased.

I returned the smile. "Just a girl who knows what she wants."

Before collapsing into bed, I made a quick trip up the familiar stairs to Diana's rooms. She had once gifted me a set of rooms near hers, which she believed I stayed in. As much as her generosity warmed my heart, I had not been able to accept them. It blurred the line between our roles far too much to be comfortable.

Diana had borrowed books from her friend Shela in the City of Scholars, and they hadn't been returned before the incident. On the few occasions I'd seen her peruse the old texts, she had been very protective of them, and I wagered that these books might be more important than I'd initially realized.

Her bedchamber was exactly how I'd last left it—the bed turned down for after the party. My heart panged. Jewellery lay out on the vanity, and shoes were haphazardly strewn across the room from when she'd been trying to decide what to wear with the glittering gown from that night. I'd dressed her and done her makeup. She'd looked like a vision, a true queen. I wondered idly if that dress had survived the portal.

I allowed myself a few more glances around the room before dropping to my knees beside the bed. Her go-to hiding spot was always under the mattress. Sliding my hand underneath proved my theory. I pulled out six books, one by one, varying in length and size.

Jackpot.

Hiding my find under my coat like a drake hoarding gold, I slipped from the room and back to my own, where I lit the orb beside my bed and set to work.

EIGHT
UNDENIABLE RESPECT

DIANA

My mouth went dry.

Urdan's ominous words from the first few seconds I had arrived sounded in my head. *"Welcome to the heart of the Unseelie."*

If this was the heart, I knew less of them than I thought.

I recognized the marble floors and the giant windows from my arrival. We must have portaled into this room. It had been empty before, but now hosted a massive round table with seating for twelve. This was nothing like the rest of Ivywall—it would have been absurd to think this room could even exist within its walls.

From the windows, I could see much more than I had from Spense's room. It was definitely a desert with sand and cacti as far as the eye could see. The fence I'd seen was a lot closer, and it was easier to make out the details now. Impressively tall and menacing with wires and spikes, it was more a wall than a fence. There was a slight shimmer around the edges that was barely noticeable—magic, I realized. Who were they keeping out of Ivywall?

Seated around the table were five fae, who all looked astonishingly alike, aside from one raven-haired female. They all shared the same deep brown eyes and sandy hair at various lengths. They watched us inquisitively as we made our way over. I smiled at Pik, who sat nearest the door, waving to me.

Spense gently pulled at my elbow to stop me beside him at the end of the table.

"Siblings," he said, a proud smile on his face. "I would like to introduce you to Diana, high princess of Eira."

Bringing up my title was not the move I'd have gone for, as two of the males' faces grew tight at his words.

"Hello," I said, meeker than I'd hoped for.

My eyes were drawn to the male who stood up to incline his head to me, the dark-haired female joining him. Immediately, I knew that these were the parents of the rapscallion Aislinn.

"Welcome, Diana," he said kindly. "I am Sorin, and this is my wife, Meske. Your presence in our world came unexpected, but we are happy to meet Spense's soul-destined at last."

A jolt went through me at that. As much as I wanted to be known as myself first, not as Spense's soulmate, the title would serve as protection.

"No need for such formality," Spense said, sensing that I had stiffened.

He pulled out a chair for me beside Pik and settled into the one beside me. My heart thundered as I took in each of his siblings.

"Sorin is the eldest of us, and he is the head of the court, meaning he deals with the day-to-day of Ivywall. Next, we have Badras, who is head of fae-folk relations."

The fae he gestured to was an absolute beast. He had wide shoulders and a strong jaw and looked like a fight was never far from his mind. He wore his hair in a bun at the top of his head. If anything, Badras looked like he would be the head of the army, not a peacekeeper between the Folk.

"Alwyn comes next, and she is the head of the drake riders."

The female next to Badras practically bounced in her seat with excitement. It was striking how, even with her tiny frame, she looked every bit the warrior that Badras did. She wore her hair back in a long ponytail with the sides of her head shaved.

"I would have thought the drakes fell under the army," I dared to say to Spense.

"He wishes." Alwyn smirked. She winked at me, and I couldn't help the small smile that escaped my lips.

Spense rolled his eyes. "Last but not least is Olys," he said, his hand coming to rest on the shoulder of the small male beside him.

Olys had looked the tensest when we arrived, and that tension had not left him. His lips were pressed thinly together, and his narrowed eyes seemed to see right through me. There was a certain air around him that made me shiver. He was not looking for a new friend.

Keeping things light despite his brother's obvious distrust, Spense said, "Ollie here heads up all the agriculture and trades. A most important job."

He clapped his brother on the back, but Olys did not break eye contact with me.

That's fine, Olys. I don't trust you either.

Meske cleared her throat delicately. She was beautiful and fair with stark blue eyes in the shape of almonds. Looking at her closer, I could see that she shared a mating tattoo with Sorin, inky-black lines weaving from their shoulders to elbows.

Spense chuckled. "Sorry, Meske. My dear sister is the head of the healers. Not to mention, she is the finest healer in Ivywall. I wasn't going to forget you, I promise." He smiled at her, receiving a satisfied smile back, before looking around the table. "There you have it. The Drakenis family."

"Did you get your surname for the drakes in your army?" It was the first time I'd heard of him having one. Not all fae did; some preferred to be known by their profession, like Ada the Baker.

"Our surnames say a lot about us, don't they, Lightbringer?" Spense winked. "Are there no more attendees tonight?"

"We thought it best for Diana to keep the meeting to the heads this time," Sorin explained. "It is overwhelming enough for her already."

"Probably wise," Spense said. To me, he explained, "We have a few more trusted members of the council. They do not have any votes, but they are invaluable nonetheless."

I looked around the table. Spense's siblings all met my gaze with varying levels of enthusiasm.

Before I lost my nerve, I asked, "Will the king not be joining us tonight?"

Everyone swung their heads toward Spense. Clearly, I was missing something.

Spense cleared his throat. "There is no easy way to describe this. Our father suffers from hysteria. More often than not, he does not know himself. He will forget things, like conversations he had yesterday or even his children. We never know what version of him will come out each day. Unfortunately, he hasn't been a part of this council for many years. Not since—"

"That's enough," Badras cut in, his voice low.

Spense stilled, looking at his brother slowly. "She has a right to know about the court she is now a part of." His tone was dangerous, and even without my magic, I could sense the shift in him.

It reminded me of the day at the stables in Eira, when he had lashed out at the grooms.

"It's a lot of information to be thrown at her right away, brother,"

Sorin said calmly. "She will learn it all in due time."

The tension around the table deflated, and I could instantly see that the eldest brother had the undeniable respect of all his siblings.

Sorin spoke to me directly. "As our father is unable to attend, his personal servant, Pik, is here as his representation."

Pik nodded. "I relay everything back to him and do my best to get his thoughts on each matter. It is … a delicate effort. But one I am proud to do."

Urdan … is not well?

"The king seemed himself enough when he attempted to invade my land," I said, my voice ringing through the room.

The siblings all took my bitter words in silence, shifting ever so slightly. It surprised me when Olys spoke first.

"King Urdan has bouts of awareness when he remembers everything. They are few and far between. He was lucid when he marched through the portal—which, if I am correct, *you* fixed so that it could be travelled through."

My temper flared. "I didn't fix it for *him*!"

Olys sneered, "Then, what was your plan with it? For Eira's armies to march upon us instead? Or were you so foolish that you had no course of action in mind when you healed it?"

My stomach dropped as I thought back to that day. My grandmother, Maeve, had appeared to me, guiding me to heal the portal. She'd said it was my destiny, that it would heal the broken lands. It felt foolish now to think that I'd had no plan. Destined fate or not, I could hardly believe the ancestors had picked me to rule Eira. Especially now.

"That's enough, Olys," Spense growled.

"No, brother, this needs to be said. She is as untrustworthy to the Unseelie as any of our enemies beyond Ivywall. She would sooner set her own armies loose here than help us." Olys's eyes glinted darkly as he glared at me.

"You think *I'm* untrustworthy? Within seconds of the portal being fixed, Urdan sauntered through, army in tow, demanded we all step aside, as he was going to take Eira from us. Then, he claimed Spense as his son, told me this was all Spense's idea, and slammed memories into him so hard that he was rendered unconscious. *Then,* he proceeded to fight the queen—*my mother*—until she had no other option but to close the portal to keep his army out! Now, I'm here, in the heart of the group that just tried to kill my fae and take my land, and you're finding it strange that *I'm* untrusting? I hardly believe that you would be this calm in my position. Kindly screw off, Olys!" I was slightly panting when I finished, and I realized I had stood up, my fists clenched.

That had felt *really* good.

Alwyn let out a low whistle. "I can see the match now."

I reseated myself and smoothed my pants. Spense reached out a hand and closed it around mine. I stared at Olys, who stared back, unperturbed by my outburst.

"Diana has been through a lot. I trust her with my entire being. That should be enough for you. I expect her to be treated with respect as she navigates this all." Spense squeezed my hand periodically while he spoke.

"I am happy to give her that respect when she has earned it." Olys folded his hands together at the table, his thoughts final.

Alwyn clapped once. "Good enough for me. Let's move on, shall we?"

Sorin cleared his throat. "I agree. In the spirit of building trust, let us be candid, as we usually are in our meetings. I would like to discuss how many attacks we've seen this month. Alwyn, as you've temporarily stepped into Spense's role, would you bring us all up to speed?"

I glanced around the table. They were going to continue as normal with my presence? There was not a chance in hell that my mother would allow Spense into her meetings, probably not even after the tattoos.

Spense nudged Alwyn with his elbow. "Been double-dipping, have you?"

She grinned. It was a look that invited adventure and danger. "I don't know what you're always going on about. It was as easy as besting Badras in a duel."

The brother in mention growled once, not a fan of their mockery. Based on his sheer, terrifying size and stature, Alwyn truly must be brave to take him on.

"In honesty though," she continued, her voice growing serious, "the regiments have seen a huge uptick in human attacks. They have continued making devices that render our magic unusable, and with that advantage, we have become evenly matched. I don't know how they're finding out where our markets are, but it is proving to be a big problem. We are full to the brim with refugees in Ivywall. We will not be able to sustain this high number forever."

Human? I had never heard of that creature before.

I looked to Spense, who had furrowed his brow, tense worry on his face.

"Things have gotten worse since my departure."

Alwyn nodded. "I have spoken to Olys and his agricultural workers, and we are consuming more than we are growing. These fae don't feel safe enough to return to the towns. And I don't blame them either."

"I will speak with my Folk ambassadors to see if any would be willing to accommodate us. Or, at the very least, be willing to supply food or aid to the army," Badras said.

Sorin nodded. "I suppose that is all we can do for now. We will not turn away any who seek shelter in Ivywall."

Spense's eyes were narrowed, his mouth slightly parted, like he had something on his mind, but he didn't speak up.

"On the topic of Folk," Badras said, his mouth tightening, "I have received an urgent call from Elfwood."

Olys groaned, dropping his head in his hands.

"Their clan leader, Kvistor, is requesting our aid. He says the humans have been getting closer to their borders and that they fear an attack soon. Their scouts have reported seeing camps not a day's ride from them."

"How much do we trust Kvistor?" Sorin asked.

Badras inhaled deeply. "It is hard to judge the loyalties of the elves. The last interaction I had with him was ten years ago, when he declared his unhappiness of The Pixie Decree."

Spense looked to me. In a low voice, he explained, "The decree stopped the elves from sport-hunting the Night Pixies. They weren't happy about it."

"They were hunting other Folk for sport?" I asked, shocked.

"Once you meet the Night Pixies, you'll understand. Incredibly destructive little things. Still, couldn't have Ivywall turn a blind eye to it. The Folk need to be united now more than ever."

I so badly wanted to know what was going on with the humans and their devices. It didn't feel right to interrupt the meeting to ask to be brought up to speed. Spense had promised explanations, and I would have to be patient.

Sorin pondered on this and finally said, "If you believe they are telling the truth, then we should send a party immediately."

"I'm not sure if I do trust him," Badras growled. "I've been on the receiving end of elvish revenge before, and it wasn't pretty."

"The risk of not bringing them aid is higher than the risk of petty revenge. What if the humans wipe out the clan while we stand idly by?" Spense demanded. "The army is mine to command. We will send out a team to help."

Badras shrugged. "Fine, Spense. Be the hero. But I don't want to hear a word from you if it goes south."

"It won't."

Alwyn turned to Spense. "My riders will accompany you. It is the fastest way to get there after all."

"Thank you, sister," Spense said. "That will be a great help."

"All right, it's settled. A group will leave at dawn for Elfwood. I trust you will organize this with Alwyn?" Sorin addressed Spense, who nodded. "Great. I believe that is enough of a recap for one meeting. My belly is growling, as I'm sure yours all are as well. Let's go to dinner."

The siblings and Pik stood and filed out of the room. Meske gave me a big smile and a pat on the arm as she passed. Alwyn looped her arm through mine, the familiarity of it reminding me of Maisie. A pang of longing for her clattered through my wounded heart.

"I like you," she said simply.

I couldn't help but laugh once. "You hardly know me."

"But, you see, I know my brother *quite* well," she cooed, looking back over her shoulder once at Spense, who followed us out of the exquisite room and back into the dry hallway. "And someone who is worthy of being his soulmate is automatically someone I adore."

It was a truly kind sentiment, one I hardly deserved.

"Thank you," I murmured.

"I cannot wait for the adventures we are going to have," she enthused, bringing her head to rest on my shoulder for a beat.

Spense's voice drawled from behind, "You don't want any part in Alwyn's so-called adventures, trust me."

I twisted my head to look at him and was surprised to find his gaze right away, his grey eyes full of an emotion I didn't quite recognize on him. He was happy, no doubt. Probably fulfilled now that he was home with his siblings, who obviously cared deeply for him.

"And why is that?" I asked. "I happen to like adventures."

In one smooth move, Spense cut in between us, edging out his sister and grabbing hold of my hand. His fingers interlaced with mine, setting my heart on a staccato pace.

Be vigilant.

"Because my adventures are much more fun and much less likely to end up with you on the wrong end of a leprechaun's pipe," he drawled, his voice tickling my ear. He sent a pointed glance to Alwyn, who rolled her eyes.

He had certainly been charming before, but this new Spense was a downright flirt. I couldn't stop the flip my stomach did at the feel of his lips brushing my neck.

"I know it's not the best circumstances," he whispered, keeping our conversation private from Alwyn, who was a step ahead. "But I am excited you're here. We'll figure out a way to get a portal again together. In the meantime, I hope you can enjoy yourself—even just a little bit."

I found myself leaning into his arm, his touch. It would be so easy to fall into this again. I was standing on a precarious edge.

"At least someone's happy I'm here," I said drily.

Spense was unworried. "Olys will come around. He'll always be the one to fight the hardest against change. Keep on being your strong, charismatic self, and he'll love you. Just like—" He coughed once. "Just like Alwyn so clearly does already."

He smiled down at me, and I couldn't help but feel lighter.

He brought our joined hands up to his face, where he dropped a kiss on mine.

"Let me show you my world."

NINE

SPARRING

AEDAN

"**A**gain!" I called out through pants.

The afternoon sun beat down on the training sand pit, where a cluster of soldiers surrounded me. On my count, they sprinted the length of the arena, dropped and gave twenty push-ups, and sprinted back.

A hand on my shoulder made me jolt. Instinctively, I threw my weight into a punch outward. If it wasn't for my father's impressive evasive skill, I would have struck him square on the jaw.

Embris chuckled. "Easy there, big shot."

I shook off the embarrassment of being caught off guard. "Feel like joining in?"

"Tempting, but no. Would hate to make a fool of myself." He smiled knowingly. It was obvious that he would not look a fool in front of the sweating soldiers. He was the captain, and his skill and prowess were unparalleled.

I bristled inwardly. Embris meant well, but his little jabs and jokes only succeeded in making me feel inferior. I poured my blood, sweat, and tears into this army, all to make him look good.

After watching the soldiers run a few more sets, I released them. "You should make them train with full armour on," Embris said, eyeing up the male who had collapsed on the ground in a pool of sweat.

"It's on the schedule to start with full gear in another week," I replied, keeping my tone calm. Of course I'd planned on getting the soldiers used to the weight of armour; I just wanted to make sure they were toned and ready for it.

"Bump it up. Every training from here on out is in full gear."

I clamped down on my bottom lip to keep from saying something I would regret. "Yes, sir."

"Good." Embris motioned to Ryen to join us. "I have a job for you two."

Ryen stood to my left, as customary for a second. He listened raptly, the sweat from training sliding down his dark skin.

"As you know, we are preparing for the worst. In the case that we have a breach and a war is started, we need to be ready."

Warily, I watched my father pull out a small, rolled-up scroll of parchment from his pocket.

"This is a letter from Queen Vera, asking the Nordians for their swords if it comes down to battle. I need you to deliver it." He handed me the paper.

"You're sending us to Mount Nord?"

"The queen is sending an *official party* to Mount Nord. You will head it," Embris corrected.

For the Nordians to accept us in peace, the travelling party was to have no more or less than five. It was part of the long-standing agreement. Instantly, a shiver came over me despite the heat. I was being given a huge responsibility.

Ryen didn't skip a beat. Bowing his head, he promised, "We won't let you down, Captain."

"I look forward to hearing of your success. You will leave for the mountain tonight. I don't expect you to come across any of the shadows on your journey, but keep your wits about you." Without another word, Embris stalked off, leaving me to make the time-sensitive, complicated plan on my own.

"What can I do?" Ryen asked loyally.

Sighing deeply, I considered what I could delegate to my second. "I need you to gather up three more soldiers to join the party. I don't care who, as long as we can trust them to be respectful, obedient, and calm around the Nordians."

"You got it. Anything else?"

"Could you also see to getting the horses ready? I'd like to leave before nightfall if possible. We can make camp at the base of the mountain before making the trek up in the morning."

Approaching the Nordian camp in the daylight would guarantee we wouldn't sneak up on them, creating trust. Although it was a foolish thought that the Nordians didn't know exactly who was on their mountain at any given time.

"Of course. I'll meet you at the front of the palace by dusk."

"Thank you, Ryen." I clasped my second's arm in gratitude.

That left me to gather supplies, choose someone to take over training, and rehearse what I would say to the warrior tribe to gain their aid. Pushing my shoulders back, I got to work.

On my way back through the palace after securing rations of dried fruits, nuts, and water for the trip, I stopped by the library. A friendly kitchen worker had told me that Maisie was there, helping Prince Leo find some tomes he was looking for. It was only fair to let her know I'd be away for a few days.

I entered the double doors into the high-ceilinged room, where walls and walls of books towered taller than me. As usual, it smelled like dust and old paper, making me wrinkle my nose. Many were fond of that familiar scent of books, but it always made me feel like I was going to sneeze.

I spied Maisie's yellow curls right away. She was descending from a ladder that ran along one of the bookshelves, holding two large volumes under her arm. Prince Leo of the South stood close to her, and as she touched the bottom step, he reached out a hand and placed it on her back, guiding her to the ground. There was something in the way she stiffened that made my blood run cold.

Clearing my throat made Leo drop his hand and move away just a step. It was subtle, meaning he was no fool. That didn't surprise me. I'd only ever met the prince in meetings, and even then, I could never get a read on him. He kept his true motives far from the surface.

Maisie met my gaze, her blue eyes confused to see me.

"Sorry to interrupt, my lord." I allowed the smallest of a head tilt, acknowledging his status over mine.

"Ah, Aedan Thesand, yes? Our up-and-coming deputy captain. What a pleasant surprise." When Leo smiled, it was the look of a predator sizing up its prey. Too many teeth. "I've heard such promising things of you."

Playing diplomat was the only way to gain footing with these officials—especially the princes. It was not something I enjoyed, but growing up in the palace, taking lessons with Diana, had prepared me well.

"That is such a compliment from one such as yourself, Prince Leo. From what I've heard, you're not one to bet against in the sparring ring. It would be an honour to have a master like you in one of the army's training sessions, if you would be so willing."

Truthfully, the idea of meeting Leo in the ring, with the freedom to plant as many facers as I could, sounded quite appealing.

Leo accepted the compliment with a wry grin, raking his gaze over me. Goose bumps erupted over my skin, but I wasn't perturbed. This was a dance, and I was leading.

"It has been quite a time since I've practiced that particular skill, but your offer is tempting indeed. Maybe once these meetings conclude, I will find myself in the ring again." He was so confident, so at ease with the part of prince that he played.

I nodded, to which he continued, "But you haven't come to cajole me into training. What can I help you with, Deputy?"

"Actually, I need a word with Maisie here. Palace upkeep, as I'm sure you understand."

For a moment, Leo stared, his intelligent eyes darting between us. He was blatantly curious; either he couldn't hide the expression or he didn't care that I knew he didn't believe me. It was probably the latter.

"Of course," he said coolly. "She is not mine to command; you do not need my permission."

I bristled. *I wasn't asking.*

Keeping a pleasant smile on my face, I touched Maisie's elbow gently and steered her toward the front of the library. "It should only be a moment."

"Take all the time you need. Palace upkeep is important after all. Just as long as I get her back. She's a favourite of mine, you know."

His languid voice brought violent thoughts to mind. Getting a shot at him in the sparring ring was sounding better and better.

When we were out of earshot, I spun us around so her back was to the prince, where I could watch him easily.

"Palace upkeep?"

I shrugged. "I thought it would sound boring enough that he wouldn't be interested."

Maisie shook her head, curls bouncing. "Leo's too smart for that." She bit on her bottom lip, staring at the wall behind me.

"Are you okay with him alone?" I remembered the interaction between them when I'd first walked in.

Maisie straightened her shoulders, looking at me with an almost-proud expression. "Of course I am. And it's not like you could do anything if I weren't—he's a prince, and I'm a servant."

"I could absolutely do something if you needed me to. Don't ever think that you're less of a fae than him. Are you sure—"

"I told you, I'm fine, Aedan. What do you want?"

I'd never seen her irritated before, and it surprised me that she had a defiance in her. I realized now that even though I'd known Maisie since we were children, I didn't really *know* her at all.

"I wanted to let you know I won't be able to meet you for a few days. Probably not until the day after tomorrow."

Maisie narrowed her eyes. "Why?"

So nosy. "I'm being sent to Mount Nord."

Her mouth tightened at the mention of the mountain. Vaguely, I recalled the time many years ago when Diana had been sent to the warrior tribe to complete her combat training. Maisie had been a wreck while she was gone, clumsy and worried and vacant-minded. This must bring memories forward for her.

"The queen is requesting the Nordians' aid should we come to a battle," I said quietly. It felt right that she should know about this development, considering our alliance.

Maisie nodded. "I'll keep an eye out for your return, and we will meet at our usual spot then."

"Sounds good to me. I'll see you in a few days."

She went to turn, but I caught her arm before she could. "What books does he want?"

"He's looking for old history, as far back as we can go. I think he's hoping there will be clues about portals in them. I'm keeping a list of the books to look through myself after."

Nodding, I released her. I watched her walk back to Leo, and when my eyes flicked to the prince, I was surprised to see he was staring at me, that adder-like smile still on his face. I nodded once and turned away. The image of Leo's face on the body of a snake haunted me as I made my way through the palace.

Perhaps it was time my father did one of his routine background checks into the Southern prince. There was an eerie, prickling feeling at the back of my head about him, and worrying about his loyalties was the last thing we needed on our plates right now.

It was nearing sundown when I met Ryen and his assembled party out front of the palace. He had not disappointed; three other riders and their respective mounts were packed and ready to go. Trent was there, his tall, lanky form impossible not to recognize. Mikale was present, as was …

Jamey.

When I reached the group, I pulled my second to the side, out of earshot.

"I know what you're going to say."

"So, save me the breath."

Ryen rubbed his face. "We needed a fifth. I talked to—and threatened, might I add—every single soldier I wanted in this damn army. Do you know how few I trust to accompany us to Mount Nord? I even started going through my less desirable options. The lady overheard a vehement no and offered to be our last member."

"And why would you think that's acceptable? She's a visiting *guest*, not a soldier."

"Listen, I know it's not your favourite idea, but she's tactful and polite, and I figured a diplomat would be a much better option than a loose cannon. I took a risk."

I heaved a big sigh through my nose, running my hands through my hair. "A diplomat is not something the Nordians can relate to."

"How can you be so sure? None of us have spent enough time there to know what they value. How they run their tribe."

He was right, as usual, and it killed me to admit that to myself. As much as I didn't want Jamey there, if Ryen thought she was the best option, that was what we would go with.

"At least tell me she got permission from the West to come."

"I don't need permission, but my grandfather is aware and accepting of my joining you."

If there was one thing I hated, it was my private conversations being hijacked.

I turned to see Jamey staring with her chin up at me, her arms crossed. What was with these females giving me attitude today? Brushing past her, I checked Kali's tack and put a foot into the stirrup, swinging myself into the saddle.

"Mount up. We'll camp at the base of the mountain tonight."

Ryen rode next to me the whole way there, apologetic, even through his stoic demeanour. I wanted to be annoyed with the Western prince's granddaughter, but I was more so intrigued. She had been my shadow lately, and it seemed out of place for her. Even her proclaimed feelings for me had been unusually forthcoming. Or maybe I had just never noticed with my eyes fixed on Diana.

I found myself wondering what the harm was in indulging her.

If she was playing me, I would see through it right away.

If she wasn't, we could potentially have a good time together. Nothing serious.

Except she seemed the type to want serious.

Ugh.

Would my life always be so complicated? I wasn't far from succumbing under the weight of all the secrets and moving parts of the palace. As future captain, would this put even more on my plate? Embris always made it seem so easy. He had raised me all alone and still worked tirelessly to build the queen's army to the best it had been in centuries, along with the horses. It exhausted me to think about. And it sent that horrible wave of nausea straight to my gut.

That was why I always told myself one thing: *One step at a time.*

Otherwise, it was overwhelming.

Otherwise, I would drown.

I kept my thoughts on greeting the Nordians and how I would gain their alliance. It kept me focused during our ride and all through the setting up of camp and building of the fire. Even as I drifted off to sleep, I didn't allow any intrusive thoughts in.

One step at a time.

TEN

AUTHENTIC

SPENSE

It was like a dream—better than a dream actually. I walked into the dining hall, hand in hand with Diana, familiar smells and faces greeting me. Alwyn walked ahead, clasping hands and laughing in her usual way.

I could feel Diana stiffen when she took in the room, and it wasn't surprising. Ivywall's dining hall was starkly different from the one gracing the palace in Eira. Here, we had long, informal banquet tables and mismatched chairs with Folk of all kinds intermingling and fellow fae who took rotations on cooking duty. It was as far from Eira's fancy and scheduled royals-only dinners that you could get.

As I watched the Unseelie interact, it solidified how similar we were to the Seelie. Truly, the only difference was the branches of magic we used. If the two races were to mingle together, we would appear as one.

Today, it smelled like fried potatoes—a recipe we had stolen from the humans. For reasons I couldn't explain, cutting the potatoes into long strips and frying them tasted *much* better than eating them baked. Lots of the spice blends and cooking techniques we used had come from watching the humans—the only thing that had proven to be good about them.

Diana took in the room with barely disguised awe. It was noisy and crowded with scraping plates and loud conversations. She allowed me to lead her to a set of empty chairs at the farthest table from the kitchens, where it was usually quietest.

Alwyn had gotten sidetracked and was nestled in the lap of a golden-haired girl, who whispered into her ear, making Alwyn's laugh ring out across the room.

"Everyone eats together?" Diana asked, her voice barely audible over the noise.

I pulled out her chair, and she sat slowly, mesmerized.

I pushed it in and leaned over her shoulder. "Yes. I'll be right back."

It was easy to manoeuvre through the tables and chairs without watching for Diana, and it took no time at all for me to slip into the kitchens, unnoticed. That was, until I started dishing up two plates.

"Well, I'll be. The lost prince, returned."

I grinned at hearing my longtime friend Jardan's voice. "In the flesh."

"Knew they couldn't keep you down." Jardan slapped me on the back. "You're too much of a survivor for that."

My smile faltered. One of the harshest parts of regaining my memory was the remembrance of the centuries-instilled hatred of the Seelie. It was the same as the prejudice Eira carried toward the Unseelie, and I was now stuck somewhere in the middle.

Two more males joined us from deeper in the kitchens, friends I recognized from growing up in Ivywall.

"Kent! Morne! I can't believe the food smells this good with you two running the kitchen," I teased.

They both shoved at my shoulders playfully.

"Don't get used to it." Kent grinned.

I kept scooping fried potatoes and green beans onto the two plates as they filled me in on Ivywall's newest refugees and how difficult it was to explain to a gnome that the metal found around the castle was not for mining. When I reached for the pot of rice, Jardan's eyes caught on my tattoo.

"I should have known the rumours were true." His jolly spirit was instantly gone, his face now guarded. "Might as well pack up now. Ivywall will be done within the month."

"What's that supposed to mean?" I snarled.

"I know the *Seelie girl* didn't come willingly. And if the rumours are true—which are proving to be—she ain't just any regular Seelie. You've brought war to us. They will come for her and destroy us all."

I slammed the lid onto the pot of rice, making the three males flinch. "The decisions I make are always for the good of Ivywall, so you'd best sear that into your brain. As for what those decisions look like or why I make them, it's *none of your damn business*. If I hear you take that tone of voice about Diana again, you can find yourself somewhere else to live."

I didn't wait to see Jardan's reaction because I had learned a long time ago that it was easier to handle my rage when I redirected. I could hear them speaking quietly as I marched away.

It was becoming crystal clear how much hate Diana had protected me from in Eira. I didn't know how I could ever do enough to repay her.

I set the plates down in front of Diana, who smiled gently. She had been observing the rush and madness of the hall, and as much as I'd hoped the busyness of it all would distract her, I could see the tightness in her eyes. A small glance around was all it took to learn why—there was a group at the table next to us with eyes locked on Diana, speaking in low tones and very clearly about her.

"I hope you like potatoes," I said, drawing Diana's attention toward the plate in front of her.

She looked puzzled. "I've never seen them cut this way."

I chuckled. "Trust me, they are so good like this."

She picked up a fork and speared a potato, giving me the opportunity to send a flare of magic toward the whispering group. Only, unlike the time I'd sent quiet magic to Aedan's plate, I took pleasure in not hiding my punishment. Simultaneously, their glassware shattered, sending pieces flying all over the table. They gasped and floundered in their seats, and a few had the decency to look embarrassed.

Satisfied, I returned to my conversation.

"I assume that was you?" Diana asked without looking up.

"Don't know what you're talking about."

She met my gaze, fighting a genuine smile that made my heart flutter.

I started on my dinner. "Do you like the potatoes this way?"

"I do. But you know what would go really well with them?"

"What would that be?" I shovelled beans into my mouth and froze mid-chew when she spoke.

"You telling the truth." She dropped her fork and folded her arms over her chest. "I want to know everything, Spense. Starting with why you came to Eira in the first place. You have the memories now. The fact that you're not telling me makes me think the worst."

It was like a stone had been dropped into my stomach. I still needed time to figure out how I would explain that to her in a way that she would understand. In a way that wouldn't make me lose her forever.

"I want to tell you everything, and I will. Just like I promised. But not here, like this."

She leaned forward, hissing, "First, you said that about the meeting, and now this. You're putting it off."

"I know it seems loud in here, but it is easy to be overheard, trust me. And this is not a topic I want just anyone privy to."

"Fine," Diana said. But she didn't look convinced.

"I can start by filling you in on Ivywall, if you'd like."

She agreed, but her shields were coming up, making me feel like I was flailing in water. She'd changed since our time in Eira—she didn't trust me anymore. And that made me ache more than I'd thought it would.

"As you heard in the meeting, Ivywall is more than a palace. It's a sanctuary, a home. We aim to provide not only for the Unseelie, but also to as many Folk as possible. My siblings and I might be considered the children of the king, but we are not royals in the way you think. We are equal to everyone here. Everyone eats together, and those who take shelter here rotate on a chore schedule. It's what keeps us going."

If she was shocked by how we worked here, she didn't show it. "Tell me about the humans. I've never heard of them before."

"They're creatures who look a lot like us, except they're smaller and rounder. They don't have any sort of magic ability, but they are highly intelligent. Most recently, they've come up with devices that can block our magic, and combined with their growing combat skills, they are formidable foes." I shuddered at the thought of my last tussle with a human.

Diana shook her head softly. "That sounds serious. Why do they fight with you?"

"That's where it gets a little fuzzy. I've only ever known a world with war between us. My brother Sorin has lived quite a long time, and he remembers playing with humans as a child. Although even he doesn't remember which side cast the first stone. He believes the humans rejected us once they learned of our magic. Out of fear or jealousy, I do not know. Only my father would remember why, and even that might well be lost forever.

"There is a city not far from here called Rathe. It is where the humans settled centuries ago and where most of the Unseelie and Folk live—in secret. As they get better at detecting us, we get more refugees in Ivywall." I paused to let her mind catch up.

"They cannot breach Ivywall?" she asked, her brow furrowed.

I could practically see the wheels turning in her head.

"They have never found it. There are hundreds of combined glamours around Ivywall, refreshed twice daily by our guard."

"The wall," she breathed. "I could see it shimmering."

I nodded. "It has kept us safe and hidden. My father built it himself when it became clear we were no longer welcome in Rathe."

Diana took a deep breath. "Just how old is Urdan?"

I had been wondering when she'd ask. "The king is over eight thousand years old, like you discovered when we were in the City of Scholars."

"How?"

I shrugged. "He has never told me while lucid. In his ramblings, he's said many things, most to do with the 'imbalance of the worlds' and 'that Seelie bitch.'" I laughed darkly. "Who's to know for sure?"

Diana's hand went to the pocket of her pants, where Jweira was trapped in an emerald.

"She's the oldest," I said softly. "Old enough that none of us ever met her. We think her imprisonment was what drove our father mad in the first place."

She swallowed. "I'm sorry."

"Don't be sorry. It's not your fault that she was trapped."

She didn't meet my eyes, clearing her throat. "How old is Sorin? You said he was the eldest by a lot."

"Let's see if I can remember them all correctly. Sorin is almost three thousand, which makes Badras around twenty-two hundred. Meske is eleven hundred. Alwyn is fourteen hundred fifty, but she'll swear up and down she's not a day over twelve hundred. Olys is next, only two hundred twenty years old." I counted them off on my fingers, making sure the math was right.

Diana's face was white. "And how old are *you*?" she whispered.

I almost laughed at her shock, but I held it in for her sake. "Don't worry; you didn't get matching tattoos with an old man. I'm only twenty-five."

She laughed weakly, relieved. "You're a baby compared to them."

"Yes, it's why they like to boss me around." I liked it when our words were lighter. It made my heart feel lighter too. And with everything going on, I would have to grasp on to these moments for as long as I could.

"I can't imagine having such a long life span," Diana admitted. "And I don't understand why the Unseelie live so much longer than the Seelie."

"It's just Urdan and his children," I explained. "All the other fae have normal life spans, like in Eira. I don't know why we are how we are. Sorin has been researching it for a long time. We used to believe our aging was incredibly slow, but now, he seems to think it gets halted at a certain point and we stay frozen at that age."

I didn't need to see her face to know what she was thinking—whatever darkness Urdan had dabbled in while at war with the Seelie queen was responsible. Personally, I'd grown up wondering if he had figured out a way to live longer in order to buy himself time to bring back his first child, the soul inside the emerald Diana carried. I'd always thought I'd ponder it more when I had lived as long as my siblings. But now, a tiny seed of fear had been planted—if I were anything like my kin, I would outlive Diana. By a lot.

I pushed that from my mind as we continued eating.

After dinner, I toured her around Ivywall. The interior was basic, out of necessity for other supplies. It was almost embarrassing compared to the grandeur of Eira's palace. It was a good reminder that the looks of Ivywall did not reflect the integral work we did here.

Our last stop on the tour was my favourite place in Ivywall. The roof.

I led Diana up the set of adobe stairs that stood behind a wall in the back of the library, tucked out of sight and rarely used. In the daytime, it was too sweltering to enjoy sitting on the roof. But at night, in the cool desert air, it was paradise.

The sun had only set a few hours ago, but the chill was already significant. I breathed it in, letting my lungs fill up. I'd forgotten how wonderful this was.

I watched Diana take in the view, her eyes wide. From here, we could see specks of Rathe, little torches signifying the city was going to sleep. Beyond it was sand as far as the eye could see, the horizon a flat line.

"Doesn't it scare you?" she breathed.

"What?"

"The vastness. It's so … open. There're no mountains, or forests, or even a hill." Diana shuddered, crossing her arms over her chest and rubbing them absently. It was hard to tell if that was chill or awe-induced.

I did appreciate the beautiful mountains and trees of the Northern Peninsula. But at times, it felt claustrophobic, like there were too many things squished into a small area. Too many places to hide. In the desert, all was laid bare—take it or leave it.

"It's all I've ever known. And honestly, I like it. Feels like there are infinite possibilities, you know?"

I sat down, letting my legs swing in the night air. Diana joined me, and I pointed out Rathe to her, a speckling of light an hour's ride away.

"Where's Elfwood?"

I pointed left of the city, where only sand and cacti were visible. "It's a few days' ride east. But by drake, we'll make it there in a few hours."

Diana only nodded, sucking on her bottom lip.

"You don't have to come if you're scared."

"I'm not scared," she replied immediately.

I smiled to myself. "Good. It's them who should be scared of you."

She chuckled quietly. Having her here, in my world, on my roof, felt like I was finally seeing for the first time. She was the missing light I hadn't even realized I was without. My magic swirled low, calling for hers to join it. But I pushed it down. I would let her come to me.

I cleared my throat. "We should be prepared that the humans will have the magic neutralizers with them. Do you feel like you want to freshen up your hand-to-hand combat training?"

Diana shook her head softly, her hair swaying around her shoulders. The moon was on its way up, and it made her chestnut strands shine. "I'd rather rest up, especially if there's a journey ahead of us."

I understood even if there was a small part of me that would love to practice with her in the training ring. Dancing the lethal steps of a fight, our bodies slick with sweat, in close proximity. Our magic mingling. Her hands deftly swinging a broadsword as if it were a twig.

I shook my head. That would have to be enough of that if I wanted to get any sleep tonight.

"Fair enough. And although you've yet to prove your non-magic prowess, I've been told you can handle yourself." I shifted closer, our thighs touching. The hand that was in her lap twitched, and I took it in my own, rubbing circles with my thumb. "Besides," I breathed, relishing in the way my breath brought goose bumps to her skin, "I would feel horribly jealous, watching you use your magic on someone else."

"*Spense*." The word came out like a warning. "Stop that."

I dropped her hand. "Stop what?"

Diana turned to look at me directly, the pain in her eyes evident. "Stop pretending everything's normal. That there's not a literal *war* on your doorstep. Stop pretending you're not affected."

"Of course I'm affected."

"Then, how can you be so flippant, holding my hand, flirting, bringing me to romantic spots? I'm so overwhelmed for you that I can hardly *breathe*, Spense."

"You're lucky you've lived your entire life in a fancy palace, never having to worry about war. This is all I know! Instead of etiquette and dance lessons, I was taught how to wield a sword and which way was easiest to gut your enemy. As a boy, I spent hours listening to my brothers strategize, and I could read a map before I could read a book. That takes a toll on you. There are few moments in my life of real, unbridled joy. So, forgive me if I try to enjoy the ones I get."

I could feel a flush creeping up my neck, mirroring the one in Diana's cheeks. I hadn't meant to get so heated. But it wasn't fair for her to think I didn't care.

Movement at the door to the roof caught my eye. Alwyn stood there, halfway through the threshold.

"Hope I'm not interrupting," she said, eyes darting between us.

"You're not." I focused on slowing my heart, clearing my mind.

"I figured you'd be too preoccupied to actually help me make a plan tonight. And I can see that I was right," my sister joked, coming over to sit cross-legged, away from the ledge. "I've organized a group of drakes and riders to take to Elfwood. We'll leave in the morning."

"Thank you, Wyn. You're the best."

"And don't you forget it." I smiled at my sister, who turned to Diana. "Can't wait for you to meet my drakes. They'll like you—I can tell."

"There you go again with your overestimation of me, Alwyn," Diana said. "But I appreciate the sentiment."

Alwyn let out a puff of air and crossed her arms over her chest. "I never overestimate anything!" She held a straight face until she met my eyes and burst out laughing. "Okay, maybe I do. But you're different."

I couldn't help laughing along. Alwyn had such a contagious laugh, along with her superpower of always knowing how to make a room lighter.

"In all seriousness though, the drakes are a good judge of character. As long as they feel your magic is nonthreatening, they turn into cuddly pets."

Diana's face paled slightly. "They can sense magic?"

Alwyn nodded. "Of course. They're subject to storm users, but they get along with just about any type."

I had forgotten to fill Diana in, as was evident in the confusion on her face.

"The Unseelie are gifted with different magic than the four of the Seelie, but the idea is the same. Here, we categorize them into storm, sun, soul, and fauna. It's why your magic might feel weird here," I explained.

Her face relaxed. "Which are you?"

Alwyn grinned. "You'll fall for him all over again once you hear."

I jabbed her with my elbow. She jabbed me back without missing a beat.

"*I'm* strongest in fauna, which is why I get along with the drakes so well," Alwyn said. "But I dabble in storm. Can't let Bad have all the lightning to himself."

The females both looked to me expectantly.

"I use soul magic. It's no more powerful than the other types."

"It's definitely more powerful. And it's rare," Alwyn supplied helpfully.

I shot her a look.

"Right now, we only know of two Unseelie that can use it."

Diana looked to me, her eyebrows raised. "Is that so? How does it work?"

Alwyn got up abruptly, brushing her pants off. "Well, I'm going to leave before I become a third wheel. Plus, I don't need to hear any more about how much cooler my baby brother is than me. See you both in the morning."

With a salute over her shoulder, she was gone as quickly as she had come. I rolled my eyes at her theatrics.

I took a breath. "Storm and sun magic draw from the energy of nature, just like the elements the Seelie use. Fauna works similarly, using the energy of the willing Folk and animals. Soul magic doesn't need anything to channel. It exists entirely on its own, a well inside its user. It might diminish or grow, but it'll never vanish."

"So, you're creating your own magic?" Diana asked.

I nodded.

"That's pretty amazing."

"It's not any different, other than the fact that I don't worry about using too much. Too much sun magic can burn you, just like too much storm magic can drown you. My only drawback is my own energy level." I hesitated before adding, "And I can draw off of others' magic as well."

"Even against their will?"

"Yes."

"Have you ever done it?"

"I have." I looked away from her hazel eyes, out into the darkness. "It's a source of eternal guilt for me."

Diana shook her head in wonder. "This is all just so much. It's entirely different from how I pictured it here."

I almost didn't want to ask, but I did anyway. "Better or worse?"

She laughed humourlessly. "I don't even know. Better, I guess? I already knew the Dark—Unseelie, I mean—aren't how they were depicted in Eira's history. But I didn't picture it to be so …"

"Ritzy? Fancy? Uptight?" I supplied jokingly.

"Real," she finished. "It's real here. You can feel it in the air. Everyone is authentic, even the palace itself. You're all in this together."

Her words were a sigh of relief washing over me. "I hope you'll be happy here, at least for the time being."

Diana held my gaze, and like I normally did when she looked at me, I felt like she was seeing into my soul. "I think I can be. As long as you're honest with me."

"I will be," I promised.

"Good. Because you know my plan is to create a portal again, right?"

"I figured."

Her face looked pleading. "I have to finish whatever destiny my ancestors planned for me. And it's all connected to having the portal open—permanently."

I knew Urdan would never agree. My siblings would have adverse reactions to that as well, not to mention the entirety of the Folk. But maybe we'd find a way for every party to be happy. For now, I had time to sort it out.

"I'll help you, whatever you need."

"Thank you," she said.

She smiled a real smile, and I could see that some tension had left her.

Was she really so surprised I would be on her side?

Then again, I'd never told her how my feelings matched the tattoos.

"Spense?" Diana asked.

When she said my name like that, I would give her anything she desired.

"Yeah?"

"Tell me why you came to Eira."

Eleven
The Curator

Maisie

The streets of Nevelyn were packed full, as usual, the patrons going about their busy days, preparing for the heat of the next few months. Of course, in the North, our heat didn't compare to the other regions, but it was still a treat for us. Many would close down their shops and spend lazy days on the River Nord or even hike into the forest to visit one of the lakes.

A notice from the palace had gone out, warning the citizens of the shadows and to stay in large groups. As ominous as it sounded, the overall vibe of Nevelyn was still cheery.

Since I wasn't expecting to see Aedan for a few days, I needed a way to infiltrate meetings without him. This meant a trip to the end of the Marketplace, where one could find all the contraband one's heart desired. Luckily, dressed in my plainest servant clothes, without any emeralds or pins placing me in the palace's service, I did not stand out. Peddlers ignored me, fae bumped into me, and none paid me any heed as I slipped past the jewellers section into the seedier part of the market.

Instantly, the air was colder from the lack of sunshine. The stalls and buildings had been built close together, allowing for almost the entire aisle to be in shadow. I wrinkled my nose against the rancid, stale smell in my nostrils and felt the hair on the back of my neck stand up.

I was being watched.

Trying as hard as I could to be inconspicuous, I glanced at the signs over doors, only giving myself a second to take in what was offered.

Nico's Night Nest.

We buy gold!

The Curator.

The last store caught my attention. Under the name, a curious line of script read, *Whatever you're looking for, The Curator has it.* It sounded like the place I needed. The blacked-out windows and dim light coming from inside made me hesitate even if it did look like one of the more well-kept establishments in this area.

Against my better judgment, I stepped into the store.

I was hit with a choking amount of incense that made my eyes water. There was a haze in the air, and once I adjusted to it, the room became clear. It was small with a closed door at the back of the room and two armchairs facing each other. A glass table stood between them, giving the appearance of a very casual office. A large tropical plant grew from a pot in the corner of the room, but other than that, it was unfurnished.

The door at the back opened, and a finely dressed young male stepped into the room.

"Have a seat," he offered, his voice smooth and low.

Hesitantly, I perched on the edge of one of the armchairs, taking him in as he took a seat across from me.

Though he was young, there was nothing immature in his keen gaze. His eyes were so dark that they could have been black, matching his cropped hair.

"I am The Curator. You may call me Kol. What is your name?"

I didn't want to give him my name. I'd rather have done this all in the dark, without so much propriety, but it was clear he had the power in this little game he played.

"Grea," I supplied.

"Grea." He rolled the name over his lips like he was tasting it. "No, try again."

"Excuse me?"

"If you want my help, you will not lie to me. I will ask again. What is your name?"

My face flushed. Kol's magic rolled off him in waves, coating the room with power—and incense. Fear flashed through me for the first time since being here.

"Maisie."

"Thank you, Maisie. What can I do for you today?" Kol leaned back in his chair, one leg crossed casually over his knee.

I felt cold all over. I was in over my head here.

For Diana, I reminded myself.

I could do this for Diana. She would do it for me.

"I need a way to listen through a magic-sealed wall."

The Curator raised a delicate eyebrow. "I see. I have such a device, but it will not come cheap."

I'd expected that, so I'd come prepared. My own meagre savings were hardly worth bringing, so I'd ... *borrowed* some jewellery from Diana's vanity. I would find a way to replace it before she noticed.

I pulled a drawstring bag from inside my cloak and handed it to him. Kol opened the bag and tipped the contents into the palm of his hand. A multistrand sapphire necklace lay there, glittering, even without the sun to magnify it.

He examined it for a moment. "It is a lovely piece. But I do not want jewels."

He dropped the necklace back into the bag and tossed it into my lap. I paled. I didn't have a plan B.

"I don't have anything else to offer you."

Kol leaned forward. "That's where you're wrong," he said, a smile pulling at his lips. He was shockingly beautiful—it was almost ethereal. "I like to deal in favours. And I would be a fool to pass up a favour being owed to me from someone who has such open access to the palace."

My heart quickened, pumping fear into my veins. How could he possibly know where I worked? "This was a mistake. Thank you for your time, but—"

"Don't be so hasty, Maisie. I thought we were friends."

Kol reached into his jacket pocket and pulled two stones from it, small and round as acorns but the deepest colour red imaginable. He held them out to me, but I didn't move.

"These stones are a device made from science. Do you know what that is?"

I hated him, hated his condescending tone. But I shook my head anyway.

He pinched one of the stones between his thumb and forefinger, allowing me to see it better. "Science is what fae use instead of magic when they are born without it."

"Everyone is born with magic," I said automatically.

"Ah, yes, so I've been told," Kol said drily, rolling his eyes. "Notice how fast those words were out of your mouth? Knee-jerk reaction, I assume?"

I swallowed.

"That's what I thought. You have been conditioned to believe that. But don't worry; it's not your fault. There are a great number of fae born in Eira without a lick of magic in them. A remnant of a very old bloodline long gone from this realm. Since their society vehemently rejects the idea of not being a magic-wielder, they become lost to themselves. In more recent years, a group has formed, calling themselves the Outcasts. They dabble in sciences and experiments, using tools and other ingredients I help procure." The Curator's lips curved in a sly grin. "They have been trying to recruit me for ages."

"Why would they want you if you have magic?"

"Now, what makes you think I am in possession of magic?"

Did he think I was stupid? "I can feel it coming off of you!"

Kol shrugged. "Call it residue. It is not mine."

It sure felt like his, the way it clung to him. I hadn't been blessed with such strong power like Diana, but I was fairly certain this earthy magic was coming straight from him.

"Believe what you want. The matter at hand remains. I have stones that will allow you to eavesdrop. In return, I want a favour. The terms are clear. Do we have a deal?"

I took the stones from him, turning them over in my hand. He wasn't lying about them not being created with magic. They felt cold and plain.

"How do they work?"

"One stone must be placed in the room you wish to eavesdrop on. The other you hold in your hand when you want to listen. They will act as a tunnel through whatever magic has been placed on the room."

It sounded real enough. And it was my best option. The idea of owing him a favour didn't sit right, but I was no stranger to using my body in unpleasant ways.

"And by a favour, you mean …"

Kol laughed. "If I knew what I wanted, it would not be a favour, would it? I do not know what I desire of you just yet, but have no fear;

I shall figure it out." He cocked his head to look at me like I imagined a lion would look at prey.

"I could offer you my favour right now," I said, stepping closer, even through my screaming nerves. I undid the top button of my dress, holding his gaze.

Kol's eyes travelled down my body and back up. He huffed a laugh. "I have a strict rule not to mix business and pleasure," he said, his slender fingers snaking out to redo my button. "Besides, I find I can get what I want in that field without having to make a deal."

I wanted to slap that horrible smirk off his face. But he had what I needed, so instead, I plastered on a smile. It had been worth a shot even though his rejection was a cool tide of relief.

"Fine. Deal."

Kol grinned wickedly. "Excellent."

The stones already in my hand, I spun on my heel and made a beeline for the exit. I'd spent too long in here. The incense was making me feel fuzzy.

I stopped at the door and looked over my shoulder, realizing something. "You already had these stones in your pocket. How did you know I'd want them?"

The Curator only put his hands in his pockets and shrugged. "I had a hunch."

The weight of two stones in my pocket had never brought me such joy. I was filled with a newfound hope, and even though they might not tell me anything at all, at least I was taking matters into my own hands. It was a breath of fresh air not to be reliant on Aedan for this.

The rest of the day, I tried to keep my smile hidden as I went through my usual tasks. I would plant the device when the queen took dinner, and later tonight, I would dedicate my time toward the books I'd found in Diana's room. Nothing could bring me down.

When Vera was called from her council room to join her family at dinner, I could barely stop myself from sprinting up the stairs.

The council room was closed, but unguarded. It was easy to slip inside, unnoticed, and I found myself staring at a giant portrait of the first Queen Diana, her green eyes boring into me.

"Don't judge," I muttered.

I studied Queen Vera's desk. The stone wasn't very big, but its colour would make it stand out on the oak. I would have to hide it.

Ducking under the desk, I felt along the slats, looking for a place where it could be slipped into. Without any luck, I moved on to the legs of the desk and the chair. Everything was smooth and flat, no hidey-holes anywhere.

Aha. A sconce for a light orb on the wall stared at me behind the desk. I reached behind the smooth surface of the orb to the ridges that held it to the wall. There was enough of a groove to slip the device into, and I was delighted to find that it was unnoticeable in there. I tapped the orb to turn it on, confirming the stone's red hue wouldn't alter the colour of the light.

Yes! This will work!

I tapped the orb again to turn it off and fled from the room. Right as I was slipping out of the doors and clicking them shut ever so softly, a voice from down the hall sent a flood of panic through me.

"Maisie? Whatever are you doing?"

Damn, crap, fudge—

"Queen Vera." I bowed my head. "My apologies. I didn't mean to intrude. I-I was looking for you," I lied, thinking wildly.

"I don't have a lot of time, but what can I do for you?" Vera's icy gaze bored into me, her narrowed eyes missing nothing.

Delios sat by her feet, his giant head swinging toward me. He always made me nervous, the talon-like claws and even bigger teeth at the queen's total behest.

I was starting to sweat with her and Delios and her two guards staring at me. My throat felt tight as I blinked nervously, trying to pull something—anything—out of my empty brain.

Tears pricked at the back of my eyes, stinging. I was going to have to fess up. I couldn't do this; I couldn't *lie* and spy on my queen.

Miraculously, Vera interpreted my tears as sadness and placed a hand on my shoulder gently. "Oh, Maisie, you're worried, aren't you?"

I sniffled, confused, as she squeezed the muscle on my shoulder in comfort.

"I'm worried too. We'll get Diana back, I promise. I'll never stop looking for her."

I couldn't believe my stroke of luck. My guilty conscience weighed like a rock in my stomach, making it even harder for me to agree with the queen. "I'm sorry to bother you with it. I know you're working hard. I just thought … if there were any news, maybe—" I sniffled again.

"Don't worry, child," Vera soothed. "Once there is news to share, you will be the first to know." She smiled sweetly, straightening up.

Sure, the queen could say all she liked about me being the first to know. But I was at the end of a lengthy list of officials, guards, her court, and anyone else who crossed her path before the servants. That was the natural way of it, an age-old way of life that Aedan and I were disrupting.

"Thank you," I said quietly, still looking down.

Vera opened the door to her council room and paused in the doorway. "I can forgive your intrusion, as I know how close you and my daughter are. And I sympathize. But, Maisie?"

I found the courage to meet her eyes and swallowed at the stern look on her face.

"Remember your place."

The words rang in my ears, even after the queen and her entourage disappeared into the council room. It was a hammer dropping, a heavy hit to punish me for trespassing. I was no stranger to those words, and they usually sent me aflame with guilt and the drive to do better. Those feelings were there now, but they were overshadowed by something that I was afraid to feel about my queen.

Defiance.

I was the worst servant in Eira for having the desire to spy on my queen, even after she'd just comforted me.

But I could be a horrible servant if that meant getting Diana home safely.

I had been making for the kitchens, where I could fire through my evening chores before taking a look at those books, when I passed the queen's seneschal, Solis. He gave me a curt nod as he walked briskly in the direction of the council room.

Thinking that was what Vera had meant when she said she didn't have time to speak with me, I turned on my heel and followed Solis back to where I'd just been caught.

I watched from down the hall until the door closed and then retrieved the device's other half from my pocket. The stone was smooth and cold in my palm, making no sign that it was working. I grasped it tighter, willing anything to happen.

Just as I was about to give up, I heard a crackling noise. It tingled in my ear uncomfortably until the crackling turned into voices.

"… just came from the Unclaimed Land," Solis was saying.

I couldn't believe the stone I held wasn't magic. I could hear the speaker as clearly as if I were in the room.

"We have received word of why Lord Nimshar left without warning."

"Gaia knows he just wanted to cause a scene," Vera sighed.

No one had told me he was gone. I hadn't seen any of the East's servants around the last couple of days, but with everything going on, I hadn't made any note of their unusual absence.

"Unfortunately, My Queen, it is a bit more serious than that." Solis cleared his throat. He sounded nervous.

"Spit it out then, Solis."

"Lord Nimshar has been called back to run the Eastern court in the princess's stead. We are to prepare for Princess Hollaina's imminent arrival."

TWELVE
SOMETHING HEAVY

DIANA

Spense looked like night embodied as he swung his legs off the roof of Ivywall. His inky-black hair melded into the sky, and his pale skin glowed like the moonlight. Only the light from the stars silhouetted the horns jutting from his curls.

Even waiting on him to potentially drop a bomb, I couldn't ignore how achingly beautiful he was.

He took a shaky breath and dragged a hand through his hair. "The memories have been … difficult to sift through. It's taking a while to sort everything out. It feels like my room was upended and none of my belongings were put back in the right spot, you know?"

I didn't know. But I nodded anyway.

"And I want you to know that I'm not the same fae as I was before. You've changed my life, and I couldn't be more grateful."

Spense was really laying it on thick. I barely resisted telling him to just spit it out.

"Growing up here was hard. I'm a lot younger than my siblings, so I was alone most of the time. My father oversaw my lessons. He expected nothing less than perfection from me, as his plan was for me to someday take over for him—a sore spot with my brothers and sister at the time. He hardened and shaped me into a soldier, his hatred for the Seelie contagious. I grew up to think, like most of the fae here, that the Seelie were malevolent tyrants who drove us from our realm in pursuit of power."

I swallowed. It was still hard to accept that as the truth after so many years of false history shoved down my throat. As shameful as it was, I still found myself wanting to defend my ancestors.

"Urdan's plan was always to march on Eira and reclaim the land. His only problem lay in getting back there. Between not having the power to do it himself and experiencing more and more bouts of forgetfulness, he struggled to find the right way to make a portal. I-I wanted to please him so badly. And I thought this was the way to earn his respect.

"So, I spent a year researching and talking to any historian I could find. I was able to piece together what had been missing. Creating a portal takes a lot of magic, and most times, the user will become exhausted before completing it, thus causing a rift. It made sense, but something didn't sit right with me. Portals had fallen out of practice after the war even though it was widely known how to make them. Surely, *someone* in Rathe would have had the power to open one and bring the army back to Eira.

"And I was right. It took a lot of convincing, but I was able to get my hands on a very old, very withered journal from a long-since-passed soldier who had been in the Unseelie army when we first arrived in Rathe. He wrote about hundreds of attempts to get back and how my father spent years working with researchers to understand why they were unsuccessful. Finally, a scholar was able to get a read on why the magic didn't work—the Seelie queen had sealed Eira. I still don't know how she did it, but it was written that whatever she did must have come with a huge sacrifice."

I tried to absorb what I was hearing while suddenly feeling the urge to move back from the ledge. I didn't trust my shaky arms to keep me upright.

Spense took a breath before continuing, "That sacrifice meant there was a loophole in the magic. I had a hunch that whatever this grey area was, it would be hard to find. Rare even. And through more research, I found out that the closing and sealing of the portal had been done on a lunar eclipse. Right away, I just *knew* this was the loophole. I'd never been surer of anything.

"So, on the next lunar eclipse, I went to my father. We began the creation together, fuelling our magic into the portal. It was more than enough, and it was *working*. Until Urdan called it off. Now that he knew how to get around the seal, he wanted to get his army prepared and a plan in place for the next eclipse." Spense swallowed, his breath shallow.

"But I … I had just spent so long researching and figuring this out, and we were finally so close. I kept going, even after my father stopped. I told him that I could go now, as a spy, and infiltrate the court. And when he didn't react, just kept watching me, I thought that meant I should keep going. If I could create it on my own, he would be so proud of me. When it was done, I could tell something was off. It felt … sticky. But I couldn't stand the thought of facing my father after that. I'd taken a risk, and I had to see it through. So, I stepped through the rift."

A single tear slid down Spense's face. "The first thing I remembered when I woke up back here were the last words he had said to me as I left."

I reached out and took his hand gently. If he noticed, he didn't react.

"He said, 'You are my biggest failure.' "

My heart clenched for him.

Spense squeezed my hand, wiping his face with his other. "And he was right."

"No, he wasn't." My voice felt thick, and it sounded far away when I spoke.

"You don't have to say that. I know what I did."

I curled one leg up so I could twist to face him better. "Spense, you were mistreated by your father. It's understandable why you did what you did—"

"I wanted to infiltrate your court, Diana! I would have, too, if Urdan hadn't taken my memories. I would have lied through my teeth and used whatever I had to. I would have seduced you. I would have used glamours on those who questioned me—*I was not good.*" Spense dropped my hand, reaching both arms behind his head as he grabbed at his hair.

The words hung in the air for a moment, Spense's loud breaths the only sound in the quiet night. It was everything I'd been determined not to believe of him. But the disappointment I expected to crack through my chest was only a small thud.

"Do you regret it?"

"Of course I do! I have never felt so low in my entire life, even when I was the brunt of my father's disappointment. The guilt I have over betraying you, your trust, it's going to swallow me whole."

"You didn't betray me," I said, feeling oddly calm.

"But I *wanted to*, Diana. The only reason I didn't was because I didn't remember a damn thing besides my own name."

I'd never seen Spense so shaken up. He had always been the constant cool since I'd known him, ever confident, taking everything in stride. We'd switched realms, and our personalities seemed to do the same.

The irony was not lost on me.

"The fact that you regret it means you changed. Do you feel like the same fae you were before you came to Eira?" I didn't pause long enough to let him answer; I already knew what he would say. "Without your father's influence, you became free to be who you really are—and that is someone good and pure and just. It was always in you, just a little hidden."

"It's nice that you believe in me," Spense said softly. "Maybe one day, I will too."

It was heartbreaking to see him so crushed. In that moment, I realized how impossible it was to keep myself at a distance from him. I couldn't. We were magnets.

"I can never apologize enough for starting all this, Diana."

"If you hadn't, I would never have known my life was a lie. I would have lived on a throne built from lies, believing myself a ruler of peace, never knowing the atrocities that I had been born from. I would never have met you. So, please, don't apologize for saving me."

Spense's face softened for the first time, as he finally believed my words. Those grey eyes were as piercing as ever, storm-coloured in this light. "You are the best thing to ever happen to me."

My heart fluttered, and I knew he meant every word. The air between us was full of a tension that I couldn't put a name to, soft and sweet but also strong and unrelenting. It was a pull that would never go away.

"Thank you for being honest with me," I murmured.

I knew if I leaned in right now, I would be close enough to kiss him. I also knew he wouldn't be the one to initiate it. The moment was calling for it, our gazes locked, our burdens shared. And I wanted to. I missed the feeling of his lips on mine, his hand in my hair. The smell of him all around me, our magics wrapped up as one. I could be brave enough to kiss him on this rooftop.

And so I did.

Soft and hesitant at first, just a light brush. Spense relaxed into it, but let me be in control. I deepened it, an understanding of the heaviness that had just been shared. It was exactly as I remembered, the pressure and fit of his mouth against mine sending tingles down my back.

I felt his magic reach out, enveloping me in that sweet smell of chocolate. Not even the pull of it could call my own to the surface.

He leaned back when mine didn't respond. "Are you okay?"

Here I stood again, on the precipice. It was time to return the deep share of trust that Spense had given me.

"I haven't been able to access my magic since being here," I admitted, feeling safe enough not to look away.

His expression crumpled. "What?" Instinctively, his gaze dropped to my wrist, probably checking for a magic-binding bracelet, like the one that had been forced on him in Eira.

I shrugged. "It's not like the band you wore. It just feels like it's … sleeping or something. I can't even pull the tiniest amount without exhausting myself."

"But why? What could do this to you?" Spense seemed to be talking more to himself than me, which was good because I couldn't answer his questions.

"You don't think your father could be behind this?" I asked hesitantly.

He shook his head. "I've never heard of such a thing. And if it could be done, I have no doubt he would have used it on me as a training tool."

My heart clenched at the thought.

"I'll ask around, see if I can find anything to help." He reached out and took my hand. "We'll fix this, I promise."

I nodded, smiling a little. Something heavy lifted off my chest. If anyone understood the pain of living without magic, it was Spense.

After a moment, he let out a soft sigh. "I have to admit, I'm relieved to hear that it wasn't about me."

I searched for the words to say that no matter how mad I got at him, I didn't think I could ever keep my magic from his. But my brain wasn't letting me say them—at least not in a way that I liked. So, instead, I just shuffled closer and leaned my head on his shoulder. That seemed to be answer enough for him, as he rested his head atop mine gently.

I remembered something as we stared out at the dark horizon. "Hey, Alwyn mentioned that there are only two fae that you know of with soul magic. Who's the other?"

"My father." I felt his voice rumble through us.

Of course. I should have guessed.

"It's the biggest reason why he always wanted me to take over after him. None of my other siblings share the affinity in the slightest."

"Well, there goes my theory that you were adopted," I joked.

Spense pulled away to look at me, his face scrunched in adorable confusion. "What made you think that?"

"For starters, all your siblings look exactly alike. All golden-haired, brown-eyed, sun-kissed ..."

Spense let out a real laugh, hearty and full. It was lovely and made my heart sing.

"So, you're saying I'm the unfortunate-looking one of the bunch?"

The twinkle I remembered had returned to his steely eyes.

"You said it, not me." I laughed.

Spense shook his head, hair falling in those bouncy waves. His smile was lit by the moon. It was magical. "My father thinks the fact that I look so shockingly different from my siblings is a sign from the gods that I'm meant to rule. Especially with me having horns that match his wings. It fuels him."

Gods—plural. I had only ever grown up knowing one—the goddess, Gaia. I would have to dive into that later, but I wanted to ask something else first.

"What about your mother?"

Spense blew out a breath, toying with a strand of fabric fraying off his shirt. "I don't know who she is. All of us have different mothers, and Urdan will not divulge any information about any of them. Says it creates divided loyalty. In truth, he doesn't think them important after losing his soulmate in the war. It is why he became so twisted after losing her and their daughter." He looked pointedly at my pants pocket, where Jweira sat heavy against my thigh.

"I never knew my father. I understand what it's like to grow up with a piece of you missing."

Spense smiled ruefully. "I never knew how much of me was missing until recently."

We sat on the rooftop for a while, until the moon was high in the sky and the chill that crept along our skin became too cold to enjoy. With one last look over the endless sand horizon, I allowed the boy with the moonlit skin to lead me inside.

Maybe I was too caught up in digesting everything I'd just heard, but it didn't occur to me until we reached Spense's rooms that said chamber might pose an awkward situation.

Pik was waiting in the hallway, his crisp, dark suit a stark difference to his blue skin. When he saw us, his face lit up in a smile. He swept into a bow, his legs so short that his nose almost touched the floor.

"Prince Spense! Lady Diana! I believe you will be quite happy to know that I have seen to the modification of your rooms; another armoire has been brought in, and I have arranged for a vanity to be delivered tomorrow as well."

Horrible, stiff tension poured between us. I had never shared my room with anyone, and while the trust between Spense and me had been carefully rebuilt, I was in no way ready to combine living spaces yet. Thankfully, he looked like he was thinking similarly, as he cleared his throat twice before speaking.

"That is incredibly thoughtful of you, Pik, and I appreciate your efforts. It's just, uh, I think the lady would be more comfortable in her own rooms. Er … if you're okay with that." He aimed the last part toward me.

"Oh my," murmured Pik, looking pointedly away from us. "I should not have assumed."

I nodded, trying—and likely failing—to give a nonchalant vibe. My cheeks burned, my face undoubtedly beet red.

Spense grinned, shaking his head. Not a lick of embarrassment showed on his face, which only made mine worse.

"No problem at all. My mistake, my mistake! My lady, if you will please follow me, I can escort you to our most esteemed guest chambers!"

"I'll come get you in the morning," Spense said, brushing the faintest of kisses to my temple. "Be ready to ride a drake."

"Good night," I called to him, stomach churning in excitement as I followed Pik away. He was remarkably fast for his size.

"Good night, Diana," he said softly, and his smile made everything else fade away.

Thirteen
Under Your Command

Aedan

By the time the five of us had made it to the entrance of Mount Nord's camp, I was struggling to keep my panting inaudible. The Nordian who had met us at the halfway point of the mountain had not even broken a sweat the entire day's journey to the top. My other companions were not faring nearly as well; Ryen, Trent, and Mikale at least had the determination to pretend not to be tired while Jamey was several paces behind, puffing and entirely red.

The air was so cold and clear that it burned my nostrils and throat. I'd started the day with a scarf around the lower half of my face, but my breath had made it too wet to get air through. The Nordian, introduced as Fiwey, wore furs and many layers of thick clothing and kept a long beard that trailed in a braid to his chest. Facial hair was probably a great asset against the constant cold.

"Stop. We're here," Fiwey grunted, bringing his total word count of the day to about a dozen overall.

Peering around his massive body, all I saw was the same thing I'd been staring at all day—snow and boulders. Except, as I watched the spot Fiwey stared at, a mist began in the air, cloaking us all until my vision was limited to my own hands.

I'd known the mountain had magic of its own variety, but I'd never witnessed it in person. It was breathtaking to behold, nothing tying it to any source, coming from nature itself.

All at once, the mist dissipated, and I was in the middle of a bustling camp.

Mount Nord.

Wooden corrals held chickens and pigs, and circular firepits were spotted throughout. Shelters and huts made of the same dark wood had been built into the side of the mountain, where homes had been carved out of the rock. A strong gust of wind pushed through us, whipping our hair and jackets. Looking up, I could see the hazy shapes of the famed pegasi resting on the peaks surrounding the camp, wings folded in against the cold.

Everyone was working. Some sharpened weapons or roasted food over pyres. Warriors sparred with swords at the far end of the camp; children mimicked their moves with long sticks. All the Nordians were lean and toned, their hair long and braided, muscular even through the furs they wore. True warriors.

Feeling suddenly inadequate, I motioned Ryen to my side. He stood on my left as Fiwey set off to announce our arrival. He disappeared into a large tent, and when the flaps finally opened again, he was joined by another large Nordian.

I bowed my head and accepted the tree trunk of an arm that was offered to me.

"You must be General Oppen. It is my honour," I said, remembering the reverie with which Embris had told me about the fearsome general.

He laughed gruffly. "Do I look a hundred years old to you?"

I frowned. My father had never mentioned how old Oppen was, but considering that he had been the general when Embris was young, I should have known he would be older than the male standing before me.

"My apologies," I said smoothly. "Might you be able to point me in the general's direction?"

"Not to worry," the male replied, his eyes narrowing amusedly. "What's your name, soldier?"

"Deputy Captain Aedan Thesand." The words flowed easily, but while it was usually a title I was extremely proud of, I got the feeling it held no meaning here.

"Nice to meet you, *Deputy Captain*." The male grinned. "I'm Maverick, the new general."

I was instantly irritated. He'd been stringing me along, making a fool out of me. These power-hungry males were the worst kind, especially when they were in leadership positions.

"Ah. I was not aware of that change. I look forward to working with you." I gestured to my companions. "This is my second, Ryen, and this is Trent, Mikale, and Jamey. We come on Queen Vera's behalf about an important matter. Is there somewhere private we may speak?"

Maverick looked us all over. Then, he nodded at Fiwey, who backed away. "By all means, come with me."

We followed the general into the tent he'd come out of. I ducked to avoid the flap hitting me in the face after it was not held open for me.

This was clearly a space designated for meetings. There were a dozen cushions on the floor, circling a firepit. A glance upward confirmed there was a hole in the tent roof right above to let the smoke out.

Maverick sat down in one of the seats, his large frame almost laughable to see cross-legged. I followed suit, and my party did the same. The general lit a pipe and took a deep inhale. Even without catching a scent, I knew it was not just tobacco by the way his face relaxed. He offered the pipe to me, and I politely declined.

Shrugging, Maverick said, "So, what is so important for you to make the trek up our mountain?"

He blew smoke through almost-closed lips, and I watched it form swirls in the air before disappearing upward. From my angled view, the lines on his face appeared harder, sharper. The scruff on his cheeks couldn't hide their hollowness.

I reached into my jacket pocket and held out the rolled-up letter penned by the queen. Maverick wet his lips and stared at my palm for a moment before gruffly taking it from me. He broke the seal, unravelled it, and I watched as his eyes danced across the paper.

When he was done, he crumpled it up unceremoniously and threw it into the firepit. Within seconds, a healthy flame erupted, hungrily devouring the parchment. Mentally, I thanked Gaia that all my colleagues had managed not to flinch.

"You valley folk sure love following the exact words of the peace treaty. Vera using lines verbatim was a nice touch." Maverick scoffed while I cringed at his flippant use of the queen's name. "Let me see if I have this straight. You let an Unseelie warrior into the loving arms of the palace, who then turned around and stole your princess. And now, you're preparing for a war and want our weapons."

"In so many words," I replied through gritted teeth.

"Hmph." Maverick leaned back and took another long intake of his pipe. "That sounds like a *you* problem. Why should we bail you out of a mess you made all on your own?"

If I had known the new general would be this much of a prick, I would have stayed home.

"Because the queen has requested it, and anyone would be a fool to go against her."

Maverick smiled wolfishly. "Is that a threat, Deputy? The way I see it, you should be on your knees, begging, before you have two enemies to deal with."

I took a deep breath before unlocking my teeth to speak—something I had been practicing since I was just a boy who liked to talk back. "General Maverick, I mean no offense. We are in utter need of all our forces if we stand a chance at getting the princess back in Eira safely. I agree it was a mistake to let the … *trespasser*"—my nails dug into my palms when that male's punchable face flashed in my mind—"so close to the heart of Eira. But the price of that mistake is not something we are willing to pay. Diana is the high princess, the heir to the entire realm. Handpicked by the ancestors. Without her, we are lost."

Without her, I'm lost.

"We acknowledge that you have your own governing body in Mount Nord, and we don't want to ruin our working relationship with the Nordians. All we ask is for you to stand at our side should it come to a war."

Maverick leaned forward, his brows knitting together. The smell of the herb in his pipe wafted my way, making my eyes water. Gaia, how much *gotu kola* could one ingest before passing out?

"You act like what you're asking for isn't the precious lives of my warriors. A war would see a great many from all sides fall. My Nordians aren't pawns. They are the last possible option, used only when peace cannot be made with words."

I hadn't expected such poetics from the general. He was rough around the edges, but it made sense now why he had been chosen to lead.

"I understand your desire to keep as many lives as you can, and I agree. As a soldier myself and as someone who has been working with my own army for many years, I respect that you don't treat your warriors as toys. They are not. There are real lives at stake, fae with husbands and wives and children. Eira would not see our forces used thoughtlessly."

Maverick nodded slowly, the tent quiet, save for the crackling fire that was still burning without even a twig to kindle it. "All right. The Nordians will fight with the queen's army."

I smiled, sagging slightly in relief. "That is great to hear—"

"On one condition."

"Name it."

The general stared straight through me, as if he could see into my soul. "We will fight, but only under your command."

I—what?

"I can assure you, Captain Embris is by far the best male for the job. He has many years of running the army under his belt. He—"

"I do not care." Maverick waved his pipe through the air. "I don't know Embris and therefore don't trust him. You, on the other hand, I trust. You see war as it is—a bloody waste of life. Many glorify the art of war, and I feel confident, knowing that you and I are in disagreement of that. So, the Nordians fight under you or not at all."

He sat back and cocked his head to one side, perfectly at ease to watch my internal struggle.

For a moment, I was too stunned to think of an appropriate answer. I could feel everyone's eyes on me, but I didn't dare look away from the fire. It was horribly wrong for me to even consider agreeing when it meant usurping my father. It was a damn mutiny. Treason even. But sitting here in this dim tent, across from the herb-smoking general of a feared warrior tribe, I knew there was no other way to gain their swords. Maverick was a male who knew what he wanted.

I was going to be in huge shit for this.

But I would be worse off if I came home as a failure. There was no chance in hell I was trekking down the mountain and riding back into Nevelyn without what I had come here for.

The lesser of two evils it was.

I stuck my hand out to Maverick, offering a clasp of agreement. "You have a deal."

He grinned, smoke falling out of his mouth like a drake. "Excellent."

FOURTEEN
WILD AND UNFORGIVING

AEDAN

Nordians were terrible singers.

That was what I'd thought at first anyway. But now, after a few good puffs from a dubious-looking pipe, I was starting to enjoy the shanty being belted around the fire.

O fee, O fie,
O sun be nigh
Wind be rough
Swords be tough
Grant us glory in battle!

The song itself wouldn't be so bad if there was a consistent key. Everyone sang it in their own variation, the result being intelligible, drunk shouting through the camp. I was surprised their children could sleep through it.

Honestly, I would be surprised if the sound didn't carry all the way into Nevelyn.

I nudged Ryen beside me. "Think they cause many avalanches from this?"

He laughed, his eyes twinkling with amusement. "Are you saying you *don't* wish we had our own song to sing after training? Because I think we need one now."

"I think my father would actually rather die a gruesome death."

Whatever herb I had smoked was making my edges feel soft, every laugh that came out of me heartier. I welcomed it.

I even welcomed the gamey, unidentified meat that was passed around the fire. I had succeeded. And what was better: I had done something Embris could not have accomplished.

So, when Jamey sat beside me, I let our thighs brush. The herbs told me that I should, and how could I deny them? For hours, I'd let them open me up enough to make friends with our new allies.

The allies *I* would be leading.

And, damn it, I *deserved* this. I was finally allowing myself to enjoy the fruits of my labour.

Eventually, Maverick quieted everyone down to formally introduce us to the group around the fire. I'd seen him pound back drink after drink, pipe after pipe, but the male didn't so much as slur his words.

"We side with Eira to get the fair Princess Diana back from the evil clutches of the Unseelie," Maverick jeered to the group around the fire, earning some hurrahs and stomping of feet in agreement. "We fight for honour, for glory, for *us!*"

The circle went up in cheers, primal and wild. It was contagious.

Then, the general smiled slyly, one side of his mouth tipping much higher than the other. "Maybe the princess will be so grateful that she'll come up here and rekindle our old flame."

My head snapped up. Others laughed, patted him on the back, while I sat, frozen, cold washing down my spine.

The circle was raucous once more, and I suddenly felt sick.

A warm hand was on my knee. "Are you all right?"

They had been together? It wasn't possible.

Yes, it was. Diana had spent a whole summer up here when she was sixteen.

Could I have really been so blind not to see her affections for another?

You were blind about Sp—

I stood suddenly. Jamey's hand fell from my leg. She looked up at me with troubled eyes.

"Were you lying about your feelings for me?" I asked.

Light from the fire danced across her face as she shook her head. "Not at all."

Wordlessly, I offered her my hand, and after a moment, she pressed her palm in mine, light and questioning. I led her away from the fire, unnoticed, except by Ryen, who gave me a rather judgmental look as we passed. I didn't let it bother me.

We got to the guest tent we'd been assigned—a small square boasting only two single cots, set up with furs draped over them.

As the flap closed behind us, I closed the gap and fitted my mouth to hers. She gasped into it, stiff at first. I almost pulled away out of fear of being too forceful when she returned the kiss, becoming fervent and strong in my arms.

Wind howled through the tent, shaking the sides. Jackets fell to the floor, but I didn't feel the cold. We became as wild and unforgiving as the mountain, kissing and biting and pushing. She dragged me to the cot, and I crawled over her. I broke our kiss only when she lifted my shirt over my head and only again when hers was next.

"Aedan," she whispered into my lips, "are you sure about this?"

"I want this if you still do," I managed to say.

Jamey only nodded, using her momentum to rid herself of her remaining clothing. Mouth dry, I followed suit.

We melted into each other and into the night, my mind gratefully occupied, my body happily fulfilled. And even when we finally collapsed beside each other, almost falling out of the tiny cot, I was blissfully void of any and all thoughts that had once consumed me.

Jamey tucked into my side, her breath a gentle sigh on my chest.

I could deal with thoughts later.

I would enjoy tonight.

"Feeling under the weather?" Ryen smirked as I squinted against the sun glaring off the snow.

I mumbled a cuss—one I'd learned from the soldiers in the army—under my breath, to which he laughed. The sound only made my head pound harder.

After leaving Fiwey at the edge of the Nordian camp, I had heard nothing but teasing from my second. I supposed I should just be grateful that he'd waited until we were out of earshot to commence. How he'd stayed so sober I didn't know, and he made sure I knew how much better he was faring than me.

To be fair, mixing the Nordians' pipes with drink had probably not been a wise decision on my part.

Jamey had not said or done anything incriminating, but the tension in the group made it obvious enough that everyone knew which bed we'd ended up in last night.

I had expected regret to bloom in my chest, but it never came. Not even guilt. And so I ignored the smirks from Trent and Mikale and shrugged off Ryen's pestering.

The trek down the mountain seemed longer than the way up. It was hard to ignore the chill in the air, making me shiver on top of my cold sweats brought on from the night before. I wasn't a fan of the heat, but I found myself longing for the sunshine that had been blessing Nevelyn for the past week.

I made the executive decision to skip lunch, saying my companions could eat as they walked. If I stopped walking, there was a good chance I'd curl up in a ball and stay that way for the rest of the day. Only the thought of a soothing ginger tonic and my own bed kept me going.

At one point, Mikale caught up with me. "I just wanted to say that I was really impressed by how you handled the general. You made him feel like he was the one winning even though you got what you wanted."

"Thank you, Mikale," I said. "But I wasn't trying to con him. It was just luck that we both shared a common goal."

"Don't sell yourself short, A!" Trent called from behind us. "Not many can say they've successfully handled negotiations with a warrior tribe."

My chest swelled with gratitude. I had good soldiers, worth every sentiment I'd given Maverick.

"One problem remains." Ryen's voice cut through the air like a knife, and I flinched inwardly as it rattled through my head painfully. "How are you going to break it to Embris that you're taking his job?"

My father didn't need to know until the last possible minute. It wasn't like I was taking over his whole army, just the Nordian division. But I knew the captain would still be seething mad. He'd see it as a play for the army, no matter what I said. It still wasn't known if we would even be fighting. It was possible we wouldn't have to call upon the Nordians at all, and he'd never have to know.

"Let me worry about that. Not a *word* from any of you—is that clear?" I turned to stare each one in the eyes before continuing my pace. Each nodded, even Jamey. "If I find out any of you has disobeyed me, your tongue will be removed."

Probably a touch dramatic, but it got my seriousness across.

We made our way down Mount Nord. When we reached the end of Spike's Passage, I finally called for us to rest a moment. The last of the trek would be a steep decline, and we would not be able to stop until we were back on level ground.

Trent and Mikale collapsed on the path, leaning against snowy boulders while they chugged the last of their canteens. Jamey sat delicately on an edge, sweat sheening on her brow.

Spike's Passage was named for the rocks that jutted up like the sharp teeth of a predator. It was treacherous to go around it, so the only way down was through the skinny path. Tedious, but it also boasted the best—and only—view of the North. In Mount Nord, only snow was visible, unless you were airborne.

Carefully, I picked my way around the spikes and looked out into the valley, expecting to see the familiar green of the forest, the River Nord snaking through, and the palace tips poking through the trees.

All I saw was white.

Snow everywhere.

Snow lining the trees, covering the ground, even fluffy flakes falling from the sky. The river was frozen, and the absence of its roaring made the wintery scene ominous.

This wasn't possible. Eira was in full bloom, about to transition into the heat of summer. How could this be?

"Ryen."

My second joined me, stiffening when he saw what lay in wait for us.

"Tell me my eyes are playing tricks on me," I said quietly.

"What in Gaia's name?" Ryen breathed.

The others came up behind us, each voicing their own confusion.

"This has to be a glamour of the mountain," Trent guessed, his voice unsure.

"It's no trick." Jamey spoke for the first time in hours. "The North is frozen. The ancestors are punishing us for what happened with Diana."

The words hung in the air like heavy clouds. Maybe she was right, and whatever powers that be were trying to get a point across. Or maybe the mountain was responsible, and at the bottom, we'd be welcomed by green grass and sunshine.

Something deep in my belly warned me that the latter was wishful thinking. For whatever reason, nature was out of balance.

Silently, we marched down the mountain, not talking when we got to the bottom and were greeted by more of a tundra than we'd thought. Not when we mounted our horses and trudged through the snow. Not even when we got to the gates of the palace and saw that it was halfway covered and stuck closed and only the back gates were in use.

Nevelyn was a whiteout.

FIFTEEN
TWO GOLD ARM BANDS

MAISIE

It was late and damn cold with the freezing wind blasting through my coat.

Five more minutes, I told myself. *Five more minutes, and Aedan can shove it.*

I rotated between crossing my arms over my chest and tucking my hands inside my pockets when they lost feeling. Neither really helped with the cold, but there hadn't really been time today to search through my stored winter clothes. The sudden pivot from almost summer to full-on winter had caused a panic in the palace, servants running around all day to make sure fireplaces were working smoothly and to grab the officials' coats from storage.

The lobelia that had been blooming was almost invisible, weighed down by snow. I reached out a hand to brush some away, trying to catch a glimpse of the purple flowers in Diana's favourite garden, but yanked it back when someone shouted behind me.

"Hey! What are you doing out there?"

I was relieved to see the voice belonged to a palace guard. He was not one I was familiar with, probably a new hire, but I was counting myself lucky that it wasn't someone who might want to escort me inside. Once he saw I was a servant, he would likely leave me alone for the warmth of the palace.

"You'll catch your death out here," the guard said, stopping just outside of the garden alcove.

"I was just hoping to see the flowers I love," I said, wincing when I realized how dumb that sounded while standing in the middle of what would likely become a blizzard soon. "I'll be in soon; don't worry."

His eyebrows knitted together. His head swung to the flower bed and then back to me. Finally, he shrugged and turned to walk away. But he paused a moment and looked over his shoulder at me. "I've heard about you. Mary, is it?"

I didn't correct him.

"The word in the guard is, you're the favourite whore of the palace officials."

If there had been any blood left in my body to chill, it would have. My heart kicked up in speed, sending cool sweat under my pits.

"Hmm." He crossed the distance between us and took my chin in his gloved hand, turning it from side to side. I yanked away, and he tsked quietly under his breath. "Feisty. I like it."

Every warning bell in my head was going off, but I was—almost literally—frozen. If I made for the palace now, he could follow me. Or worse, see it as an invitation. But if I stayed out here, I'd most certainly lose my fingers and toes—maybe more.

Swallowing, I tried to think of Diana and straightened my back. "Even if that were true, it would hardly be any of your business."

The guard laughed and grabbed my arm, roughly dragging me closer. His stale breath was warm on my face, and a tremor broke out through my body.

"I've been looking for a way into the inner circle, what with me being new and all." He winked. I fought the urge to gag. "I think some personal experience would gain me favour with the boys. You don't mind, do you?"

I fought to get out of his grasp. This was getting too close to the point of no return. I'd seen it on too many faces not to recognize it now.

"Let—me—go!" I pulled and pulled and even tried to summon some magic, but my fear made it too hard to grab on to. I was getting close to tears now, and I knew once they started, I would shut down, hiding away in my own mind, only to find myself in a stranger's bed in the morning.

"C'mon now. Won't take long." He fumbled with undoing his belt and also keeping me in his grip.

I could already feel the fight leaving. Draining. This was my job. It was expected of me.

One tear slid down my face.

"HEY!"

The guard turned just in time to catch a fist in his face. Blood spurted from his nose and cracked lip, and he stumbled backward, yelping.

Aedan.

Fresh, wonderful, clean air found its way into my lungs. He wouldn't let me disappear.

I could only watch as Aedan sent another punch to the guard's gut and grabbed his shirt collar. He breathed something into his ear that had the male's face paling, his eyes widening in fear.

Without another word, Aedan dropped the guard, who scrambled to his feet and fled through the snow, tripping and stumbling.

Instantly, he was at my side, sliding his arms free of his coat and draping it around my shoulders. The smell of pine enveloped me, warm and comforting.

"Are you all right?" Aedan's eyes were deeply concerned, the blue standing out even more against the white of the snow.

This was the part of him I'd thought might disappear along with Diana. The sensitive, gentle, caring piece of him that had somehow managed to escape his father's influence.

I nodded, too close to breaking down to risk speaking.

He put an arm around my shoulders—gently, ever so gently, as if I were made from glass—and guided me into the palace. The warmth was a relief, and I blew on my hands to help start their revival.

"Why were you out there?"

"Our meeting spot, of course." I shot a disdainful look his way. Had he really forgotten?

"Well, yes, but I figured the extenuating circumstances might change things." He gestured to the window, where big flakes of snow floated through the frame. "I was waiting by the door to the gardens for you until I thought I should check the spot, just in case you had gone rogue and decided to test your body's ability to pump blood to your toes."

"I'm glad you checked," I said quietly.

"I am too."

We walked through the palace and up to the royal family's wing. I was grateful for Aedan leaving me in peace, the only sound our footsteps echoing off the marble. He didn't ask me about the encounter, nor did I want him to. I'd always found tranquillity in the silence between friends; I was lucky to have such a bond with Diana. It surprised me to feel it with Aedan now.

"What did you say to him?"

His voice was full and unforgiving. "I made it clear he was unwelcome in the queen's guard. He is … awaiting punishment from my second."

"You don't have to do all that for me."

"You deserve to feel safe in this palace—everyone who works here does. The guard made it clear he did not belong with our collective. There is no room here for scum like him. I have zero tolerance for those who think they are better than everyone."

Aedan's face was set, his jaw clenched.

All the males I'd ever met were the same at their roots—greedy, arrogant, entitled. Except for him.

Why didn't Diana ever fall for you?

With a start, I realized we were outside his rooms. I'd never been in his or Embris's rooms, but as a longtime resident, I knew where they were. It was a coveted spot—the closest one could get to the royal rooms without being one.

"I thought we would be more comfortable in my sitting area," Aedan explained, pausing halfway through the threshold when he saw my face. "Is that okay with you?"

"Your reputation, not mine," I said weakly, my words not quite hitting the humorous tone I had been going for.

The unsaid words hung between us: my reputation could do much worse—and had.

Aedan opened the door wider for me to enter. "I couldn't care less about the palace gossip."

He shook his head, and I watched a piece of golden hair pull loose from its perfect hold.

Heart lightening, I took in the room. It was not unlike Diana's antechamber—large enough to have guests, a few armchairs settled around a fireplace. A desk faced the wall that shared the door into his room. It was neatly organized with a stack of papers and a large map that depicted Eira. A few pieces of artwork hung on the walls, which had been painted a mossy green that did not match the rest of the bright white theme of the palace. It was like a forest, an embodiment of Aedan.

I liked it.

I made myself comfortable in one of the armchairs, enjoying the proximity to the fire. Aedan settled across from me.

"This snow is pretty unbelievable," he said, shucking off his scarf and gloves.

"I thought I was dreaming when I saw the first snowflake fall," I admitted. "For a while, we thought it was some trick or glamour."

Aedan shook his head. "And I was really looking forward to the sun after Mount Nord. The queen's official stance is that the snow is an act of Gaia. She's using it to her advantage to sway any still not on her side."

I frowned. "How so?"

"From what my father told me, Prince Leo is still actively disagreeing with how the queen is going about the portal. He thinks we need to be acting faster, and … well, he has been throwing accusations around that Vera knows the secret to the portal and won't share it."

"That's absurd. If she knew, we'd have Diana back already!"

Aedan shrugged. "Just telling you what I've heard." He stared into the fire, a muscle twitching in his jaw, and I remembered the day he had pulled me from Leo in the library. He clearly had no like for the prince.

"Was Mount Nord successful?" I asked, hoping to steer away from the topic of Leo.

Something like a wry grin flashed across Aedan's face before he could hide it. "Very much so. We have the Nordians' support should we need it."

"Good work!"

"Well, I certainly had to work for it." He grinned. "The new general, Maverick, enjoyed making me sweat."

I felt my eyes widen. "Maverick is the new general?" I breathed.

Understanding flashed on Aedan's face. "You know."

Unable to think of anything that would help the situation, I just nodded.

"How … how long did it go on?"

"Just the summer while she was there," I said gently. "It didn't end well."

Aedan nodded, his lips pursing, and he stared at the wall with the desk like he was trying to bore a hole with his gaze.

"What's on your neck?" I squinted, trying to get a better look.

When he'd turned his head away from me, a small bruise had stood out against the light of the fire. But it looked too light to be a bruise and in such a weird spot.

"Is that a hickey?" I gasped, incredulous.

Aedan slapped a hand to his neck. "It's nothing."

I laughed at the absurdity of it all, even as something deep inside me clenched painfully.

"The buttoned-up Deputy Captain Thesand with a hickey on his neck. What are you, fourteen?" I teased.

Heat rose in his cheeks. "It was strong herb," he grumbled, which only made me laugh harder.

He eventually joined in despite himself, and for the first time in a long time, laughter was the only thing on my mind.

When we finally subsided, Aedan asked, "What about you? Did you find anything while I was gone?"

I filled him in on the books I'd found in Diana's room from the academy and that the first two I'd read didn't help beyond explaining what portals were. I hoped to read another one tonight. Given my limited spare time and the dryness of these books, it was a miracle I'd finished the ones I had.

"But I have other news."

I had the sudden urge not to tell him about my trip to the Marketplace. It wasn't that I wanted to hide it from him, but would this information change our dynamic? With my device, I no longer needed him to replay the events of the meetings in the queen's council room.

It's fine, I rationed. *You still need him. There are other places he can get information. He won't go back on the alliance.*

Aedan arched an eyebrow. "Oh?"

"I visited The Curator," I said, testing the name on the air. He didn't react, so I continued, "He deals in obscure and rare objects. I was able to procure a device that allows me to hear through magic-sealed walls."

"That's impossible," Aedan said. "It was likely a scam."

I shook my head. "It works. I tested it."

I filled Aedan in on how I'd planted one stone in the council room and showed him the other that I kept on me at all times.

He turned the device over in his hand. "What did you call this?"

"Science. Apparently, there is a group of non-magic-wielding fae that experiment with it."

I expected the same knee-jerk reaction that I'd given Kol—there was no such thing as fae with no magic. But Aedan was silent as he stared at the red stone.

"If anyone found out, Maisie, you could be tried for espionage. Treason even." He handed the device back to me.

I sucked in a breath. "I know."

"Let's hope this stays secret then. Can you trust this Curator?"

Hmm. Can I?

"I think so. As long as I make good on my side of the deal."

"What were the terms?"

"A favour," I said, suddenly self-conscious of the risk I'd made.

He paused. "At least tell me he doesn't know who you really are."

"Yes. No. I don't know. Maybe." I scrunched up my nose. "It was hard to get a read on him. Very ominous guy. He *knew* things."

Aedan raked his hands through his hair, looking exasperated with me.

"Look, it's fine, okay? I know the deal I made, and honestly, I'd do it again. Let's move on."

"You're not what I expected," he said, one soft laugh escaping him. "You're so much like Diana."

Warmth spread through me, even more than the fire could. I would never be as fierce and just and strong as her. But it still felt good that he thought so.

"Do you think she's okay?" Aedan's voice was soft, unprotected.

"Yeah, I think she's okay." I thought of her on the last day I'd seen her, wearing the most gorgeous dress I'd ever seen, commanding the attention of the room with her glittering smile. She had been the embodiment of queenliness. "The Dark realm has no idea what they've just invited into their nest."

He smiled down at his hands.

I looked down at my own, to the red stone that was warm from me holding it. "Oh!" I held the stone up excitedly. "Did you hear about Princess Hollaina?"

"Embris filled me in when I returned. It was probably the last thing I'd expected to hear. They're keeping it tightly under wraps, so your 'science' must have worked," he admitted.

"Why do you think she's coming? She hasn't left the Eastern court for decades."

"I have no idea. All we were told was to prepare for her arrival.

Apparently, she's not all there anymore. Maybe the timing is a fluke."

"Or she decided that Nimshar was the worst possible choice to make decisions on her behalf."

Aedan chuckled. "One can only hope it is not serious. We need the regions to be united now more than ever."

"Well, I'll be listening," I said, holding up the stone. "But anything you can gather outside the council room will be helpful. I'll continue going through the books too."

I stood before the sleepy lull in my limbs stopped me from leaving. I made to take off Aedan's coat—I'd forgotten I was wearing it—but he stopped me.

"Take it. The hallways will be cold in this weather."

I hesitated. Anyone who saw me with the jacket, bearing the two gold arm bands of the deputy captain, would automatically assume the worst of my reputation. I didn't want that for Aedan. But he could handle himself, and the hallways would be frigid without a fireplace to warm them. So, I nodded and grasped the door handle.

I startled when I bumped into someone. Standing on the other side of the door was none other than Jamey Pinois of the West, wearing the same shocked expression that I was.

"Sorry, lady," I said instantly, bowing my head and backing into the hallway.

She only nodded, confusion on her face as her gaze landed on the jacket around my shoulders and then at Aedan in the doorway. She looked … jealous.

Ah.

I expected to feel gratified to solve the mystery of the hickey giver, but all I felt was a strange pressure in my chest.

"Thanks again for saving me, Deputy Captain," I said, summoning a meek servant voice. Hopefully, Jamey wouldn't look too much further.

Aedan nodded once. "Of course. Good night."

I could hear their murmured hellos and the soft click of his door as I made my way back to the servants' sector.

It's good he's moving on from Diana. He deserves to be happy, and she's a perfect choice for him. I told myself that over and over as I walked home and crawled into bed.

I opened an ancient-looking book called *Group Magic and Its Many Uses* and started reading.

I got through four pages before I realized I hadn't read a single word.

Ugh. Too much going on in my life lately. I touched the light orb beside my bed and turned over in the darkness, willing sleep to come. When it did, it was filled with red stones and snowy purple flowers and the smell of pine.

SIXTEEN
UNDERFOOT

AEDAN

"I hope I'm not interrupting," Jamey said, wrapping her shawl closer to her body. Her black hair was dusted with snowflakes, her nose red at the tip.

I motioned for her to sit by the fire. "Come warm up. What were you doing out in the snow?"

Gratefully, Jamey perched in the chair Maisie had just vacated, holding her hands out toward the warm flame. "I needed to see for myself. It's just absurd, what's happening."

I nodded. "Have you spoken to your court since being back?"

"I saw my mother briefly, and she updated me on the recent meetings. That Southern prince is sure a loudmouth."

Irritation prickled under my skin. "At least he is advocating for action to be taken."

Jamey's gaze flicked to me, her eyes narrowing. "I hardly think accusing the queen of not sharing crucial information warrants as advocation. He needs a reminder of his status."

Ordinarily, that would have been my cue to excuse myself from the conversation. But after speaking with Maisie, I was in a surprisingly good mood despite our circumstances. "We are all under a lot of stress right now. I think it's important we remember that as we move forward."

She smoothed her dress. "Perhaps you're right. I wanted to speak with you about what happened on Mount Nord."

I sat in the other chair, the warmth hitting my cheeks. "I should apologize, my lady. I fear the, uh, rather strong herbs might have contributed to my forward behaviour."

Jamey tilted her head, looking me directly in the eyes. "Are you saying you regret your time with me?"

My hand froze halfway toward running through my hair. I faltered, mind spinning for something to say that wouldn't offend her. Truthfully, I'd enjoyed that night on Mount Nord as casual fun—but I worried about the repercussions if she somehow felt misled. As a future ruler of the West, I couldn't have bridges being burned down with her.

"Because I don't regret it. In fact, I was hoping that you might be inclined to continue seeing one another."

Jamey's throat bobbed as she waited for my reaction. Relief cooled through me, enough that I actually huffed a laugh, my arm finally completing its journey to my hair, where it raked through the strands. It was almost too long now, but I had to admit that it was much more welcome than my usual close-shaved cut in the frigid air.

"I would like that," I told her, relaxing in my chair. "As long as you understand the pressures and time commitments of my job. This wouldn't be ... official."

"I understand. I have my own duties as well. I won't get underfoot."

I couldn't imagine what she possibly filled her day with as the granddaughter of a high-ranking region head, but I didn't question it.

Jamey stood abruptly, coming to stand close to me. She reached out a delicate hand and turned my chin to the side, revealing my neck. "How unprofessional for a deputy captain," she remarked, humour in her eyes.

"It needs to be kissed better."

She laughed. "Is that so? Well then, I must oblige. Are you free tomorrow, after dinner? I could meet you."

I pulled her onto my lap. "I have a better idea. Why don't you meet me now?"

She smiled.

SEVENTEEN
SOULWEAVER

SPENSE

un beat down on my bare back, the heat only partially responsible for the sweat coating my body. I stood in the middle of Ivywall's training ring, in a semicircle with two dozen other hopeful army applicants. Sand licked up my bare feet, coating my skin up to my ankles.

The air was sticky and unbearably thick. What should have been an easy test of push-ups, sit-ups, and planks had turned me into a panting mess.

Thankfully, I was not alone. The other applicants shared the sweaty gloss and heavy breath. We awaited our next order from King Urdan, who had commandeered this otherwise routine army testing from Sorin.

The poor other applicants. If only they'd picked a testing date that the king's son wasn't participating in.

"Being in the Unseelie army, no matter what position, rank, or division, is not just an honour. It is a duty, a responsibility, a promise to protect our fae. This should not be taken lightly. Once you join, you are no longer your own. You will answer to General Sorin and him alone. If he says jump, *you say* how high.*" Urdan paced in front of us, his hands clasped behind him, his signature cape blowing gently. His leathery wings were tucked in tight, almost invisible under the cape, save for the points that peeked out at the bottom.*

My brother Sorin stood behind him, holding his staff in one hand and using the other to moderate the sun's rays, directing more heat on us at Urdan's behest. He had graciously allowed our father to take over the testing, and only the slightest tightening of his mouth told me he was not happy about it.

His brown eyes bored into mine, and I couldn't help but feel he was trying to warn me of something.

"I think we need an example," Urdan said. "You there, come here." He pointed to the male beside me, who was tall and lanky and looked barely old enough to meet the required age.

Having turned fourteen only three days prior, I thought I would be the youngest by far. But perhaps I was wrong.

"What is your name?" he asked the applicant, who stood before him with his chin up, like he was already a soldier.

"Giro, sir."

"Giro, please kneel before this post." With a flick of his wrist, a wooden beam shot up from the ground, standing about four feet tall and as wide as a grown cactus tree.

My stomach began to churn. Urdan's face had taken on the steely, murderous look that haunted my dreams.

The boy, Giro, did as he had been asked. Urdan then instructed him to wrap his arms around the post, where he had Sorin tie them together. Even with his back to us, I could feel the fear coming off Giro. He knew now that whatever example he was about to be a part of, it wouldn't be pleasant.

"Now, I require a volunteer." My father's gaze raked over the group before landing on me, just as I'd known it would. His teeth were bared in a horrifying smile as he beckoned me up.

My legs were like lead as I joined Urdan before the post.

"Now is your chance to prove your worth to our army. Your unfailing obedience. Take this and lash our friend Giro here ten times." When he

outstretched his arm, a whip hung from his hand. It was hefty and long, the tail end positively wicked in its thinness and sharp end.

There were shuffles of feet from behind me, but no one would say a word. Not Giro, not Sorin, not anyone. We were all under Urdan's command.

Nausea bubbled in my stomach, and my mouth filled with saliva, but I refused to vomit.

There was no other way.

No other way to my father's approval.

My hand acted of its own accord, taking the whip. My fingers wrapped around it, testing the weight. I saw myself in this semicircle, standing in front of Giro's open, unmarred back, as if I were a bird flying overhead.

Sorin stood quietly, his focus unwavering, but I felt the heat around me ease ever so slightly.

"Your general gave you an order, boy," Urdan spat, lip curled. "Hesitation will be treated the same as disobedience. Follow your order, or you're gone."

The whip cracked through the air, slicing across Giro's back. He tensed, but did not yell or cry out. And he wouldn't. He was proving himself, just as I was.

His skin was warped and bleeding in some places. The more I stared, the more I wanted to empty my guts. So, I didn't look. I just reacted.

The muscles in my back and arm rippled as the whip soared through the air again. And again.

Over and over, my body listened to me, even when I wished it wouldn't.

Giro's back was never going to recover fully from this. He'd always bear these scars. I would bear them too, if only on the inside.

Three more.

Two more.

When I finished the final slash, I dropped the whip as if it had burned me. It might as well have, the way my hand felt like acid. I stepped away, *unable to look at the bleeding mess I'd created. Unable to listen to the tiniest whimper from Giro.*

"Congratulations. You're all officially soldiers in the Unseelie army." Without another word, Urdan vanished.

The words I'd always wanted to hear from my father fell empty in the air.

Two of the newly minted soldiers ran to Giro and gently untied him, cradling him as they carried him away, toward the healer's ward. With the king gone, Giro had let himself go and was crying freely, his glassy face excruciating to behold.

When everyone was gone, I bent over and heaved out everything in my stomach. A hand touched my back. Sorin.

Wordlessly, his hand strong and guiding, he led me back to Ivywall.

I sat up in bed, sweat drenched and tangled in my sheets. I ran to my bathing room, knelt before the basin, and lost last night's dinner as the hot, sticky air from my dream surrounded me.

When there was nothing left, I wiped my mouth and waited for the nausea to subside.

Finally, air became easier to breathe, and I sat back against the wall. It was still night, darkness bleeding in from my windows.

I sat there, on the cold stone floor of my bathing chamber, replaying that invasive memory over and over again until I stopped feeling the extreme guilt and heaviness. It was only when the first light of dawn broke that I was able to stand, wash my mouth, and clean the sticky, dried sweat from myself.

Heart shattered and mind empty, I dressed in my battle leather. I was an imposter in this outfit, doing up the straps and attaching my various weapons.

He would pay for what he'd done to me. I was a psychological mess, the perfect Urdan Junior. But his approval, his pride, meant nothing to me anymore. It was time for me to be my own general.

I rapped gently on Diana's door, and it slid open before I fully took my hand away. I hid a smile. She'd been waiting.

"Good morning," I murmured, taking in her desert-appropriate attire.

Someone—probably Pik—had supplied her with the clothing she would need. She now wore a lightweight, long-sleeved tunic that reached up her neck and matching pants that would be suitable for riding in the heat. Her boots would grip in the sand well, and she'd been given a scarf that she wore loosely around her shoulders to put over her mouth and nose for extra protection in the air.

I loved that she was wearing the clothing of my world, that she fit in. I loved that we matched.

"Are you nervous?" I asked as she joined me in the hall. I led us toward The Cliff, nicknamed long ago by Alwyn, where we would find the drakes.

Diana shook her head, her hair falling around her. I picked up a piece and tucked it behind her ear. She shivered at my touch.

"I love flying. Although I'm a little nervous of what we'll find in Elfwood."

Having her in my world calmed a storm that had been raging since my magic had first appeared. It opened up a little crack in my heart and filled it with warmth.

"Badras seems to think it's a trap, but I don't think so. Are you sure you feel comfortable fighting hand-to-hand? There would be no shame if you're not." Truthfully, I felt a little rusty myself, even after two hours of practice before bed last night.

"I'll be fine," Diana confirmed.

I had never seen her fight, but if I knew anything about growing up in a palace, I could trust her training had been extensive. Even if the thought of sending her into a possible battle without knowing her capabilities filled me with intense anxiety.

Alwyn met us at the entrance to the council room, bouncing on her heels when she saw us. Her brown eyes were alight, her smile a heavy contrast to the battle armour she wore.

"You look wonderful!" she exclaimed, hugging Diana. "Although you'll have to let me fix your hair. You'll go crazy if it's not tied back while you're riding."

I eyed my small sister. "You went a little heavy on the armour there."

Alwyn shrugged, turning Diana around and getting to work, her nimble fingers deftly turning the chestnut waterfall of hair into braids. "I like to be prepared." She looked me up and down. "We basically wore the same thing. It just looks like less on you because you're the size of a mountain," she said, rolling her eyes.

Diana snorted, her back to us.

When Alwyn finished weaving the braids together and was satisfied they would stay put, she turned her around again. "There. You're wearing my signature brand, which means you have to kick ass today."

"What's your signature brand?" Diana asked.

"Badass warrior princess."

Diana laughed. She looked every bit the part.

I opened the door into the council room, and they followed me in.

"Why are we in the council room?" Diana looked around the room with the same wonder she'd had yesterday, taking in the black-and-white marble with awe.

"This is the secret door to The Cliff," Alwyn said, wiggling her eyebrows.

She ran her hand along a seam of marbling until she reached a sconce and abruptly yanked it down. Without warning, the floor in front of her slid away to reveal a set of adobe stairs spiralling under the room.

Diana crinkled her nose in confusion. "The Cliff is underground?"

"No, you'll see." I took her hand in mine and started down the stairs. The familiar scent of clay and drake wafted into my nose, the char of it welcome.

We spiralled down until we'd made a complete turn. Being a full level underneath Ivywall, one would expect a dark cellar. Instead, the floor had been built into the side of a rock formation and swept out, overlooking the desert as far as the eye could see. The Cliff was a U-shape and looked out over tiers cut into the rock, varying sizes and lengths. Each and every one housed a drake, most dozing lazily in the sun that had begun to rise. The soldiers that Alwyn had rallied were busy preparing their mounts for the trip.

Diana was shocked. "This—this is *under* Ivywall? But how?"

"The Cliff was here first. Ivywall was built overtop."

Alwyn didn't so much as give us a second look as she walked to the edge and right off, her body dropping rapidly. Diana raced to the edge and peered below, where Wyn had jumped down a level.

She grinned up at us. "You coming or what?"

I jumped, landing easily in the loose dirt. I reached up to offer Diana a hand, only to find she was already standing beside me, looking out at the slumbering drakes.

"Why couldn't I see this from the roof?" she asked.

I lifted my shoulder in a noncommittal half shrug. "Because we designed it to be hidden."

Wind whipped through The Cliff, scattering sand and debris into the air. I pulled up my scarf and gestured for Diana to do the same. She was squinting against the wind, blinking rapidly at the grit that had made its way to her eyes.

I reached into my magic and pulled a familiar strand to my face, one that would act as protection from the sand, diverting it away from my eyes. This was crucial when flying; otherwise, you'd have a terrible case of dry eye when you landed.

Diana watched me, and I could tell she felt the magic. I offered her my hand and sent some up her arm to her eyes as well.

"Storm magic isn't my strongest branch," I admitted. "But it will do the job."

I kept Diana's hand in mine as we made our way along the edges of The Cliff until we stood beside Alwyn. She held the reins to Xiro, her battle-bred mount. He was incredibly large, even with his wings folded in, wholly black, with hard lines and ridges. His tail was as long as his body, and his jaw could not fully close, for the massive fangs. He was a nightmare in the flesh.

If Diana was apprehensive of the beast, she did not show it. My heart swelled with pride.

"Took you long enough. Your mounts are ready." Alwyn pointed behind her, where an Ivywall worker was hastily running between two drakes, finishing up their straps and buckles. "Mount up. We leave imminently."

Some of the other soldiers were in the air already, gliding on the wind above us. With a nimble climb up the side of her drake, Alwyn settled into her saddle and buckled herself in. Xiro's wings snapped out, scattering sand, and within seconds, he was airborne, whipping through the air like he was wind itself.

I let out a laugh of excitement as I recognized the drake waiting for me. Sensara! My grey doe stood tall and proud, her keen eyes taking me in as we approached. She had been a gift from my father when I was six and she was a baby herself, and we had grown and trained together.

I reached out to run my hand along her thick scales, and she leaned into me, huffing gently. "I've missed you too."

The drake handler who had gotten them ready handed me my broadsword, dipping his chin in greeting. I took the marble-handled blade, crudely named Bloodletter by my father, and savoured its familiar weight as I sheathed it. The handler also passed a smaller, thinner sword to Diana and a few short throwing knives, which she buckled into thigh sheaths.

"Does this one have a name?" I asked, nodding at the blade.

"Soulweaver."

I smiled. It was perfect.

The Ivywall worker offered breastplates of varying sizes to Diana. They were scuffed and used, but they would do the trick. Once she found one that fit, I helped do up the straps, impressed with how formidable it made her look.

Diana stood back, looking at the drake that was waiting for her. I recognized him right away—Keely. He was getting up there in age, but was a true master. Every drake rider's first flight was with him. He would treat her well.

"That's Keely," I told Diana as she slowly touched his white-scaled shoulder. "He will take good care of you, I promise. He will follow. Here, do you need help mounting?"

She inspected the tack, the lightweight seat, and the ridges along the girth, used as stepping stools. "This is not unlike what we use on the pegasi," she noted. Without hesitation, she climbed up the ridges and settled onto Keely's back.

I shook my head in wonder. I should stop being surprised by her abilities.

"Don't forget to buckle in," I called over my shoulder as I swung my leg over Sensara's saddle.

Within seconds, the drakes' wings were flexing, testing the air. At my urging, Sensara vaulted into the air, Keely following close behind.

Wind crashed through my ears, through my clothes, but it was welcome. We climbed up, up into the sky until Ivywall was just a speck below us. Alwyn's group had started toward Elfwood, and we followed close behind.

Going through the motions of flying, of taking off toward an unknown battle, was unbelievably familiar. Since I'd been home in Ivywall, memories came and went, some coming back in flashes impossible to ignore. Others were like this—quietly settled in the background until, one day, they showed themselves again. I'd spent many hours growing up in this very saddle, working with Sensara to glide through the air and slice down on our enemies.

The Battle of the Kelpies.

The Gnome Rescue.

The ongoing war against the humans.

That time the pixies had gotten hold of my father's sword, and we spent three days trekking across the desert, only to find it had been in his saddlebag all along.

There was so much war, so much fighting here. I had been blind to it until now. I didn't want it to be this way, but I also didn't want to march on Eira. Was peace really so unachievable?

Under Urdan's rule, yes.

He was stuck in his ways and possibly stuck in his own mind too. Nothing would ever change for Ivywall, for all the Folk, if the water remained unrippled.

The Unseelie king had ruled for eight millennia too long. It was time to create a splash.

When we were finally flying smoothly, I twisted around to see how Diana was doing. Even with her face masked, I could tell she was smiling. Her eyes were aglow. She sat with a comfortable poise as she gazed at the horizon.

Beautiful.

Her eyes snapped to mine, and I almost collapsed at the force of her happiness. She was light and free and fearless. Since coming to Ivywall, this was the closest I'd seen of the Diana I'd fallen for. All the cacti and golden landscapes in the world couldn't tear me from her gaze.

After a few hours of flying, shouts from the front of the line caught my attention. Alwyn had given the order to start descending. As Sensara dipped below the clouds, Elfwood came into sight. The city was under fire, smoke making it hard to tell what was going on. Bodies ran, and metal clanged. The closer we got, the louder the battle. Soon, we could hear the shouts from generals and cries from the army.

I swooped to Alwyn's side, and she yelled at me through the wind, "We can't risk using the drakes' fire while everyone is in such close range! We'll have to join on foot!"

Indeed, it would be decimating to all parties if the drakes let their fire loose. We would join the fray with our steel, and it would be enough.

It would have to be if I wanted to stop the waste of elf and fae life.

It would have to be if I wanted to regain my siblings' respect.

Wind racing, swords clanging, we landed in the middle of the battlefield.

EIGHTEEN
ADORNED IN IRON

DIANA

I hadn't even landed in the dirt off the side of Keely when I felt it. That tight, crushing feeling in the air, sealing the energy around us from using it. The air felt hot and sticky, and everything seemed to move in slow motion. My limbs felt slow and heavy. This was land without magic. The humans' weapon was at work.

Spense was shouting at me, trying to give me last-minute advice. Between the roaring of the drakes and the roaring in my own ears, the sounds of metal clashing and voices yelling, I could barely make his words out.

"… stick to your aim and don't hesitate …" he was shouting. "You'll know the humans by their iron armour!"

He watched me, clearly uncertain that I'd made sense of what he told me. But a soldier ran at him, and he sprang into motion.

Indeed, the human was decked head to toe in iron, which seemed both heavy and a purpose-driven choice even if that reason was unclear. It was crudely made, obviously favouring use over style, and had an owl stamped into the crest on the breastplate.

Even if he hadn't been wearing such a statement of armour, I would have known the humans because they were so vastly different-looking than the tall, twig-thin, green-skinned elves. In fact, the humans, other than being a little shorter, didn't look all that dissimilar to the fae.

I watched Spense fight the human and was wholly unsurprised to see that his skill was just as impressive with a blade as with his fists. Still though, it entranced me, how he swung and arced, easily disarming his opponent. He was fluid and—

A gasp escaped me when Spense ran Bloodletter right through the human's chest. He waited only a second before yanking it clean out, watching the soldier slump to the ground.

The human was dead.

I'd known what I had signed up for, but it was just now clicking in that I *hadn't* known. This was real.

This was war.

And I was mentally unequipped.

Beside me, Keely let out a deafening roar and swung his long tail at a human brandishing a sword at him. I narrowly avoided being tripped by the club end as it ripped through the sand, effectively hitting the human in the chest and sending him flying.

While the drake's attention was on that soldier, another ran at his unguarded flank. Without thinking, I unsheathed Soulweaver and sprang forward, muscles adjusting to the sword's weight in my palm.

Metal clanged as I stopped his blow to the drake. It was stronger than I'd anticipated, and I had to use both hands to brace against the soldier.

With my weight leaned forward into our crossed swords, I was caught off guard when the human suddenly sucked his own sword back and charged at me again.

I jumped to the side, feeling the air of his blade *whoosh* against my cheek.

You have to do better, Diana.

There was barely any time to think before I was blocking another strike. And another. I was on the defence, slowly being driven toward Keely's large hide, where I would be backed in. I needed a way out.

After deflecting the next blow, I feigned left and darted right, slipping to the side of the human, where I was able to get my own shot in. He countered it but tripped as he sought footing, and I felt a small thrill when he hit the ground on his knees, weighed down by his armour.

I pointed Soulweaver at his chest, but he parried it. On instinct, I flung my hand out, waiting for the magic I was directing at him, waiting for the pommel of his sword to drop.

Nothing happened, but there was an unexpected reaction in the human. From behind his helmet, his eyes widened in fear, and he stilled completely. This soldier had been on the receiving end of magic before.

When he realized the magic was absent, he grinned savagely and grabbed my outstretched hand, gripping it crushingly with his. "You pointy ears don't know how to fight fair," he snarled, spitting the words out in utter disgust. His voice was so devoid of pity, of empathy.

With his nails digging into my palm, he brought up his other arm and placed the cool iron of his wrist guard onto my skin. Pressing down hard, he looked eagerly at me, clearly waiting for my reaction.

It was uncomfortable, but not bad enough that I couldn't wrench my arm away and drive him backward, Soulweaver outstretched.

"Wh—how did you do that?" the human spluttered. "That's supposed to *burn* you!"

I didn't know where he'd gotten that idea, but he was mistaken. "Now, who's not fighting fair?"

I swung the lightweight sword into the air, aiming for the soldier's chest, like I'd seen Spense do. *You have to do it quick. No time to overthink this.*

When I looked into his eyes again, I saw a male utterly defeated. His face crumpled, his gaze already dead. He looked young like this, unseasoned. Would his family know why he didn't return home?

And suddenly, it wasn't the human looking at me. It was Anten, staring into my soul, waiting for me to take his life.

Bile rose up my throat. I ran backward, only sheer shock keeping me from dropping Soulweaver.

"Do it then," Anten said, his voice angry. "Kill me!"

"No, I—I didn't mean to!" I yelled. "I'm sorry. Please—"

Without warning, blood spilled down Anten's chin, and he coughed, sending red spit all over me. The point of a sword stuck out from his chest, and as it disappeared, the soldier slumped, revealing an elf with a forked tail that slashed behind him. His curved rapier dripped blood and gore.

The elf looked me up and down once. "You're welcome," he said, then pounced back into battle.

Slowly, I looked down at the body that was spilling blood onto my boots. I was able to take a full breath again when I saw that Anten's face had been replaced by the unknown human's. But pain still sat in my chest, causing each pull of my lungs to sting.

I whipped my head around, looking for somewhere, anywhere, to get more cover. I felt exposed, cracked open, out here in the middle of it all. The sun beat down, and I was acutely aware of each bead of sweat that ran down my back.

There—the outskirts of the battle. Bodies were being pulled off the sides from both parties, some groaning, bleeding, and some clearly dead. I could assist the healers. I would be helping the battle and staying out of areas where I was clearly a liability right now.

Getting to my destination was not nearly as clear-cut as I'd hoped. Humans ran at me from all angles, and I reacted, my training taking over when my mind shut down.

Except I couldn't make myself give the killing blow to any of them. Not even the ones who spat obscenities at me and threatened to pull my entrails from my body and feed them to me. I clubbed them on the head or shoved them into the path of another soldier. I didn't look back to see if they had made it. I couldn't stop seeing Anten's face on every single one.

A body rammed into me from behind, and I spun, sword out, ready to clash again.

Alwyn's grin met me. "Watch where you're swinging that thing!" My face must have conveyed my internal struggle because her brow furrowed. "Are you okay?"

Unable to even formulate a fake answer to that, I nodded, feeling like my head was bobbling a little too fast to be believable. Thankfully, Alwyn's attention was grabbed by a soldier running at her from the side, screaming wildly.

She was a viper in battle, quick and lithe. She struck without hesitation and was onto her next mark before her last hit the ground.

As I watched her, I realized the battle was waning. Bodies lined the ground, and most of them were adorned in iron. The humans were losing.

A whistle sounded through the air, calling the human army to retreat. A few of our own soldiers chased them out, but most celebrated or began to search through the fallen.

"Hey." Spense's voice was soft in my ear, his arm comforting as it wrapped around my waist. He pulled down his scarf to touch his lips gently to my temple.

When I looked up at him, I was surprised to find he looked rather clean, his face devoid of the red streaks I'd seen on other soldiers. His armour and Bloodletter told other stories, so I kept my gaze off them.

"Are you all right?" he murmured.

I could only nod as we watched the Ivywall and elven soldiers clean up the battlefield. An elf with a razor-whip tail and gleaming black eyes came up to Spense, and I recognized him with a sharp breath. This was the elf that had saved me earlier.

"Lord Kvistor," Spense acknowledged, nodding at the green-skinned leader.

Spense was the tallest being I'd ever met, but this elf towered above him, skinny and long-limbed. His pointed nose and sharp cheeks did not help the downturned set of his lips, giving him a permanent frown.

"I was not confident that you would come," Kvistor admitted, eyeing me. His accent was lilting, almost singsongy.

Under his scrutiny, I felt oddly jittery. I brushed my hands over my armour, trying in vain to wipe the blood from it.

"You asked for help," Spense replied. "Ivywall protects their own."

Kvistor couldn't help the sneer that crossed his face before he smoothed it away. "Consider Ivywall forgiven for the Night Pixie betrayal. Please stay for the bonfire and take your leave in the morning."

Spense had crossed his arms and was a commanding presence, even without being the tallest in the group. "Always a pleasure, Kvistor." When the elf looked away, he rolled his eyes.

"You just saved his entire race," I whispered as we started toward the middle of the camp, where wood was already being piled high in a pit formation. "Not even a thank-you?"

"That was actually pretty apologetic for an elf," Spense answered. "They hold grudges like you wouldn't believe."

I watched the bodies being dragged from the battlefield, and I had a grotesque image of them being used for kindling in the bonfire.

Ivywall soldiers came up to Spense, one by one, each with various questions about how we were to help or the logistics with feeding the drakes.

"I should be in the middle, dealing with all this," he said apologetically to me. "Will you be okay on your own?"

Alwyn spoke from behind us. "She won't be alone." She slipped her hand into mine.

"Come," she said, pulling me away from the death. "Let's go clean up."

Nineteen
Burn

SPENSE

Blood and gore plastered the sand, the stench of battle strong in the air. The loudness had died away to a solemn quiet, one that I knew well.

The elves kept their heads down as they collected their dead. Their energies were low, and although the battle was won, there was no celebration.

We had lost soldiers too. Not many, but a few that I had known. Trained with.

And yet I found myself without much deep thought about it.

The sadness, the heaviness, the grief of such a waste of life did not weigh on my shoulders as it did the others.

I felt lighter than I had before coming here.

It was as if the thrill of a victory, of a well-fought battle, fuelled me.

I relished in it.

Diana had been shaky and cold when we emerged victorious. I had made up my mind then that she would never have to see another battle when I could fight them for her. She was still good, still light, and I didn't want death to become a mark on her soul. Change her.

Like it had changed me.

It was easy to pick out the humans among the bodies on the ground. They wore their heavy iron armour as if it were a lifeline. I couldn't take credit for the rumour given to them a long time ago about a metal that could burn the fae, but it worked to our advantage just the same.

The elves would bury their dead, as was their tradition. Over the ridge, shovels were hard at work to create shallow graves. It was a way to honour their lost lives by having them stand guard over their loved ones, never far away.

The humans did not deserve such an honour. They were foul, horrid creatures, whose only qualm with us was that we possessed something they did not.

They had hurt us, insulted us, and driven us from Rathe. They had killed fae. *My* fae. And no matter how much I wanted to shove it down, there was a part of me that blanched at running away from this fight even if it were to go home.

I was finding my way back to myself in pieces, some jagged and rough as they chafed against who I'd become in Eira. But some pieces were effortless and smooth, as if they had never left.

Those pieces were loud today. They reminded me not to get soft. That death—*killing*—was only a natural part in winning a war. The gods could not fault me for protecting my own.

"What shall we do with the bodies?" a soldier's voice called from over my shoulder.

I stared down into the lifeless eyes of a human, his mouth caught open in surprise.

There would be a bonfire tonight to send off the fallen elves.

"Burn them."

It was only fitting.

TWENTY
GREATER PLANS

DIANA

Alwyn led me through the sand hills until Elfwood was visible, little houses and buildings positioned in a circular pattern.

The city was sombre, the patrons watching us from windows as we made our way through the streets, but it was not lacking in beauty. Cool white stone adorned every building, desert flowers blooming between the cracks. I was not sure how plant life was possible in the intense heat, but I didn't have the energy to think any harder about that.

When Alwyn stopped me, I realized why Elfwood had been built in its circular fashion. We stood before a lagoon of the bluest water, as big as a lake. All the homes had been built around this pool, all pointed to it.

Alwyn motioned to an elf who waited near the adobe steps leading down into the water.

"Welcome to The Oasis," he greeted, bowing at Alwyn. "Will you be requiring a private section?"

"Please."

The attendant led us to a different set of stairs that had been carved into the side of the lagoon. Trees with massive leaves that I did not recognize leaned over the water, sheltering the area from the sun's rays. More cleverly planted trees provided a screen of leaves around it as well, giving the look of makeshift walls. As I looked over the lagoon, I saw there were a dozen private sections just like this. It was whimsical and lovely, but the part of me that would have enjoyed seeing it was trampled down beneath layers of exhaustion and grief.

"Clothing is not permitted in The Oasis," the attendant said, dropping robes at the steps. "You will find a variety of soaps and scents on the side here. I hope you enjoy the relaxing tranquillity of the water." He paused at the top of the steps and added, "And thank you—for coming to help us. I don't know if Elfwood would have been victorious without you."

Alwyn smiled softly as he left us at the stairs. She unbuckled her breastplate and placed it on the ground, making a haphazard pile of her armour. I followed suit, and soon, we were just left in lightweight shifts. When we got to the bottom of the stairs and disappeared into the coverage of the leaves, we discarded the shifts as well.

I sank into the cool water, slipping all the way under. I stayed there for as long as I could, until my lungs burned. When I emerged, Alwyn was leaning against the wall of leaves, her eyes closed and her head tipped back. Her dusty-blonde hair spread like a halo around her.

"The Oasis is sacred to the elves."

I could understand why.

"The water has healing properties," she continued. "I'd move to Elfwood just for this lagoon if I could stomach their food."

Muscles twitched at the side of my face, and the pull felt weird. *Gaia,* had this day wiped away my ability to smile?

"Have you killed before?" Alwyn's voice was low, soft, but hung in the air. She had lifted her head and was looking at me with those familial brown eyes.

"Yes." My chest caved in. Saying it loud made it so real. As if it hadn't been real before, as if I could pretend that I had dreamed it. "But not today."

Alwyn nodded once. "I understand. Killing is no easy thing. It shouldn't be taken lightly."

"No one on the battlefield seemed to think that." My mind's eye replayed the ease in which Spense, Alwyn, the elves had made their final blows.

The warrior's face hardened. "That's not a fair judgment for you to make. We have lived with this longer than you've even been alive. Yes, the act of killing has become somewhat of a second nature to me. And I believe I speak for most when I say that each life I take leaves a mark on me. I don't want this. But it's the way it is and has been for millennia. There are no current solutions to it either, not with your queen in charge."

I bristled, emotion finally returning. "This is not my mother's fault. Urdan is just as much to blame."

"They both are. The difference is, we have a plan to remove Urdan from the throne and make amends with the Seelie. I doubt such an idea of peace has occurred to those in power in Eira."

This was the first I'd heard about removing the Unseelie king from power. Could such a thing be possible? He was ancient and powerful with an infatuation with his throne.

"It didn't really work so well when your father burst into our land with an army in tow." I couldn't stop the bitter words. I was still stung and confused.

Alwyn shook her head in annoyance. "The plan was blown to shit when Spense ripped into Eira on his own. He was so young and eager. The rest of us siblings, we're old. We've been around for centuries and seen enough fighting and war for countless lifetimes. After all these years of waiting, we knew Spense was the key to bringing peace back. Our father doted on him like he had been gifted from the gods. And for what? Because he had finally sired a child who looked remotely like him?" She scoffed. "After he gained Urdan's unwavering trust— or what trust was possible from him anymore—we planned to make him our spy. Our sheep in the wolf's den. Even if it took a hundred years, we were banking on his conscience and sense of justice to turn him against the father he aimed so hard to please."

I said nothing as Alwyn retrieved a tube of soap from the side and began washing her hair. Fingers methodically ran through her scalp, her braids coming undone.

"Of course, we tried to intervene when Spense figured out the key to getting around the portal seal. He wouldn't listen, but we didn't worry too much when he went straight to Urdan. Even if the king was having a good day, he wouldn't march on Eira until he concocted a plan. And that would require having a rational train of thought for days in a row—impossible for him. It was sooner than we'd planned, but we decided to bring Spense in on everything that night. We never got to, obviously, because he jumped headfirst into that unstable rift like an idiot. We thought he was dead for sure."

Alwyn handed the soap to me and began rinsing her hair, dipping her head back in the water so she looked up at the leaves bent over us.

"So, no. Urdan's march on Eira was a shock and the thing we were trying hardest to avoid. The absurd coincidence of him being lucid at the same time the portal was healed was unfortunate, considering most of us were out of Ivywall as well. Now, we scramble to make a new plan. With Spense back and the addition of you, we might actually stand a chance at making change."

"Spense has no idea about what you're all planning." The words came out flat, an accusation instead of a question.

"I'll admit, we are still not fully sure where his loyalties lie."

"You speak as a group. *We.* Do you all share this thought?"

"I know what you think. That Sorin and I are the good-natured ones and that Badras and Olys are the opposite. Everyone thinks that at first. But we all share the same notion toward Spense, and I can promise you that. We all love him dearly and have no idea what has or has not changed in him since returning home."

My throat felt dry. "I … I think I understand that. I have been finding it hard to relate the Spense here with the one I knew in Eira. He has been through a lot, I know. It's just … confusing."

"It is, and I doubt it will get much clearer before we are forced to take action."

I poured soap into my palm and deposited it into my hair, working it into a lather. The action was comforting, bringing some relief to my tension. Lavender filled the air, and I dragged the smell into my lungs, chasing away the stench of the battlefield.

"Why are you trusting me with this?"

Alwyn was thoughtful for a moment. "Because I believe there's a reason for all this. Spense leaving, you being dragged here. A wrong was done many moons ago, and I'd like to think the gods are finally rectifying it. Soulmates are no small thing; they mean something. There *has* to be a greater plan at work. If I don't believe that after all this time, what do I have to keep me going? Plus"—she smiled—"you seem more levelheaded than my brother."

My tattoo glinted at me from under the water. Below the surface, the lines wiggled and squirmed, making them come alive. Maybe Alwyn was right. Was I part of some retribution plan? My ancestors had told me I had a destiny to fulfil.

I didn't know if that made me feel better or worse.

"It's probably no surprise that I want to return to my home in

Eira. What you might not know is that before everything went down at the portal, my ancestors spoke to me. They told me the only way the realm would survive was if we brought balance back to it." I paused, gauging her reaction, but Alwyn only watched, intent. "I want to help you bring the Unseelie and all the Folk back to Eira. But I can only work with you if you promise not to target my mother."

The warrior tilted her head to the side, reminding me of a hawk as she drank in my words. "I cannot speak for all my siblings, but I'm sure an agreement could be made. But, Diana, if she goes after us, we might have no choice."

"I understand. I'll make sure it doesn't happen."

Alwyn looked at me through narrowed brown eyes, her gaze unflinching. After a moment, she smiled. "Then, welcome to the team."

The cooling water and fresh scents did wonders for my morale. I still felt the ring of death like a dull ache in my chest, but rational thought had at last returned. Wrapped in the soft clothing provided by The Oasis, sitting in front of the biggest fire I had ever seen, I almost felt like myself.

The elves were an intriguing bunch to watch. Most had long, thin tails, like Kvistor, and they used them as a third arm, wrapping it around firewood or passing food back and forth. They spoke in their own language, soft and melodious. The fire danced and cackled, bathing them in swaths of orange light. When it hit their green skin, they looked almost iridescent.

"Here, take this." From beside me, Spense held out a brass cup, stirring me from my observing.

I took it and wrinkled my nose upon inspection. The contents looked murky and brown, and the smell of dirt wafted from it. "What is it?"

He chuckled. "I promise it doesn't taste like it smells."

I stared at him. "Was that your attempt at convincing me to drink this?"

Spense's smile stretched up, up, up until it reached his eyes and made the corners crinkle. I was struck by a sudden pang in my stomach, and I couldn't look away.

He leaned closer, his dark curls spilling over his forehead as he tipped his head toward me. Shamelessly, I waited with bated breath as his lips touched my neck and trailed upward.

"Drink it, please," he whispered, barely audible. His voice tickled my ear, sending shivers crawling down my spine.

Okay, so that was decidedly more convincing.

Feigning flippancy, I stepped back, looked Spense dead in the eye, and drained the entire contents of the cup in one motion. I almost pulled off a smooth finish, but the drink had other plans. My mouth filled with a taste so rancid and sour that I definitely would not have been able to swallow had it not already been halfway down my throat. I coughed violently, the burning in my mouth only intensifying.

When it finally subsided, I threw the cup at Spense's chest, which he deftly caught. "Are you trying to kill me or something? What *was* that?"

Spense laughed, full and deep. "I'm sorry, but if it makes you feel better, everyone has that reaction at first." He gestured to Alwyn across the fire, who sent me a grinning thumbs-up. "It's a tonic the elves have made for centuries. It is their belief that taking it after a battle will heal the soul of the violence. I thought you might want to partake," he added softly.

Warmth bloomed in my chest at his kindness, spreading through my limbs pleasantly. Or maybe the drink was already working. I didn't speak, just enjoyed his presence as we looked into the bonfire's flames.

Spense pressed closer to me, slipping an arm around my waist and pulling me against him. There wasn't anywhere our sides didn't touch, and I savoured the feeling. He pressed a kiss onto the top of my head.

"I'm proud of you," he murmured against my hair.

"Proud of me?" I scoffed. "For what, drinking dirt?"

I felt his chuckle reverberate through my body.

"I'm proud of you for coming to Elfwood, for fighting, even when you were dealing with your own demons. I'm proud of you for navigating your new surroundings so gracefully. I'm proud that you're mine, Diana."

Neither of us had so bravely put those words out there, allowing them to float on the air without truly knowing where they'd land. But I liked how they sounded, how they felt on my skin. Light and airy, almost like I was flying.

Words did not feel like enough, so I took the arm on his other side and brought it to my lips. I pressed a soft kiss to his wrist, to the swirling ink that marked us as each other's.

We sat like that for a while, watching the bonfire slowly shrink. Watching the elves cautiously engage with the Ivywall soldiers. Watching the ease that had drifted over the camp, blanketing the pain and loss.

An ease that was shattered when a drake flying low came into view on the horizon, accompanied by fervent shouting. Immediately, arrows were nocked, and weapons were drawn. My heart raced, only to be flooded with relief at the sight of the Ivywall colours on the rider.

Spense ran to meet him—Alwyn not far behind—as the beast glided to the ground, worry etched on his face. Although relieved it wasn't the humans returning, I couldn't imagine the bad news that might cause a runner to come all the way out to Elfwood in the midst of a battle.

I drew my bottom lip into my mouth, waiting while my stomach coiled around like a snake. When the runner turned and took to the air in the direction they'd come, Spense and Alwyn spoke briefly, their heads bent together.

The elves around me murmured in their quiet language, every pair of eyes peeled.

When the siblings began walking back, Alwyn signalled to the Ivywall soldiers, her hand in the air. Whatever it was, they calmed, sheathing their weapons and retaking their seats.

Spense walked straight to me and grabbed my hand. "Get whatever you need ready to ride. We're heading back to Ivywall with a small party—immediately."

I struggled to keep up with Spense's long strides as he started toward the hill the drakes had chosen to nest under. From the corner of my eye, Alwyn spoke with Lord Kvistor, her tone low.

"Is everything all right?" I asked once we rounded the hill.

"It will be," he replied, sending a high-pitched whistle into the air. The drakes were alert at once, standing up and shaking the sand from their leathery hides. "We just need to get back to Ivywall."

Spense wasted no time getting Keely saddled and moving to Sensara right away, who leaned down on two legs so he could reach her better. Around us, half a dozen soldiers were saddling their own mounts, Alwyn included.

"Up you go." Spense motioned for me to mount, and he climbed up onto Sensara's back.

I got myself situated, then looked over to the camp, where the elves were all still sitting easily around the fire. None even spared us a glance.

"You're scaring me. What's going on?"

Spense motioned for the party to take to the air, then turned to me as Sensara's wings snapped open. "My father is lucid."

TWENTY-ONE
IRREPARABLE DAMAGE

DIANA

'm about to meet the real Urdan.

My stomach was in knots, the ease The Oasis had coaxed into my muscles completely erased. The ride back felt significantly shorter than the way there, made worse by not being able to ask Spense all the questions that had built up inside me.

What's going to happen when we get there?

What will Urdan say to me? What if he wants me gone?

How long do they expect him to be lucid for?

If the king I'd met in Eira was the real version, I could expect him to be cold and cynical. He wanted the Seelie to pay for their exile. I worried what reaction he would have toward me, toward Spense, the battle at Elfwood.

No one said much when we arrived on The Cliff or as we made our way up into Ivywall. Spense felt tense, and Alwyn's mouth was hard, the lines on her face set deep.

Their brothers met us in the council room.

Badras strode forward, clapping Spense on the back. "One way to ruin the high of a battle win, huh?"

I was instantly filled with distaste for him.

Sorin was his usual composed self. "The report on Elfwood can wait. Come. Father is asking for us." He set his gaze on me. "All of us."

Fear was a jolt in my stomach, but I straightened my back, nodding.

The six of us made our way to a part of Ivywall I had never been through. It was quiet and dark with a surplus of guards lining the hall. They all nodded to us as we passed, although I felt lingering gazes on me as I gripped Spense's arm.

When we arrived at a set of double doors, the party halted. At the front, Sorin appeared to take a deep breath before knocking. Spense threaded his fingers through mine. I leaned in toward him.

"My share of chores for the week says Father doesn't even notice me," Olys muttered drily, earning a snicker from Badras.

The doors opened, and we were ushered in. Urdan sat on a giant black throne, his wings impressively splayed out behind him. He stared at us from dark eyes, sunken and heavily bagged. Even with the air of power around him and his commanding sneer, there was something off. His skin was pale and sickly.

We approached the throne, which, up close, I realized was made from solid, glittering obsidian. I wanted to pull back, stand farther away in the safety of the doorway, but we walked right up to the base of the throne and fanned out in a line so he could lay his menacing gaze on all of us.

And he did.

"Sorin." His voice was calm and collected.

"Badras." Cool and light.

"Alwyn." Thin and bored.

"Olys." Short and tight.

"Spense." Urdan drew the *S* out, pausing his assessment on his youngest son. "You have returned. And, I take it, you were unsuccessful?"

Spense didn't say anything, keeping his gaze trained on the wall behind his father. I remembered Alwyn's words about his desire for Urdan's approval.

"Then again, here you stand, with the Seelie princess on your arm. Some might call that a success." Urdan stood from the obsidian and walked closer to Spense, stopping when their noses were inches apart. They stood at almost the same height, impossibly tall and alike in shape.

"You know what I think?" the Unseelie king hissed. "I think you were too *weak* to do what needed to be done, and that's why we aren't already in Eira."

"I don't care what you think," Spense replied, his voice harsh.

Urdan chuckled, deep and gravelly. The rest of the siblings watched from their places.

"Look at you, finally gaining a backbone. Fall in love and think yourself grown, hmm? You still have so much to learn," he sneered. Casting another look down the line of his children, he added, "Still, you might prove useful yet." A clear snub toward the others.

Then, Urdan's gaze landed on me. It felt heavy, like my shoulders were already bearing its weight. "And you. Whatever will we do about *you?*"

I kept my chin up, even as my hands shook at my sides. I didn't trust myself to speak, fearing anything would come out meek and shaky.

After staring at me for what felt like hours, Urdan took his spot back on the throne. He rubbed his temples. Snapping his fingers, he called for a servant. "I need my tincture—now. My head cannot take much more of this."

"Father," Sorin began, clearing his throat, "it's been some time since you were last … awake. We would like to discuss some things with you."

Urdan waved his hand impatiently. "Once I have my tincture, I will be able to concentrate."

"Right, of course. It's just, sometimes, the tincture makes you drowsy. I worry about how much time we'll have with you."

"Sorin, you are wearing my patience thin. Are you suggesting your king cannot handle a few herbs for an old ache?" Dangerous. His tone had changed, the air growing electric.

I looked to Spense, who was working his jaw. Faintly, I could feel magic seeping from him, crawling toward his father. With both of theirs in the air, it was hard to differentiate the two. They were more eerily similar than I'd realized.

"Of course not, Father."

"You've been alive long enough to know I can handle myself, boy. Besides, we both know there is no lack of days in our futures. Not with the bitch still out there, creating evil with every breath."

That sparked my interest. "Your life is tied to someone?"

All eyes swivelled to me, and I realized how bold I had just been. Wanting to shrink inside myself, I bit down on my lip.

Finally, Urdan let out a snuff of laughter. "I will forgive your rudeness because I want to rectify what you have been told about the truth. Long ago, when the Seelie queen waged war on me and the Unseelie race, she knew she was losing. The Folk had sided with me, and she was no match to our joined forces. To even the playing field, she took my daughter. My pride and joy. She used insidious, *dark* magic to bind Jweira's powers to hers. She was quite extraordinary, my girl. More power than this bunch combined. I suppose that is what comes from a child born of a true soulmate." Suddenly, his mouth turned up into a sneer. "I seem to recall you had her last."

I swallowed the urge to touch my pant pocket, where the emerald was warm and heavy against my leg.

"Talk or don't," he continued. "No matter. She *will* be returned to me."

I could feel Spense's eyes on me, all the siblings—who had probably not known that Jweira was in my possession. But I couldn't look at any of them. Roaring had started in my ears.

"But where was I?" Urdan was a terrifyingly compelling storyteller. He stroked the stubble at his chin in thought before speaking again. "After the Seelie queen took my army general, the Folk ran. Jweira had been the one to rally them to our cause, and without her, they scattered. We fought, but we were not fighting a fair fight. Our enemy was—*is*—a cheat, and a liar, and of the vilest kind.

"We were shoved into this wretched land and forced to watch as the portal to our home was closed in our faces. But in doing such an unspeakable act, causing such unbalance to nature, the queen did irreparable damage to her soul. The only way to keep herself from shattering into fractured pieces was to bind herself to a soul of equal power. Mine." Urdan's disgust was clear as he spat the last word. "I cannot die until she does, and she cannot die until I do. It is a completely unbreakable loop. There is no way out. I can only pray that the gods will take pity on my soul and release me from her toxic grasp."

My chest felt impossibly tight. This story matched what Jweira had told me. All this time, I had been on the wrong side of history.

"You're saying the Seelie queen still lives?"

"Have you not been listening? The bitch lives, right under your nose."

A servant broke into the room, hurrying toward the king with a small vial of red liquid on a tray. Bowing, he extended it toward

Urdan, who swallowed it down in one gulp. He licked his lips, which had turned blood red, and tossed the vial at the servant, who only just managed to grab it before it shattered on the floor. From the feel in the air, someone's magic had had something to do with that.

If I hadn't been scanning the siblings already when Urdan took the tincture, I would have missed Sorin's shoulders drop, followed by Alwyn's almost-inaudible sigh.

"But who … who is she?" I pressed.

If their reactions were to be believed, the tincture messed with Urdan's lucidity.

The Unseelie king laughed, a glossy look coming over his face. "Ilysia. That is her name. The Seelie queen who condemned us all."

He sat back in his throne, the rigidity gone from his posture. His eyes had glazed over, and he stared unseeingly at the wall behind us.

"Come." Sorin motioned for us to follow him. "Our time is up."

PART II

TWENTY-TWO
LOOPHOLE

DIANA

Out in the hall, the siblings dropped their rigid postures immediately. Alwyn even shook her shoulders out.

"Guess you'll be doing your own chores after all." Badras pushed Olys teasingly, who pushed him back, until they were roughhousing right in the middle of the hallway.

"Are you kidding with this? Now?" Spense hissed.

Badras looked up from where he had his brother in a choke hold, rubbing his knuckles into Olys's hair. "I can't believe you still take him seriously. He's just a senile old male who lives for telling us how disappointing we all are."

"He is still our king." Sorin's voice was laced with warning.

"And the sky is still blue, and the sand is still white," Badras retorted. "It hasn't changed, and it probably never will. We'll all be living in an endless repetition of blue skies, white sands, and a senile king until we turn to ash."

"Then, why don't you *do something* about it?" Spense had not taken his brother's lax tone of resignation. If he were an animal, his hackles would be raised, a snarl not far away.

Alwyn and I caught eyes for a moment, and she gave the slightest of nods.

Sorin was eyeing the king's guards in the hall, who had all tactfully turned away from the quarrelling siblings and were pretending to focus on cracks and fissures in the adobe walls. "We need to talk, but not here."

The eldest brother led us back into Ivywall, to the marble council room sitting atop The Cliff.

When we were all seated around the table, Meske joined us, her brow furrowed. "Should I summon Pik?"

"No. This is family business." Sorin pulled out the chair beside him, and his wife sat.

Spense leaned forward over the table. "What's going on?"

"Please tell me you're not doing what I think you're doing." Olys shot an incredulous look around the table at his siblings, landing on his sister.

"He should know," Alwyn urged.

Olys shook his head, running fingers through the sandy locks. "What happened to waiting for the perfect timing?"

"Now's as good as we're going to get."

Bewilderment clouded Spense's tense face, and I took his hand under the table, squeezing lightly.

"*Someone* just start talking," Badras cut in, his tone dry.

Sorin shot an ungrateful look his way and cleared his throat. "Spense, this might come as a shock to you, but the rest of us have been … planning. For centuries, even before you came along, we knew something had to be done about Urdan. It would be no problem for us to remove him—the guards are loyal to us, and his magic would be no match against all of us together. Even our Unseelie would follow. But our father alone possesses the memories of true portals and how to create them. He also holds the knowledge of the Seelie forces and how to aim the best attack."

Spense sat upright in his chair, to which Sorin waved a hand calmingly.

"I know what you're going to say—we cannot march on Eira." And maybe I was mistaken, but his eyes wavered to me for a half second. "Let me continue to explain.

"It left us with a bit of a predicament. Even on his best days, Urdan would never share that information with us. We were at a loss—that is, until you were born. He brought you up as his prodigal son, the one that would inherit everything because of your likeness."

I spared a glance around the room, but none of the siblings held any contempt in their gaze. They had all moved on from the hurt of their father.

"Our plan was simple—wait until you gained Urdan's full and complete trust and use you as the turning piece in our revolution. With your inside knowledge, we would be able to return to the realm we had come from. We would do whatever necessary to ensure the Unseelie were never uprooted again. Perhaps nature would be righted as well, and Urdan would finally know peace." There was sadness there, as though Sorin sympathized with the king's too-long life.

Spense ran his fingers through his messy curls, the black colour so unlike his siblings. "Well, damn." He blew out a sigh. "Why didn't you bring me in on your plan from the beginning?"

"It's not that we didn't trust you," Alwyn said, her eyes soft. "We thought that given your desire to please him … you might accidentally let something slip. We just didn't want to take any chances with something that was so long in the making."

"I guess that plan's out the window now anyway," Badras grunted. "Whatever you did that night you left for Eira, Urdan's not happy with you. How's it feel, being one of us?" He grinned.

Alwyn sent a small but mighty elbow into his ribs.

"So, we come up with a new plan." Sorin folded his hands together on the table. "Adapt. It's what we do."

Spense took a shuddering breath, looking at me once before facing the others. There was pain in his gaze, as though he knew that with his next admission, he was leaving his father's devotion behind. I gave him a small smile.

I'll be here with you, every step.

"The night I went to Eira might have thrown me from Urdan's good graces, but it was not in vain."

The siblings looked at each other.

"Not only do I know how to get around the sealing of the realm, but I know how to make a fully functioning portal as well."

Alwyn gasped delightedly. "Oh, Spensey!"

"Do tell, brother," Olys drawled from his spot across the table. "I find it troubling that you were able to do something in one night that all of us could not do in the better part of a thousand years."

Spense bristled. "It wasn't one night, Olys. I put a lot of energy and research into finding the information that I did. And I'm happy to explain it all once you've agreed to my conditions."

Badras chuckled darkly under his breath. Olys sneered, opening his mouth to hurl what I was sure would be an insulting string of words, when Sorin spoke first.

"I promise you, brother, we all want the same things. But if agreeing to terms makes you feel as though you can trust us, then let's hear them."

Olys threw his hands in the air.

"One, I want to be involved with planning from here on out—and Diana as well. No more leaving me in the dark. Two, I want to avoid a war with the Seelie."

The words hit the air and immediately soured. Alwyn looked

down at her lap, shaking her head gently. The brothers were more outspoken, Badras in particular.

"We are already in the middle of a war, brother. You expect us to return to that abuse with our tails tucked? We need to show up and make it known that we are not to be messed with ever again. I'd like to see the Seelie sent here, see what they make of this scorched earth!"

A fire ignited in my core, and I fought the urge to leap to my feet.

"The Seelie don't want a war. Diana can attest to that. We would be able to find our place there again with her help as high princess."

Heads swivelled to me.

"I was visited by my ancestors, who told me the realm was out of balance. In order to bring nature back to how it was supposed to be, we have to unite both races. And the Folk must return as well. I was not able to explain this exceedingly well before I was brought here, but I know my mother will see sense. Our ancestors' word is law."

It was easy to see that Badras was not on board. But he wisely kept his mouth shut and allowed Sorin to speak.

"We will agree to go there peacefully," he said, his words carefully plucked. "But if there is war against us, we will not back down."

Sorin and Spense locked eyes across the table for an electric minute until Spense relaxed his shoulders and nodded.

"Fine."

I wasn't sold on the peaceful interaction between the Seelie and Unseelie, but it would have to do. I could de-escalate when the time came.

"Any more terms?" sneered Badras.

"Yes, actually." Spense glared. "I don't want to go back until Diana's magic has returned."

Shock rippled through the room, including my own. I ground my teeth as I shot him an incredulous look. Spense placed a hand on my arm, unbothered by my annoyance.

Alwyn leaned over the table to look me in the eyes, her brows knitted together. "What happened to your magic?"

I swallowed. I already wasn't sure where I stood with Spense's siblings. Their eyes on me made me nervous, especially now that they knew I was weak.

"Since I arrived here, it's been gone. Well … not gone, I suppose. I can still feel it, way deep down. But it's like it's stuck. Every time I try to reach even a little bit, it weakens me to the point that I nearly pass out."

Badras grunted. "Makes sense now. I wondered why your magic hadn't intertwined with his." He looked between Spense and me. "I thought you were both just prudes—"

Alwyn's eye roll and elbow in the side, earning a low growl from her brother, stopped him from continuing to embarrass me, even as I felt a flush creep up my neck. I wasn't sure if our magic would be intertwined with the soulmate tattoo alone. Usually, it was only after a pairing's first coupling that their magic became inseparable from the other's, twisted in, creating an entirely unique new one.

In some cases, a traumatic event or act of love was enough to kick-start the merging process. Considering we hadn't exactly had a second to adjust after the tattoos appeared, I wasn't sure what our magic would look like once mine returned. Considering Spense and I had never—

Discreetly, I pulled my hair away from my neck to try and cool the warmth spreading there.

As usual, Spense was unflappable. "It's important we get it back before we go to Eira."

Olys's eyes narrowed. "How do we know she'll even get it back at all? Maybe she's not compatible with this land, and it will return once we're back in Eira."

"I agree, Spense." Sorin rubbed at his face. "There are a lot of ifs in that term. We don't know what's blocking her magic, and it could very well be the distance from her realm, as Olys said. Perhaps as high princess, her magic has become tied to Eira."

That had never crossed my mind before, and I begrudgingly had to admit that it made sense. Hope was a small flutter in my chest.

"Maybe so." Spense pursed his lips. "But if that's the case, it doesn't bode well for our situation."

"What do you mean?" Sorin asked.

"The loophole of the seal is that it was created on a lunar eclipse. So, in order to negate the seal, the portal has to be made on the same naturally occurring moon," Spense began.

"Surely, over eight thousand years, *someone* must have attempted a portal on a lunar eclipse, whether they meant to or not. They're not that rare." Olys crossed his arms, leaning back in his chair to stare down his brother.

Spense nodded. "I had that thought as well. It wasn't until recently that I realized what finally made the difference. It has to be another part of the loophole. Just using the eclipse would be too easy. There had to be blood involved too."

At his siblings' lack of expression, he waved his hands emphatically. "Think about it—the portal takes enough magic that two are needed. Even with powerful fae trying, nothing worked. And then, when I try with Urdan, suddenly, it works? It has to be connected to the seal. If the Seelie queen offered a blood sacrifice, then only her blood would be able to undo it."

Alwyn frowned. "But neither of you is of her blood."

"Correct. However, she tied her life to our father's. I think that caused the seal to see his magic as hers. And since I am of his blood, mine was also accepted. So, now that we don't have Urdan, we'll need Diana. She's a direct descendant of the Seelie queen."

Who's still alive, apparently. That still blew my mind. Had I met her? Was she masquerading as one of us or off hiding and biding her time? My gut leaned toward the latter. Surely, someone would have noticed that kind of power, let alone a fae who never aged.

"Wouldn't any of you working together be able to get past the seal, considering you are all of Urdan's blood?" Meske asked. Her hands were in her lap, where she toyed with the seam of her sleeve.

Spense dipped his head in acknowledgment. "It's possible. Unfortunately, I think magic plays a big part in it, and none of you share the soul designation."

"So, you're saying that it *has* to be you and Diana," Sorin confirmed.

"Yes."

My heart kicked up a notch. Silence fell while everyone stewed on the words. Spense's thumb rubbed soothing circles over my hand—a silent comfort. Eventually, all gazes landed on Sorin. Whether or not he was officially the leader of the bunch, he was who they all looked to.

"I have a plan," Sorin said finally. "I need to know now, are we all still in? Once we start, there's no turning back."

Each sibling enthusiastically shared their agreement.

"It's time we go home for good," Alwyn chimed.

Sorin smiled. "Just what I wanted to hear. Olys, when is the next lunar eclipse?"

The head of agriculture thought for a moment. "I can get you an exact date later, but I expect the next one is about two weeks away."

Spense blew out a breath. "Can we be ready in two weeks?"

Olys nodded. "Of course we can. The longer we wait, the more chance Urdan will get word of it. And we can't let him interfere, memory or not."

Sorin nodded. "It's decided then." A wicked grin crossed his face, one so uncharacteristic for the calm, measured male. "Take half an hour to gather supplies for notes and food. We're going to be in here awhile."

TWENTY-THREE
A THREAT

ÆDAN

The birds did not seem to understand the sudden weather change. They still sang every morning, calling when dawn broke. The sun came up as usual, but the warmth from its rays felt impossibly far away. I woke to the sharp call of the morning lark and felt any hope in my chest putter out at the sight of the white flakes still falling outside my window.

Prying myself ever so gently from Jamey's grasp, I crept from bed and dressed for the day. Princess Hollaina was expected today, and I was to meet with Embris and Vera before she arrived.

It did not take long for me to get ready, and I contemplated if I had enough time to squeeze in a jog before the meeting. But the paths had likely not been shovelled this early in the morning, and I had no desire to use the hallways of the palace as my track.

I stole a glance at Jamey as I opened my wardrobe. She slept like the dead every night, which was advantageous for me to avoid the awkward morning shuffle. It wasn't that I didn't enjoy spending time with her. I just found that after large amounts of her, I needed space.

So, I tried to keep quiet as I rummaged among my jackets. *Where is my deputy coat?*

Ah. I had given it to Maisie last night.

I wrestled with the thought of taking a trip to the servants' quarters to retrieve it from her. She would likely be awake, helping the palace get ready for the day.

But was it a slight, asking for it back? Females confused me in the weight they put into certain actions and not others.

I was probably overthinking this.

Giving my head a shake, I grabbed the overcoat I only wore for tradition's sake in special ceremonies. It was a bit flashy, but it would have to do. At least no one could fault me for being underdressed.

When I knocked on the door to the queen's council room, my father opened it and ushered me inside. "Ah, Aedan, good. We have important matters to discuss. The scouts tell me the Eastern party will arrive within the hour."

They were making good pace then. Or attempting to catch us unawares.

Queen Vera stood behind her mahogany desk, a hand absentmindedly stroking her chin as she stared at the obscenely large portrait of Queen Diana over the fireplace. She looked guarded, her brow furrowed, as she ran her other hand through her wolf's scruff.

Embris cleared his throat once. "Shall we get started, My Queen?"

Vera snapped from her trance immediately. Her usual queenly demeanour radiated from her as she gave me a quick smile. "Yes. Please, sit."

My father and I took up the armchairs across from the queen's perch. Without a formal setting, we could enjoy the extravagant upholstery that rarely got used.

"I hope you both ate because I've instructed that we are not to be disturbed for refreshments."

My stomach panged hungrily in response.

I took a cursory glance around the room inconspicuously,

wondering if I could spot the other half of Maisie's red stone. I still couldn't believe she'd had the bravery to plant a listening device in here. But then again, the more I learned about her, the more I realized everything I'd thought was wrong.

"We have not seen the East visit since Hollaina became the ruling princess. She is reclusive, erratic, and introverted. I have met her on many occasions during my visits to her court, and I can say with full certainty that she suffers from a traumatic past."

Embris grunted. "So, the rumours are true then."

Vera crossed her legs delicately. "Not necessarily. Since no one alive, save her, was witness to the event that killed her parents—Prince Helvig and his wife, Lidya—we cannot know for sure. The only thing we know to be truth is that she was present at the murder of her parents when she was only fourteen. From the reports that I have read, the official stance is that they were assassinated by mercenaries from the Unclaimed Land. Hollaina was also attacked, but survived by starting a fire that ended up consuming half the palace. You will see the remnants of that night by the scars on her face, but it is important you do not react. She is sensitive toward them."

We both nodded.

"She seems harmless enough," Embris commented. "The East has never been much of a problem, except for that pest Nimshar." He scowled.

Vera nodded absently. "That is where we must be careful. For all intents and purposes, Hollaina has been nothing but amiable toward us. But when I was at the Eastern court, I heard whispers of a much darker tale. One where she killed her parents herself and set the fire to hide her tracks. I am not one for idle gossip, but there were many accounts of her dallying with Dark supporters while growing up."

"That's enough grounds for treason," my father growled. "Is it not possible for you to dethrone her if you don't trust her?"

Vera's face soured. "Even if my findings were enough to make a case against her—which they are not—I cannot go against the word of the ancestors. She was chosen to lead, and so she shall until they appoint someone else."

I almost laughed. What was the point of the title of queen, leader of all the regions, if there was no real power attached to it?

Embris nodded. "We will be vigilant, as usual. I can assign extra guards around the palace if you wish."

I bristled. As deputy captain, shift assignments were my domain. If he had given me a moment to speak, I would have suggested it myself.

"These are unprecedented times," Vera said. "Having more guards would be good, so long as we do not start to feel cramped. There are a great number of officials staying here right now. At this rate, we might have to delegate some of the assistants to the Nevelyn Inn."

The absurd amount of fae in the palace was starting to get to me. Between the snow keeping everyone cooped inside and the constant small talk around every corner, it was getting hard to find a peaceful, quiet spot.

"It is pertinent that this information stays in this room." Vera's icy-blue gaze bored into mine.

I expected to feel a shiver of guilt, knowing what was planted somewhere between these four walls, but I felt steady, calm.

"Nevelyn is honoured to have these guests from the East, understood?"

Again, we both nodded. Her captain and deputy captain dutifully taking orders.

"Good." Satisfied, Vera stood and went to the door. "Bring in Maisie, please."

This time, my heart leaped. Had she been found out? How could I save her from this?

Maisie entered, wearing her usual servant attire. She always looked well kept with tidy clothes that fit her well. What she couldn't keep tidy, however, was her head of unruly yellow curls, which always managed to break free of their ties. Even now, she tucked a piece, which had come loose around her face, behind her ear.

"I am appointing Maisie to be Hollaina's personal maidservant while she is visiting," Vera announced, earning a shocked look from us all. It almost upstaged the relief that flooded through me.

Turning directly to Maisie, she continued, "Considering you do not have as many duties right now, this is the perfect opportunity for you. Not only do you know this job well, but it will also give you a chance to spend time with the servants that she brings. In fact, I encourage it." She smiled at Maisie, who managed to school the surprise from her face and nodded.

Vera returned to her seat, heals clacking on the marble. "Thank you, Maisie. I know you will do us proud. That will be all."

With the briefest look toward me, Maisie murmured her goodbye and left. I watched the door close behind her, leaving us in silence.

"Aedan."

My attention snapped to the queen.

"You and Maisie … you are close, are you not?"

My brow furrowed. Where was this going? "We have spent many hours together as a result of her serving Diana. I would not say we are all that close, however." Even as I said the words, I realized how untrue they had become in a few short weeks.

Vera chuckled quietly, making my heartbeat rise to a staccato. "It is nothing to be ashamed of. I am aware of the girl's reputation. Not much goes on in this place that I'm not aware of." She aimed a knowing look at me, and I suddenly understood.

My father turned to me, surprised. "The maidservant? What happened to Lady Pinois?"

I cleared my throat, which turned into a cough. I could feel the red heat blooming up my neck, behind my ears. It had surely settled into my cheeks by now.

I felt warm enough to take my coat off, but considering its collar was keeping the atrocity on my neck hidden, I opted to sweat instead.

"I, uh, I think you are mistaken, My Queen." I was able to get the words out without spluttering even if I had to stare at a point behind her on the wall. "I see Maisie as a professional—that is all."

"Mmm." Vera pursed her lips together. "It is none of my business, I admit. I only ask because there is something I'm hoping you'll do for me. You see, I have been waiting for an opportunity to strike, where you would have the chance to prove yourself as someone I can trust. Someone in my inner circle." She looked to Embris, who nodded, puffing out his chest in a proud manner.

I swallowed. It was news to me that the queen did not see me as someone she could trust. In fact, it was quite a sting to hear, considering how I spent my life serving her to the best of my abilities.

"Aedan," my father said, "don't you want to make your queen proud?"

I looked between them, their watchful faces. All of this pageantry and politics, it took up so much time and effort. Time and effort that could be used to get Diana back. A sudden distaste rose in my throat, sour as bile. The more I learned about royalty, the less I wanted to be involved with it.

But I could bide my time. I already had the support of the Nordians, and Embris could not lead forever. When he was gone, when Diana was queen, we could make things better. We could change Eira together.

"Of course. What do you need from me?"

Despite the roaring fire and the ample amount of bodies in this room, I felt cold. Chilled right down to my bones.

I sat beside Amatha, the wife of Prince Kashdan of the West. Also known as Jamey's grandparents. Thank Gaia she was not in attendance. If my father knew of the time I had been spending with Jamey, then it was likely no secret to them either, and I could not handle talk of an official courtship right now.

If ever.

On my other side was Prince Leo, whom I had a strong distaste for despite his always being civil toward me. He was incredibly observant and smart, which made him dangerous when he had opposing views.

Plus, he was a real snake.

Only the princes and a select few officials had been invited to Hollaina's arrival. Before today, I would have said that this was the queen's inner circle, her most trusted. But now, I wasn't so sure.

It had taken a surprisingly short amount of time for the large table and chairs from the queen's office to be set up in the throne room. I didn't see the need for such grandeur, but as we had not received the Eastern princess in her entire reign, Vera's advisors wanted the impressive throne room to be the first impression.

It was infinitely odd to be seated around the table while the queen sat upon her throne. But if anyone else thought the same, they hid it well. The table was filled with hushed whispers and rumours. No one in this room, save for Vera, had met the princess personally.

A guard ducked into the room to announce the arrival of the Eastern party. From the opened doors, footsteps could now be heard ringing in the halls. Everyone sat up straighter, adjusting themselves as they craned their necks toward the door.

Eastern officials I recognized entered the room first, spreading out along the wall. They wore the usual blue attire with the eagle emblazoned across their breast pockets, which made it easy to spot Hollaina instantly.

She wore a dress of deep blue with long sleeves and a high neck that touched her chin. Her white-blonde hair was pulled away from her face but trailed down her back loosely. Magic swirled around her, so light that it was almost invisible. I did my best not to stare at the scars on her face, which were deeply grooved and ran from temple to chin on the left side. But even more shocking than that were her eyes. Light blue, pale and resembling the snow-filled sky. At first glance, she appeared to have no irises at all, giving a terrifyingly haunted look.

No doubt about it, Hollaina was eerie.

She stood with her hands clasped in front of her as she took in the room. Her eyes landed on each of us before finally resting on the queen.

"Princess Hollaina, we are so honoured to have you join us here in the North." Vera rose from her throne and descended the dais to greet her. "I trust you had a good trip."

"I would have preferred not to leave the safety of my court." Hollaina's voice was soft and airy, like it was carried on the wind. "Believe me when I say, this situation was in dire need of redirection."

Vera's face twisted into something much less welcoming. Through pursed lips, she gestured to the table, where we all sat, staring. "Why don't you have a seat, and we can walk you through our decision?"

The two stared at each other for a moment before Hollaina nodded, accepting a chair pulled out for her by one of the Eastern officials. She sat gracefully, hands folded in her lap, and looked down the table toward Vera.

Up close, she was even more striking. She was young and beautiful, but there was something in her eyes that looked ancient and haunted.

She's been through an atrocity, I reminded myself.

Prince Kashdan leaned across his wife to give the newcomer a welcome, his smile as warm as ever. "It is good to finally meet you, Princess." He looked like he might try to offer his hand across the table but thought better of it. "The Western Shores are honoured to have the opportunity to work with the true head of the East."

Hollaina cocked her head to one side, taking in the older prince. "Has Lord Nimshar not been satisfactory?"

Kashdan cleared his throat. "Ah, no, that's not what I was implying. He has been perfectly fine, although I do believe, sometimes, his opinions don't reflect—"

"He speaks for me, and I trust him wholeheartedly to represent the opinions of my court. From what he's told *me*, he is rarely taken seriously. And I must say, that is disappointing to hear indeed."

Wisely, the Western prince did not reply, only swinging his head to look at Vera. If I could see his face, I was sure it would have been pleading.

Coward. So much for the grizzly bear on his chest.

"Nimshar can come across brash and outspoken, as I'm sure you are aware." The queen caught Hollaina's attention. "I have spoken with him many times about it. If he feels we are not taking him seriously, then he should consider his lack of tact."

"Your words are so pretty, Queen. But I am only reminded of the fact that no matter how pretty the buttercup might be, it is still a weed."

Everyone in the room suddenly found the table extremely interesting and kept their eyes averted.

"We can certainly discuss Lord Nimshar, but now is not the time," Vera cut in, her queenly voice icy.

Hollaina did not say anything, just kept staring with that unflinching gaze.

"I suppose you have questions about the snow." Vera folded her hands together on the table.

"No. I know why the snow is here, and so do you. What I'm confused about is why several weeks have gone by since your daughter's disappearance, and here you sit, playing politics and hosting parties, as if you do not care. Why have you made no move to retrieve her?" Hollaina gestured to the empty throne beside Vera's, where Diana had taken up her spot since her ascension.

The queen visibly bristled. "How *dare* you say that I do not care about Diana's disappearance! We are doing everything we can to learn about portals so that we might retrieve her as soon as possible. As well as battle the insidious shadows that plague our lands more and more with every passing minute. We have been called to rescue and evacuate many small towns—including ones in the East."

Hollaina delicately leaned back, seemingly content to have hit her mark. "The shadows are indeed troubling. But that does not change the fact that the heir to this realm is missing. It should be the top priority. One might think there are ulterior motives at play."

Instinctively, I looked to Kashdan, whose constant need to protect the queen would normally have him sputtering in contempt right about now. But he was silent, not daring to even look at the Eastern princess. His wife clutched his arm, as if to question his silence.

Vera's face was venomous. "It is clear you do not wish to converse, only to accuse. I believe you should retire for the night and think on your words before you say something you will regret."

A threat, clear as anything. It hung in the air like fog. No one seemed to breathe.

Hollaina only smiled, such a strange look on her pale, haunted face. It made her scars stretch and shift. A shiver worked its way down my spine as she laughed softly. "Are you so fearful of your lies coming to light that you would banish me? You've gone soft." She stood abruptly, her Eastern subjects following. "You've also forgotten that isolation is the furthest thing from punishment to me."

Practically gliding on air—which, now that I thought about it, was definitely part of the Eastern air magic—she stopped to whisper something into Vera's ear.

Considering all the fae in the room were naturally gifted with heightened ears, she must have used her air magic to funnel the sound because I couldn't hear a word. And based on the looks of everyone else, they didn't either.

The queen, however, soured at whatever was spoken to her. She stared straight ahead, her eyes glaring daggers, as Hollaina left the room, her officials in tow. It was only when the princess disappeared through the doors that I felt air returning to my lungs, the room lighter.

No one spoke for a moment that felt like an eternity. Vera unclenched her jaw, took a deep drink from the glass of water in front of her, and straightened herself.

"Princess Hollaina and I have a lot to discuss in private. If you'll excuse me."

With the grace and calm of a regular day, Vera stood and left.

Embris was the first to speak. "We will reconvene at a later time, likely over dinner. You're excused."

Chairs scraped as everyone stood, talking quietly to each other about what they had just witnessed. Unwittingly, I locked eyes with the only one left sitting—Leo.

He grinned savagely. "Unprecedented times, aren't they, Deputy?"

I held his gaze, unflinching. The prince of the South rose slowly, his lips still stretched in that awful smile, and left the room at a leisurely pace, hands in his pockets.

Leo's unspoken words were clear to me. Vera had met her match. What would happen if the East refused to bow to her? Would the ancestors step in, or would we be forced to make them submit?

The more I stewed on it, sitting alone in the silent throne room, the more I felt like we were barrelling toward something that was too late to stop. A chain of events had been set into motion when Hollaina left her region, and change was coming, swift and unapologetic.

It was clear the Eastern princess wanted Diana back even if her strange words and accusations made her untrustworthy. She was not in the queen's graces right now, but I couldn't help but feel delighted that the words in my heart were being voiced. Maybe they would help spur the group into motion.

Or maybe they would doom us all.

TWENTY-FOUR
Dilemma In Etiquette

MAISIE

The quiet, familiar motions of getting a room ready was soothing to me. With the palace filled almost to the brim, it was a relief to be on my own. I spent a little longer than necessary getting Princess Hollaina's room ready, taking care to straighten the bedcovers and wipe the mirror. There were no flowers to be found that weren't under giant snowbanks, so I swapped the empty vases in the room for dishes of various fruits and rosewater potpourris.

Pleased with my work, I grabbed the pile of sheets that I'd changed and stuffed them into a basket so I could bring them down to be washed. This room hadn't been used since Spense had been in it, and I wanted to make sure his rich, overwhelming scent was long gone. It had seared my nostrils when I first walked in, fresh tears stinging my eyes as everything I'd pushed down came roaring back.

Usually, I would ask someone else to make up the room. But this time, there was no way out since I had been assigned by the queen herself as Hollaina's personal maidservant. So, I'd put my head down and gotten to work, breathing through my mouth until the smell of roses began to cleanse the space.

The shock of being picked for this role was still settling even if

I understood that it was mostly out of convenience. My mother had been so proud when I told her, and a couple of the girls had hugged me and wished me luck, but I did not feel pride for the role. Not like I had when I served Diana.

Basket perched against my hip, I made it halfway to the door when I realized I'd dallied too long. Footsteps sounded right outside, and soon, the handle turned.

Crap. This was not how I'd wanted to introduce myself to Hollaina. It was entirely embarrassing to be caught in the middle of making up a room. We were supposed to be stealthy and quick so the guests never knew how much cleaning up after them we really did.

As the door opened, I set the basket down and tried to wrangle the pieces of my hair that had come loose.

The most ethereal being I'd ever seen floated through the threshold and paused when she saw me. I was so entranced in her light pallor, her airy essence, her unapologetically displayed scars that I almost forgot to bow my head.

"My apologies," I mumbled, trying to grab the basket and move toward the door with my neck craned down.

A cool hand cupped my chin and lifted it gently. I found myself looking right into Princess Hollaina's pale eyes. They almost swirled as they took me in. They looked bottomless.

"Do not apologize. I am grateful for your service."

No one had ever told me that before, save for Diana.

"What is your name?" Hollaina continued.

"I'm Maisie. I've been assigned as your maidservant while you are visiting."

Usually, eye contact with a royal was something scarce and terrifying for me. But I didn't find anything in Hollaina's gaze that I wanted to flinch away from.

Finally, she released my chin and stepped back. "Well, Maisie, it is a pleasure to make your acquaintance."

I nodded, making toward the door now that I was free. "Should you need anything, please just touch the orb here, and I will come." I gestured to the light orb that was on the wall close to the door.

When touched, it would light up a twin orb in the servants' quarters, and I would be notified. All the rooms upstairs had them.

Hollaina surveyed the room and stopped to dip a finger in one of the dishes of potpourri. Hopefully, the smell was enough to get rid of any lingering Dark.

"Thank you. I apologize in advance that I might be needing much of you. I expect Vera will not want me to leave this room often." She laughed quietly to herself, the sound like a gentle breeze.

"I'm sure that's not true," I said, surprising myself. "The guests here are free to go wherever they'd like in the palace. We have a wonderful library, if you're interested."

"You are too kind." Hollaina took a seat in one of the large chairs in front of the fireplace. Even with her thin, wispy stature almost being swallowed up by the cushions, she still commanded respect, her features strong. She was young, but something about her made her seem like she had been through centuries of life. It was almost familiar, the haunting quiet in the magic around her.

It's the scars. I knew she'd been in a fire, but I didn't know how severe. She must have seen some horrible things.

"But can I be called a guest when the hostess does not truly want me here? An interesting dilemma in etiquette, don't you think?"

I didn't really understand, and instead of just nodding, like I normally would, I contemplated. For some reason, I felt like there was more to her words beyond discussing formality.

"I would say that perhaps the word *guest* has many different meanings."

Hollaina smiled, her scars bunching up. "I look forward to picking your brain, Maisie. But for now, you should depart. Unless, of course, you wish to meet the queen in the doorway."

Sure enough, footsteps were starting to grow from outside. I almost questioned how she'd heard them so early, but one look at that all-knowing smile, and I just bowed my head and darted out.

I think I like the princess of the East.

Vera did not stop to acknowledge me in the halls. She likely did not even notice me with how determined her steps were, hard lines in her face as she stared down Hollaina's door. The princess must have done something severe to earn a personal, angry visit like that.

What I would give to have my red stone planted in that room.

I ran into Aedan, lurking outside the entrance to the kitchens. He must have been waiting for me because he straightened when he saw me approach.

"Come looking for a snack? You're going to ruin your dinner."

"Actually, I was waiting for you, but a snack sounds amazing. I haven't eaten anything today."

"And yet you shouldered on bravely." I placed my hand over my heart in mock sympathy. If only he knew how many meals I had skipped while on this job. But I gestured for him to follow me into the kitchen anyway.

He smiled, dimples pinching. I stared at them a beat longer than what was probably polite before wrenching my gaze away.

The kitchen was surprisingly quiet considering how many mouths we were feeding. But as we were in the lunch descent, everyone was either up serving the tail end of it or finding other things to do before dinner prep began.

I raided the cabinets and found some crackers and jams, not

bothering to plate them. Aedan didn't seem to mind, gratefully dipping his knife in the strawberry jelly and spreading it straight onto the cracker in his hand.

"Enjoy. That might be the last strawberry you get for a while."

This jelly was the last of our stores; we hadn't had a chance to make a batch yet this year. The strawberries had been days away from being ripe when the snow came.

Aedan shook his head. "There must be something we can do to clear the snow. I've heard that we're waiting on shipments of fruit from the South, but it'll take a bit for them to fill such a large order."

I nodded passively. I'd heard that too. It was such a shame, seeing as we only got fresh fruit in the North during this one time of year.

"I'm guessing you coming to see me is related to the very angry queen I saw marching toward Hollaina's room?"

Aedan rubbed a hand over his face. "That meeting was a shit show. It was basically a battle for dominance between the queen and Hollaina."

"Who won?"

"I'm kind of inclined to say Hollaina." He popped another cracker into his mouth.

"She's sure something," I agreed.

Aedan paused, raising a brow. "You've met her then?"

I nodded, leaning across him to grab my own cracker. I didn't complain about the clean pine scent that washed over me from being so close to him. "She came to her room as I was finishing getting it ready for her. Kind of odd and a little scary, to be honest. But I … I think I like her. Is that treasonous to say?"

The deputy captain laughed, the sound warm. "I like her, too, so I won't tell if you don't." More dimples. "I'm just worried about what will happen if she and Vera don't put down their weapons."

"What were they even fighting about?"

"Hollaina is angry that there haven't been more efforts to get Diana back. She thinks Vera is hiding something from us, something that pertains to Diana's absence. I can't imagine that to be true, but then again, she's still missing."

The words marinated in my head, turning over and over. Immediately, I wanted to reject the thought of the queen being secretive, but I remembered the time I'd come across her in a shadowy midnight meeting with Embris.

"Everyone has secrets," I said carefully. "That will always be true, no matter what role you play in society. I just don't understand why she would keep something about Diana hidden. She wants her back the most out of anyone."

"That's where I'm stuck too. It feels like we're missing something big. Have you had any luck with those books?"

"No. I read through every single one, and I've found nothing important."

"Hmm."

"Yeah."

"The Well has frozen over."

I groaned, "Of course it has." There would be no water coming out of there anytime soon.

Aedan put the lid back on the jelly, the crackers demolished. "I guess we'll keep digging around and observing then."

"Should we decide on a new meeting spot?" I thought of the snow that would easily be up to my waist, covering Diana's favourite garden.

"I think it'll be impossible to find somewhere quiet with how busy the palace is. It worked out pretty well today," Aedan said, glancing around the empty kitchen. "We can make it work wherever we need to."

I nodded, following him to the door, even as a weird disappointment settled in my stomach.

"Oh," he said, looking uncomfortable as he paused. "Would it be possible to get my coat back?" He looked down at the fancy, embroidered lapels he wore. "I can't help but feel a bit overdressed."

I flushed. I should have returned it first thing this morning. What if he thought I was holding on to it for some absurd, creepy reason? "Of course. I'm sorry. I can grab it right now."

He followed me to the servants' quarters, even going so far as to follow me down the stairs, where most royals preferred to remain at the top.

We got more than a few stares on the way down, my face feeling warmer with each one. I knew what they must think, and I didn't want that for Aedan. When we reached the common room, I told him to wait for me there.

It didn't take long for me to make the well-memorized trip through the twisty hallways to my room, where I grabbed the jacket, which I had folded neatly on my desk so it wouldn't crinkle.

Grea caught me as I was hurrying out my door, grabbing my arm. "I don't know what you're doing, but you need to be careful."

"What are you talking about?" Instinctively, I thought of the books I'd borrowed from Diana, now safely stored back under her mattress, where I'd found them. Had someone seen them in my room?

The young brunette jerked her chin in the direction of the common room. "A few of us have noticed you spending more time with the deputy captain. Are you two …"

"No! Gaia, no, it's not like that. We both lost someone important to us; it's just easy to be around someone who understands, you know?"

Grea flicked her eyes back and forth from the hallway to me, clearly not believing me. "I'm glad to know he's not treating you as some of the other royals here do."

I flushed, my gaze dropping.

"And I believe him to be a decent male. But, Maisie, you have to remember that at the end of the day, he's basically royalty, and you're not. Even if he doesn't mean to hurt you, he'll always put the Crown first."

I frowned. "I know all this."

Slowly, she nodded, letting go of my arm. "I don't mean to upset you. I just … I know how you were with the princess. And now that she's gone, I worry you'll attach yourself to him and get hurt. Whatever this is seems like more than grieving together." She pointed a glance at the jacket in my arms.

I was almost too stunned to speak, caught somewhere between anger at Grea for inserting herself into my life and embarrassment for being called out on something I was more than likely doing.

"I appreciate your concern." With a terse nod toward her, I sped back down the halls, feeling her eyes burning into my back.

Aedan *was* a decent male. Better than decent. If anything, spending time with him was helping me, not hurting me. I knew enough to keep the line of royal and servant clear between us. It was something I'd been doing with Diana for years.

When I reappeared in the common room, Aedan smiled. And damn if my gaze didn't go right to those dimples. It acted like a shock to my system, and I remembered Grea's words.

Shoving a professional smile on my face, I handed him the jacket and pulled away before our arms could touch accidentally. "Guess I'll have to find another way to get one of these snazzy jackets," I joked.

"If you wanted to join the army, you should have just asked," Aedan teased. He leaned in conspiringly. "I have an in with the head recruiter."

Ignoring the flip in my stomach, I managed to laugh and pull myself away, heading back up the stairs. He followed me up and stopped at the top.

"Hey, Maiz, can I ask you something?"

I blinked. No one had ever called me anything but my full name or the occasional *hey, you*. I liked the way it'd rolled off his tongue so easily.

"Of course."

Aedan glanced around the palace. "It's more than a little suspicious that Hollaina is here. We don't know her motives or how long she plans to stay. If she says anything strange to you, would you please tell me? It's an important part of palace security to stay well informed."

"Yes, definitely." I had already been planning to. Did he not trust me? We were working together on this. I watched his tall frame walk down the hall while chewing on my bottom lip.

Later, at the end of another long and busy day, I tucked myself into bed and stared into the darkness. It was only then that I realized how true Grea's words had been.

TWENTY-FIVE
FUNDAMENTALLY DIFFERENT

AEDAN

The sounds of grunting and heavy breaths filled the room. My skin had a layer of sweat coating it, my hair stuck to the back of my neck.

"Must you do that in here? I'm trying to read."

I looked up from my push-up position to where Jamey sat, legs crossed, on my settee. Her raised eyebrow only fuelled me to continue my workout.

"There is a library here, you know. Huge one in fact."

"There's also a training arena."

If you don't like it, go read in your own room and give me some space, I retorted in my head. But I had not yet become so brazen with her, so I settled on, "The arena is frozen, and the palace is filled to the brim with officials. I need to work out before bed, and this is the biggest part of my room. You can sit in the antechamber and read if you prefer."

Jamey pouted. "It's cold in there."

With my head down, she thankfully couldn't see the way my eyes rolled. Why bother complaining about the noise—which was silent as a mouse, considering my usual environment—if she wouldn't take any of my suggestions?

"Why have you been working out so much anyway? Surely, your twice-a-day sessions are enough to keep you fit."

I finished my set and brought my knees up to catch my breath. "It settles me," I admitted. "It's the one thing I can control right now."

Jamey closed the book in her lap. "What's on your mind?"

I flipped to my back, pulling my knees up so I could begin a set of sit-ups. The motion gave me a moment to stall. Jamey was offering counsel, to listen and help, but I wasn't sure if I wanted to talk to her about it.

Still, maybe it would help to get some things off my chest. "I'm worried about war."

"I doubt it will come to that."

"There doesn't seem to be a plan in place to avoid it," I replied between pants.

Jamey scoffed. "Just because the queen does not confide everything to the officials, it doesn't mean she has no plan. She's the smartest and sharpest mind in Eira. I have complete trust in her."

"If a queen cannot confide in her inner circle of officials, then what are they even for? Decoration?" My voice came out more bitter than I'd hoped, but with my breath caught between sit-ups, it was the best I could do.

"You just don't understand royalty," was Jamey's reply. Her tone was not harsh or mean, but the words fell sour on my ears.

Sure, I had been living in royalty, training in it since childhood, serving as a deputy captain, but I knew nothing of a royal court or how to belong in it.

I understood all right. More than she did. With my outside view, I could see the Crown exactly for what it was. A posturing of power and political moves to fool everyone else into thinking they were falling behind. Because when you were constantly playing catch-up, floundering to make sure you were not the odd one out, you missed the obvious.

In this case, the obvious was that Queen Vera had no plan.

"Agree to disagree," I said quietly.

Done with my workout, I began my stretches. I often thought that stretching was the best part of working out, when your limbs were satisfyingly weak and the sleepiness came from pulling your muscles.

"I didn't mean to offend you, Aedan." Jamey rose from her chair, hands clasped in front of her. "I'm just trying to share the optimism I have. There's no need to be so bleak. You simply don't have to worry about it—that's what I do, and it gives me great peace."

It was all I could do to hold in my snort. *Here's how to feel better: just don't be bothered by it.* As if it could be done that easily.

That was why Jamey and I could never be something serious. We were fundamentally different. I didn't fault her for it. But she would never get me.

"Are you ready for bed?" I dropped a kiss on her head because that was the only way to get her to think all was fine between us. Then, I pulled back the coverlet and headed to my bathing room. "I need to clean up, but I'll only be a few minutes."

As I scrubbed water over my face, the delightful, tired pull of my body settled in—exactly the effect I aimed for with my numerous workouts. My mind was far from ready to sleep, but it was no match for an exhausted body.

TWENTY-SIX
BUOY IN THE STORM

SPENSE

Tipping my head back, I drained the contents of the drink Pik had passed to me for energy. It was bitter and acidic, like lemon rinds, but if it kept me awake during this meeting with no end, then I would bear it.

"Thank you, Pik." Sorin drank his own tonic, grimacing once at the taste. "This was much needed. Now, with the logistics of Father's travel settled, I think we should move right along to our next order of business—the Folk. Badras, I'll let you take the lead."

As head of the fae-folk relations, Badras nodded, shoving his empty drink across the table and unfolding several parchments. He cleared his throat. "I don't anticipate any struggle from the Folk. Elves, gnomes, goblins, brownies—they have all made their unhappiness known to me in recent years. I believe they would jump at the chance to go home. The problem lies with the Folk that are … less than easy to communicate with."

Memories came swirling back to me in a haze. "Meaning the nymphs and dryads."

Badras nodded. "As well as the pixies and the leprechauns. They are not impossible to speak with, but I anticipate it being a struggle— and a time suck. The pixies alone require me to go through their three-day trial to be granted an audience in front of their council. I will have to get started immediately."

"We will help in whatever way you need, brother," Sorin said. "We can split up the more difficult Folk and each take one."

"That would be extremely helpful."

Olys coughed. "We're forgetting about one."

The faces around the table dropped.

Badras's lips thinned. "The kelpies will not come easily."

"Are we sure we really want to bring murderous, camouflaging carnivores with us? Maybe we could accidentally forget them," Alwyn joked.

I thought of the river creatures who delighted in tricking innocents into the watery depths. Their faces full of teeth and webbed fingers made me shudder. I wouldn't miss the foul things if they didn't make it—and the gods knew they could hold their own against the humans.

Sorin sighed. "Where we go one, we go all. We're not leaving anyone behind."

"And how do you suggest we contain them while we travel? They will die if their skin touches the air." Badras folded his arms across his chest.

"We will make up containers that can hold them in water while we cross the portal. It doesn't have to be anything fancy—just enough to keep them healthy until we find a body of water in Eira that they will enjoy. I'm sure Diana can aid us with a solution for their new home." Sorin jotted notes down, his eyes lit with ideas for this new invention.

Badras shook his head. "I will need to get a head count to be sure, but last time I checked, there were over three thousand kelpies still thriving. You will need to make a lot of containers, brother. Are we sure it's worth it? Perhaps we can take a small group to continue the population over there."

Our eldest brother was not hearing it. "Nonsense, Badras. We are *not* leaving our subjects behind, and that is final. We will have our soldiers and patrons of Ivywall help with the construction of the containers."

Badras shrugged but kept his mouth shut.

"And how will we convince the kelpies to get into the containers?" Olys asked. "They are hardly known for their agreeable nature."

One by one, my siblings' heads swivelled to me.

"No."

"Come on, Spensey." Alwyn batted her eyelashes at me. "This won't work without you."

It was my turn to cross my arms. "What happened to soul magic being devious and inhumane?"

Sorin cleared his throat. "While I will be the first to agree that bending the will of another is inherently wrong, this is one case where the good outweighs the bad. This is the only way to save the kelpies."

"Glad your moral compass still points north, brother."

"Are you really going to be a stick in the mud about this? What's the harm?" Badras's tone was getting annoyed. And he had no right to be.

He didn't understand the addiction of soul magic. Of how one use led to two, which led to four and five, and eventually, it wouldn't cross my mind whether it was right or not.

I didn't want to go back to that place. Eira had purged me of it, and I was unlikely to get another chance like this to live without its greedy hands on me.

The council room doors swung open suddenly, and a small child raced in, laughing with glee as she outpaced her tutor.

"Aislinn!" Sorin exclaimed as his daughter launched herself into his lap.

She snuggled in and looked up at him with her big brown eyes. The ones she had gotten from him.

"Hi, Papa," she said sweetly.

Her new tutor came to the door, puffing and red-faced. Colour that quickly drained when he saw what his student had interrupted. "My apologies, Princes and Princess," he stammered, twisting his hands around a book of history he was holding. "She has been rather excitable today."

"The little fox just wanted to take her rightful place among the council." Alwyn smiled.

"Can I stay with you, Papa?" Aislinn's little voice was almost enough to break Sorin. "I want to help."

Sorin smiled gently—a look that was reserved only for her. "Your ideas would put us all to shame, I'm sure."

Aislinn grinned. Her father smoothed back her raven-black hair, taking care to tuck it behind both ears.

"But the best thing you can do to help us right now is to make sure your studies are up to date. Can you do that?"

She deflated, jutting out her bottom lip. "Victar is boring. Can you get me another tutor? Can Wynnie tutor me?"

Alwyn laughed genially. "Now, now. Victar can teach you a lot more than I can. When you're ready to wield a sword, that's where Auntie Wyn comes in."

Aislinn grumbled but agreed, kissing Sorin once on the cheek before sliding off his lap and trudging back to her tutor. When she passed me, she stuck her little palm out.

Grinning, pleased she remembered our game during my time away, I tried to make contact with her hand. She whipped it to the side before I could and laughed.

"Too slow—again."

"I'll get you one of these days," I told her as she gave me a sassy hair flip.

"See you later, little fox," Alwyn called as Victar bustled her away.

We were silent for a moment, soaking in the happiness of Aislinn before it faded away to responsibility once more.

My niece was a light in this darkness, a buoy in the storm. Everything we were doing, it was with her in mind. Her future, her inheritance of our duties. I wanted it to be easier for her than it was for us. I wanted her to know peace.

"I'll do it."

Sorin loosed a sigh. "Thank you, brother."

Twenty-Seven
History Class

DIANA

I stared down at the sword pressed against my throat, following the lines of the metal all the way up the handle and to the arm of my assailant.

Alwyn grinned. "Another point to me."

I grumbled as I caught my breath. A full week of joining the siblings' dawn training sessions, and I still hadn't been able to best her. I'd gotten a win against Sorin and Olys and a few on Spense—but I wasn't counting those because I was pretty sure he had been going easy on me—but the viper of a female was too quick and lithe.

Frustrating as it was not to win all the time, the sessions had been really good for me. Since Urdan's lapse of lucidity, he had not returned, and no one was inclined to hold their breath for a reappearance anytime soon. Which worked to the advantage of the siblings, considering their plan hinged on him being in the dark.

Being up before dawn, sweating and using muscles long forgotten, gave me an outlet before spending hours planning in the council room. It was at least some semblance of a schedule, a routine. It was the only thing keeping me from falling apart.

That, and Spense.

He smiled knowingly at me as I picked up my sword from where it had been knocked from my hand and dusted off the grip. "Don't beat yourself up. You know they have thousands of years on you."

That didn't stop *him* from being able to keep up with them. I stuck out my tongue and headed to the shady alcove for some water.

The sun was only just starting to rise, but already, the heat was intense. Being up on the sandy plateau behind Ivywall was so enjoyable in the dark twilight of the mornings. The air was fresh and frigid—a stern reminder of how easily the desert could take it away.

"One more go before we head back?" Spense held Bloodletter loosely at his side, the challenge in his voice contradicting the ease of his stance.

I remembered how it had felt this morning to spar against him, our movements in sync, our timing nearly perfect. It was all too easy to get swept up in it, in how, if I twisted a little more in my turn, my shoulder would brush his chest. And how that small motion would cause him to pause for a split second, his breath shifting.

My stomach flipped at the thought. I took one last swig from my canteen, ready to join him, when Badras spoke.

"Why don't we see what she's capable of against someone who actually knows what they're doing?"

I hadn't seen him approach the alcove. He usually kept to himself during training and never once asked me to spar. Or talked to me at all really.

Alwyn growled from where she sat against a rock, "I take offense to that."

Badras held up his hands in surrender. "No offense meant, sister. I only thought to challenge her without the advantage of being a sword's length apart."

"You want to go hand-to-hand?" Spense asked. "Not entirely fair when you're double her size."

Badras only shrugged. The three looked at me. Even Sorin and Olys had ceased their sparring a few feet over to watch.

I considered the brother in question. He was a hulking male, no doubt about that. All muscle and mass. But someone that size would have trouble being swift.

I thought of Alwyn, with her tiny frame and warrior spirit, and raised my chin defiantly. "You're on."

Badras grinned. "We'll do old-school rules. No magic—on my part, of course. First to pin the other wins," he called over his shoulder.

Once in the chalk circle, he pulled off his shirt and tossed it at Spense, who scowled.

"Is that really necessary, Bad?"

"What's the matter, brother? Worried you won't compare?"

Spense just worked his jaw, staring him down. I took in the sight of Badras, golden skin that smoothed over ridges and planes of muscle. His long sandy hair was half in a bun, the other half skimming his shoulders, and he stood steadily, like a building, smirking at me.

I snorted at him, at his surety that I was checking him out. "Hardly a comparison worth making."

Low laughter sounded from behind us, and Badras curled his lip. "Let's find out."

He charged at me without warning, and I barely leaped out of the way in time. Spinning around, I was able to catch my balance before he came at me again. I ducked and shifted as he sent blow after blow my way.

My idea of being swift and nimble to get the win was quickly disintegrating. Badras was *fast*, and he was not letting up.

I couldn't spend the entire time on the defence, so after I ducked his left hook, I struck out with a punch of my own. It didn't meet flesh; in fact, it barely met the air before Badras had it in his grip, yanking it so that I was turned around and he had his trunk of an arm around my shoulders, pinning me to his chest.

His voice was soft and dripping in male arrogance as it tickled my ear. "How long has it been since you trained without your magic, Princess?"

I brought my elbow up hard, effectively hitting his windpipe and causing him to loosen his grip around my shoulders. I wiggled out and spun to face him, trying not to smile at the way he gasped for breath.

"A while," I admitted. "But the kind of training I have had is not one you forget overnight."

Taking advantage of his limited air, I charged. I brought my fist up like I was going for a punch to the gut and instead swept down and kicked out his legs. He tripped, not falling as I'd hoped, but in his unbalance, I was able to get behind him and deliver a kick to his lower back that sent him to his knees, his hands braced out in the sand. If I'd had my magic, I would have sent it to keep him pinned down in this moment. But I didn't, so a tackle would have to do.

Before I could convince myself not to, I leaped in the air and crashed into his back with the entirety of my weight. He hit the ground with an *oof,* and I scrambled up, placing my foot between his giant shoulder blades.

"I believe that's a pin."

Alwyn hollered from the sidelines. Spense laughed delightedly, his face lit up. Even Sorin clapped a few times. I knew that the biggest part of my win had been taking advantage of a moment when he dropped his focus to taunt me, but I held on to the pride. I'd still taken down the behemoth of a male, in hand-to-hand, all by myself.

No offense to Alwyn, but that trumped our swordfights any day.

Badras rolled over in the sand and stared up at me, his face contemplative. I offered my hand out, and he accepted, jumping to his feet with grace.

"Interesting," was all he murmured as he retrieved his shirt from Spense and made for the alcove.

"About time someone knocked him on his ass." Alwyn tossed me my canteen, grinning, and I drank heavily.

I shrugged. "I know I won't be able to do that again, but it still felt pretty awesome."

Spense's arms wrapped around me from behind. "A win is a win." He spoke into my neck, planting a kiss there. I leaned into it, savouring the naturality of it. "Want to go cool off?"

Something told me what he had in mind would only raise my heart rate.

"Oh gods, gross," Alwyn groaned. "Now, I won't be able to use the pool ever again."

Normally, her words would start a blush in my cheeks, but something piqued my interest that I'd forgotten about. "Over here, you all say gods—plural. In Eira, we only have Gaia. Do you recognize different ones?"

Alwyn patted the space beside her in the shade of the rock, beckoning me to join her. "Welcome to Alwyn's history class. Please have a seat."

Chuckling, I settled in the sand beside her, grateful to be out of the sun. I chugged more water from the canteen and watched as Spense used his shirt to wipe sweat from his brow, exposing a line of muscled skin at his waist. He caught me watching and smirked as he took a seat in the sand across from us.

I was starting to regret not taking him up on his earlier offer.

"Gaia is the goddess of the earth and everything it encompasses. And, like in her races, there must be balance. Her counterpart is Ouranos, god of the sky and sea. They are the two gods we worship.

Perfect balance of feminine and masculine, creating order in all the realms."

"I've never heard of him," I said, mostly thinking out loud.

"It makes sense," Spense mused. "Gaia, being the light side, was the patron of the Seelie. It doesn't surprise me that Ouranos was erased with the Unseelie."

"In addition to those two, we also recognize their children." Alwyn twisted to show me a tattoo on her shoulder. A star with four points, each one swirling up into its own design. "The children of the gods, which we call deities, brought magic into the lands. They are each responsible for one branch."

She pointed to the top point. "Demekol. Firstborn, gifted with earth magic. It's only conjecture, but we believe the counterbalance to this is the fauna branch."

Alwyn's finger dragged down to the lowest point. Even with limited vision over her shoulder, she knew this tattoo inside out. "Lazansus. Secondborn, given the fire magic. This one is harder, but we believe its partner to be soul."

The point on the left was next. "Are you ready to have your mind blown? The thirdborn deity was a daughter, named Ilysia."

I gaped. "The Seelie queen?"

Spense shrugged. "Potentially. We don't know for sure. Could just be a shared name. It's unlikely that the deity Ilysia would have fared this long without punishment from the others. The deities are forbidden to interfere with the worlds."

"Let's hope she's not—neutralizing an honest-to-goodness *deity* changes our plan. A lot. As in we no longer have one." Alwyn's joking tone was only half-hearted.

Mind whirling, I could only listen as she continued, "Ilysia was given water magic. I believe this is paired with our sun distinction, but there are some"—she coughed in Spense's direction, who rolled his eyes—"that will argue that sun belongs with fire. We don't have much of the old texts to go off on, but I don't think sun and fire are compatible. They're too similar. Water and sun go much better together, don't you think?"

She didn't wait for me to give a response, which was fine because I wouldn't have been able to formulate one anyway.

"Lastly"—her finger landed on the right side of the tattoo—"we have the fourthborn, the goddess of air magic, which balances out storm. Her name is Ilex."

After a few moments, Alwyn sat straight again. "It's not like any living fae have ever seen one. For all we know, they don't exist in physical bodies, but more on the ancestral plane. But this lore is what has been passed down to us for generations."

Thoughts whirled, too fast moving and vague for me to hold on to. "So, there's no record of the deities ever living among the fae?"

Alwyn shook her head. "If they did, it wasn't public knowledge. Don't worry," she added, noting my frown. "The Seelie queen is not the deity Ilysia. They only share the name. If she had committed such a crime against nature, then her siblings would have stepped in to fix it. And if they couldn't, then Gaia herself would have."

"Well, then why haven't they intervened after all this time? How can they sit and watch such damage happen to their world?" Confusion had slowly melted into a prickling anger, warm and tight on my skin.

I pictured rulers draped lazily over thrones, watching as the world they had created turned into chaos before their very eyes. It made me feel ill. Suddenly, an image of the Seelie queen from Jweira's memory settled in my mind, her eyes of ice glinting under the wolf mask. She was still out there, in *my* home, continuing to spread evil.

"It is something that has been heavily philosophized, but really, it's simple. No intervening means no intervening. Correcting a wrong from another deity is not the same as the gods changing the course of the world at their whim. They can only watch and find other ways to help. Like, for example, using your ancestors to send you messages." Alwyn looked me dead in the eye, her eyebrow raised.

Spense cleared his throat from across the sand after I failed to respond, my jaw slack. It was a crazy notion. The gods—the *actual gods*—sending messages to me? I couldn't be that important.

"Hate to break Alwyn's history class short, but we really do have to get going. There's another meeting with the army generals we don't want to be late for." He stood, brushing sand from his long legs, and I slowly uncurled my own, dread weighing down my limbs like water.

Spense worked hard to get me into every meeting and didn't tolerate any maltreatment toward me. And I was grateful for him, for his big heart and loyalty to me. But these meetings with the functioning pieces of Ivywall, they were so important. The more I attended, the less I felt comfortable. I knew they didn't trust me, and I worried they weren't saying what they truly thought, for fear of Spense's retaliation. For our plan to work, we needed one cohesive team. I couldn't help but feel I was a rock, stopping the river from flowing smoothly.

"Why don't you go on ahead without me?" I squinted up at him. "I'm really beat. I think I'll sit this one out."

He frowned, shielding his eyes from the sun so he could see me clearly. "Are you sure? You have every right to be there, you know. Did someone say something? I—"

"No, no, that's not it." I mustered a loose smile. "I just, uh …" What could I say that wouldn't make me sound like I was too immature to have a place here? Or leading my own kingdom for that matter? Maybe I'd have to fake an injury or illness—

"Diana already promised she'd come with me to see Benton." Alwyn strung an arm through mine, effectively saving my ass. "He loves meeting pretty new girls. It'll help sway him to our cause. Plus, you don't get to keep her all the time, you know. I know she's your soulmate, but you have to share."

"Are you sure you're okay with going into Rathe?" Spense's steel-coloured eyes bored into mine, and I willed away the guilt in my stomach. "I know you can handle yourself, but it's still dangerous. I'd rather be with you."

I had not anticipated Alwyn's plan to include leaving the safety of Ivywall and heading into the human-infested city of Rathe, but there was no turning back now.

I stood and put a hand on his arm, smiling. "You go to the meeting; it's important. I'll be fine. I'll be with Alwyn, remember?"

"Yes, that's what worries me," Spense mumbled, to which his sister laughed to herself.

"I'll see you at dinner." I stood on my tiptoes to give him a quick kiss, and even then, he still had to lean down to brush his lips against mine.

After fixing his sister with a stern look, Spense headed back toward Ivywall, leaving Alwyn and me alone in the heat, which was only getting hotter.

"Thanks," I murmured, almost afraid to meet her eyes, worried what she'd think of me blowing off Spense.

To my surprise—and relief—she only gave a half shrug. "I can tell when a female needs a break from all that testosterone. And I really could use your help with Benton."

"Don't you need to be in the meeting with the army generals?"

Alwyn scoffed. "When those boys finally string together a *real* plan, then I'll get involved. I'm not wasting my time listening to them talk in circles. Besides, no one would dare tell me how to direct my drakes. They don't have the balls."

We started off to Ivywall, where we would inevitably change into more suitable clothing for going out in the scorching sun.

"It's not that I can't handle being the only female in a room of males," I finally said after a few minutes of silence. "I want you to know that I'm fully in this—your plan—whatever it takes. I'm not … I'd never shirk off responsibilities."

Alwyn nodded. "I know."

"I just know what they all think of me even though they would never say anything because of Spense. And I would hate to think they aren't speaking their true minds about all of this because of my presence." Words were rambling out of my mouth, and I probably sounded desperate, but I couldn't stop. I needed Alwyn to know, to respect me. She was my friend and my ally. And, I supposed, family too. "I thought it would be good for them to meet without me. That way, everyone could be comfortable."

Alwyn's hand reached out and grasped my shoulder, stopping us. "Diana"—she laughed breathily—"I get it. Being the only female in the room is no stranger to me. I need you to believe me when I say that I trust you, okay?" She smiled and dropped her hand, continuing her pace.

"Sometimes, I forget how young you truly are." She shook her head gently. "I spent many, many years trying to prove myself, my worth, to others. The day I learned that worth comes from within was the day I was finally set free. So, when I say that I trust you to be a fully functioning member of our team, I mean it. I'm not questioning your decisions, and you shouldn't be either."

We reached the entrance into the adobe palace, and even though the cool air filled my lungs, Alwyn's words were warm in my heart.

"Thank you," I murmured.

She bumped me playfully with her shoulder. Even with her eyes trained ahead, I could see a smile grace her lips.

"You might not be thanking me later. Benton is a shameless flirt."

"Who is he anyway?"

"I'll tell you on the road." We stopped at a forked hallway, one I was finally beginning to recognize. Our rooms were in opposite directions. "Wear the heat-resistant clothes. And don't forget the headscarf. It's important our ears stay covered—you'll see why. Meet at the stables in twenty."

"We're not flying?" I called to Alwyn's back, as she was already on her way.

"Flying would give us away. We're taking camels!" She threw me a grin over her shoulder, one that was positively wicked.

She disappeared before I could ask what camels were, so I hurried on my own way. Despite the serious threats in Rathe, excitement bubbled in me like a brook at the thought of going into enemy territory. Alwyn had said she needed me, and even if that was an exaggeration, it felt good. Right.

Having a goal, a purpose, filled my soul with an intensity I'd never imagined. Spense, Alwyn, Sorin, even Badras and Olys, they were up front, and there were no secrets between anyone. It made the dark seriousness of the situation just a little easier to manage. A little lighter on my heart.

There. A whirring deep in the pit of my stomach, accompanied by the sweet snow-white pull behind my eyes.

It was gone as quickly as it had come.

My magic.

Hope flared in my chest, warm and bright. I could do this. The eclipse was coming, and I'd be ready.

Eira, I'm coming home.

TWENTY-EIGHT
SWAY

AEDAN

"Here, here, and here." Solis, the seneschal of the queen, stood over a map and pointed at spots around the North. Two were in a quiet town near the Unclaimed Land's border and one in the middle of the forest on a trade route. "The most recent shadow attacks have been rapid and quiet. Only seven fae were affected, and all have been sent to the South's treatment camp."

I cursed under my breath. The shadows were getting more powerful.

Vera sighed. "Thank you, Solis."

"What can be done of the shadows, My Queen?" Kashdan asked, his purple robes looking a little duller today.

"It pains me greatly to say this, but we do not know. Not yet anyway. As much as I am eager to send an attack team, we know nothing about the shadows' weaknesses or how to abolish them. I fear it would be a death sentence."

There were solemn murmurs around the table.

Embris cleared his throat. "For now, we strongly advise you to stay in large groups and in more populated areas. For the time being, we are limiting trade routes by half, and all parties must be four or more when travelling."

Everyone nodded, the region heads all relaying the information to their officials to send back to their courts. Except Hollaina. She shook her head, a soft chuckle slipping through the noise.

"Is there something you find funny about our fae being attacked?" Embris snapped.

Hollaina smiled, scars stretching tight. "Not at all, Captain. No, what I find unbelievable is how you can all sit around and ignore the obvious."

"Please enlighten the council." Vera seethed.

"The shadows are clearly a reaction of the realm. Just like the snow. An utter imbalance. Something that cannot be solved without the high princess. As I said before, it is a huge mistake not directing all available power toward making a portal."

"I agree with the Eastern princess," Sir Radtar said, his voice wavering once. "I know you are doing your best, My Queen, but I cannot shake the feeling that these atrocities we are facing are related to Diana's absence."

"Thank you for your concern, Radtar. As a long-standing official of the North, I respect that you are as desperate as I am for my daughter's return. However, I have made my intent clear. I cannot sacrifice the lives of Eira in an attempt to get her back. Diana would not want that either."

I bristled. How dare she say what Diana would want!

"Furthermore," she continued, her voice turning icy, "the shadows have been surfacing since before Diana's disappearance. And there are *many* teams at work, attempting to create a portal. We are doing the necessary steps, and for some reason, they are not working."

"This is the first we're hearing of it." Hollaina did not seem to care about the warning tone in which the queen had spoken. "I am concerned that you did not seek our counsel. Surely, there are texts or perhaps scholars that are able to lend their minds to such a problem. Had I known, I would have sent for my own, and we would be all that much closer."

Heads swivelled between the two females, who stared each other down.

Radtar spoke up bravely. "I will send word to the Academy to update them."

Vera shot him a look, one that said, *If you're not careful, you'll soon be looking for a new job.*

It grated me to see how much of a dictatorship the council had become. Wasn't that the whole point of appointing one—to give *counsel?*

"No need, Sir Radtar," Vera gritted out. "I assure you, I have taken those steps already."

Hollaina leaned back in her chair, her white hair spilling down it. "If those steps have been taken, then am I to prepare for an Eastern emissary's arrival?"

Embris cut in before the two could escalate further. From the way they stared knives at each other and the smell of lilacs filling the room, they were not far from fighting with more than words. "Let's go over the plans for when the portal is open, shall we?"

Vera's gaze flicked to him, and she settled back into her chair, a docile smile appearing on her face. "A great idea, Embris. Please, proceed."

The queen could pretend all she liked, but she was losing control over her officials. Hollaina was not going to make it easy, and from the way Sir Radtar had spoken up, it seemed she was swaying others to her side.

Getting high hopes for change was not something I wanted to dally in, but it was hard not to when Hollaina spoke as she did. I couldn't help but feel as if she knew something we all did not. If so, it hardly made her better than the queen.

As I tried to pay attention to army lines and strategic positioning, one surety was blatantly obvious: something big was coming, and we'd better be ready for it.

TWENTY-NINE
THRILL

DIANA

If someone had told me two months ago that I'd be sitting on a lumpy creature in the middle of a desert, riding into a death trap with my soulmate's sister, I'd have laughed in their face.

Even now, a bubble of laughter escaped me at the sheer absurdity of it all. I never would have guessed that camels were just slow, hump-backed versions of horses. Or that riding them felt like swaying and even made me a little dizzy.

Alwyn twisted in her saddle and gave me a quizzical look over her shoulder, to which I just shook my head, unable to school away the smile on my face.

Maybe it was the nerves making me giggly—that was definitely not foreign to me. But the closer we got to Rathe, the more excitement took over. Yes, it was a city full of enemy humans who wanted magic eradicated, but it was an adventure. The last time I'd felt this open freedom in my chest, I had been …

I was sixteen, in Mount Nord, I realized with a start.

It wasn't often in my life I was left to my own devices, that I didn't feel watched, and I hadn't realized how much I craved it until now.

Surveying the thick sandy braid peeking from Alwyn's headscarf, I felt a warm tug of emotion. She was not the type to smother or babysit. Her confidence made me confident, and she didn't expect me to be anything other than myself.

I'd grown up surrounded by lots of family my whole life, but somehow, being with Alwyn felt familial, like I'd never known before.

Instinctively, I swung around in my saddle to look over the unassuming lines and slopes of Ivywall. When we'd ridden away, I had been delighted to see that the front of it did appear to look more like a real palace with big inviting doors and a huge pond—or as commonly phrased here, a *watering hole*.

Only it wasn't there.

I blinked, thinking maybe there was a grain of sand in my eye, playing tricks on me.

Ivywall was gone. The entirety of it had disappeared, the sand in its place smooth and bearing no signs of a former palace on it. I remembered Spense's words from my first night in this realm, how much glamour was placed on Ivywall daily.

"Alwyn."

She swivelled again, chuckling when she saw my expression. "Pretty cool, right?" She slowed her camel so we could walk side by side. "It's the only thing that's kept us safe from the humans."

I shook my head in wonder. "I've never seen a glamour work like that. How is it done?"

Alwyn grinned. "If I tell you, I'll have to kill you."

I rolled my eyes, smiling. "How will we get back in?"

"Oh, Diana, ye of little faith." She tsked. "Leave that to me, and focus on staying in your saddle. You're looking a little wobbly."

I grumbled under my breath. Riding terrifying drakes *through the sky* was no issue, but this docile, hump-backed creature was my bane? Not fair.

The sun beat down, causing wavy lines to appear on the horizon.

Even in the clothing specially designed for the heat, sweat trickled down my back. Thankfully, the ride from Ivywall was only an hour. Rathe was in view, full of adobe structures with angled roofs not unlike the palace.

We rode through the outpost, nodding at the uniformed guard at the gate. Clearly, two young females coming into town on camels were nothing to be concerned about, because he barely even looked us over before waving us through.

Too bad for him because he missed the finger Alwyn casually flipped over her shoulder when we passed.

We stopped to tie our camels up in a shady spot, where a small young human was collecting coin in exchange for watering and watching the beasts. Finally back on solid ground, I was able to take in Rathe even if it felt like I had sea legs.

It … it looked like any other city. Apart from the obvious desert modifications, it was laid out in a crosshatch pattern with shops and vendors down the streets and homes above them. It lacked the hustle and life of Nevelyn though. The humans looked alike to the fae, maybe a bit smaller and stockier. The reasoning for our scarves became clear—their ears were tiny, little, rounded things. Barely even noticeable on their heads. If I didn't know better, I would have loved to get a closer look.

Hardly any humans were out, and I realized why—this was not a climate where you dallied outside unnecessarily.

"Where to?" I turned to Alwyn, but she'd already started off down the sand road. "Hey!"

She led us down through the busier part of Rathe, where if I peered through the windows, I could see lots of interactions happening in stores, markets, and pubs. What caught my eye was the seemingly surplus amount of blacksmiths offering their services.

When I mentioned it to Alwyn, she leaned in and spoke low. "It's absurd. A city this small needs *maybe* two, considering they don't even shoe their horses here because it makes them slip on the sand. So, why do they need so many metal workers?"

I met Alwyn's chocolaty eyes. "They're making weapons."

"Exactly. A war is coming, much bigger than we expect. If I had to guess, I'd say the viceroy of Rathe has been working with legions across the water, expanding his army. My spies haven't been able to get a confirmed yes, but I can feel it. Something big is happening, and if we don't get out soon, I fear we might be taken by surprise."

My gut hollowed. "They won't be able to find Ivywall though. Surely, that can tide the win in your favour?"

"They've already done enough harm without storming us at our heart. They've driven almost all the Folk out of Rathe entirely, and they continue to hunt us out. Like Elfwood. Why couldn't they have left the elves alone? They weren't bothering anybody. Ivywall is full to bursting with the Folk finding sanctuary with us, and if worse comes to worst, we won't come out of this fight. The humans are vile, evil tyrants who won't stop until the last sliver of magic has been wiped out." Alwyn spat on the ground to drive her point home.

I knew it was bad, but the fervour in her voice, mixed with the eerie lack of magic in the air, churned my emotions. They didn't deserve to live in this kind of fear. The thought of my citizens in this situation filled me with terror and a drive to protect them so heavy that I could choke on it.

"We'll get out of here," I assured her, placing my hand on her arm.

She smiled gratefully, calming. Placing a hand over mine, she replied, "I know we will."

An emphatic voice from across the street spun our heads in that direction.

A large human woman was handing out parchments to passersby, and when she noticed us, she began shouting, "Demons! Demons have infiltrated our cities! Protect yourself!"

She waved her paper at us with wide eyes, and though Alwyn kept walking, I took one from her, careful to keep the scarf in place around my ears.

"Don't let their magic condemn your soul. A pretty girl like yourself should take extra care to stay out of their demonic webs." She stared right at me, continuing to watch as I picked up a little pace, trying to put some distance between us.

The parchment in my hands was crumpled and faded, but the words were printed clear enough. If I could read them.

"What language is this?" I hissed to Alwyn.

She snorted. "Old Unseelie. They are eager to erase us from their culture and yet are happy to ignore where all their customs and languages came from. Do you think they built Rathe to be this large and successful on their own? Pfft. Before we arrived, the humans were basically heathens."

I frowned at the parchment. "What does it say?"

"It just spouts some crap about how to spot a *demon* and who to alert about it. Totally useless." Alwyn's eyes focused on the road beside me. "Keep your head covered. We're being followed."

Fear kicked up, sending spikes through my belly. It was everything I could do not to turn and glance where Alwyn had just been looking. My hands shook on the parchment, and I folded it over and over to keep them busy.

We walked deeper into Rathe. Our pace might seem leisurely to an outsider, but our strides had gotten longer, covering as much ground as we could for our small frames without drawing too much attention. At one corner, we turned, and I was able to get an inconspicuous look back and quickly noticed our follower. He was the only other body in the road and was in no rush to get to the cool interior of a shop. With a hood covering his features and an intent clip to his pace, there was no question about it.

I took a shaky inhale, trying to tap into the place inside me that could stay calm in battle. Without my magic, I felt exposed. Anything remotely left of my bravado had been shredded by my failure in Elfwood.

"We're almost at our destination. We're only safe because he doesn't know for sure what we are. If he did, we'd have been attacked already."

I followed Alwyn's lead, trying to keep my steps even with my breathing. A small wind picked up as we turned, hitting a cross breeze. My hood flipped up, and I snatched it back down before it could come off my head entirely.

"Do you think he saw anything?" I hissed under my breath.

"No," murmured Alwyn. "But that's actually a good idea."

"What are you talking about?"

Without any explanation, Alwyn's magic crept up my neck, landing on my ears. It tingled softly as a glamour took place. Another wind blew toward us—stronger than before, thanks to Alwyn—and both our hoods were ripped away from our faces.

"Are you crazy? What if there are no-magic devices around?"

The female had a fake smile plastered to her face, giggling in a way I'd never heard from her. "We're going to be full of sand after this!" she remarked, raising her voice enough that it carried down the road toward our follower.

I dared a glance over and saw that he had paused, rigidity gone from his posture. By the time we righted our hoods and started walking again, he was gone.

"That was fun." Alwyn grinned. "Really gets your heart rate going, doesn't it?"

Yes, and not in a good way. I was still trying to get my breathing under control.

I shook my head in relief. "It shouldn't surprise me that you're one of those thrill seekers."

She elbowed me. "When you've lived as long as I have, nothing's really a thrill anymore." Her tone was joking, but something about the severity of her words settled heavy in me.

Living and fighting for over a thousand years was no small feat. It would be draining on anyone. But Alwyn was full of life and wit. And once we got back to Eira, she could be free to live whatever life she wanted. I would make sure of it.

I took her arm in mine as we continued down the road, heart thudding when she leaned her head against my shoulder.

We entered a small shop with heavy curtains drawn around the window and door.

A bell rang as we stepped inside, and a voice called from the back, "Be right with you!"

The walls were lined with odds and sods, parts, knives, clothing, and just about anything that could fit. There was hardly a space big enough to see the paint colour on the wall.

"What is this place?" I whispered to Alwyn.

"To the humans, this is Benton's Consignment. The shop that literally has everything." She grabbed the parchment from my hands and chucked it into a mountainous pile of papers and torn books in the corner.

A tall, older male ducked under the flaps covering the back room, wiping his greasy hands on a rag. He clucked his tongue when he saw Alwyn. "You promised I wouldn't have to see you again for a few months. It's only been two weeks."

Alwyn batted her eyelashes. "Are you sure? That doesn't sound like me."

Benton shook his head in resignation, fighting a smile. "What do you need this time? I've already received your birthday invitation."

"Why do you always assume I need something? And you'd better be coming to the party, by the way. It just so happens I've come to introduce you to a very special friend. This is Diana."

She swept her arm toward me, and Benton took me in. I stepped forward to offer my hand, but he took it in his palm and dropped into a bow, placing a kiss on my knuckles.

"What a pleasure to make your acquaintance, Diana." His gaze swept up and down lazily, and he grinned as he dropped my hand and stepped away, a gleam in his eye that unsettled me.

Alwyn rolled her eyes and stepped over to yank the sleeve of my shirt up, revealing the black ink on my arm. "Down, boy. She's taken—"

Benton shrugged. "Wouldn't be my first set of soulmates."

"By my brother."

His lips thinned. "So, you come to my shop in the middle of hostile human territory to rub it in my face that she's not available? This is low for you, Al."

She walked up to the tall fae and reached on her tiptoes to flick his nose. "You need to get your head out of the gutter. We're here to talk."

"This'd better not be on official business again. The council *hates* when you sidestep them."

"It's official, but it's not business. This is a friendly chat, and whether you relay what you heard to the council or not is up to you."

Benton groaned, "You are the biggest pain in my life, you know that?"

"Are you going to offer us tea or not?" Alwyn sashayed over to a stack of furniture that almost reached the ceiling and carefully removed a stool from the pile. She sat, watching Benton expectedly.

Grumbling under his breath, the shop owner disappeared behind the curtain again.

"He's one of the good ones even if he doesn't let it show on the surface," Alwyn promised.

I was still on the fence, but it meant a lot that she trusted him.

"When we first walked in, you said that, to the humans, this was a consignment store. Is it something else to the fae?"

Benton's deep voice sounded from behind as he reappeared, holding a tray with Alwyn's requested tea. "To the Folk, this is the official face of the Seelie Quadrant."

THIRTY
WATCHED

AEDAN

I sat atop Kali, scowling at the back of a Southern representative's head. I had only been awake for a few hours, and I was already in a foul mood. Trekking through yet another dumping of snow to the training arena to find the locks damaged by ice had been the start of it. Then, only half the army showed up for training because the other half had been commandeered by the palace to work on shovelling pathways. The workout thankfully helped bring my boiling rage down to a simmer.

But the true icing on the cake had been when I was given *escort duties* to the party of officials that were leaving to free up some space in the palace.

Escort duties. As if I were still a boy, trying to prove his worth.

Embris had not been in a mood to push—something in the air today, it seemed—so I gritted my teeth and dutifully accompanied the group. It was a day's ride to the edge of the Unclaimed Land, where all the regions met in the middle. The land that overlapped each one belonged to no party in particular; in fact, it had its own wild magic within those borders. Something to do with the magic of each region meeting there like a current. There was probably a more in-depth explanation, but history had been my least favourite subject, growing up.

With a clang in my chest, I thought of Diana, who would probably chastise me for forgetting and give me an entire lesson on it while we rode.

It was hard to think of her. It was tangible, a physical ache in my body, one fuelled with regrets and guilt.

By the end of the day, we would reach the border, and by midday of the next, I could wave goodbye to my charges. Without any other guards with me, I would be able to travel through the night, hopefully returning in time to make that evening's meeting. And one day closer to bringing the princess home.

One step at a time.

When we reached the outskirts of the Northern border, it was well into the night. I'd endured enough hemming and hawing from the group to almost give in just for some peace and quiet, but I was glad we'd pushed on. They wanted back to their court, and I wanted back to mine. They could endure a sore ass for a day or two. Gaia knew they'd been enough of a pain in mine.

The officials were too tired to do much more than eat a quick meal, so I didn't bother making too large of a fire. Once we passed into the Unclaimed Land, the balmy, moisture-thick air had us shedding all the layers we could.

"So strange," murmured one of the Southern officials, staring at the snow coming down just across the clearing.

There was a clear line where it did not dare fall, and crossing it had made me tingle all over. The magic here always put me on edge.

"Rest up," I told them all as they departed into three small makeshift tents—thankfully put up with magic; otherwise, it would've taken them until dawn to get them assembled. "We leave at first light."

There was some grumbling, which was to be expected, and in

truth, I didn't care what they thought of me. As long as I was doing my duty to escort them safely back to the Southern Isles, they could dislike me all they wanted.

I curled up on the now-spread roll I'd attached to Kali's saddle, favouring the night air and the sporadic breeze that came with it. Plus, this way, I would be better alert to any changes and could keep an eye on the horses as well.

Staring up at the stars, I willed sleep to come. It was peaceful, listening to the orchestra of the frogs and grasshoppers. It lulled me, pulling my eyelids down, and I was almost asleep when it suddenly went quiet.

Silent.

I jolted upright, every nerve in my body on edge. It was easy to slip into my training, slowing my breathing until it was inaudible and carefully getting to my feet. The knife I'd slipped under my roll was held loosely at my side. Nature was one thing you could never outwit. Animals suddenly going quiet meant there was a threat nearby.

I scanned our entire clearing twice more before I ventured farther out. The hair on the back of my neck stood up, bringing my magic to the surface, ready to lash out.

The horses started to shift among themselves, and Kali's entire focus became locked on one bush in particular, her ears never wavering from their upright position.

I crept toward the bush, releasing a wave of magic to swim out ahead of me, sheer and shimmering, to absorb any surprises. The leaves were rustling. With a deep inhale, I plunged my knife into the bush, my arm catching on the branches.

The knife met no resistance, and from the bottom of the bush shot a rabbit. It raced away, disappearing into the night.

Cheeks flaming, I yanked my arm from the foliage, cursing

myself for letting fear take such a strong hold on me. At least no one had witnessed it.

"Except you," I muttered, locking eyes with my grey mare.

She snorted once, and I could swear the look she gave me said, *You really fell for that?*

Even with the apparent threat of being nibbled on now gone, I didn't sleep. I leaned my roll against a tree and stared into the darkness, trying to convince my body to calm down.

But no matter what I tried, I couldn't shake the feeling that I was being watched.

"Thank you for the escort, Deputy Captain. You sure made good time."

The Southern guards had ridden to meet us at the border, pleasantly surprised that they wouldn't have to wait another day on the outskirts.

"Please tell the queen we are most grateful she sent her finest to accompany them," another said, nodding her head in appreciation.

I returned the gesture. "It is important to the North that we treat our guests as our own."

Kali carried me swiftly back into the Unclaimed Land, surefooted and unbothered by the previous day's travelling. We were easily cutting our time in half. As we drew nearer to the Northern border, something shrill called through the air. Eerily resonant and high-pitched, unlike any bird call I knew. It threw Kali off as well, causing her to spin around in search of the noise. She was a war mount, bred and trained for bravery in battle, and she was always on guard.

"Screw this damn forest."

I dug my heels into my mare's sides, and we took off again. Every minute longer I spent in this creepy land was setting my teeth on edge. The sooner we were back on Northern soil—or snow, rather—the better.

In the distance, I could see white rimming the horizon. "Come on, Kali. Let's go home."

She added another burst of speed, and even though I should have been relieved to be getting closer and closer, I felt an increase of panic settle in. It was absurd, but I had the innate feeling I was being chased.

"Come on. *Come on.*"

That shrill call sounded again, and I whipped around. If I saw what the culprit was, I didn't make any sense of it.

Because there was a sharp twinge in the back of my neck, and suddenly, the world went dark.

THIRTY-ONE
DEMONSTRATION

DIANA

Alwyn sipped her tea politely, thanking Benton when he produced chairs for us all to sit. My legs moved on their own, seating me, and it wasn't until a cup was placed in my hands that I remembered where I was.

In the headquarters of the Seelie Quadrant.

"Has she never had tea before?" Benton half whispered to Alwyn as I stared into the steaming drink unseeingly.

The female chuckled. "You know, I'm not sure. Maybe she's never seen it. Do your Seelie drink tea over there, Di?"

Benton sat up straight. "You are from the lost land?"

I nodded, finally finding the muscles to clear my throat. "I had no idea there were Seelie over here. I thought the fae were completely separated during the war."

"Our oldest stories say there was a group of Seelie that was displeased with how their queen was ruling, so they joined forces with the Unseelie in hopes of dismantling her. They came over with the mass exile all those years ago. Of course, our numbers are dwindling. There are very few left who have the original Seelie magic."

"Wow," I breathed.

"Benton is one of them," Alwyn added. "No need to be so modest, old friend."

The male grunted. "It's a sensitive piece of information. Having magic in this gods-forsaken town is bad enough, but if it were known that I wielded the kind of magic that had sent the Folk to their deaths here? I would be hunted down."

"I thought the Folk knew about your store? And what it truly is?" The tea in my hands was likely getting cold by now, but I didn't want to lose focus for a second.

Benton sighed. "The Seelie Quadrant is not as well respected as it used to be. The Unseelie and other Folk see us now as more of a sympathizers group than a real force. To the public, the true Seelie died out centuries ago, when their magic left."

My heart sank. "So, the Seelie magic is not viable here anymore?"

"I didn't say that." Benton raised a hand in the air, and the front door swung open.

Gusts of wind came barrelling through, pulling my hair free and sending it flying. The air was crisp and cool and smelled of home. Each drag of air into my lungs felt like I was back in Eira, deep in the forest, riding as fast as Finnvarra's legs could take us.

The air died down, and as the door slammed shut, so did my heart. There was a gaping hole inside that I hadn't allowed myself to fall into, and I wasn't going to jump now. Not when we were so close to getting home.

Alwyn was grinning, her sandy hair in knots. "That will never get old! The storm wielders can shape wind, but nothing like that! That's air magic, through and through. Wouldn't you say, Diana? You're the expert after all."

I laughed hollowly. "I wouldn't say I'm an expert anymore. That was pretty impressive though."

Benton drained the last of his cup. "I doubt it compares to what the air users in their true homeland can do."

"Trust me, you're right on par with them. In Eira, the air wielders live in the East, on this giant plateau by the ocean. It is the windiest, most open-aired place I've ever seen. I don't think I got the salt out of my hair for weeks."

Benton smiled wistfully. "What I wouldn't give to see that."

"That's why we're here," Alwyn said gently. "To bring you home."

"You paint a peaceful picture, and yet you only plan to use us in your war."

Alwyn shook her head. "That is not true. We want to bring everyone back, all the Folk, to be reunited where they're supposed to be. Diana has given us her word that the Seelie will talk."

"How can you promise such a thing?" Benton swung his head to me.

I tried to sit up straighter, feeling like an imposter. "I was the high princess there. Heir to the throne."

"You *still* are," Alwyn corrected. "The queen is her mother. She will listen to Diana."

I nodded, even as a slimy unsureness gathered in my gut.

Benton's eyes widened. "Can this be true?" he breathed.

"We need the Seelie Quadrant's support. When we make the portal, they have to be ready to go. Ready to play nice with everyone. It's going to take a huge effort, but if we're united, we can make it home." Alwyn's voice took on that of a leader before a big battle, prepping her soldiers. It seemed to be working.

"I will speak with the council. When they learn of this, they will be willing to do as you say." The male turned to me. "Perhaps, if you could do a demonstration before the council, show them that you are truly of Seelie magic, it would help drive the point home."

I faltered. "Uh, well, I would love to do that, truly. But the problem is, ever since arriving here, I haven't been able to access my magic. It's sort of … stuck, I guess."

"I've been told the original Seelie settlers had trouble adjusting at first too."

My head snapped up. "What?"

Benton nodded. "The journals I've read say that quite a few struggled with the realm change. The magic is much different over here."

"Do you know how long it took them to get it back?" I urged, fully aware that I had perched on the edge of my seat and was inching closer and closer to him. Hope cracked open in my chest, a wild flight of relief.

The Seelie rubbed his hand over the back of his neck. "I'm not entirely sure, but it was different for everyone. I'd say the average was anywhere between a few months and a few years."

The hope in my chest plummeted to my feet. The eclipse was in a week. We couldn't wait months for my magic to return.

Alwyn grabbed my hand in hers. "That doesn't mean anything, Diana. From what Spense has told us, you were extremely powerful. The heir. That timeline likely doesn't apply to you."

I just nodded, unable to meet her eyes or Benton's. Alwyn began making plans with him, tactfully taking over so I could process. When we stood to leave, Benton bowed his head to me.

"I cannot tell you how happy you both have made me. I look forward to serving you as my high princess one day."

Tears pricked at the back of my eyes. I wanted to be a good leader, one who would bring peace to Eira and unite the fae once more. I wanted it more than anything. But how could I do that without my magic? How could I protect an entire realm when I had failed in the only real battle I'd ever seen?

And maybe I couldn't. A weight lifted from my shoulders at the revelation.

But I would still try.

THIRTY-TWO
SCARS

DIANA

After Benton had waved us out of his store, Alwyn complaining loudly about how he never visited her, we took a different street than the one we'd come down.

"I can't wait for you to meet them," Spense's sister said emphatically, squeezing my arm.

"Who?"

She only gave me that wicked grin of hers and tugged my hood up higher on my head. She pointed out Folk residences as we passed. "That's the pixies' pub. It has a secret basement that's off-limits to humans. There, that's the apothecary that everyone in Rathe goes to. The healer there, Mora, is a brownie and has to apply glamours every day to appear human. They always come sniffing around, hoping to find something incriminating in her shop. But all she keeps on display are ingredients, the same that the humans use. She'll make you custom potions from her home, if you need."

We stopped in front of a corner building, the faded letters reading *Slote's Winter Accessories.*

I looked to Alwyn in confusion. "How is this shop still in business?" Although, as I peered through the dusty windows, it didn't look to be inhabited at all by the broken shelves and empty walls.

Alwyn tugged me to the door. "It's abandoned. At least to the non-magical eye."

She pulled me into the store, and my eyes watered as an entirely different scene slowly came into focus. Barren, cracked walls became whole and bright white. The debris on the floor disappeared, leaving small tables and various toys in its wake.

Children were everywhere, sitting cross-legged or playing with each other. Older patrons kept close eyes, helping and stepping in when needed. It was a quiet sort of chaos.

"This is the future of the Folk."

I gripped Alwyn's hand, my heart fluttering. These children were not just Unseelie. There were blue goblins like Pik, chubby gnomes, even tiny sprites flitting about.

"It's beautiful."

"Alwyn!" A lovely female smiled widely as she greeted us. "What a pleasant surprise."

"Nemani, this is Diana. She's my new sister, and I was hoping to introduce her to our lovely little rascals. Diana, this is Nemani, headmistress of the Home for Folk Youth."

The dark-skinned female took my hand, her eyes shining. "Sister? Congratulations. It's a pleasure to meet you, Diana. This is the only orphanage in Rathe. We are proud to have you visit."

"This is amazing," I gushed. "It can't be easy in this city."

"Not always." Nemani smiled wistfully, looking out to the group. "But it is necessary. And we are so honoured to do this. The children are the very best of us. Anything we can do to set them on a path to success in life, we will."

A small girl came up to Nemani, sniffling as her eyes watered. She reached her arms out, silently requesting to be picked up.

The headmistress obliged, cooing, "What's wrong, Addie?"

When she rocked the girl to her chest, I noticed the child's ears. "Is Addie human?"

"Yes." She tucked a piece of brown hair behind the girl's ear. "We don't turn any child away. In fact, being able to shape young humans might prove to be one of the ways we find peace in Rathe again."

"The magic here doesn't affect her?" I wondered.

Nemani shook her head. "Children have the wonderful gift of completely open minds. She has not started shutting off those pathways in her brain yet. And with our help, she won't."

I was speechless, my heart warm.

Alwyn gestured to a group colouring at a round table together. "Why don't you sit with them for a few moments? I need to speak with Nemani."

She pulled the headmistress aside, presumably to inform her of Ivywall's newest plans. I gladly made my way over to the children, crouching near their table. Three fae and one gnome looked up, questioning. A male sat with them, probably around my age, with kind eyes. He smiled at me when I joined them.

"Say hello," he guided the children.

They all chimed in various greetings, their curiosity dimming.

"What are you drawing?" I asked the boy closest to me.

"It's a drake," he told me proudly. "I'm going to be a rider one day."

I chuckled. "With that confidence, I have no doubt you will."

The supervisor extended a hand to me. "Welcome. I'm Giro. I overheard that you joined the Drakenis family. I have always been curious to know who Badras would end up with."

My cheeks flamed. "Oh, um, actually, it's not Badras. It's Spense. Do you know the family well?"

Giro's face darkened, his smile slipping. "I do. I was in the Unseelie army for ten years. I served with Spense. Or under him, I suppose I should say. My apologies. I was under the impression he had gone away."

Immediately, I felt as if I was wandering into dangerous territory. But it was a chance to learn more about who Spense had been before he came to Eira.

"He was away," I ventured. "But he's back now."

Giro made a noncommittal grunt. "Not even a soulmate could keep him from the power, huh?"

My brow furrowed. "Are you talking about the soul magic?"

The ex-soldier shook his head, his gaze lost to memories. "I'm talking about the power of the army. Of being the one who controlled everything. Urdan gave him full rein of it, even while Sorin was still technically its head. There was not a move made that Spense had not orchestrated. By the end of my time there, it had consumed him. He didn't even do anything for fun anymore. It's part of the reason I had to get out. All darkness and no light takes its toll. I just couldn't do it anymore." He looked to the children, who had resumed their artwork. "Here, I smile every day. These children don't know darkness, not yet."

My shoulders caught on a deep inhale. "I'm sorry he made you so unhappy."

"I don't blame Spense, and you shouldn't either. It was the power. It corrupts. During our younger years, he was one of my greatest friends. We had a rather traumatic experience during our trial that bonded us, and I never held him accountable for the work his father was forcing him to do. Him being the king's personal right hand—that was something we were all proud of at the time. We just grew up and became different fae." Giro studied my face and hastily added, "I'm not trying to upset you. I'm sure he's changed. In fact, I'm positive of it. The Spense I last knew would not have had any time to find himself a soulmate."

I attempted to match Giro's small smile. "A lot has changed in him, and I think he's trying to figure it out as much as I am."

One of the children leaned across the table to grab a coloured pencil and knocked several others onto the floor in the process. Giro leaned over to scoop the rolling utensils, and with his back to me, I was unable to hide a gasp when his shirt rode up, exposing harsh lines of scars across his skin.

He righted himself, depositing the pencils back on the table. He looked at me, a sadness in his face. "Don't worry; they're old. Traumatic experiences and all that," he joked weakly.

Bile crept its way up my throat. *Gaia, please don't let those scars be what I think they are.*

"Were—were they from …"

Giro took my hand gently in his own. "I hold no ill will toward Spense. These scars are from the army. We all carry them, whether you can see them or not. I would wager Spense's run much deeper and more painful than mine."

"Do you want to colour my drake?" the little Unseelie boy asked me, shoving his paper down the table. "The wings have to be black, but you can pick any colour you want for the body."

"I would love to. How kind of you to offer," I replied, choosing a green from the communal pile. I began shading in the oval body, grinning at the size of the misproportioned head.

"That was wonderful sharing, Javeel. Well done," Giro praised.

I listened to the children chatter for a while, Javeel instructing me on staying within the lines of his drawing, and by the time Alwyn joined us, my smile had become permanent.

"I think Diana needs a career change," the female remarked, leaning over my shoulder. "This drake is exquisite. It looks just like the ones at Ivywall."

Javeel preened. "I know. I'm going to ride them one day."

Alwyn grinned. "Well then, may I keep the drawing? That way, the drakes will remember how well you depicted them when you come to join the riders."

The boy's face lit up, nodding so hard that his head could have come clean off his shoulders.

"Thank you, Giro." I stood, ruffling Javeel's hair. "I needed that."

He smiled. "I wish you and Spense a life of peace together."

"I'll tell him you're doing well."

Giro inclined his head. I waved to the children and to Nemani and followed Alwyn back out into Rathe. She was tactfully quiet as we made our way back to the camels, letting me bask in the happiness of the children for as long as I could.

Because the moment we rode out of the city, reality was back. And it was harsh. But this time, I held more hope in my heart. Determination. Those children deserved a future where they wouldn't have to hide in a glamoured shack. I wanted nothing more than to see them free to run and play in the beauty of Eira, unburdened by war. I would bring that change for them.

It was possible. That was evident in Spense. Change was in the air, strong and heady like magic, and I was ready to wield it.

THIRTY-THREE
PRECIPICE

SPENSE

Six days. Only five more sunsets and six sunrises until the eclipse was upon us. It was my first thought every morning, and it did not leave my head all day.

All the preparations had been keeping me far from idle, and I was thankful for it. Throwing myself into plans for an entire race to leave the realm was no small undertaking. Where I could see the stress starting to manifest in my siblings—most especially Olys, who was close to reaching his limit—I was thriving. Never in my life had I felt such purpose, such drive. And toward a goal that benefitted literally *everyone*.

The thread that hung in the balance: Diana.

She was trying, and, gods, I knew she was giving it her all. But her magic had yet to make an appearance. Between her meditations with Sorin, her drills with Alwyn, and all of us taking shifts consulting every one of the texts we had in our library, I worried that she might be too exerted to be able to reach it now.

"We need to discuss alternate plans," Sorin remarked quietly to me.

He had silently joined me on a shady bench, looking into the training ring. Diana swung a sword around in the middle, darting around as Alwyn tried to win a point against her.

I chewed on my bottom lip. "You mean, wait for the next eclipse? I can't imagine how we can go another few months like this. Not to mention having to tell everyone that it's not happening now."

We hadn't wanted to tell the general public about our plan to leave Rathe in the literal and proverbial dust, for fear of getting hopes up. But it didn't seem fair not to give them enough time to get their ducks in a row.

It was another reason I had been subtly keeping Diana away from the busy areas of Ivywall. The buzz about finally returning to Eira was flying, and I didn't want to put that pressure on her.

"I know, brother, but we might not have a choice."

"Is meditation not going well?"

Without warning, Badras plunked down on my other side, effectively squishing the three of us together. "Of course meditation isn't working. It's glorified napping. What she *needs* is to jump-start her magic into coming back."

Sorin rolled his eyes. "I don't even want to ask."

Badras grinned, that savage smile that brought fear into those who were against him. "Come on, brother. Surely, you can see that, in all your years of wisdom? What she needs is a high enough adrenaline rush that will allow her magic to override whatever's keeping it locked up tight."

"Diana has flown drakes, fought humans, gone undercover into Rathe, all while being an outsider in a strange realm. Surely, her adrenaline would have kicked in by now," I deadpanned.

"Maybe we're all a safety net. Anytime she's been in that kind of danger, she's been around someone with magic. Someone who will protect her."

I turned to Sorin, waiting for him to take my side, but he was pensive.

"Maybe you're onto something."

Badras huffed, gloating.

"You think Diana needs more surprise and high stakes in her life? I thought your stance was that she needed to find inner peace, become one again, all that." I didn't want to see her in any more upheaval.

Sorin watched the aforementioned princess spar in the ring. "No, I think her upbringing gave her a great deal of training in keeping calm in dangerous situations. But can you think of a time where she lashed out, was out of control?"

I went silent as the memory Sorin had referenced played in my mind. "She killed someone who was going to kill me. She hadn't meant to."

That day in the forest—as we stared into a fully formed portal, Diana's wild and beautiful magic swirling around us like a warm bubble—was a day I'd never forget. She'd lost control when she tried to save me, and one of her guards had been killed.

That act of protection—of *love*—had given us our tattoos.

Badras stroked his chin, where stubble had now started to speckle his jaw. "I think I see where you're going with this. And if that's the case, I want the first pass at Spense."

"Very funny."

"All joking aside," Sorin interrupted, "it might be something to consider if nothing progresses in the next day or two. We would have to make it seem real, of course, so brothers sparring would not work."

Badras grumbled while I considered this. In the ring, Diana stopped for some water and looked at me quizzically. I smiled and offered a thumbs-up.

"Let's do it."

"Really?"

I nodded. "She would do it for me. Besides, I won't be in any real danger. She just has to believe that I am."

Badras smiled, positively wicked. "I have the perfect idea."

Three hours later, I stood at the highest point of The Cliff, the wind whipping through my face the only reprieve from the sun beating down.

I could make out Sensara below in her nest, staring up at me. Hopefully, she would not try to rescue me, or the plan would be ruined.

Olys stood beside me, a hood around his face. He hardly needed it, however. We would be moving fast enough and far enough away that Diana wouldn't be able to recognize my attacker from the entrance under Ivywall.

"I would like it known that I do not approve of this."

I waved a hand in the air. "So you've said."

My brother's glare could break glass, but I ignored him as I took one last look at the bottom of the chasm, where Sorin and Badras waited in case Diana's magic failed.

Was it a great idea? No. I could admit that. But it was worth a try.

After training, Alwyn had suggested flying to cool them down. Her only part in this was to tell Diana to meet her at The Cliff, and we would do the rest. She couldn't come, or Diana would expect her to step in.

There.

Movement at the entrance caught my eye. Long chestnut hair flew around in the wind, and she looked around for Alwyn.

Immediately, I ran at Olys, allowing our swords to clash loudly. The wind would carry it down—with the help of Badras's wind.

"You'll never get away with this!" I cried, feeling the words slip into the wind.

Olys pursed his lips as he swung at me. "That was dramatic."

I shrugged and allowed his next swing to push me back, inching toward the cliff. "Is she looking?"

"She is. Can't tell her expression though."

It would have to be enough. We sparred, and I let him drive me closer and closer to the edge. When we stood on the precipice, too close to each other to use the swords, I grabbed at his shirt. With his free hand, Olys shoved me. I wavered, every instinct in my body urging me to move, to regain my balance, but I let go.

And then I was floating.

Diana's scream ripped through the air, breaking my heart in two.

Why had we done this?

She was going to hate me for causing her this anguish.

Floating soon turned into falling. At this speed, I was no longer able to control my movements, and that sparked panic. I could only stare at the rocky ground as I got closer and closer. I was truly falling to my death.

Air blew from below and cushioned around me. The tingling magic of Badras wrapped protectively over me, and I could suddenly breathe again. My brothers wouldn't let me fall.

As I slowed and turned upright, I caught Sorin's expression—the opposite of the relief that was spreading through my body like a warm drink.

My feet touched sand. Breathing heavily, I laughed when Badras clapped me on the back. My head felt light and airy.

"You should get up there," warned Sorin. His grave voice brought me back to reality.

Diana's magic hadn't worked.

And she thought I was dead.

I whistled to Sensara, knowing she was on alert for me, and within seconds, I mounted up, urging her to The Cliff's entrance. When she touched ground, I launched myself from her back.

Diana was crumpled on the ground, head in her knees, incoherently whimpering.

"It's okay. It's okay, baby." I ran to her, kneeling to gather her in my arms. "I'm here. I'm okay."

When she brought her tear-soaked gaze to mine, my shoulders collapsed.

"Wha—how?"

She was too relieved to be mad right now, but I knew it would come.

"I'm sorry. I'm so sorry." The words spilled out. I couldn't think of any other ones.

We clung to each other, and it was only a minute before she put it together.

"You did that on purpose?" The hurt in her voice was a dagger in my heart.

"I'm so sorry. I wasn't thinking. I—we—we thought it would work. I'm so sorry, Diana. I never wanted to cause you pain."

"I thought you were *dead*." She pushed away from my chest, rising on her knees so we were at the same level. "And I was useless. I couldn't save you."

Fresh tears sprang from her eyes. I reached out to brush them away, but she grabbed my wrist.

"Don't." Diana got up and stalked back into Ivywall, her cedar scent carrying back to me.

I sat on my knees, entirely hollow for a while until Sensara nudged me with her great nose. My brothers had gathered a few feet away, each displaying a look of varying pity. I couldn't stand it.

"She just needs some time. Her emotions are extremely high."

I shook my head. "What do we do now?"

Sorin came up beside me and heaved an arm under mine, pulling me up. "We rest, and we think. Don't worry, brother. All is not lost yet."

As I walked through Ivywall on numb legs, I couldn't help but feel very lost indeed.

THIRTY-FOUR
FALSE PEACE

AEDAN

When I opened my eyes, the first thing that computed was the thudding ache in the back of my neck, as if someone had taken an anvil to it. It made my eyes bleary, and the blinking to try and clear them only made my head pound.

I was in some kind of way. Judging by how quickly I had succumbed to whatever had been injected into me, I must have been drugged. Not many poisonous plants grew in the North after the queen had blazed them to the ground, so whoever had done this must have known what they were doing.

A fly buzzed close to my face, and when I went to swipe it away, I only pulled at tight bonds. My hands were bound behind my back, around some sort of post I was leaned up against.

Get it together, Aedan. Focus. Where are you?

It was so hard to concentrate when it felt like my eyes were made of molasses. I peered around, trying to make sense of what was in front of me.

A clearing. Trees—lots of them. Hot and sticky air. Worn-in dirt path.

Any weapons? The tree trunks were bare, and the branches started much too high up to be of any use. The ground had some rocks scattered around. Maybe if I could kick one toward myself—

"You're awake already?"

A deep voice from behind had me twisting abruptly, sending shooting pain up my neck.

The voice chuckled as it got closer. "Although I shouldn't be surprised. The dose we use is curated for an average size, and you're quite beefy, aren't you?"

A male came into view from my left side, stopping when we were head-on. He was tall and lanky—skinny even. His grey hair was short and thinning in a few areas, and he stared at me with such open authority that he had to be a leader.

The stranger held up his hands. "Now, don't take that as an insult, of course. We just don't see many fae around here built like they could wrangle a bear." He smiled, clearly amused. "Oh, where are my manners? The name's Pawl."

When I didn't respond, he cocked his head to the side and toed my boot. "Not the chatty type, huh? You know, the polite thing to do when someone gives you their name is to reciprocate."

"It wasn't very *polite* when you drugged me and tied me up," I growled. My voice was gravelly and scratched my throat the entire way out.

Pawl laughed again. "Apologies for the dramatics. We mean no harm, just couldn't catch you to talk. You were riding awful fast through here. Tearing it up like you were being chased or something."

"Who's we?"

"The Outcasts, of course."

"You say that as if you expect me to know who that is."

Pawl looked affronted. "Well, you certainly should. We were formed many centuries ago, when the fae born without magic were tired of being treated like we were lower than everyone else."

Maisie had mentioned the fae without magic. They had made her listening stones out of science. If this was the same group, they were dangerous.

"And you've made the Unclaimed Land your home?"

Pawl grinned, a face full of teeth. "The Unclaimed Land is not just a home, but a provider as well. The magic here is wild, untied to any region, and the land shifts to create everything we could ever need."

"What does that mean?"

"It means that we can continue our work in the privacy and shelter that the land makes for us. But that has been jeopardized. And I take it, you know why."

"Why would I know that?"

Pawl finally looked annoyed. His happy-go-lucky demeanour dropped. "Don't deny it. We've seen what's happening in the North. All that snow is rather uncharacteristic this time of the year. Not to mention the abnormalities happening in the other regions. It has spread here too."

My mind whirled. Everything still felt hazy. Save for the shadows, the other regions had not reported anything out of the ordinary. Only the North faced Gaia's rage.

"I see what they say about the North is true. You all think you are the centre of the universe."

Pawl rolled his eyes before reaching toward me. On instinct, I reared back, bringing my knees up as high as they could go to protect myself.

"Relax. I'm going to loosen your bonds so I can turn you around."

The tension around my wrists slackened, enough for me to stretch them out. Pawl gripped my shoulder and pushed. If I hadn't helped swivel, he probably would have been there all night.

Facing this way, I could see into a camp. Bustling with fae going about different works, shelters made into hills and a large copse of trees, and smoke billowing into the sky from a giant firepit. None looked my way, except a pair of sorrowful, deep brown eyes.

"Kali! What have you done to my horse?" I leaped forward, but Pawl had already tightened the bonds again.

"She's fine. Just a little herbal mixture to keep her calm. She was terrorizing the camp—a danger to herself."

I looked my mare over as best I could from this far away. Thankfully, it was impossible to hide blood on a light horse, and she looked untouched. Sleepy but well.

How dare they lay a hand on her! They would pay for that.

"Listen, Pawl. I'd like to get back to my home, and I'm sure you'd like to be rid of me. Why don't you tell me why I'm really here?"

"Straight to the point—I like it. Maybe we'll be through before I have to administer your second dose."

He had to keep me with enough drug in my system that my magic would be dampened. But how would he know if it returned? I reached down deep and tugged, feeling a tiny quiver. My magic would be back soon—enough to fuel an escape. As long as the Unclaimed Land's wacky energy stayed out of it.

"I assume you don't know about the prophecy then." Pawl didn't wait for an answer. "Back when the fae were separated, our ancestors gifted us with hope. The exact words have been lost over time, but we know that they warned the war was far from done. *And when two become one and the world turns over, the final battle will begin.*"

"Let's say I believe you about the whole prophecy thing. Are you saying that a war with the Dark fae is coming?"

"No! Two becoming one means the Seelie and the Unseelie will finally be reunited."

"If we're united, who are we fighting against?" I tried to keep the sarcastic edge out of my voice, but this was quite the tale.

Pawl's mouth opened and closed like a fish. "Have you been taught *nothing*? The Seelie queen is the root of evil. She must be taken out. *She* is the final battle."

I laughed. "The Seelie queen? You mean, the original queen of the realm, who's been dead for over eight thousand years?"

"Of course your history books would say that. She has been controlling the narrative for millennia. Yes, she is alive! You have been living in a false peace for *centuries*, happily gobbling up all the lies as long as it means you don't have to put any real thought into it." Pawl's face had gone red; he was practically spitting as he spoke.

"If the Seelie queen lives, who is she? If she is as malicious as you say, surely, she would not have allowed others to take the throne while she sat idly back."

"I do not know her face, only her name—Ilysia. For all we know, she could be pulling the strings from behind a powerful figure. Or she could be biding her time, glad to sit tight in the world she's created. I don't know. But if we aren't ready for this battle, Eira will be lost forever."

It was clear that Pawl stood behind his thoughts with pure conviction. Swaying him to see reason was out of the picture, so that left only one tactic for me to get out of here alive.

"And how do you expect I can help with that?"

"You have the ear of the palace, judging by your uniform. And those gold bands—that means you're high up, doesn't it? With you in our ranks, the Outcasts could stand a chance at saving everyone."

Pawl was frighteningly confident.

"Suppose I wanted to help you out. I can't very well risk my position and trust at the palace if you don't have a real plan or force to back you up."

Pawl had said the Unclaimed Land was a provider, but based on the half-starved look of the fae in this camp, it wasn't a very good one. My soldiers, powerful and trained impeccably, would squash the Outcasts without even having to resort to magic.

Pawl laid a hand on my shoulder, a knowing smile turning his lips. "Now, my boy, don't you worry about us. We've got friends all over the courts. All we need from you is to be our signal when the time is right."

Spies. The Outcasts are organized enough to have infiltrated the courts?

"Signal for what exactly?"

"You think I was born yesterday? I'm not giving away our whole plan before you agree, Aedan." Pawl ripped away, his hand falling to his side as he clenched his fists.

Even as the fog still lingered in my head, a tingle of awareness floated up my spine. He'd just called me by my name.

And I hadn't given it.

Pawl realized his mistake at the exact moment I did, and the jolly demeanour vanished completely. "Freya, you'd better take over. I've screwed it up."

"Oh, my love. You did so well. This is not an easy task." A soft, smooth female voice sounded from my back.

How had I not heard someone come up behind me? Her back to me, she walked over to Pawl and placed a hand on his cheek, which he leaned into.

Her voice—it was so familiar.

"Besides, I think it's time Aedan and I were reacquainted."

She turned to look at me, and suddenly, I couldn't breathe.

Staring back at me, brown hair greying and body as lithe as the fae in the camp, her scent so sweet and floral, was my mother.

THIRTY-FIVE
SALVATION

DIANA

My hands were numb as I gripped the glass of water between them, my fingers turning white at the ends from the pressure. I had been frozen in this spot for an hour, staring out my entirely too-tiny window at the endless sand.

The betrayal and hurt after the events on The Cliff had begun to pass, but I clung on to it. I was desperate to feel them, to feel angry at Spense, rather than acknowledge what I was truly feeling.

Fear that my magic didn't work, not even in the moment I'd needed it most.

Guilt over the lives that would be affected if I failed to create a portal.

Desperation for someone—*anyone*—to take over this whole thing and tell me it was going to be okay.

But mostly, I was afraid of the shame that crept up like a tide, inevitably spreading.

Spense had been so worried, so untrusting in the magic training, that he'd done something abhorrently mean in a last-ditch effort.

They all thought I was a lost cause. And that was the worst feeling of them all. My hands pressed into the glass, squeezing tighter and tighter until I thought the cup might shatter.

A knock on the door pulled me from my thoughts. I knew who it would be, and I considered pretending I wasn't in here before sighing in resignation.

"Come in."

I stayed where I was, and Spense made no move toward me as he slipped inside and shut the door behind him. Grief was sketched clearly on his face, his head bowed, wavy black locks spilling down his forehead.

"Are you okay?" His voice was soft and gentle. And I hated how pitied it made me feel.

"Not really."

"I can't even begin to tell you how sorry I am. It was so stupid. *I'm* so stupid."

I shook my head. "It was incredibly hurtful, yes. But I understand why you did it."

Spense took a few steps closer to me. "I wasn't thinking. I didn't consider how you would be affected if it didn't work, and that was wrong of me. I was so sure that it was the jump-start your magic needed to come back. Just like how you had saved me in the river that day."

I remembered that afternoon in Nevelyn, when he had changed my opinion of him. Jumping into the freezing, rushing River Nord to save a young girl. I relied on my readily available magic to help pull them out to safety. That moment had made me feel strong, useful, important.

I'd never realized how much I'd taken my magic for granted until arriving in Ivywall.

"I can't believe it didn't work." My voice came out tiny, weak.

"That's what you're upset about? Not about what we ... what *I* did?"

"Believe me, I'm mad at you for that," I confirmed. "But mostly, it scares me. If trying to save you didn't even bring my magic back, what can? I don't want to fail, not when there's so much on the line."

Spense crossed the remaining distance between us and pulled me into his arms. Surrounded by his warmth, his smell, I finally released the tension in my shoulders, leaning into him. The cup slipped from my fingers and landed with the tinkling sound of broken glass, but neither of us made any notice. I pulled my arms in tight and allowed him to wrap around me fully. There, in the cocoon of his arms, I let myself cry.

What started out as silent tears turned into shuddering sobs before long. Every single emotion—good, bad, scary—rose to the surface and was let go. Spense shouldered it all for me. He stroked the back of my hair and whispered in my ear that I was okay, everything was okay, *we would be okay.*

When there was no more and I was a hollow pit emotionally, Spense guided us to the edge of the bed, where he sat and pulled me onto his lap. I lay there for a while, my head on his chest, listening to the steady thud of his heart.

"We're going to get through this, you know," he said. "Whether it takes a few more days or a few more years, we're not going to stop trying. We're going to take everyone home."

"What if it never comes back?"

"It will." His chest rumbled with fervour, sending shock waves through me everywhere we touched.

"I'm afraid of what will happen if we don't make it in time for the eclipse. Everything that follows will be my fault."

"It would absolutely not be your fault, Diana. And I'm sorry if I or any of my siblings ever made you feel like this rested on your shoulders alone. It was our decision to make these plans, to push for the upcoming eclipse. If anything, the pressure of it all might be hindering your magic. Please don't ever feel like you are to blame for the fate of those who live here."

He pulled my shoulders back to look at me. His grey eyes were open, comforting, but still holding that steely reserve I knew so well. "I mean it. You are a gift to us. To me. You're my salvation. My redemption."

My throat worked on a swallow. Tears threatened to spring free again even though I was sure there couldn't possibly be anything left. Even without my magic, the emotion coming off him was palpable. In that moment, I was as confident in him as I could be.

I touched his chin gently, sliding my hand to the nape of his neck. My fingers curled in his hair. "I love you." The words came out sure and clear, just as I was. Just as I had been feeling for a long time now.

Spense shuddered, releasing a sigh—maybe of relief? He touched his forehead to mine. "I love you too. *Gods*, I love you. I have since the moment I met you."

I smiled, my heart warm. "That can't be true."

His chuckle reverberated through my body. "Of course it is. I sat in that hospital bed with absolutely no memory, and you came in, all quiet and observing. We made eye contact, and I swear I felt something spark. We were always meant to be."

I glanced down at our arms, twined together. The black ink swirled from one to another seamlessly. Like they had been made for each other. Like they were two halves of one whole.

"Fate."

I looked up at Spense, who smiled gently, in the way I knew was reserved for me, before he leaned in to brush his lips against mine. It was soft, tentative, allowing me to slip away into an easy existence.

When he finally pulled away, it was only because there was a rap at the door.

"That'll be Alwyn," he said. "She'll be making sure none of us miss her party. I can tell her to leave."

"Wait, I don't want to be rude. It's for her birthday, isn't it? If she wants us there, we should go."

Spense gently peeled me from his lap and set me back down. The bed was high enough that we saw eye to eye while he was standing. It was a much different view than I was used to seeing, and I loved it. Loved feeling equal. Loved him.

"Believe me, she won't notice our absence. Or anyone's for that matter. Her parties always get rowdy."

While the thought of staying in with Spense was hugely appealing, I was navigating a new friendship with his sister, one I intended on growing.

"We can leave before it gets too rowdy."

He eyed me. "Are you sure you're in a party mood?"

I really wasn't. I felt like I had been tipped over and emptied out. I was exhausted and worried and about a hundred things in between. But maybe a little bit of letting loose would help.

With a shrug of one shoulder, I told him, "Not particularly, but I am in need of a distraction."

Spense grinned. "I could think of better ways to distract you."

I swatted at his arm, even as my stomach dipped. "Tell her we're coming."

He planted a kiss on my nose and went to the door. I could hear Alwyn's approving hurrah and her telling Spense to make sure we weren't late.

Smiling to myself, I flopped back on the bed and stared up at the ceiling. A good sleep was probably the best thing for my body right now, but the best thing for my mind? For my morale?

That would be a good party.

Thirty-Six
Dead Body

Maisie

The undeniable sounds of an emergency outside my room yanked me from sleep. I bolted out of bed and swung open my door. Chaos reigned. Servants ran to and from while others gathered in bunches, heads bent low, whispering.

Immediately, the day of Diana's disappearance rushed back to me, filling me with a horrible sense of dread in my stomach.

I caught at the sleeve of Jilly as she hurried down the hall. "What's going on?"

Her eyes were wide as she shook her head. "There's a dead body in the library."

"Who?" Waves of fear rolled through me as the faces of those I cared about flashed through my mind, one by one.

"I don't know—some official. The queen is there now."

I took off down the hall, weaving and bumping into what had to be the entire servant staff.

Guards stood at the staircase leading into the palace. I recognized them from years of serving, but didn't know them well enough to persuade them to let me through.

My mother sat in the common room, pouring tea for herself and a few older servants who sat with her.

"Maisie," she called. "Come. Have some tea."

I squished in beside her, feeling the small couch made for two, *possibly* three, sway under the combined weight of five of us. Ada wrapped her arm around me, and I leaned in close, savouring the safety that I'd never felt from anyone else.

"Do we know who it was?" I asked the group.

"Sir Radtar."

I knew of the male, one of the North's own officials. Aedan had mentioned in passing that he was one who had been vocal about his dislike of the queen's plans.

"I heard it was a murder," Grea whispered conspiratorially.

"Do you think it was the shadows? Could they have breached the palace?" another asked, looking around wildly as if a shadow might pop out from the corner of the room.

"We don't know anything for sure yet," my mother hushed. "He was very old—it could have been health-related."

Lorsey, seated across from us, shook her head. "I talked to Kella before they took her upstairs for questioning—she's the one who found him—and she said he had white foam around his mouth. That is a poisoning—no doubt about it."

Ada's mouth thinned. "No need to get everyone upset over something we don't know yet, Lorsey. Until the queen's statement is made, all we know is that an official died."

The older females bickered among themselves while I sipped my tea absentmindedly. They might never know what had really happened, and in a week or two, they would move on to something else.

But I had Aedan's insight, and he would be there right now, getting all the classified information.

My heart stuttered. No, he wouldn't be. He was on an escort trip and wouldn't be back until tomorrow.

I didn't like being on the outside of things. I wasn't sure when, but somewhere along my secret meetings with Aedan, I had gotten accustomed to insider knowledge. It should be comforting for me to slip back into my role of ignorance-is-bliss servant, but for the first time in my life, it frustrated me.

A high-ranking official was dead.

From the whispers around me, that frightened a lot of the servants, especially the younger girls. They worried about being next.

I just wanted to know what was going on inside this palace. Summer snow on the outside, mysterious death on the inside. Something was going on, and I just hoped we could figure it out before it was too late.

THIRTY-SEVEN
GOOD TIMES AT A COST

SPENSE

Diana loved me.

That was a banner running through my mind all night. I liked to think I had known all along that she felt how I did, but hearing her say the words—first!—had lifted a weight I hadn't realized was bearing so heavy on my chest. She thought me deserving of her love. And I would prove to her every day that it was true.

She glanced at me from across the room, smiling to find that I was already watching her. I hadn't been able to stop all night. With her hair down and a glass of lavender-coloured pixie wine perched gently in her hand, she was the picture of radiance.

"Brother, are you even listening?" Sorin's voice snapped my attention away.

Badras snickered. "Sor, he hasn't heard a gods-damn word you've said all night."

I returned my brother's grin, unapologetic. The lights were starting to go down in the banquet hall, which signalled the end of the polite social hours and the beginning of the *real* party.

Snatching a freshly topped-up flute of wine from Olys's grasp, I started toward Diana. "Excuse me, brothers."

"You owe me for that drink!"

"Put it on my tab." Without looking back, I crossed the dance floor, which was already starting to get busy.

A few self-proclaimed musicians had struck up a melody in the corner of the room, entirely offbeat but somehow charming nonetheless. The room was less than impressive style-wise, following Ivywall's adobe look, but it was filled with camaraderie and playful energy. Something the palace in Eira could never replicate.

I approached Diana from behind, snaking my arm around her waist and pulling her against me. I savoured the way she settled into me, as if without conscious thought.

"How old are you turning, Alwyn?" she asked.

"Today is my twelve hundredth birthday!" Alwyn shrieked, to some applause of the group of females around them.

"Funny," I said. "I remember you having one of those last year."

My sister gave me a mocking face. "You know what? My bad. It's my twelve hundred first birthday."

She put her glass up in a cheer, which all her friends obliged. I recognized them from the drake unit in the army.

Diana laughed with them all. She had a lovely blush along her cheeks, and her eyes shone. The others were the same, laughing with an easy, relaxed glaze over their faces.

"How many of those have you had?" I murmured in Diana's ear, looking at the near-empty glass in her hand.

The purple liquid had been full in her flute all night, and I'd thought she'd been nursing it. Now, I wondered how many times it had been topped up.

She twisted in my arm to look up at me, the green in her hazel eyes almost gone in the dim light. "Are you worried I can't hold my liquor?"

I chuckled, dropping a kiss on the top of her head. "I have no doubt you can handle it just fine. But pixie wine is no ordinary liquor, darling."

She shivered at the use of the pet name, which I found delightful. She shrugged and downed the last of the flute.

"You're right. It's *extraordinary.*" Diana giggled.

My mouth popped open at the sound coming out of her mouth, both extremely cute and shocking.

"You might want to think about slowing down," I said, trying to hold her focus, as she now wiggled along to the tune coming from the corner. "This stuff has knocked me on my ass more times than I can count. I don't want you to suffer that."

Alwyn waved her hand in my face. "Spense! Let the girl drink! She deserves one night. It's my birthday, and I say we DANCE!"

Her friends cheered in solidarity. They all pulled Diana away and led her toward the dance floor, where I lost sight of her, save for the top of her chestnut hair in the sea of bodies.

I pursed my lips. I was happy to see Diana enjoy herself—gods knew she deserved a break. But the pixie wine was made by tricky little beasts who provided good times at a cost. Last time I'd overindulged, I had a splitting headache for three days, unable to eat anything for two. Eventually, the high had stopped becoming worth it. Especially when army training couldn't care less about the state of your hangover.

The eclipse was in less than a week. If Diana was out for three days because of the wine, that was all time lost from training. Swallowing the lump in my throat, I watched the group dance and tried to keep an eye on Diana.

"Still going, huh?" Badras appeared at my side, clapping a hand on my shoulder.

"She needed to let loose," I murmured.

Indeed, the dance floor still boasted a small crowd even though the tempo of the music had begun to slow down. Little curtains had popped up around the outskirts of the room, creating makeshift rooms and seating areas. The shades conveyed a false sense of privacy, which many, *many* bodies were taking advantage of.

Diana seemed not to notice as she laughed along with Alwyn, a fine layer of sweat covering her.

"Clearly," Bad grunted. "Good luck with that." He nudged me with his shoulder as he walked away, aiming toward a female at the door, who watched him with half-lidded eyes.

In a similar fashion, Alwyn left the dance floor to enter one of the curtained rooms, kissing Diana on the cheek as she left. I started toward her, thinking this would be a good time to wrap up the evening.

Joya, a lieutenant in one of the first drake units, pulled a long roll of *joggu* from her pocket and lit one end with a wave of her hand.

"Oh no." I hurried my pace, knowing that in the state she was in, Diana would not deny a puff of the roll, which was three or four different types of psychedelic mushrooms, crushed down and mixed with a few other herbs. That was not something she needed tonight on top of the pixie wine.

I made it just in time to watch as Diana put the *joggu* to her lips and pulled deeply from it.

"Shit."

I put an arm around her shoulders, steering her away from Joya, subtly plucking the herb mixture from her fingers. "You're having quite a lot of fun tonight, aren't you?"

Diana shook her head, blinking rapidly. "Whoa," she said, her voice slurred. "What is *in* that thing?"

Joya laughed and snatched the *joggu* from me. "Enjoy the ride!"

Only Diana did not look to be enjoying the ride at all. Her eyebrows scrunched together, and the red blush left her face, leaving her pale. She began to sway, her mouth opening and closing.

"Hey, hey, are you all right?" I took her elbow gently. "Let's go sit down."

I almost turned away, but was glad I didn't. Diana's eyes rolled back, and her head lolled. I pulled her into my arms, catching her as she collapsed.

THIRTY-EIGHT
LEMONGRASS

AEDAN

Suddenly, I was three years old, staring into the honey-brown eyes of my mother as she lay sick in a hospital bed. My tiny hands wrapped around her arm, clinging for all I could. She was thin and gaunt, and when she coughed, it made a rattling sound in her chest.

That sound had haunted me all through my childhood. Kept me up at night, fuelled my darkest dreams and saddest thoughts. I'd never forget the sound.

My mother smiled at me, familiar eyes crinkling in the corners, and I could only stare. The smile that I'd all but forgotten, fallen away to the bottom of my mistiest, earliest memories. She was my mother, and yet she couldn't be.

My mother was dead. I'd been there when she died.

"What kind of sick magic is this? *This* is what you thought would sway me to your side?" I spat on the ground. "How dare you!"

Freya stepped forward, and I leaned farther back, my skin digging into the post. "My son, never one to give his trust freely. I taught you that, and even as you scorn me, I am proud of it. I have no doubt it has served you well."

"You taught me nothing. You are not my mother."

Freya tsked. "Now, now. We don't have the time for all this back-and-forth. I can promise you that I was the one to carry and birth you almost twenty-five years ago. You were born in the middle of a summer storm, and a tree caught on fire outside our home after being struck by lightning. We took that as an omen of the strength you would have. Of the important path you would walk in your life. We lived in a home on the River Nord that had a swing in the backyard. Have I convinced you yet?"

"Anyone could know those things." I remembered the swing in the yard—one of my favourite ways to pass the seemingly endless hours Embris spent at the palace.

But truthfully, I had no recollection of the lightning story. Surely, my father would have mentioned it.

Freya pursed her lips. "You have a birthmark on your left hip. Your magic first displayed when you were two, trying to get an apple off a tree. You refused to wear clothes for a month—"

"Okay, stop."

"You have heard enough?"

"What would my mother be doing in the Unclaimed Land with a group of no-magics? *She* had her own magic. Lots of it."

"Once, I did." Freya smiled softly. "The Outcasts' cause is important. It is not just about fae born without magic. It is the new era they are creating, the work they are doing to fix this world. When I heard of it, I knew that was where my calling lay. I do remember my own magic. It's blue, like yours, and when I used a lot of it, the house smelled like fresh rain."

I was silent.

"Now, do you believe that I am your mother?"

"That is a strong word for what you are. A real mother wouldn't have abandoned her family to go live in the forest with a radical group of crazies."

Pawl stepped forward, his jaw locked, but Freya held out her arm to stop him.

"I can understand why you are hurt. You believed me to be dead. I did not want that for you, but I could only imagine the heartache you would feel if you knew I had left. You might have tried to follow me. It was better this way."

I laughed quietly, humourless. "Better? To spend my whole life grieving for my mother? To have nightmares of the day you died? To watch everyone grow up around me with their mothers to give them love and advice? You took off like a *coward*. You left me behind to fend for myself. You are nothing to me." And even as the words left my mouth, they stung like acid in my throat. I didn't want to hate her. But I did. I had to. Anger was the only emotion I could trust right now.

Freya nodded slowly, taking a minute to readjust her ill-fitting tunic and straighten her pants. "I am sorry you feel that way, Aedan. Every decision I made was out of love. I wanted to protect you. In all honesty, I fully assumed Embris would remarry, and you would not be without a mother figure. I hoped I could usher in this new world and still find a place in yours. Perhaps I was wrong."

I didn't want to meet her eyes. Couldn't. "Please just let me go."

"I might not be anything to you anymore, but that doesn't mean we're done here. There is work to do, and you can help."

Heat rose in my core, fuelling rage through my nerves. "Why on Gaia's green land would I help *you*?"

"Because without the Outcasts, you stand no chance of seeing the girl you love ever again."

My heart leaped and flopped and did about a million other things before settling into a somewhat-normal pace again. "That sounds like a threat."

Freya shrugged. "It is the farthest thing from that. It is the only offer of help you're going to get."

"The Outcasts expect to be able to make a working portal with absolutely no magic? Using your *science*?" I scathed.

Deep down, a whirring movement sparked to life. My magic, sleepy and groggy, was stirring.

"We do not pretend to have abilities that we do not possess. A portal has to be made by magic and a certain type of it. What we have planned will not only allow for one to be made, but it will finally release the truth into the world. That is the only way we can get Diana back."

I stretched my arms as much as I could with them bound behind me, willing my magic to wake up and start moving. "Why do you even want her back? Some prophecy that might or might not even be about her?"

"It is not just some prophecy," Pawl growled.

Freya ignored him. "It is absolutely about her. The Seelie queen, Ilysia, had a daughter named Diana. It is no coincidence that our princess is named for her. It is a sign. The prophecy speaks of a merging between dark and light. Diana received a soulmate marking with the Unseelie boy, did she not?"

Bile rose in my throat. I shoved the memory of that day down as far as it could go. "How could you possibly know that?"

Only Vera, Embris, and I had left the forest with that knowledge.

"As Pawl told you, we have spies everywhere." She cocked her head, a look of pity crossing her face. "I'm sure that was a hard day for you, having to watch the one you love become mated to someone else."

"My feelings for Diana are of familial love. She was—*is*—my closest friend."

Freya nodded knowingly, and I gritted my teeth.

"And how does the palace intend to retrieve their heir? I am happy to let you go if there is a closer plan in place than ours. I'm sure the queen knows that the portal must be created on the upcoming eclipse and what magic is needed to fuel it. We are probably worrying over here for nothing." She shared a smirk with Pawl.

"I don't trust anything you say to be the truth."

Unease had begun to prickle in my skin. The Outcasts, insane as they were, had a plan. Whether their ideals were true or not didn't change the fact that we were sitting on our asses in the North, wasting days.

"Why would I lie to you? I am taking a huge risk in divulging this. I know you could have the queen's army—led by my ex-husband, no less—here and shutting us down within hours of your return. But I know you see the corruption in the palace. I know you feel it, as I did. Nothing will happen there, not until it's too late. Are you willing to take that chance on your precious *friend*?"

The words sat in the air and in my skin for a few minutes. Every bone in my body wanted to reject my mother and be done with all this. But I couldn't shake the feeling that she was right.

"Well, Aedan, I can sense that your magic is close to returning," Freya started. Pawl jumped to attention, worried, but she waved him off. "We won't need that second dose. He is free to leave."

"*What?*" Pawl spluttered.

"There is not much more we can say that will change his mind if we haven't already. Take a few days to think about it, my son. Our plant in the palace will be making their move soon. We need your help to see it through smoothly."

Freya came over to me and bent at the knee, so we were eye to eye. She reached around, and at first, I thought she might be going for a hug. But she tugged at the rope tying my hands together and freed them, her hair tickling my shoulder. The smell of her, floral and sweet and nostalgic, filled my nose.

I pulled my hands into my lap, stretching and rolling my wrists. Angry red marks dug into the skin. They would likely take a few days to heal.

When my mother stood, she nodded to me. "If you choose to help us bring Diana home, you can meet with our spy by using the code word *lemongrass.*"

"Can't you just tell me who it is?"

Freya only smiled.

"I haven't decided what I'll do yet," I stated.

Slowly, watching Pawl warily, I got to my feet. My neck had a horrible kink in it, and my back felt raw from rubbing against the post. It would be an uncomfortable ride back to the North, to say the least.

"I understand. Thank you for your consideration, Aedan."

She was confident that she'd swayed me—there was no doubt. In her patronizing words, in her smile, in her utter lack of fear in untying me. And I wanted to prove her wrong. I wanted to show her that just because she was my mother, it didn't mean she could waltz back into my life and control it. Me.

But I thought of Diana, and she washed away the pettiness.

I just needed a clear head and a good sleep to think through all this.

Pawl and Freya walked with me into the camp, which had gone quiet, and watched as I saddled Kali.

It was only once I mounted and got my bearings toward the direction of the palace that I stopped and turned back to look at Freya. "Did my father know?"

"Know that I was not dead?"

I nodded.

"No. As far as I know, he never found out."

I wasn't sure what I'd expected to feel from that answer, but something like relief washed through me. With one last look at the honey-brown eyes from my childhood, I urged Kali into the forest, away from the Outcasts.

We didn't slow until we reached the line of snow and entered into the North. My good mare trudged through the thick layer, picking up her legs high to push through the dumping of snow. It was getting dark, but I wouldn't stop until we were back.

As the high spikes of the palace came into view atop the snow-covered trees, it occurred to me that for the first time in my life, I wasn't running away from something.

I was running toward it.

THIRTY-NINE
FUEL

DIANA

I *must be floating.*

My limbs felt free and weightless. My head was clear. Nothing in the world could pull me down right now.

White was all around me. Or was it black? I giggled. It didn't really matter anyway.

Those starry lights were familiar. They bobbed closer and closer to me, and I reached out my arm, hoping to grab one. They looked soft and gooey. I wanted to touch them.

An orb got closer and warped before my eyes. It stretched impossibly fast and tall, and soon, there was a female standing before me, light pouring from her.

Diana.

"Oh, hey." I felt my eyelids struggle to stay open. "I know you."

The female was Iave, the first of my ancestors to visit me during my ascension. She was the same ethereal beauty that I remembered.

"How you been?"

There was a musical sound that vibrated through my body, and I realized it was laughter.

Oh my. It seems you are not quite as recovered as we thought.

"What are you talking about?" I slurred. "I feel *great.*"

I'm sure you do. Joggu *has that effect.*

Joggu? Oh. Iave must mean the herb I'd smoked at Alwyn's party.

Wait. I didn't remember leaving that party. How was I with my ancestors again? There was no Sacred Pool in Ivywall.

Oh, damn. "Please don't tell me I'm dead."

Iave laughed again. *You still have much to accomplish before you join us. Don't fret, my child.* Joggu *contains* gotu kola—*an herb you have particular experience with, do you not?*

"You could say that," I grumbled.

It was commonly used to aid meditations, but I had a somewhat-rare reaction to it that caused me to feel the effects a little too well. Meaning I was usually hallucinating for days. I'd never ended up here though. Wherever *this* was.

"How long have I been out?"

Three days. You are close to waking, which is why I am able to communicate with you now.

Three whole days? That meant the eclipse was only another three away. We'd lost so much time, and I was no closer to regaining my magic. I buried my head in my hands and realized how different this was from the first time I had spoken with my ancestors. I'd been without a body then, unable to move. I was just a being. Now, it felt like I was dreaming, and my body had been cut and pasted into this strange landscape.

Why do you worry so?

"Where do I even start?" I almost laughed as tears pricked my eyes. "Surely, you have been watching me. You know how I struggle to fulfil the destiny you have laid out."

Of course we have been watching. We are always with you. Even to this strange realm, we followed you. A destiny is not something you have to force. It is what will be, no matter how you try to change it.

"But how will I reunite the dark and light without my magic? How will I get them home?"

You are not without your magic, Diana.

"It won't work. Something's wrong."

You are in full control of your magic. Unwittingly, you sent it into a deep hibernation during the portal closure. You need only to will it forward again.

"I never knew magic could go into hibernation. I must have used too much."

It is by far the opposite. It is a punishment you have bestowed upon yourself.

I wished she would elaborate more. All the interactions I'd had with my ancestors made me feel like I was prodding for every tiny bit of information.

"What do you mean, punishment?"

Iave cocked her head to the side. *Tell me, are you still unable to wield a weapon against another?*

I closed my eyes, shame filling me from the inside out. "Yes. I can only see his face."

And what weapon did you use when you harmed Anten?

A gaping hole opened inside my chest where my heart should be. "My magic," I choked out.

Tears flooded down my face. I'd used my beautiful gift for evil, and now, my subconscious was cutting me off from it. Because of me, the entirety of Ivywall and all the Folk were endangered.

"How do I get it back?" I asked finally, when I had stopped the shaking that racked my shoulders. "Whatever it is, I'll do it."

It is not unlike any time we hold back from being our best selves. You must forgive yourself, truly and deeply.

I shook my head. "I don't know if I can, Iave. I did a horrible thing. I don't want to feel like his life didn't matter." My voice came out small, cracked.

Of course his life mattered. And forgiving yourself will not change that fact. Anten fulfilled his destiny. He lived a good, true life, and when it mattered, he was going to spare the life of your soulmate. He has earned a place of honour here.

I lurched forward, looking around at the nothingness. "He's here? He's … at peace?"

He is. And he would be saddened to know that you are holding back because of him.

"I didn't want to hurt him," I cried, trying to speak through the sobs. "Anten was my friend."

I know. He never stopped being your friend.

I wanted for a moment to step into Iave, to feel the warmth of a hug and her calming words in my ear. But innately, I knew that she was not a form that I would be able to touch. I was aching for it. The touch of a maternal figure. For … for my mother.

Use this anguish and fear. Turn them into strength. You can conquer this, as you have conquered all obstacles in your path so far. Let Anten fuel you, not hold you back. The world still needs to be righted. Do not let his death be in vain.

I let Iave's words sink into my skin, my soul, and warm me. She was right. Holding myself back now was not doing any good. It wasn't helping Anten, and it wasn't helping me. Grief was a heavy weight on my shoulders, but I could bear it if it meant getting the Folk back to Eira.

Iave smiled, light pouring from her in waves.

"Thank you," I told her. "Thank you for never letting me be alone."

You are the very best of us all, my dear. But you are not alone, not when your soulmate walks beside you. It is a privilege, you know. Not many will feel the pure joy of life with a partner handpicked for them by Gaia herself.

I smiled to myself. I was lucky to have Spense. He made me better, challenged me, completed me. "He must be worried. He doesn't know about my reaction to *gotu kola*."

My ancestor chuckled. *He has not left your side.*

Around me, the world began to fade and blur at the edges, as if the horizon were stretching.

"I should go to him."

I was weightless. I was floating. I was falling. Spinning.

Good luck, Diana Lightbringer.

The world around me faded, and I fell into black.

My eyes flew open and immediately found his.

Spense leaped from the chair beside the bed I was lying in. "Diana," he breathed, relief flooding through his face.

I could barely concentrate on his beautiful smile, the messy curls, the grey eyes, like a storm cloud right before it rained.

Because I was warm—everywhere. In the best way possible. My limbs tingled. The hair on my arms stood up. I was electric. I was breathing air so crisp and clear. Clarity I'd never felt before.

Magic flowed through every orifice, and I laughed in joy as the sensation flooded me. It flew up and down and out. It sang a melody in my heart that I had been missing for so long.

Finally, when the rush died down and settled into a hum around my body, I looked to Spense with an open smile, which only grew at his look of awe. Of love.

He leaned in to place his forehead against mine, laughing gently. "You're back."

His magic reached out, and mine greedily pulled it in, enveloping us both in a mist of lavender. The ink on my arm flared with heat.

"I'm back."

PART III

FORTY
REPRIEVE

SPENSE

"**W**ell done today, everyone. I will see you all at the same time tomorrow for our final preparation session."

Soldiers filed out of the training camp as I dismissed them. They were fighters at their peak, warriors bred for battle. They were ready, and I was filled with pride.

A few friendly faces clapped me on the back as they passed, others waving as they headed out. When the sandy alcove was empty, I picked up the shirt I had left draped over a rock.

"Interesting method," a voice drawled from behind me, filling me with icy dread.

I turned. "I'm surprised you could find your way here, Father. Who let you out?"

Urdan sneered, his wings flapping out behind him angrily with a snap, "Insolent boy. I seem to remember you leaving with a lot more manners."

"What you remember is my fear and unattainable desire to please you. Since my time away, I've realized that I don't care about your opinions anymore. I know who I am without you."

"Is that so?"

I didn't have to endure my father or his prattling about whatever nonsense he had come to bother me with. I made to push past him, but his hand shot out, catching my shoulder in a vise grip.

I bared my teeth. "Get your hand off me."

"I think not. You have been ignoring my summons, and that gives me the right to punish you as I see fit." Urdan brought up his other fist, and a haze of magic swirled from it.

Suddenly, his twisted face disappeared from my sight, and I was transported to a day much like this many years ago.

My father held me by the shoulder, but I was much shorter, looking up into his angry eyes.

"I'm sorry, Father. I'll do better," I pleaded. "I promise. Please don't hurt her."

Urdan dropped me, the sand rough on my knees. "Use the soul magic correctly, and no harm will come to your precious beast," he sneered.

He'd never understood the bond I had with my drake.

Sensara stared at us off to the side, her eyes questioning as her large head swung between us.

I blew a breath through my lips and bit back the tears that pricked my eyes. My throat burned with the heat of the desert, and I dreamed of the moment I would be released from training so that I could be allowed to gulp down water again.

In the distance, I concentrated on the figures crossing the dunes. They were humans, on a trading trail, and would be arriving in the city of Rathe within the hour. Their camels pulled wagons of goods, and most walked beside them, pulling them back onto the path when necessary.

"Focus, Spense," my father urged, his voice echoing in my head. "Think of how they wronged us. Ivywall will suffer because of their plan to cut trades with the West to spite us. Without the herbs that only grow in forests,

we cannot survive. This group cannot make it into Rathe with the order."

In my heart, I knew there must be another way. These humans were messengers, not responsible for making the order.

Or maybe they are, *a voice argued. It was deep and sinister, the voice of the evil within.*

My head was going to explode if I had to keep thinking about this. About what I was doing. So, I reached into the pull of the soul magic, accepting Urdan's help as he tunnelled us down farther. I let it wash over me, into me, numbing all my senses.

Finally.

I settled in the lead human's mind, easily landing in his subconscious. They were notoriously unguarded. He froze, aware of something wrong, but unable to figure out what.

"That's it," Urdan praised. "Now, search for his life force—there. End him."

I blanched. "But I can erase the order from his mind. He won't remember anything to do with the change in the trade route."

"They need to be taught a lesson. The Unseelie cannot be seen as weak. This is your job, Spense. One day, it will be you who has to protect Ivywall, and you cannot falter. Do it. Now."

He was right. Ivywall needed me. We would not be reduced to nothing, slave to the whims of the humans and their hatred for magic.

The male's life force shimmered before me, mostly grey with tints of darker spots. Those dark spots told a tale of vile acts, unconscionable behaviours. He deserved this.

It was all too easy to snap the line. I blinked, and the human fell.

Urdan's pride bled through the soul magic into me, and I thrived from it. This feeling was the best in the world, and no one could convince me otherwise.

"Again."

I ripped myself from Urdan's touch. "Stay out of my head," I spat.

He chuckled. "When will you realize that you cannot keep me out? The more you stuff down the soul magic, hide it away, the stronger it will become. It calls to me, begs to be let out. Surely, you will not deny your father the reprieve of answering its beckoning."

"That darkness will not destroy my mind anymore. It's nothing more than a parasite that's crying as it dies out."

I shoved past him, the shakiness of the memory finally lifting from my limbs. I would never succumb to soul magic again.

"You might try to resist, but you'll never keep it out for good," my father called, his voice amused. "Better embrace it now. It will come for you—mark my words."

FORTY-ONE
TILL THE END

MAISIE

Something wasn't right.

There was a wrongness in the air, a tight vibration that held like a noose around my neck. As much as I wanted to shake it off, it clung to me.

The worst part was that no one else seemed to notice. I told myself I was just feeling the stress of the palace and working so hard. But I didn't really believe it.

Today marked the third morning since Aedan had left to escort the Southern officials home. Which was a normal amount when making that particular trip, but he'd sworn with fervour that he'd be back for last night's meeting.

My plan to stay a bit more detached from him hadn't taken into account how I would be struck with worry for the deputy.

I'd attended Princess Hollaina after she returned from the meeting yesterday evening, and she offered to share her brandy with me, even going so far as to pour me a glass after I refused. I didn't touch it. Prince Leo joined her in her suite, casting stares at me all night from where I stood by the door. Hollaina had not dismissed me, even when she spoke of her vehement disregard for the way things were being run in the North. Leo had watched me with his snake eyes, waiting for a reaction.

I couldn't help but feel as though I were being tested.

But for what?

Maybe this was leading to the slimy feeling in my gut. Whatever it was, I wanted Aedan's opinion. He was one of the only voices I trusted now.

If he wasn't back today, I would … well, what would I do? Bang on Embris's door and demand he send a search party for the deputy captain?

No. In what world could I ever do that?

They know what they're doing, I chided myself. *Stay in your lane.*

Rounding the corner into the breakfast hall, I sidestepped servants carrying fresh plates of eggs and fruit. Normally, I avoided the hall at all costs during the busy morning rush—made even busier now with all the guests—but Hollaina had asked for a pitcher of orange juice to be brought up to her.

And much to my dismay, the kitchen had sent all the juice to the hall to cut down on trips back and forth.

Squeezing myself between two bodies, I moved to the front and beelined for the drink table. Thankfully, orange was still available. Having to make up a fresh pitcher of juice right now was the opposite of appealing. While wrapping a napkin around the condensation of the glass, I recognized the voice of Ryen Sarton, Aedan's second.

"… not back yet. It's starting to make me nervous."

A voice I didn't know joined him, low and quiet. "What does the captain say?"

Ryen scoffed. "You know Embris. His stance is that if Aedan can't manage a simple escort trip, then he shouldn't be deputy captain. No, if we want to go looking for him, we have to do it outside of the army."

"Count me in."

"Are you certain? This is serious, Kinney. It could be seen as treason to go against the army's orders. At the very least, we could be stripped of our ranks."

Their voices got lower, more urgent. I strained against the noise of the breakfast hall to hear them, stepping backward while making myself look busy moving things on the table.

Kinney's tone was insistent. "I don't care for how the army is being run anymore. Everything that happened with the rift and now the princess's disappearance—it doesn't sit right with me. Aedan doesn't think the same way as the royals. *He* is the only one I want to follow."

There was a clapping sound, assumedly the males shaking hands.

"If he's not back by tonight, we ride out for the Unclaimed Land. I have a group of soldiers I trust. They feel the same as we do. We will back Aedan till the end."

"Till the end," Kinney echoed.

Even though the idea of being in the knowledge of a possible treason was anxiety-inducing, I couldn't help but feel a rush of pride for Aedan. He deserved this loyalty. And it was thrilling for me to know that they would take care of him. I wasn't the only one who'd noticed his absence.

I fought a small smile as I carried the pitcher from the hall and up the stairs to the guest wing. Nothing could stop me from keeping optimism today. It felt renewing to know there were others like me, feeling the same things that they shouldn't be feeling toward the royals.

With my hip, I guided open Hollaina's door. Nothing could bring me down. Not even—

"In order for this to work, Vera *must* die."

Well, shit.

FORTY-TWO
PLAYING WITH FIRE

MAISIE

The glass pitcher slipped from my hands and shattered on the floor, sending orange juice spilling across the marble. My mouth opened and closed soundlessly as I tried to make my muscles do something—*anything*—to move, get out of here, run. But I was frozen.

Princess Hollaina and Prince Leo stood by the fireplace, and their heads whipped around at the sound of the break.

No, no, I had misheard her. *Don't freak out. You just heard her wrong. She definitely did not say she wanted to kill the queen.*

I had only the small, already-damp napkin with me, but I bent anyway and dropped it into the mess. It was instantly soaked and useless.

"Maisie."

I looked around in vain for something to mop it up, ignoring the sound of blood rushing in my ears.

"Maisie."

I craned my neck up and met Hollaina's eyes. I hadn't noticed her move. How had I not noticed her standing in front of me?

"I, uh, I'm so sorry for the mess. The glass—it-it slipped. Uh, let me just get this cleaned up for you."

"That won't be necessary."

With a wave of her hand, the glass pieces pulled themselves back together, skittering across the floor, and reformed the pitcher. The orange juice seeped back into it, and when it was done, I could only stare, dumbfounded, on my knees.

Hollaina bent to pick up the pitcher and took my arm, guiding me up with her.

"Do not be alarmed by what you heard, my dear," she said, her voice soft. "It was only a joke, nothing to be taken seriously."

Her words were like honey, coating together sweetly and thickening in my head. It was a slow tide of relief; I was completely unburdened by hearing her voice.

Leo sighed impatiently. "You are really going to throw away this chance?"

Hollaina gritted her teeth. "I told you how I wanted to do this."

"The gods have given you the perfect chance. Why fight it? At this rate, it could take another few months before you have her on your side."

Their voices sounded very far away, thick and warbly. In some absent place in my mind, I wondered if this was a dream.

"Fine."

Like a pail of cold water being thrown over me, everything snapped back into focus. The honey-thick buzz was gone, leaving me to breathe in what felt like frigid air.

What was *that?*

"Maisie," Hollaina started again, reaching forward to take my face in her hands.

Instinctively, I jerked back, yanking out of her grasp.

She held her hands up, backing away a step. "I didn't mean to alarm you."

Everything was too much. Too much sound, too much smell, too much feeling. Tears pricked at the back of my eyes, but I didn't know why I was having so strong of a reaction.

"What you're feeling is normal. It tends to happen when being pulled from a glamour. And I do apologize for that."

Hollaina must be beyond powerful if that glamour was all her own doing. I had never felt anything like it. I had crumbled instantly to her will.

Swallowing deeply, I focused on the Eastern princess's pale eyes, biting my tongue to keep the tears from overflowing.

"I know you heard us talking. And I don't want to scare you. But the queen is not who you think she is. In order to make everything right, she must be out of the way."

"So, you mean to *kill* her." My voice shook, but I held my conviction.

Hollaina looked at Leo, who raised an eyebrow and shrugged. "It is not an ideal situation. Let me explain fully before you judge what you are going to do."

I looked between the two royals, who stood confidently. Neither of them was worried about being overheard making plans to *kill. The. Queen.*

"You won't let me leave this room, will you?"

Leo smirked, his eyes narrowing. "That depends on you, darling."

His voice skittered up my back, leaving little snake bites in its wake. I shivered.

"Don't scare her, Leo." Hollaina tsked. "We will not harm you."

"You think I won't tell anyone of your plan?"

The princess sighed thoughtfully, taking a minute to collect herself. "I believe you are in great upheaval with yourself, Maisie. Unsure about your footing in the midst of this big dilemma. Given the right motivation, you might be swayed to a different cause."

"And what cause might that be?"

"We are only acting on the words of the prophecy. Our hope is to bring Diana back to Eira and that, with her return, the realm will see balance once more."

Every nerve in me that was the servant Maisie screamed to get out, to alert somebody of the rebels in the palace. But the part of me that was a friend, a dreamer, a *believer* listened intently. I was not so unlike Ryen and his band of soldiers, I realized. They were loyal to Aedan, not the army. I was the same.

I was loyal to Diana, not the Crown. I would always choose Diana. "I'm listening."

Hollaina grinned.

Feeling dazed and a strange sense of pride, I stumbled from the guest chamber. It was well into the afternoon, and I'd be expected to help with dinner chores soon.

Even with the knowledge of Hollaina's extensive glamour abilities, I knew I was in my right mind. It filled me with renewed hope, a purpose to reach for. I couldn't help my smile as I ventured down the palace stairs, wishing the snow would just stop for long enough that I could take a walk in my favourite garden.

At the end of the hall, someone ragged entered through a back servant door. I hurried over to the massive body, dirty and hunched. They stood at the door, brushing snow from a ratty coat.

"Hey! You can't come in this way! Visitors have to use the front entrance."

The figure looked up, and I stopped in my tracks. Aedan's blue eyes looked pained as they searched mine. They were hollow and shaded purple underneath.

"Oh Gaia. What happened? Were you attacked?"

I could only take in his downright ruffled appearance in shock. His cloak was ripped, his uniform dirty, and his usually perfectly styled hair was hanging around his face haphazardly.

He grabbed my elbow and led me away. "We need to talk in private."

I hurried along to keep up with his long strides. "Don't you need to see a healer? Or alert someone?"

Aedan shook his head, barging into a supply closet without warning. He swung me around, and we were suddenly face-to-face, chests pressed together in the tight space. The door clicked shut.

"Did you know about the Outcasts?"

"The—what?" I spluttered.

"The no-magic fae. When you got the stones, did the dealer mention anything to you?"

I thought back to that day. The incense of The Curator's store and the whirlwind of the following days made it all a blur. "Actually, yes, I think he did say something about a group called the Outcasts. That they had been trying to recruit him forever."

"Yeah, well, turns out, they aren't a real friendly bunch."

I gasped, placing a hand on his arm. "They did this to you?"

"It was more neglect than force," Aedan muttered. "I was tied to a post. Anyway, it doesn't matter. They knew who I was. They wanted me to join their forces. Some crap about a prophecy."

Butterflies danced around in my stomach—and not just because I could feel Aedan's heartbeat in my chest with how closely we were pressed.

"A prophecy about bringing balance back to the realm?"

He cocked his head, stunned. "You've been busy while I've been away."

"You won't believe this, but Hollaina and Leo just told me the same thing. I'd accidentally walked in on them discussing their plans to murder the queen—"

"*What?*"

"We'll circle back to that." I waved him off. "They have this whole plan to open a portal and get Diana back. They think she's the meaning of this prophecy, that she's destined to save us all."

Aedan nodded. "That sounds like the same thing the Outcasts were saying."

I shook my head in confusion. "But save us from what?"

"I might have more on that than you. According to the Outcasts, the Seelie queen still lives and needs to be taken out." At the look on my face, he continued, "Yeah, *that* Seelie queen. The original one."

Rubbing my hands over my eyes, I loosed a heavy sigh. "Do you believe any of it?"

"Honestly? I'm not sure. It sounds crazy, but up until a few months ago, I never would have thought I would see a Dark fae or a portal in my Gaia-damned life. I don't know how to feel."

"Yeah."

"But I think … I think it might be our best option to get Diana back," Aedan whispered. He spoke as if he were afraid to admit the words aloud.

I nodded. "I agree. She's worth whatever trouble we're inviting by getting involved with the Outcasts."

"And they *are* trouble. My mother is one of the leaders."

Aedan's mother? "I thought she passed when you were young," I ventured softly.

His face was grim. "That's what I thought too. Turns out, she abandoned her family to join their cause."

"I'm sorry." *Say something else, brain! But, ugh, what can I even say to that?*

He shook his head. "I can't focus on that right now. It's a later issue. The good thing to come out of that strange encounter was the fact that she trusts me. I'm supposed to meet up with her contact in the palace."

We looked at each other. "Hollaina."

"I guess I'll have to make contact soon then. When does she spend the most time in her room?"

"She literally never leaves unless it's for meetings. Her meals all get brought up. She says it's because Vera hates her. Can you imagine how much more she would despise Hollaina if she knew what she was really up to?"

Aedan chuckled. In a heart-stopping, utterly shocking sweet move, he leaned down and placed his forehead against mine. "No matter what happens with the royals, the rebels, or anyone in between, it's you and me in this together. It's our plan, our responsibility to bring her home."

He leaned back again, and I could only nod. He had this way of making me feel seen, talking to me like I was more than a servant. In moments like this, I didn't question his sincerity. I never did, even when I constantly wondered about everyone else's.

It was getting impossible not to notice that I was feverish everywhere we touched. The hard planes of his chest and the steady thud of his heart sent mine into a staccato rhythm.

This was adrenaline. Pure adrenaline, nothing else.

Right?

"This feels like playing with fire," I admitted.

Aedan's eyes danced. "We can put each other's flames out. Maybe all this snow will be good for something."

A smile crept up my face, so rare these days that it felt like it was stretching my cheeks.

"So, what do we do now?" I asked.

"Probably get out of this closet."

"I don't know. I'd love to see the look on Diana's face when we tell her we came up with a master scheme to retrieve her while squished in a tiny supply closet."

He smiled. Damn those dimples.

"I have to get cleaned up before anyone sees me like this and asks what happened. I don't want anyone to know about the Outcasts."

I tried to lean back against the shelving to make room for him to pass, but it really was a tight fit. He ended up having to move us together, sliding sideways out of the closet.

"I take it, Hollaina and Leo believe you're with them?" Aedan asked once we were free.

I nodded. "I said I would help them. I'm not vital to their plan, obviously, so they didn't give me much intel. But I will have a job when the time comes."

"And you're sure you're okay with this? If it doesn't work, we'll be in shit. I'm kind of banking on the fact that Diana will save us from a treason verdict."

I took a deep breath. *For her.* "Let's do this."

Forty-Three

Loyalty

Aedan

I needed a drink.

After stripping off my ruined clothes—and tossing them straight into the incinerator pile—I managed to make myself presentable enough to make the traipse down to the soldiers' compound. I stopped briefly in the stables to make sure Kali was given a mash after her long trip and an extra blanket and made my way to the barracks.

Ryen must have seen me trekking across the snow through his window because he met me at the entrance and ushered me inside.

"You had us worried," he said, clasping my arm and pulling me into a quick hug. "What took you so long?"

I cast a quick glance around the room. It was too busy. Soldiers milled about, and others lurked near the edge of our conversation, looking for a way in.

"Let's go upstairs."

My second led me up to the third floor, where only his room and a handful of other higher-ranked soldiers resided. It pleased me that he had taken over the room meant for the deputy captain with its own bathing room and sitting area. I probably would have given it to him anyway if I wasn't so lucky to have lodgings in the palace. Loyalty should always be rewarded, and Ryen was as good as they came.

"Sir Radtar died yesterday."

I faltered a half step. "How?"

Ryen lowered his voice. "The official ruling is a heart attack, but there are rumours that he was poisoned. One of the servants who found him said he had white foam around his mouth."

I furrowed my brow. The male was generally well liked and respected. He had served as a Northern representative for a long time, longer than I'd been alive. But a niggling thought at the back of my mind reminded me how much he had been speaking up in the meetings lately.

"Interesting."

Ryen opened the door to his room. "Very."

Once we were seated around his fireplace, which was unlit—he would have sent all extra resources to the palace because of course he would—I filled him in. Ryen had my full trust, but I left out any parts that could be used against him. Hell, I even left out how Maisie was involved. I didn't want her being used for the information. The thought of it made me inexplicably hot with rage.

This all had to go off without a hitch.

When I was done, Ryen blew out a breath. "Whatever you need, I'm with you."

"I appreciate that. But hopefully, I won't have to drag you into this. If the plan goes south, I don't want you going down too. Someone needs to lead the army."

"Embris would never pick me as his deputy."

"He would," I countered. "I think, as your own second, you should pick—"

"I don't need a second because you're not going anywhere."

"We can't possibly know that."

Ryen stood abruptly. "This is real, Aedan. There's a group of us—a big one. At this point, it's the majority of the army. We're loyal to you and only you. We'll stand up with you, fight with you, whatever you need from us. We're not going to march blindly under Embris anymore."

Something thick and heavy lodged in my throat. I was lucky. What I was doing was reckless and risky and possibly the stupidest thing I'd ever done, but I was lucky. The support behind me was more than I had ever dreamed of. I couldn't let them down. The swelling in my chest wouldn't let me.

"You're right; this is real. And I can't think of anyone better at my side. You are irreplaceable to me, you know."

Ryen sat again, a red hue creeping up his neck. "Well then, now that that's settled, what's next?"

I inhaled deeply. "I make contact with the rebel in the palace."

My second nodded, a gleam in his eye. "When I was young, I always wanted to be a spy. I guess working with a rebellion right under the Crown's nose is pretty damn close."

"I'll make sure your epitaph reads *spy extraordinaire and rebel accomplice*." I chuckled.

"As long as you don't have to write that epitaph for many years, my friend."

Sobered, I gave him a grim smile. Hope indeed.

"Begin!" Ryen's voice called through the ring.

Immediately, two soldiers sprang into action, swords clanging.

"Thanks for coming," he said to me. "It boosts morale to have you here."

I shook my head. "It's my job to be here. I'm glad they fared well while you were in charge though."

We watched as the female soldier darted through her opponent's blind spot, slamming him on the back of the head with her elbow.

"Nice shot," Ryen murmured. "So, you meet up with this contact tonight, right? How will you know where to find them?"

"I have a code to use to make sure. But I have a good idea of who it is."

Ryen nodded. "You'll be careful." He said it as a statement, not a question, but I knew his worry all the same.

"I will."

"Good."

In a rush of swords and maybe a too-fierce battle cry for a training session, the female ran at her opponent, who easily cut her off at the knees and disarmed her. In a frantic move to get her sword back, she reached blindly for the hilt and missed, slicing her hand a lengthy way along the blade.

"Go get that cleaned up," I ordered, watching blood leave bright trails through the snow as the defeated soldier marched up toward the palace.

Ryen's mouth twitched as he took me in. "Can't believe you let her leave. Last week, you would've jumped in and made her run through her mistake over and over, bleeding hand be damned."

I lifted a shoulder. "No use bloodying up the training ring." Or what was left of it, I supposed.

We cleared the snow every day and used magic to keep it from icing over, but it was still only half of what I would have liked for training.

"Mmm." My second picked up the close-combat knives and handed them to the next set of sparring partners.

We watched silently as they trained.

"Come to think of it, you haven't been doing much extra training yourself."

I glanced sideways at him. "If you've got something to say, just say it. You're using your insinuation voice."

"I just think she's good for you. I'm glad you're finding some peace in all of this."

Immediately, a flash of panic sliced through me. Had he seen Maisie and me together? I thought of her honey-yellow curls and how they stood out. They were beautiful, to be sure, but maybe we ought to have thought of better hiding spots—

"I never much liked her, but, hey, if it gets your mind off Diana, I'll take it," Ryen continued, utterly genuine.

I frowned. "How can you dislike Maisie?"

Ryen's brows knitted together. "Maisie? I'm talking about Jamey, you dolt."

"What about Jamey?"

The subject herself had appeared behind us, as if from thin air. Normally, it irritated me to no end when she just showed up places, but I couldn't be more grateful for the distraction as I avoided Ryen's narrowed eyes.

"Jamey," I greeted, bringing my diplomatic smile forward. "How nice to see you."

She ran a hand down my arm possessively, and I fought the urge to pull away. "Likewise. It has been a while since I've seen you."

Ryen cleared his throat. "You'll have to blame me, Lady Pinois. Been keeping the deputy busy with training."

Loyal.

Jamey inclined her head gently. "Of course. The work you do is so important. And as we know, there can be no slacking during this time."

She gave a knowing look, and I pursed my lips. Her grandfather, Prince Kashdan, must be generous in updating her on palace meetings. Loose lips were never prudent to ignore. I would keep an eye on that.

"Perhaps you might find yourself with a spare few moments for lunch today?"

"Ah." I looked around the training arena helplessly. My absence wouldn't be missed, but the thought of a stuffy lunch with royals and a grand feast of a meal churned my stomach. Really, I could do with some plain old crackers and jam right about now.

"We are expected to lead a bow staff tutorial later, Deputy Captain," Ryen interjected.

"Yes, that's right. Lunch won't work, I'm afraid." At Jamey's pout, I added, "I won't be late for dinner though. Promise."

"All right." Jamey gave me a peck on the cheek and waved at us over her shoulder as she sashayed away.

Ryen's stare was a burn on my skin.

"Shut up," I grumbled. "I can only take her in small doses."

My second only shrugged. "I didn't say anything."

One of the soldiers in the ring fumbled through a movement and dropped his weapon.

I jerked my head at Ryen. "Just get in there and teach him the move."

He laughed under his breath as he ducked under the training rope.

Later, when the sun—what we could make out of it through the white haze anyway—had set and the palace was dark and quiet, I slid out from under my covers. I placed the blankets back gingerly, making sure not to rustle Jamey.

The light of the moon peeked through my blinds, giving me

enough visibility to slip on dark clothing. The thought of meeting with a rebel spy set my heart on a roaring pace, but it felt right. Diana would have done the same for any of us.

I grasped the door handle and twisted it, wincing at the familiar creak it made.

"Where are you going?" Jamey's groggy voice called from the bed.

"I'm feeling ill. I won't be long." I opened the door to my antechamber.

Jamey sighed. "Please don't make me do this."

I faltered. "What?"

A thick coating of magic filled the room.

"I'm sorry," she said.

And then I dropped to the floor.

FORTY-FOUR
SINKING BRIDGE

SPENSE

A filthy curse left my mouth at the sight before me.

"Was this done by them?" Diana asked, coming around my shoulder to see the scene.

"Most likely."

What was left of the Dewy Bridge splayed out across the water. The river was human-made, supplied originally by the mountain range many days away and spurred along by water mills along various points. This made trade routes longer, ensuring a safe water source to fill up along the way.

But this route in particular might be out of commission for a while. The wood splintered in jagged lines, clearly ripped and torn by the creatures dwelling below. Not even half of it was salvageable.

"They must have been desperate to destroy the bridge," I commented, toeing over debris that had likely once been a cart.

Oranges and lemons lay spotted around, some squished but not decaying, indicating that this hadn't occurred too long ago.

"Do you think … do you think anyone survived?" Diana's throat worked on a swallow.

I peered into the water, unsurprised to see a line of bubbles breach the surface. We were being watched.

"No. Stay back from the edge," I told Diana, walking us back a few steps. "Their skin is poisoned by the air, so they won't come up. But I've personally seen them risk their hands, thinking an ankle was close enough to grab."

She nodded, biting down on her bottom lip.

My magic moved on its own, reaching to touch hers gently, envelop it. I still wasn't used to hers being back, the joy that came with that feeling. I didn't think I'd ever get used to it.

"I don't want you to see me like this," I admitted.

The only reason I had agreed to let her come with me to convince the kelpies to civilly enter magic containers was because my siblings were all busy with their own convincing. As trepidatious as I was to let Diana see such a raw, uncomfortable part of me, she had brought me back from the edge before. Maybe she was the piece I needed to keep myself from the grips of soul magic.

I wasn't going back to that dark place. With her here, I would hold myself to it.

She cupped my jaw gently, tilting her head back to look me in the eyes. "I'm right here," she promised. "I'm not going anywhere."

"I love you," I murmured, pressing a soft kiss on her lips.

"I love you too. Now, do what you have to do."

I placed my hands over hers and removed them from my face. Turning away, I walked to the edge of the water, close enough that it lapped at my shoes.

Don't.

The magic settled in me without much thought. It was ready, greedy, to return to me.

The hand—no, multiple hands—that had been about to snatch at me froze right below the water's surface.

I knelt, getting a better look at what lurked beneath the safety of the water. Large mouths with razor-sharp teeth spilling from them; tiny, beady eyes; webbed hands; scales; and gills. The part of me that might have shuddered at the sight was pushed down by the prevalent new voice.

Bring me your leader.

The kelpies struggled, each trying to resist.

But they wouldn't be able to. Not when I dug deeper and twisted, sensing the taste of their souls. It was salty and coppery, filling my mouth with saliva. I was close to full control over them. All it would take was another step forward.

We govern ourselves, a kelpie finally answered. *We recognize no leader.*

This was going to take more than I'd thought.

Then, I need you to relay this message to every single kelpie you can.

The one who had spoken hissed, her claws tearing at the magic wrapping around her willpower.

There is danger coming, I continued. *For the survival of your race, you will need to leave the water.*

We cannot leave the water. We will die.

The kelpies were submitting, lessening their fight against me. It fuelled a satisfaction deep in the worst parts of me.

In two days, the Unseelie will come with containers to keep you alive while you travel to your new home. I pulled tighter at the magic, letting this next sentence be the strongest conviction they would receive from me. *You will not resist. You will go without fighting. And you will bring every kelpie to this surface to make the journey.*

The magic glazed over them, settling deep into their subconscious. My heart beat strong, pumping adrenaline through my veins. This was possibly the best feeling one could experience.

We will do as you say.

I inhaled deeply, releasing them. Immediately, they shot off, strong tails sending water splashing over me.

Soul magic coursed through me, making me feel strong and powerful. Unstoppable. Why had I ever given this up? Who would purposefully keep themselves away from such a high?

There was a tug at the end of my magic, and it filled me with the scent of cedar. I stopped myself just before I shoved it away. That was Diana's magic, and it was good. Slowly, it crept up until I had no choice but to release the soul magic to welcome hers in.

And when I did, fresh, clean air filled my lungs.

I turned, catching her in my arms, resting my chin on the top of her head as I breathed her in. "Thank you," I murmured.

"I felt it work," she said, her voice trapped against my chest. "You have something incredibly powerful."

"I wish I didn't."

"Hmm?" She pulled back, searching my face. "Are you okay?"

I kissed her once. "I am—because of you."

"I have every faith in you." Diana trailed her hands down my chest, eliciting a line of sparks in her wake. "It can't take over anymore. You're different now."

Her constant, loyal trust in me was something I wished I shared. Certainly, I was not the same male that I had been before going to Eira. But one could only change so much. At some level, there was a part of me that begged for soul magic, thrived on it. I had never kept it at bay, never wanted to before. But for the good of the beautiful girl in my arms, I had to.

I pushed all my worries far away and instead filled my mind with Diana. Her kisses, sweet and tender. Her love, all-consuming.

I let it take over as I kissed her, turning the stress into passion.

She sighed a breathy sound as it deepened, and I felt it all the way from my head to my toes.

"You're so beautiful." I ran my mouth along the curve of her neck, peppering her delicate collarbone with kisses.

She looked at me with hazel eyes turned molten, bunching handfuls of my shirt and pulling me back to her.

I cupped her back in one hand and her silky hair in the other, delighting in how her fingers snaked under my shirt and explored my chest. They lingered over the raised scar on my abdomen from my rift experience—the one that had brought me to her in the first place.

I wasn't sure when or how it had happened, but suddenly, she was backed against the old post of the bridge, her mouth opening in shock at the force. There was an unmistakable groaning noise from the broken wood, and I barely caught Diana in time before she fell with it.

We both stared as it crashed into the water, along with several more parts of the bridge.

She ran a hand through her hair and started laughing. It was impossible not to join in, and we didn't stop until the last of the bubbles from the sinking bridge disappeared from the surface.

"Good thing the kelpies won't be here to eat the humans when they try to rebuild this."

"They would deserve it," I scoffed.

Her brow furrowed. "You know that's not true. Not all humans are in this war against you."

"Against *us*," I corrected.

"I'm just saying, it's not fair to judge all of them based on the actions of a few. I didn't judge you when you came to Eira."

I kissed the top of her nose. "And I love you for it. But you're not going to change my mind about the humans. I've seen children play *kill the fae* before."

She sighed. "Let's get out of this stupid realm."

"I couldn't agree more."

FORTY-FIVE
VOLTAGE

DIANA

"It's like he's an infatuated teen," Badras grumbled.

I looked over at him from my spot in the training ring, where Spense was gingerly helping me sit down. The *gotu kola* had done one hell of a number on me mentally, and working to pull Spense from the soul trance had drained me physically. But only two days away from the eclipse, there was no way I was sitting this one out.

I stuck my tongue out at the giant grump, who rolled his eyes.

"That's because he *is* an infatuated teen." Alwyn laughed. She swung a sword around in an arc, testing its weight.

Spense glared. "I'm twenty-five," he muttered darkly.

Olys snickered. "In our years, you would still be considered a baby."

He let out a huff of laughter as Spense tackled him to the ground. They scuffled while the other siblings shook their heads, smiling softly as they prepared the arena.

There was an easiness today. Even though we were so close to such an important moment, the tension had lightened. They were as relieved as I was that my magic had returned.

"Who wants to go first?" Sorin called.

He had brought Meske with him today, whose raven-black hair was tied in an elegant braid down her back, ever the picture of grace. She smiled nervously. It was commendable that she was out with us today, brushing up on her self-defence.

"Why don't you boys show us what we have to beat?" Alwyn declared, plopping down beside me.

Badras grinned. "Such spirit, sister. We'll see how that holds up." He yanked his shirt off over his head and tossed it to the side, revealing golden-tanned skin and muscles speckled with scars. He pointed to Spense. "Lover boy, you first."

Spense shucked off his own shirt and threw it directly at my face, which I caught just in time. His pale skin was so unalike his siblings, making him look ethereal. Since returning to Ivywall and recommencing his daily training, he had started to fill out, packing muscle and definition onto his lean frame. His scars were like branding on him, where they were decoration on Badras. And his tattoos—swirling lines, delicate scrawls, old Unseelie languages—were stark against him. My stomach flipped over itself while I traced the lines with my eyes.

The brothers squared off, and Badras made the first move, as expected. A little behind us, Meske gently lowered herself to the ground.

I patted up beside me. "Come sit front row with us."

I took her arm in mine once she settled back down. "Is this your first training session in a while?"

She laughed, the sound like tinkling bells. "You could say that."

"Couple hundred years, but who's counting?" Alwyn supplied from my other side.

Meske leaned in toward me. "In truth, I am no fighter. I much prefer healing, supporting from the sides. But Sorin was adamant I be able to protect myself and our daughter when we make the trip. He's right, of course. I just get nervous, using my magic in this way."

We watched as Badras and Spense fought with bare fists, using wisps of magic to supplement moves. With all my being, I hoped that Meske would never have to use the training she was here for today. My mother was not the fae I'd thought she was, but I would do everything in my power to adhere to the good-natured side of her.

"Where is the little fox today?" Alwyn asked.

Meske tsked. "I wish you wouldn't call her that. You know it only eggs her on."

Alwyn grinned.

"She's with her tutor right now, helping make lunch for everyone. So, please remember to tell her how delicious it is."

Alwyn scoffed. "If it's delicious, I will tell her. But if it's a horrible invasion to my taste buds, I will also inform her. The girl's got to grow tough skin if she's going to make it in this world."

Meske looked slightly alarmed, pursing her lips while she calculated if her sister was joking or not. Eventually, she sighed. "I wish she did not have to face the burden of such a world."

The sadness that enveloped her words caught me by surprise. "Aislinn is a firecracker, just like her relatives. She will not only face the world; she will change it."

Meske patted my arm. "You are kind, Diana. I admit, I have lost my passion over these long years." She smiled lovingly at Sorin, who watched his brothers spar intently. "I have been blessed beyond what I deserve with him. And we would not take anything back, not even Aislinn. Not even her, though I hate to think of her life spanning as long as ours have."

Alwyn was quiet beside me, absentmindedly drawing in the sand with her index finger. In the time I had known her, she was never one to leave a silence unfilled. The words must have affected her.

"I didn't realize your life span had been lengthened as well," I murmured.

Meske nodded. "She was a surprise. We weren't going to have children," she admitted, voice barely above a whisper. As if she were talking to herself. "We decided it would be too cruel. Heartbreaking. It's a lot to pass on to someone—eternity. Even if Aislinn has a normal life span, how can I watch her grow old and eventually"—she gulped—"die while I have to keep on living until the world fades into nothing? How can I survive that?"

My heart felt heavy, threatening to snap in half for her. She held a huge burden on her shoulders, one I wouldn't wish on anyone. Alwyn's sigh beside me was proof she knew the weight of it. Lived with it every day. Meske's hands fiddled in her lap, and she pulled at her sleeves.

"Perhaps that will be mended when we go back to Eira. Urdan said his life was tied to the Seelie queen's. Maybe when we bring balance back to the realm, it will be fixed. We have to have hope, Meske."

"Hope is something I stopped believing in many moons ago."

Alwyn placed a hand on my shoulder and shook her head once. *It's okay*, she mouthed.

My belly felt like there were giant rocks weighing it down. A sudden, new realization came on like a light in my brain, sending me into a cold sweat. If Spense was like his siblings, he would also live an unthinkably long time. And if the fresh, swirling ink on my arm was any indication, so would I.

Gaia help me, I thought, the old words coming to me before I remembered there were others I could pray too as well. It didn't seem quite right though. Like we didn't have the same history that Gaia and I shared. *Help me figure this out. So everyone can be happy.*

The three of us sat in silence as the males fought impressively.

The high of my magic had faded a little, but I was still excited at the prospect of using it. Like an itch that hadn't been scratched in much too long.

Badras was winning. Although matched by height, he was twice as heavy. And he used it to his advantage. He had Spense on the defence, walking backward slowly until they reached the ring line in the sand. He sent a right hook into Spense's gut, who grunted, bending over slightly.

At the millisecond of vulnerability, Badras jumped. He had Spense in a headlock and was holding him tight, fighting against his brother's squirming.

Then, right as I thought Spense would tap, Badras let go. Stiffly. Absurdly fast. Like he had been burned. He sent his fist into his own gut and doubled backward, landing in the sand.

I stood. What was I seeing?

"Sore loser!" Badras spat, turning onto his hands and knees and trying to catch his breath as he stood.

The smell of Spense was heavy in the air, hitting me like a blast of wind. It was sharp, his usual sweetness, but with a twist of something darker underneath. I recognized the flare of his magic and how it enveloped him at a deeper level than his normal indigo flare.

This was soul magic.

"That was uncalled for, Spense," Sorin reprimanded, joining the circle. "Hardly honourable. Not to mention irrelevant for training. If you attempted to compel every one of your enemy's magic on the battlefield, you'd run out of energy before getting through the first line."

My stomach leaped. Compelling another's magic felt a lot like a glamour. It wasn't sitting well with me. One's will was sacred. And from the sounds of it, Sorin was not unaccustomed to seeing this side of him.

Spense's jaw was clenched tight, a muscle ticcing. His steely eyes were dark, his attention rapt on Badras. His prey.

Sorin stepped in front of him. Pushed his shoulder lightly. "Hey, Spense. Snap out of it."

Spense reacted quickly, shoving out of his brother's grip. "Well, I won, didn't I?"

Around me, his siblings were shifting. Frowning. Whatever change was happening in Spense, they had seen it before.

Without thinking, I set off into the ring, ignoring Alwyn's warning to stay put. I marched up between the brothers on wobbly legs and craned my neck up to look Spense straight in the eye. His gaze was still locked on Badras, even when I reached out and grabbed his hand.

"Hey." It was only when I sent a tendril of magic to him that he shuddered, blinking, and looked down at me.

Immediately, he softened. Returned to the Spense I knew. He stared at me as he wet his lips and took a shaking breath.

He focused back on his brother. "Sorry, Bad," he muttered.

Sorin looked between us, his brow raised. "Take a break, Spense," he said, gentler now.

The male looked sheepish, running a hand between his horns to ruffle his black waves. When he looked at the ground, a pained expression crossed his face. I was going to have to keep an eye on this.

"My go," I declared, taking the attention off Spense. "And I can't fight physically, so it has to be all magic."

I looked to Alwyn, hoping she would volunteer, but she held her hands up.

"I fight with weapons. Magic is not my specialty. Plus, I don't think my ego could handle getting my ass beat by someone who hasn't practiced magic in weeks," she added cheekily.

To my great surprise, Olys stepped forward. "I'll take you on."

There was a collective change in energy as the lithe male rolled up his sleeves. It was a punch in the gut to see a swirling mating tattoo along his forearm, faded and grey, barely visible, if not for the skin that was raised along the lines. It looked like more of a scar now.

Olys had lost his soulmate. It sent an immediate pang to my heart.

He caught my stare and curled his upper lip. "Paint a picture, why don't you?"

Spense's voice tickled my ear. "He doesn't like to talk about it."

I nodded. Down to business then. "What kind of magic does he use?"

"Sun mostly. But he uses storm well too."

"Got it." I stepped forward, facing Olys head-on.

I squared my shoulders. He cracked his neck.

The others backed away, leaving us alone within the lines of the ring.

From what I knew of the male, he was quiet and reserved. He held his own opinions, but was never the first to speak up in a crowded room. He would wait for me to make the first move.

So, I did. I sent magic skidding along the sand, rustling up dust and impairing his view of me. Olys was quick to react, pulling water from a nearby cactus to settle the swirling sand. It was a flashy move of storm magic, one that could have used less energy if he'd wanted.

But maybe the energy was well spent because in the half second it took me to contemplate his move, Olys sent a blast right at my chest. The streak of magic was the same sandy-brown as his hair, tinged with the grey of a soul once intertwined, and I threw up my hands with the hopes of absorbing it.

This magic, whether it be Unseelie specialty or just my lack of practice, ignored the energy field I had created in my palms. It travelled through my hands and up my arms, sending a jolt of electricity thundering through me. I stumbled back, bracing my hands on the ground to try and empty the storm into the sand.

My fingers curled in the sand. Earth magic—this was my distinction. My strongest suit. Surely, it would work similarly in Rathe as it had in Eira.

I sent my magic deep into the ground, delighting in the freedom that coated my bones. My soul was singing, dancing joyfully in the return of its very essence.

I pulled from the sand, from the clay and the dirt beneath. It readily awakened, heeding my will, rising through the surface around Olys. Higher and higher, the clay rose, dark and sticky, encasing the fae's legs and midsection. He sent blast after blast into it, but to no avail, and I paused, ready to accept his surrender.

Olys's gaze lifted to mine, twisted in concentration. He closed his eyes, taking a steadying breath, and when he opened them again, they were pure lightning.

Lightning that cracked in the sky, terribly out of place among the blue horizon, not a cloud in sight. Lightning that forked down with the voltage to raze an entire forest, landing in my clay creation.

There were shouts from around me, but I didn't hear them. I could only hear ringing in my ears as the electricity travelled through the clay, along my magic line, and straight into me. Jweira, a constant presence in my pocket, grew warm. Hot. Scalding. But I couldn't move, couldn't speak, could only stand there, arms outstretched, while lightning poured through my veins.

Green tinted around my vision, as if I were seeing through the emerald. Images played in the back of my mind—a wolf mask, a throne room, a ceiling crumbling down. The same blast of storm that was spinning through me, around me, *with* me.

The sweet, cooling weight of Jweira's consciousness settled into my core.

With her magic wrapped around mine, we absorbed the singeing magic. Calmed it, gentled it, and released it. The icy heat travelled down into the earth from me, and as the last bit of it licked my toes on its way out, I took a shuddering breath.

"You're alive," I breathed.

Jweira chuckled. *Did you really think you could get rid of me that easily?*

FORTY-SIX
REPURCUSSIONS

MAISIE

Espionage had turned me into kind of a badass.

Sure, the near-overwhelming shadow of anxiety about getting caught kept me company like a fly to honey. But I finally felt like I was doing something important. And that made *me* feel important.

It was this notion that kept my chin tilted a little higher than usual as I performed my daily tasks around the palace. Normal, mundane chores that I would snore through regularly became a cover story, an exciting way to keep my true intentions hidden.

Princess Hollaina—who had asked me to call her Holly, but I was definitely not that bold—summoned me to her chambers routinely to "refill her tea." I shouldn't enjoy plotting treason this much.

The plan was simple in theory. Tomorrow's eclipse was crucial to the creation of the portal, so there was no room for error. Hollaina felt confident enough in her followers that she could borrow some of their magic to help create it. She was certain that once the portal was open—or at least working—Vera's officials would jump to help, leaving the queen in a position where she would have to show her cards. Either she helped or made a move to shut it down.

The room for error was alarming, but I was not well versed in war and politics. Aedan trusted the plan, and I trusted him.

"We are out of options, Maiz," he'd said. "This is the basket we're putting all our eggs into. It's a leap of faith."

Last-ditch effort it sounded more like. But here I was, putting my eggs into it anyway.

Were the Outcasts really sure they wanted my eggs? They would probably end up being runny, not like Hollaina's and Aedan's. Theirs would be fluffy and light, perfectly scrambled.

I shook my head. *Egg metaphors, really?*

I was on my way through the palace to bring another tray of tea and snacks to Hollaina and Leo, who, despite the relieving fact that he'd mostly left me alone, still gave me the creeps. Perhaps they were together, I realized. It would explain his sudden disinterest.

Weird choice, Princess, but I'm not complaining.

A servant stopped me in the hall. "Excuse me, Miss Maisie?"

I kept walking, holding my tea tray, and he jogged to keep pace with me. "I told you, Hulo, I can't help you with evening turndown. I'm much too busy with my own charges."

Hulo shook his head, pink staining his cheeks. "It's not that. The queen has requested your presence."

I stopped dead. My heart thundered in my chest. "The queen?"

The young servant nodded. "I will take this for you—for Princess Hollaina, I presume? You must go right away; she is in the throne room and said it was time sensitive."

The time it took for me to dump the tray into Hulo's arms and set off at a clipping pace down the stairs toward the throne room was mere seconds. It felt like hours though, each step adding weight to my limbs.

It's nothing, I told myself. Even as I couldn't shake the horrible pit in my stomach. The one that was never wrong. *Everything's fine.*

When I reached the massive double doors, the guards stationed outside opened them immediately, reaching behind to twist the oversize gold handles.

The effect of the throne room was no less than the first time I'd ever seen it. Jaw-dropping architecture, floor-to-ceiling vines crawling up the walls, and a window behind the dais with a view of the frozen River Nord that was unmatched. The throne was ivory white, and Queen Vera sat like she was made from it, elegantly resting her arms on the sides. The emeralds in her crown winked at me as I knelt before her.

"Maisie," she cooed. "Thank you for your haste."

There was something in her tone, the too-sweet facade, that sent shivers running down my spine.

I kept my eyes on the marble floor and swallowed once.

"I'm not one to drag things out, so I'll get right to it. We're both busy females, aren't we? Rise."

On shaky legs, I stood. Looking at her directly, however, was a different matter. My eyes betrayed me by staying trained on the floor. They were locked. I couldn't make them move if I wanted to.

Vera didn't seem to care. "In fact, it seems you've been *quite* busy. Serving our Eastern guest has you running all over the palace these days."

I dared not say anything. The tension in the air crackled. The queen was only beginning her performance.

"As queen, it is my greatest wish that all my subjects are satisfied. Including my guests. Which is hard to do when they are plotting against you."

And there it was. The drop. My breath came in tiny sips; my ears had a dull ringing to them.

"It was, sadly, not all that surprising to discover Hollaina's nefarious plans. But the true shock came from those closest to the Crown. Individuals I had complete trust in."

I squeezed my eyes shut. *Gaia help me.*

Suddenly, the queen was in front of me. Her hand wrapped around my throat, forcing me to look up into her gaze. She was utterly terrifying. Her beautiful face had twisted in contempt, her teeth bared, her icy-blue eyes burning into me.

"You disgrace my daughter. My goodwill. Your actions will come with repercussions tenfold," she hissed.

Oh goddess. She was going to kill me. Right here, in the throne room. I'd never see another sunrise. When was the last time I'd admired the sun?

Her hand snaked from my throat to my chin, nails digging in. The heat on my neck suggested she'd drawn blood, but I was numb. "Look at you. No fight. It's pathetic. If you're going to plan a rebellion, you should at least stand with your conviction."

I wanted to be strong. If only I could be like Diana, with wits and magic and strength to speak my mind. But I was weak. I was a useless servant who had thought she could take down an ancestral-blessed monarch. I could almost laugh at myself.

"Just kill me already," I begged. The pull to stop resisting had long since taken over, sliding across all my nerves and settling in.

Vera sneered, "Killing you would be a mercy. You've already given up—what's the fun in that? No, I will make sure you *feel* your punishment."

Of all the ways I had contemplated my life going, dying by torture had not crossed my mind.

A single tear slid down my face as I thought of my mother. Sweet Ada, who had devoted her entire life to the palace kitchen. Any harm to her would be entirely my fault.

"Let's start by visiting an old friend. Shall we?" In a swift move that sent me falling forward, Vera released my face and started for the doors, her dress train swishing behind her.

I stood, rooted to my spot, watching as the guards pulled open the heavy wood.

"Either you come with me on your own two feet or you will be brought by methods much less comfortable," she called over her shoulder.

The guards started toward me, sporting matching smirks.

I darted forward and kept a few paces behind the queen as she floated through the halls. Why were we unaccompanied? Did she really trust me not to run?

But there was nowhere for me to go. She knew that. Even without the treacherous piling of snow, the one place I could hide where the Crown did not reach was the Unclaimed Land, and I had no idea which direction to even start in.

And so I followed Vera, feet carrying me on shaking legs, shame lighting my insides like fire.

It became clear we were heading to the cells under the palace, which filled me with oily fear. As we made our way down the slippery, moisture-ridden steps, the dank air coated my lungs. It was so hard to breathe. Wet and hot, like a blanket I couldn't take off.

"Here, you will find the beginning of your punishment. Our old friend here is about to begin his own trial."

We had reached a block of cells, and as Vera swept her arm in a grand gesture, the body in the prison became clear.

My heart fell to my feet with a thud, and I gasped.

FORTY-SEVEN
LOSING SIDES

SPENSE

Excitement kicked up in my belly, flying around like drakes on a windy day.

It was finally here. Today, Diana and I would open the portal to usher in the new era.

In all the planning sessions with my siblings, we had gone over every minute detail. And I felt good about our choices. Confident. Except for the one—rather large—piece we weren't sure would fit.

My father.

Slapped together out of necessity and perhaps a lack of intent to dig any deeper was this rocky plan: we would bring him over on a high dose of his herbal mixture.

Sorin didn't like it. He was always eager on doing the right thing. But this wasn't his choice to make alone. And Urdan was a loose cannon that jeopardized the entire plan. He hadn't been lucid since the day we'd returned from Elfwood, and while the others felt they were safe from his brutal mind, I certainly did not. It would be just like him to get his mind back the very day we needed him quiet.

And since it had been my idea, the responsibility to slip him a larger-than-normal amount lay in my hands. Diana had offered to come with me, of course. Her kind soul was the only constant I could count on. But she was needed in Rathe to get the Seelie Quadrant out safely and without detection. It was an important job, and as much as I wanted to be selfish with her, this day was too vital to us.

It was probably best I faced my father alone anyway.

Pik met me outside the king's chambers at dawn. Grey circles under his eyes were impossible to hide on his blue skin. It was clear he hadn't gotten any sleep either.

"My Prince," the goblin greeted, bowing deeply. "The overnight workers report the king has had a fitful night."

"He will surely enjoy his nap then."

It did not surprise me that Urdan was restless, considering how much my siblings and I were linked to our father. Our life spans, our magic—it all stemmed from him. Of course he would feel the unrest of our emotions the night before such a momentous day.

Pik did not smile, only ushered me into the antechamber. Guards watched as we passed—perhaps a beat longer than was appropriate. But as the king's private guard, they always felt more entitled.

The door to his room was open with his healer performing his morning health check, as was the daily routine. It was dark in the room with heavy curtains still in place against the windows, but the hulking silhouette of my father and his giant wings were impossible to miss.

"I will be back with your tonic," the healer, Jatan, said softly.

"No."

Pik put his head in his hands, and I took a step closer to the room.

"I'm sorry, sire, but it is by your own instructions that I must insist."

"It is my instruction *now* to keep it away from me. I am not in the mood for that today."

I pursed my lips. "Is he always like this?" I asked Pik.

He shook his head.

Vindication roared through my blood. Deep down, wherever the thread that tied my father to me lived, it was pulled taut. I knew him because I was a part of him. Our magic was one and the same. It was the only one he could not fight.

I walked into his bedchamber as if I were floating, Pik and the guards remaining in the antechamber. The world was quiet, slightly blurred at the edges. When I reached his four-poster bed, we locked eyes. Father and son. Twin flames.

I did not hear Jatan leave, but the door clicked shut, and we were alone.

I pulled the mixture I'd made this morning from my cloak. "Now, Father," I said, dumping the packet into the cup of water beside his bed. Magic licked from my fingers into the glass, following my fingers' motions as I stirred the air. "Why don't you be a good boy and take your medicine?"

Urdan's eyes were deeply angered as he took me in. "Spense," he spat, "your betrayal should surprise me, but I have grown very used to the disappointment of my children."

I smiled—maybe too much. "Betrayal? That is hardly fair. We are taking you with us after all. Truly betraying you would be leaving you behind to rot alone in this hellhole."

"It is *my* army, *my* war to fight. How dare you take that from me!"

"Maybe it was thousands of years ago. But now? Your time is over. Your disappointing children have found a way to save the Unseelie and the rest of the Folk. Without you. How does it feel to be irrelevant?"

Urdan shook his head, a dull laugh rattling from his chest. "You think that you have it all planned out, hmm? You have no idea what to expect on the other side. Without me, I can guarantee you will be unprepared. Let me help guide you."

A small tug of his magic pulled at my own. I slashed down, severing the tie. This was one of his favourite tricks. With his thousands of years mastering the soul distinction under his belt, as well as the familiarity between us, my magic found it only intuitive to give in to him.

"My wisdom would be invaluable," Urdan continued, his voice low.

He was right; maybe we should use his experience. It could be the difference between lives lost. Between a loss and a *victory*.

"How do you expect to defeat a Seelie army without the knowledge of one who has bested them before?"

The illusion shattered.

I stepped closer, jaw clenched. "Defeating them is not what we're doing. With the Unseelie and Folk returned to Eira, balance will be restored. Only then can we live peacefully."

My father burst out laughing then, the sound so unnatural and jarring. Between wheezes, he wiped at his eyes. "Peace! You will not find peace with the Seelie."

Grinding my teeth, I waited for him to settle down.

"If that is truly what your plans are, then you have already lost. You might as well leave me here for all I care. I'd rather rot in this bed than in a cell."

"You're giving up."

"*You* are the one giving up. I don't play on losing sides."

"Then, you are doomed."

Urdan grinned. "So be it." Without warning, he grabbed the

mixture and tipped it back, swallowing it in one gulp. He lay back on his pillows and flicked his hand lazily to gesture me out.

I took one last look and left, letting Pik close the door behind me.

"I want him ready for transport in an hour."

The guards looked at each other quizzically, but nodded as I passed.

Time to go home.

FORTY-EIGHT
HEADED FOR THE GALLOWS

AEDAN

The stench was the first thing I registered. Dank and mouldy, thick. It coated my nose and lungs. The surroundings were no better. I'd been down here enough times on the other side of the bars to know exactly where I was. And what that meant.

We'd failed. And I was probably going to be tried for treason. Considering I wasn't dead yet, it was unlikely they'd kill me before the trial. No, the queen would want to make a lesson out of me.

And my father—well, hopefully, he would argue for my life.

I was certain he would.

Ninety percent certain.

Eighty-five?

I tucked my knees in close to my chest and considered my options. Escape seemed unlikely unless I had help from the outside. So, that left me with two options: beg for forgiveness or stand unapologetically and go down blazing.

I knew what the smart move was. But I also knew I wouldn't do it in a hundred years.

Sometime later, when I'd given in and rested my head on the

slimy wall, voices began to echo down the hall.

I recognized Vera right away.

"Our old friend here is about to begin his own trial."

What I hadn't expected was to clash gazes with familiar sky-blue eyes. Maisie let out a gasp as she took me in.

"No!" I jumped to my feet. "Maisie did nothing wrong! Leave her be!"

Vera chuckled. "Relax, dear boy. I am not going to imprison your little friend. We are only here to pay you a visit."

Maisie's face was taut, fear etched in the lines around her mouth. She kept looking at me and looking away.

"I should have guessed you two would be trouble for me. But as my daughter's closest friends, I hoped you would put her above your greed for power."

"We had to do something while you sat around, picking your nails, letting Diana fend for herself in an enemy realm," I spat.

Vera smiled, that icy stare chilling. "Not trusting in your queen is treason in itself."

I shook my head. "Were you ever going to even *try*? All those meetings, talking in circles, achieving nothing. I'm shocked more haven't turned against you."

"I'm disappointed, Aedan. I thought including you all these years in training and meetings would have prepared you better. Surely, you understand the diplomatic approach by now."

Suddenly, my ears filled with ringing. Slowly, I stood, placing my hands around the bars of the cell wall. "You were never going to get her back."

Maisie looked at Vera, eyes widening.

The queen took a step forward, leaning close. "Diana is *gone*. She was gone before she went through the portal. She had been compromised and turned against the Crown. It is a kindness to all to leave everything alone." Her stare was strong but empty. Vacant.

My gaze flicked to Maisie, whose eyes had gone glassy. Her arms were wrapped tight around her chest as she looked between us.

"It is hardly a kindness to deprive your kingdom of the princess they love. What happens when they find out you have no plans to rescue her? That the almighty, ancestor-touched *queen of Eira* chose to leave her only daughter and heir in the clutches of the enemy?"

"Glamour." Maisie's voice was quiet but sure, shocking me.

Vera snapped her head around to stare, surprised as well. "Not such an innocent bystander, are you?"

Maisie swallowed, but did not flinch.

Vera chuckled. "A glamour of this size would hardly be feasible. The amount of magic it would take to convince all of Eira to forget about Diana would require a heavy sacrifice. Don't you worry about the optics. I have handled worse with success."

She was toying with us now, enjoying her win.

"So, you want to pin it on me then?" I ventured.

The queen reached out and stroked my arm once. Shivering against the touch, I pulled away, but her magic kept me in place, a frozen vise. The air had a stale sweetness to it.

"I certainly don't want to. It is a bad look to have to label the deputy captain of my own army a traitor. I know you weren't working alone. Give me a name, and you will be absolved. You don't have to go down for this."

Calm settled through my bones like a gentle crash of a wave. I could—and would—die happily, knowing that the Outcasts were still anonymous. Their mission could still go as planned, and Diana would return. Whoever had given up my name made a mistake. I had been caught too early, before they could use me to flush out the others. It was as if Gaia herself had placed a soothing hand on my back and told me that everything was going to be okay.

"You will pay for what you've done. I might not be around to witness it, but you will see my face as the false world you've created crashes and burns in front of you."

Vera clenched her jaw and stepped back. "You have spent my last nerve. I had hoped that you might show remorse, that you might be pardoned with rehabilitation. But I can see that you are too far gone. Diana's illness spread to you a realm away, and that is dangerous."

I slid my arms through the bars, letting them hang as I pressed between the slimy steel. "So, you plan to kill me then? Like how you killed Sir Radtar for his defiance?"

It was a shot in the dark, but my aim was true.

The queen growled, her face twisting, "You will stay here, out of trouble, until I decide what to do with you. It is only out of respect for your father that I don't condemn you on the spot. Think of that when you drone on about your *corrupt queen.*"

She gathered herself and turned to leave. Maisie locked eyes with me once before moving to follow her. I needed her to be okay. I needed her to keep strong even if I wasn't there.

Don't shut down on me now, I prayed.

"What of Maisie?" I called because I couldn't help myself.

Vera looked at me over her shoulder with a deathly smile. "Congratulations are in order. Your little friend has found herself in a new position—maidservant to the queen. She and I will be inseparable from now on. And if she moves against me, it will be on your head."

Maisie had collapsed in on herself. She was a shell; she had given up.

"Do what has to be done," I told her quietly. "I'm headed for the gallows either way. Bring her back. Don't let this be in vain."

Vera laughed, the grating sound echoing off the walls.

Maisie stared blankly, and I swore I could see her retreating farther and farther away from me.

"You're stronger than her. I believe in you, Maisie."

One last glance at empty blue eyes was all I got before she walked away.

Forty-Nine
When This Is Over

DIANA

It was exhausting, having two voices in my head.

Jweira had been understandably thrilled to be with her siblings, whom she had never met, but was so excited to talk to—through me.

"Why don't I just give you to one of them, and you can talk directly to them, like you do with me?" I'd asked after relaying an entire conversation from her to Alwyn.

I am bonded to you, Diana. To pull away and bond with another, over and over, would be an unwise drain of my strength. When all this is over, I would like to get to know them each better, if they'll have me.

Her voice had been stronger, clearer, than I'd ever felt it before. Her consciousness remained wrapped—coiled—around mine, almost as if it were clinging for dear life. As glad as I was to have her, the tightness on my chest was beginning to weigh on me.

Cool wind whipped through the dark desert, ruffling the scarf around my hair. Across the horizon, the sun was beginning to rise, already spreading a reddish hue over the sand. It wouldn't be long before the sun was covered by its counterpart. The swirling dust was tame compared to the swirling in my stomach.

Spense's hand gently wrapped around mine. "We can do this."

I looked up at him, only his eyes visible through the protective scarf. "We have to."

"I have no doubts. The magic between us is unrivalled. We *are* power." His voice sent shivers down my spine.

Lately, something in him had shifted. Confidence radiated from him, coming through in every little action he did. I worried about how the soul magic might be affecting him, but with his focus needed on this, I would have to leave it for now.

"How much time do we have before the others join us?" I asked, watching the sun begin its ascent.

The eclipse was upon us, mere hours away from one of the greatest realm shifts the world had ever known.

We'd been sent ahead on eclipse watch. Sorin, Badras, Alwyn, and Olys all manoeuvred much more difficult jobs—gathering every last of the Folk and bringing them here.

Spense unclasped the scarf from around the lower half of his face, revealing a devilish grin. "Enough time to do this." His fingers deftly unwrapped my own scarf and tilted my chin up. Leaning down, he pressed his lips to mine.

As it always was with him, the world stopped moving. Nothing could compare to this. How he reached for me, wrapping his hands around my waist. How my own body reacted, trying to get as close to him as I could.

If everything else failed today, at least we had this. Each other.

I snaked a hand up inside his scarf to tangle my fingers in his soft hair. When I reached up and ran my index finger along one of his horns, Spense's breath caught in mine, and he pulled me closer. I could feel him everywhere, and it still wasn't enough.

The kiss deepened, and the snake in my stomach disintegrated into a million butterflies. Spense's hand at the nape of my neck pulled me to him. His tongue brushed along mine, and my pulse skyrocketed.

My other hand, resting on his chest atop his rapid heartbeat, moved lower. Lower still—

I broke away with a gasp as Jweira began writhing around uncomfortably, trying to get my attention. "What are you *doing*?"

I'm sorry. I tried to just ignore you. But things were getting heated. Do you know how weird it is for me to have to experience what you're feeling for my brother?

"What did I do?" Spense's voice was full of concern as he searched my face.

"It's not you." Still panting slightly, I stepped back into Spense's embrace, resting my weight against his sturdy chest. "I forgot we aren't quite alone."

His eyes landed on the emerald around my neck, which was glowing faintly. Understanding dawned on his face. "Ah. Yes." He gave me a quick peck on the lips, nipping once playfully. "You won't have to wear her forever, will you?"

I heard that.

I chuckled. "When this is over, she's taking a trip to Alwyn's consciousness."

FIFTY

SOMETHING MALEVOLENT

AEDAN

It wasn't possible. There was no way it had been Ryen.

Of those who could have possibly turned me in for rebellious activity, Ryen should have been at the bottom of my list. But process of elimination had left him at the top. The only one who could have known.

And that sent me into a spiral.

"Hey. You."

The gruff voice of a guard pulled my head from its spot between my knees.

"I'm not hungry." Had I really been wallowing that long? I would have thought dinner was still hours away.

"It's not that." He gave me a disparaging look and moved farther down the hall, keys jangling. "You have a visitor."

Great. The queen was back to kill me for real this time.

I settled into the wall. If she wanted me dead, she'd have to retrieve me from this dank cell herself. It would bring great pleasure to see her dainty shoes slip in this muck.

"Aedan."

My gaze snapped up. "*Jamey?* What are you doing here?"

Of course she had found a way into the dungeon. An army couldn't keep her out of a room she thought she was entitled to be in.

Jamey gathered her skirts and looked at the ground disdainfully, gingerly choosing a path with the fewest puddles toward the cell door. "I had to see for myself. The palace has labelled you a traitor."

I shrugged. "They have no proof. Not that it matters. The queen's word is law."

"They have a witness, Aedan."

Damn it all to hell. It *was* Ryen.

"I'm a dead male walking then."

"Sitting more like."

I cocked my head to the side, taking in Jamey's appearance. She wore a typical, everyday dress appropriate for the palace with her light hair pinned back, as usual. So, why did she seem so different?

She regarded me quietly with her air of importance. Only … she no longer had that longing look in her eye. The one I'd seen for weeks now, eager and besotted for my attention.

"Is there another reason you're here, Jamey?"

Slowly, a smile stretched across her face. "I just couldn't help it. I had to see for myself that I'd succeeded."

My stomach flipped. "What are you talking about?"

She rolled her eyes. "Come on. I know I'm a good actor, but did you really think I was *that* into you?"

Jaw clenched, I steeled myself. I was looking at a storm cloud, and it was about to start raining.

"When Vera asked me to do a special job for her, I figured it would be something more diplomatic—easily put on a résumé, you know? But having this type of experience will be invaluable to me in my new role."

"You got played, Jamey. The queen used you."

"Hardly," she scoffed. "The plans are already in motion."

I shook my head. "So, what? You pretended to like me because Vera had asked you to? And then you came to kick me while I'm down?"

Jamey stared at me for a second in disbelief. "You really don't get it yet, do you? I thought you were at least of mediocre intelligence. *I was the one who sold you out, idiot.* I was keeping a close eye on you the entire time we were together and even before that. You never seemed to notice because you really didn't care for me, did you? I was just keeping your bed warm until you tired of me. Still, the invisibility proved useful, as much as I despised being treated like a common whore. Like your Maisie," she sneered.

Instantly, I was on my feet, hands at the bars. "Keep her name out of your mouth."

Jamey laughed. "Finally, a reaction. Nothing at learning of my treachery, but a slight toward a *servant* gets you in a rage? My, how we've fallen. Where have all the good ones gone?"

"They all ran from your wannabe-princess act the second they could," I spat.

Her mouth set, and she brought a hand up to inspect her nails. "Well, it won't be an act for much longer."

"Excuse me?"

Did she mean to say—

"That's right. Vera is rewarding my loyalty by allowing me to become the new princess of the North. Her heir."

If smug could be defined by one look, it was the one Jamey was wearing right now.

"The fae will never accept you. Heirs are chosen by the ancestors."

She sniffed haughtily. "Once they realize that Diana is not coming back, they will accept me as their own. I am skilled at the art of persuasion, if you'll remember."

My jaw felt like it could snap with how hard I was clenching it. "When Diana *does* come back, you'll deserve every punishment you get."

And there it was. The shit-eating grin. She'd been waiting for me to give her an opening.

"Even if your precious princess finds a way back to this realm, she won't be alive long enough to reclaim her throne."

I growled, "She's more than capable of fending off an attack. And how could you possibly arrange for one when you have no idea where the portal will be?"

"That's where our plan comes in. Did you really think that in all those meetings, we were just sitting around, twiddling our thumbs, talking in circles? No. When the excess group of untrustworthy officials were dismissed, that's when the exciting stuff happened. What, shocked you didn't get an invite?"

When Vera had spoken to me weeks ago about testing me for her inner circle, I had dismissed it. Stupid. I should have been on my game. Of course she would send a spy to me. How had I not thought of that?

I had been arrogant enough to believe I could lead an army.

"Whatever plan you cooked up with the rebels, it will be no match for what we've done," Jamey continued. "At this point, it hardly even matters. It can't be undone. And I really want to see the look on your face when you finally realize that you've lost."

The joke was on her. I had fully accepted my failure.

"You have that much trust in this grand plan? You don't even know what the rebels are capable of or how many there are."

"The rebels want a portal opened. From what we've gathered, they might have found a way to do that. And since we cannot stop the eclipse from happening, we have set a safety measure in place."

"A safety measure?"

"Oh, yes." Jamey smirked. "Last night, while you were taking a little nap, the trusted members of the queen's council performed an intricate, ancient rite of protection. One that envelops the entire realm. If a portal is made through the wards, it immediately snaps through the connection—killing the user instantly."

Blood roared in my ears. I couldn't believe what I was hearing. "You'd see Diana *dead*? Just for trying to return to her home?"

Jamey did not look deterred. "Diana is not the princess she once was. With her unholy connection to the enemy, she can no longer be trusted. And if she tries to bring them back to reclaim Eira, she will be thwarted."

"This is a mistake, Jamey. Please, do something while there's still time. She doesn't have to die. Can't you see that there's something malevolent at play? The queen we know would never abandon her daughter and banish her from returning home. She would never kill her. *Please*," I pleaded.

The petty back-and-forth no longer mattered to me now. I didn't care if begging meant Jamey had the upper hand. She had to *do something*.

"This isn't a good look on you." The Western princess gave me one last up-and-down, gathering her skirts. "And this air is coating my lungs. Goodbye, Aedan. I'd say thanks for the good times, but I was faking them all anyway."

With a flip of her hair, she sashayed away, deaf to my pleas.

Later, when my throat was hoarse and the guard had beaten me twice for not shutting up, I let myself cry.

The salt from my tears wet my lips. And the salt in my wounds screamed in agony.

FIFTY-ONE
BESTOW

SPENSE

"A little help would be nice."

Alwyn's tiny form crested over the hill of sand, dragging what looked like enough packs to hold all her earthly possessions over her shoulder.

"*What* is all that?" Sorin stalked toward her, his lips moving as he counted how many bags she had in tow.

Badras's shoulders shook with silent laughter.

"Sometimes, I worry your brain is aging even though your body isn't. These are packs. We store things in them."

Our eldest brother clenched his teeth. "What's *in them*, Alwyn? You were told to pack light."

"Excuse me for being sentimental."

"You're leaving half of it. End of story."

Olys's arrival thankfully put an end to their bickering, and even as I stifled a laugh, I couldn't help the nerves that jittered in my stomach. We were moments away.

Those would have to be pushed way deep down. Diana couldn't see me like this. I had to be strong for her so she only had to worry about herself.

"Soak it up, brother." Olys's voice was uncharacteristically soft beside me. "Things might never be the same after this."

I looked at the beautiful girl with a huge grin on her face, watching Alwyn try to wrestle a pack out of Sorin's grip. No, things would never be the same. But as long as she was with me, we could handle it. Together.

"That's what I'm counting on, Ol."

Olys whistled through his teeth, the sharp noise ringing across the sand. The group looked to him, Alwyn hastily releasing the pack she had been holding, sending Sorin teetering off-balance.

"Are we about finished? We have maybe half an hour before we lose our window, and I want everything in place by then."

Indeed, the moon was nearly touching the sun. Shadows had begun to dance across the plain.

Together, the six of us came to the edge and looked over the sandy hill at the subjects gathered below.

The Unseelie.

Some Seelie that had survived in Rathe far longer than they should have.

Elves, goblins, brownies, gnomes, leprechauns, druids, pixies, nymphs. The Folk.

The energy radiating off the crowd was nothing short of overwhelming, prompting me to shove walls up around myself, keeping my magic safely within.

The Elfwood creatures stood in their own group to the side, barely moving, barely speaking. They stared straight ahead, battle armour ready, waiting for the call.

The gnomes had made themselves comfortable on the ground, already having unrolled blankets and passing around drinks. I smiled to myself, knowing their drinks would only fuel their ferocity in battle.

A few hundred giant metal containers sat upon wheels, dark and opaque. The soldiers assigned to moving them and making sure the containers did not lose their integrity kept a solid distance. When I'd inspected them earlier, the kelpies sloshing inside of them were not happy. The thudding they made by slamming on the walls was enough to scare the bravest soldier.

I followed Diana's gaze and found the group she had been so passionate about—the orphanage. The children clung to hands of supervisors, taking everything in warily.

Diana's hand slipped gently into mine, and I squeezed it once. These Folk were hers to rule over now too. She would be the best ruler of us all.

Near the edge of the group, some of the king's guard stood closely together, a long case shielded between them. It hovered a few feet off the ground, a nearly invisible force field of protective magic around it. Urdan's resting place until we were able to deal with him.

I looked over at the line my siblings made beside me. They all wore their armour and weapon of choice and squinted at the almost-covered sun that was now high above us.

Sorin looked to me and nodded once. He stepped forward and cleared his throat.

"Subjects of Ivywall, the time has come to return home." His voice echoed through the desert, carried by the wind of Badras's magic.

Immediately, cheers erupted from the crowd. Feet stomped, and weapons were raised in the air to accompany the cries.

"We have been victims of the past for far too long," Sorin continued. "It ends today. Just as we are not the first group to settle here, remember that on the other side of the portal are those who did not commit the atrocity that sent us here. We go in peace, as is our way. And with it, we will flourish as we settle back into our home."

The cheers were less invigorating as our subjects shifted between themselves.

They wanted bloodshed. To see vengeance for the punishment we had suffered. And I understood it wholly. If it came to it, I would lead them into revenge and see us win.

I would see the Unseelie to their rightful place on top and sit on a throne of bones, Diana at my side.

I squeezed her hand again, and she looked up at me, worry dancing in her eyes.

"Have no fear." I leaned down to murmur in her ear. "I will ensure peace."

"It's not you I'm worried about," she whispered back, chewing on the inside of her cheek.

She was so kind, so good, to be scared for her mother. The same mother who had isolated her, ignored her, and repeatedly trampled over her thoughts and opinions. The mother who would have killed me in front of her.

Vera did not deserve her daughter's love.

Or the quick death I was going to bestow upon her.

"We have less than a minute until the eclipse is at its strongest."

Olys's voice cut into my thoughts. He led Diana and me away from the others, Sorin's voice still echoing behind us, issuing orders for when the portal was opened.

We stopped in a patch of shadow, a few paces away from my siblings.

"Here." Olys dragged his foot through the sand, creating a circle. "This spot is a direct line to the sun."

Wordlessly, Diana stepped inside, pulling me gently with her. We stood, facing each other, hands clasped. Already, a tingling sensation started to spread through my body. The eclipse was powerful, feeding off the magic humming between me and Diana.

It was almost easy to start pouring it into the space between us, the circle accepting it hungrily. Diana's eyes had shut, her face concentrated as she sent her own magic spilling into mine.

It was utterly intoxicating.

Her cedar scent crashed into me, and the lovely purity of her magic pulled at every sense. She was perfect in every way, her soul light where mine was dark.

The power that grew between us crackled with energy. Everything faded away. It was just her and me. Nothing else mattered, except for this growing ball of magic between us.

When Diana opened her eyes, they were pure white. She was giving herself to the magic.

I grinned and let myself follow.

FIFTY-TWO
INVITING

DIANA

Nothing could have prepared me for the feeling of absolute power that creating a portal sent soaring through my veins. Shock waves of pure electricity fed my senses, making a triangle out of three points—me, Spense, and the portal.

It was exhilarating.

The magic coming from Spense flowed through me before pouring into the slowly growing vortex, and it filled me with endorphins. Iave was right; there was no feeling quite like having your soulmate at your side. His magic was a call that mine answered, a wild cacophony of love, power, desire, strength.

There was nothing we couldn't do together.

Slowly, the portal grew until it forced us to step away. We broke contact on one side, moving so that my right shoulder brushed against his as we stared at the growing magic.

Behind us, the siblings had grown near. Garbled voices carried over our shoulders, bouncing off the portal and rebounding.

The magic pouring from us stemmed, slowing to a trickle. When it finally released us, my shoulders sagged. It had been more taxing on my body than I'd realized.

A hush went through the desert. A shining portal, beautiful and full, stood proudly before us. Even through the darkness that the eclipse provided, its essence was incomparable.

"We did it," I breathed.

Spense lifted me into his arms, my feet coming off the ground. "You're amazing," he said, burying his face in my neck.

I couldn't help the laugh that bubbled out of me. Here we stood, after enduring so much, in front of the solution to our problems. We hadn't failed.

I hadn't failed.

Last time, my ancestors' voices had flooded my head, but this time, it was inexplicably quiet. Worry turned in my stomach. It felt strange.

Jweira pulsed once at my neck. *Something's not right.*

I reached through my magic and inspected the portal. It seemed fully functional, no fissures or impurities that I could find.

Cheers sounded behind us. The Folk had started inching forward, closing in.

"Let's go home!" Badras roared.

The soldiers were pushing back the stragglers with gaining difficulty. We were on the brink of losing control of them.

"Hey, hey, wait." I grabbed Spense's arm, but he was sucked into the mob.

His grin was almost unrecognizable as he drank in the emerging chaos hungrily.

Alwyn reached my side. "They're getting uncontrollable. It's now or never."

"I think something's wrong with the portal. We shouldn't go through yet."

Alwyn eyed the crowd pushing in, eyes glazed as they struggled to get to the portal. Their shot at a new beginning, at safety. She then looked at the portal. "How bad?"

"I don't know. I need time."

"You aren't going to get it." She squeezed my arm. "But the magic feels okay. And I trust your abilities." She took a step forward.

"Alwyn, *don't*. I have a bad feeling about it."

She surveyed me, brown eyes gentling. "And I have a feeling like I need to do this. It'll be okay, sister." She cupped my cheek once and leaped back, fire returning to her gaze. She lifted her broadsword in the air. "*For Ivywall!*"

With a last shriek, she took off at a run and hurtled herself into the portal. The lines shimmered around her body, and then she was gone.

"How did she get by first?" Spense pulled me toward the portal.

I tensed, waiting for something insidious to happen. For it to shake and rumble and turn dark. To spit Alwyn back out. But all was quiet. Inviting even.

If something *had* happened to Alwyn on the other side, there was only one way to get to her.

Taking a deep breath, I gathered my magic around myself like a protective shawl.

I looked to Spense, whose excitement was coming off him in waves.

I nodded.

"Let's go home."

FIFTY-THREE
TRAP

MAISIE

"Stand down." Vera's voice cut through the clearing, as powerful as ever.

The soldiers creeping toward the portal stopped in their tracks and retreated.

It stood proudly in the forest, large enough for two to walk in side by side. It had appeared in a few minutes total, the queen's wards alerting her to a disturbance.

She'd immediately set off with me in tow. "Don't get any ideas," she'd hissed in my ear, clutching my wrist uncomfortably.

Embris was at her side, his face unreadable. By now, he had to know his son was currently in the underground cells, awaiting a death sentence. How could he stand loyal to his queen now?

"The trap is set," Vera said, her eyes narrowing. "Now, we wait. It won't be long."

"How do we know it's them?" the captain asked quietly.

"Do not question me. Especially in the wake of what has happened."

Vera's icy tone made Embris flinch, but it no longer had the same reaction for me. Now, it just thudded around in a dull chamber. There was nothing left that the queen could take from me. She could command my body, but there was no part of me that cared anymore.

"There—someone's coming."

The portal was shimmering in the middle, creating waves through its magic. A formless blob became more and more defined—until a body tumbled through.

A sword fell to the forest floor with a thud, its red metal glinting.

The body was female and small with sandy-brown hair that was tied up tightly. She was dressed in battle armour that had been no use. She lay on the moss, limbs akimbo, her face unseeing. As horrible as it was to see the queen's trap played out, a shudder of relief washed over me. It wasn't Diana.

"Who is this?" Vera roared.

"Is she alive?" Embris asked, bending down to feel for a pulse on the female's wrist.

"She's wasted the trap." The queen seethed. "We fall on plan B. Let's go."

Embris frowned. "Are we going to leave her here?"

"Let her serve as a reminder to my daughter of who she's dealing with." Vera paced in front of the portal, staring into it like a predator.

Embris's gaze flickered once over me before he motioned to one of his soldiers to take the unconscious intruder. "Get the head healer out here," he murmured in the soldier's ear, his voice barely audible. "See if this is reversible."

In my heart of hearts, I knew it was not. Vera had constructed this trap with the sole intention of winning the war for good. If Diana had come through and been the victim, it would have been no more of a casualty than a pawn in the game.

It made me sick.

Vera stopped abruptly. "They're coming." She set off at a quick clip back through the woods, leaving me stumbling to keep up. She began rattling off orders to her captain. "Gather the army. Send notice to the Nordians that they are expected immediately. We will take our planned places in the palace. They will not stand a chance against us from outside the fortress."

"What about the cities?"

"Close them down. Send runners to board everything up. Everyone should shelter in place. If we do this right, it will all be over soon."

Vera tugged at my wrist. We were almost running, getting back toward the palace, where she could make yet another trap, like a coward.

Behind us, glowing light was coming from the portal. The queen cursed under her breath. She picked up her speed.

We were almost out of sight, and I craned my neck over my shoulder, causing me to trip over roots and branches.

Right before we rounded the corner out of the forest, I saw it.

Two bodies emerging from the portal.

TO BE CONTINUED ...

ACKNOWLEDGMENTS

It's crazy enough to think that I've written a book—and now, I've written *two*? Insane. Thank you, God, for the stories inside me and the ability to tell them.

I would be lost without my amazing husband, Evan. Your never-wavering support has fuelled me as I pursued this career, and I am eternally grateful. Thank you for comparing my book to a Netflix show you'd want to keep bingeing.

I could not have asked for more amazing parents, who continue to be cheerleaders and advocates as I chase my dreams. You guys rock.

My sissy, Hayl—Never change. I love your fervour, your passion for enjoying everything in life, and your ability to turn my rainiest day sunny. My twin, born two years later.

Milo & Lucie—Even though you'll never read this, I love you more than I can put into words. The unconditional love of a dog is someone everyone should be lucky enough to experience. And to my other four-legged baby, Finn—Thank you for being my real-life warhorse.

Publishing this book was a huge step off the high diving board for me, as I pursued the avenues all on my own. But of course, I was never alone. I had my village with me to help each step of the way:

Jovana Shirley of Unforeseen Editing—Your skills are top-notch and everything I never knew I needed. Seriously, you helped turn this fledgling sequel into a fully grown series instalment. (Book three, let's go!)

The team at Books & Moods—Thank you for the gorgeous cover and chapter artwork. I'm still amazed that you were able to take the half-coherent ramblings of a non-artistic girl who had very little specifics to give you, only "vibes," and turn it into something insanely beautiful.

My friends and family who shouted from the rooftops about this series and gifted my books—I am so grateful for you.

Also, thank you to MK Williams, whose YouTube channel taught me how to do all the back-end indie-author things. You saved me a lot of stress and time!

Finally, thank you to the readers who loved book one and came back for more. Diana, Spense, Aedan, Maisie, and the entire crew (including me!) are so grateful you want to spend time with them and witness their story unfold. It's been sitting in my head for a very long time, and as vulnerable as it is to see it out in the world, I could not be more thrilled it's *you* reading it. Thanks for taking this journey with me. Where we go one, we go all.

If you enjoyed *A Kingdom of Cursed Lies*, please consider leaving a review on the platform of your choice. They go a long way toward helping indie authors like me!

The third and final book is coming, and it's shaping up to be the biggest and wildest book I've ever written. Trust me, you'll want to see how this ends. To stay updated on all things Eira, as well as what comes after this series, follow my Instagram @authorlaurenlowther or check out my website with the QR code below.

ABOUT THE AUTHOR

Lauren Lowther is the author of the Dark Truths fantasy trilogy. She has been reading and writing since she learned the alphabet. She has a love for stories with adventurous storylines, unique plots, and sweeping romance. She lives in the Pacific Northwest with her husband, two rescue pups, and a sassy chestnut mare.

To stay updated on book announcements and more, follow Lauren on Instagram @authorlaurenlowther or visit her website laurenlowther.com.

www.ingramcontent.com/pod-product-compliance
Lightning Source LLC
Chambersburg PA
CBHW061059210726
48294CB00001B/213